MY BROTHER'S GIRL

AN IRISH KISS NOVEL

SIENNA BLAKE

My Brother's Girl: a novel / by Sienna Blake. – 1st Ed.
First Edition: April 2020

ISBN: 9798788101149

Stock images: depositphotos
Proofreading services by Proof Positive: http://proofpositivepro.com.

Created with Vellum

1

KAYLEIGH

*A*ll the girls at Dooley's knew to avoid the mistletoe hanging from the low doorway between the kitchen and the bar.

Balancing a tray laden with thirteen empty wobbling pint glasses and holding a stack of grease-covered baskets that stank of frozen fish, we would all press ourselves as tightly as possible against the door frame so the shrivelled red berries overhead didn't graze the tips of our plastic elf ears. From inside his crammed, cluttered office that smelled of whiskey-sweat and salt and vinegar crisps, Andy would stick out his balding head, lick his crumb-covered lips as we passed by with hurried steps and say, "Almost got you that time, love. Almost got myself a kiss."

It was quite safe to say that bartending at the sleaziest bar in Cork and working for the sleaziest boss in history was not exactly what I would call my "dream job". I didn't draw stick figures of bleary-eyed men, farting and scratching their asses at a bar, back when I wrote Kayleigh with a backwards "K" and couldn't even fathom how to spell Scott. When teachers asked, "What do you want to be when you grow up?", I didn't recall ever responding by saying, "Why be an astronaut or artist or anthropologist when one could be a harassed human bottle opener?"

But it paid the bills...sort of.

I tried to ignore the image of stacked white envelopes marked with red *overdue* stamps waiting for me on my kitchen table once my shift ended. "Jingle Bell Rock" blasted over the cheap stereo system. I tugged up the top of the seemingly child-sized elf costume Andy insisted the all-female staff wear through all of December and most of the time into January. The two men I served Guinness to didn't even try to pretend they weren't drooling over my tinsel-lined cleavage.

Tell them to fuck off, I told myself. *Tell them that I whispered in Santa's ear to give them coal and they know right where to shove it.*

"Who's next?" was all I said, to which seven debit cards waved frantically in the twinkling red and green lights.

Before I could lean over the bar to get the first drink order shouted in my ear, Tina called my name as she lugged a fresh bucket of ice around the bar.

"Boss wants to see you," she said, adjusting her elf ears and wiping her forehead.

"Me?" I glanced around her jingle bell-covered miniskirt as she dumped the ice, catching a glimpse of a beer belly reclined in a torn and faded leather chair in the glow of a porn-filled computer screen. I shivered despite the fact that the windows in the stuffy bar dripped with condensation, making the street lamps outside nothing more than a hazy glow. "Why?"

"What's that?" Tina leaned in to shout into my ear as Mariah belted out what she wanted for Christmas.

"Why does he want to see me?" I shouted right back, voice already hoarse, and it was only a few minutes past midnight.

Tina shrugged and wiped her hands off on her red felt skirt. "Didn't say."

After an empathetic pat on the shoulder, Tina scooped up an empty tray and disappeared into the sweaty, drunken crowd. I rubbed at my eyes, only remembering the red sparkly eyeshadow Andy made part of the dress code when it came off on my fingers. *"How else am I supposed to make you girls look festive if you refuse to smile like I'm always telling you to?"* he'd said while scratching at his balls.

A series of boo's resounded down the bar from the impatient customers when I turned to leave. Hey, it was either make them happy or my boss, and my boss paid my bills...sort of. Squishing myself up against the doorframe, I went to evade the infamous mistletoe only to find it suddenly absent from the rusty nail driven between one of many graffitied penises and a faded sticker for the local rugby team. After glancing once more over my shoulder back at the spot where the mistletoe should be, I knocked on the door to Andy's office, now just barely cracked. It had been open only moments before.

"Andy?" I called. "Tina said you wanted to see me?" I strained to hear over the drunken chorus of "Rudolph the Red Nosed Reindeer", not daring to lean my ear closer to the door that would surely glow like a Christmas star under a black light. "Andy?" I called. "Hello?"

"Kayleigh?" Andy finally responded.

"Yeah," I said, shifting from toe to toe on my uncomfortable heels bedecked with tinsel. "Do you need something? We're kind of packed out here."

"Come inside."

I stared up at a constellation of dried gum on the low ceiling. "Just tell me," I tried. "I've got to go serve."

"It's about your bonus."

I frowned. "My bonus?"

I thought I heard a little giggle, the kind eight-year-old boys make when they learn you can spell BOOBS on your calculator. "Your Christmas bonus."

Fuck. I didn't want to go in there. I didn't want to see Andy's pasty, hairy gut spilling out from beneath his two-sizes-too-small pit-stained t-shirt. I didn't want to smell his breath or watch him lick his lips or count the number of times his eyes darted to my tits.

I also didn't want to disobey my boss. I didn't want to make a stir. I didn't want to start a confrontation.

And I *definitely* didn't want to have to ask Santa for rent money this Christmas.

With a sigh, I pushed open the office door and slipped inside. The lights were off and Andy was in his chair facing away from me at his computer. Three flickering candles illuminated the over-flowing filing cabinets and stacks of invoices littering the dirty floor.

Lifting an eyebrow, I asked, "Are you sure a fire in here is up to code?"

Andy ignored my question. "Close the door, my little Kayleigh-bells."

I wanted to tell him I hated when he called me that. I wanted to tell him it was demeaning and unprofessional and inappropriate beyond belief. I wanted to tell him there was no fucking way in hell I was closing that door.

But my mother taught me keeping the peace was always more important, so I nudged the door closed with my heel.

Taking one step closer, I started, "Andy, look, we're slammed tonight and I really should be getting back to—holy fuck!"

The beat-up office chair swivelled around. I was subjected to a sight that would take me years of therapy to get over (even if I could afford it). Andy sat there with the missing mistletoe held between his teeth, butt-ass naked, save a Santa's hat perched tentatively over his crotch.

I was too stunned to do anything except stand there and stare at the white puff atop Santa's hat, a symbol of my childhood innocence, hanging between Andy's meaty, hairy thighs.

Andy said something I couldn't make out.

"Huh?" Why couldn't I look away? It was like a car crash on the side of the highway. I wanted to, but I couldn't. I just couldn't. What the actual *fuck*?

Andy repeated what he'd said. But with the mistletoe wedged in his mouth it came out garbled and entirely incomprehensible. When he saw that I still clearly hadn't heard, he growled irritably and pulled out the mistletoe. "You know the rules, my little Kayleigh-bells." Andy quickly replaced the mistletoe between his lips and gave me what I think was supposed to be a seductive face. It just looked like he was constipated, which he probably was in fact.

"What rules?" I asked, dragging my eyes to meet his.

Again he garbled around the mistletoe.

"Huh?"

His irritation grew as he pulled the stem out of his mouth and said, "You have to kiss beneath the mistletoe. *Beneath*, my little Kayleigh-bells."

To emphasis his point even further, Andy wiggled his hips at me, dangerously shaking Santa's hat.

"*Beneath*," he managed to say around the mistletoe.

"Yeah, yeah," I quickly said to stop his gyrating as the hat slipped down an inch or two. "I got it, I got it. But An—"

"Call me 'Daddy'."

"Holy shite," I muttered while holding up a hand to block Andy's crotch from view. "What I was going to say was that I'm really busy right now, you know, out there with the bar."

Andy scooted the chair closer to me even as I inched back toward the closed door.

"I'm the boss, my little Kayleigh-bells," he said. "The other girls can handle it."

"Yeah, but—"

"I've seen the way you've been looking at me." Andy had pulled the mistletoe from his mouth and swirled the mouldy berries over his nipples.

"Um, Andy—"

"Daddy."

"Don't you think this is may be just a little bit inappropriate?" I said with a tiny shrug, my fingers fidgeting with the hem of my skirt.

A flash of anger immediately distorted Andy's features, and his already red cheeks deepened to a purple. I reached back for the door handle. Andy stretched his hand forward and grabbed my wrist.

"You're not going to make a stink about this are you, my little Kayleigh-bells?" he said, his voice no longer seductive, but threatening. "Because what you just said? That's upsetting me. Do you want to upset me?"

Do you want to upset him, Kay? Is that what you want? You want him to leave?

I shook the distant echo of my mother's voice from my head and forced a playful smile on my red lips.

I shook my head and said in the sweetest voice I could manage given the present situation, "No, no, I just meant... Is it appropriate to do this without whipped cream?"

Andy's eyes, unfocused probably from the half-empty bottle of Jameson next to his sticky keyboard, narrowed before he laughed.

"Right you are, my little Kayleigh-bells." He winked up at me and I thought I might vomit. Nope, I did. Right there in the back of my throat. "Right you are."

"I'll go get some," I said. It was hard to keep my voice from shaking.

Andy lifted my hand to his lips and pressed a stinking, slobbering kiss to the back of my hand. A dog's mouth would have been cleaner.

"Don't keep Daddy Nic waiting long," he called after me as I slipped out of the office and resisted the urge to slam the door shut behind me.

I ignored Tina shouting after me for more pint glasses and hurried past the tiny kitchen filled with pounding hip hop and clattering pots and pans. My fingers shook and tears pricked at my eyes as I climbed the narrow, twisting staircase half filled with boxes of Guinness, and headed toward the alley exit.

I shoved the back door open, startling a couple smoking behind the trash bins. I wasn't sure where I was going. I just knew I couldn't go back into that office. I couldn't confront Andy.

So I was running, running somewhere. Somewhere where I didn't have to fight.

Out on the sidewalk, I glanced around for where I parked my car as the crowd parted irritably on either side of me. A light snow fell and I shivered in my skimpy costume, feeling my heels unsteady on the treacherous ice. My snow boots and coat were back inside the bar, but I knew there was no way I would go back in for them. That would mean coming face to face with Andy again. I would rather risk a broken ankle and hypothermia than *that*.

Wreaths hung from the lamp posts. Lights strung across the road swung gently in the evening breeze. I spotted my car parked across the street. Glancing nervously back toward the alley exit, I pushed the "cross" button and shivered as I bounced up and down, praying Andy's bare ass got stuck to the leather seat of his office chair.

The traffic signal above the street took forever to cast a red streak across the slick road. The door to Dooley's opened and I feared it was Andy, but it was just a big guy stumbling out after a night of drinking to cross the road. The pedestrian light flashed and I followed after the guy to cross when I heard the distinct screech of brakes *not* braking.

My eyes quickly found the pair of careening headlights as a car slid uncontrollably toward the crosswalk. Without thinking, I reached out, snagged the back of the man's coat, who seemed not to notice the car, and yanked him back and safely out of the way. Torn off balance, he slipped to the icy asphalt and in the process pulled me on top of him so I was staring down into his eyes.

"You saved me," he gasped.

I laughed nervously from a mix of adrenaline and awkwardness.

"I guess I did."

The man stared up at me in amazement and then said, "I love you."

I blinked. "Wait, wha—"

2

KAYLEIGH

*H*is lips were on mine before I could process what was happening, and then it was my first year of college all over again in a warm, dreamy haze: peppermint Schnapps and sticky sweet chocolate syrup and a mountain of whipped cream from an aerosol can all mixed together like an eternal Christmas on my tongue. My eyes fluttered closed despite my surprise, because this stranger kissed me with the passion of a soldier reunited with his lover after years of never knowing if he would ever return home alive from war. One hand clutching the small of my back and the other cupping my left elf ear, the nameless man kissed me like he might never stop.

I was gasping for air when I finally managed to pull away, my lips still buzzing with the sting of alcohol. A hot, fast blush swept across my cheeks when the man with startling green eyes and lashes thicker than mine shook his head and whispered, "You're the prettiest thing I've seen in my whole entire life."

"Oh, I don't kn—"

"You're an angel," he insisted, eyes bouncing around my face like he couldn't decide where to look. "You're *my* angel."

Pushing myself up proved difficult with this stranger's strong, muscular arms still wrapped around me, but I managed to squirm off of him and plop right back down on my ass on the ice. The man scrambled to sit up with the exuberance of a child rushing down the stairs on Christmas morning to see what Santa left him. He reached for my hands and squeezed.

"You're my *guardian* angel," he insisted.

Concerned onlookers and a wave of excited whispers that spread like the plague were moving toward us. I wrangled a hand free and pointed at my ear.

"No, no, I'm not a guardian angel." I smiled nervously as people circled us in the street and pointed eagerly at the stranger in front of me. "See? Elf."

The man burst out into laughter at my lame joke. He held on tight when I tried to pull my hand away to get up, up and away.

"You're funny, too! Gorgeous and funny." He pumped his fists, my arms flailing with his like we'd just won some world championship. "I knew, I just *knew* my soulmate would be funny."

His words startled me more than the out-of-control car, more than his very unexpected kiss, and perhaps, just perhaps, even more than Andy's entirely unwanted Christmas present.

"Wait, did you just say—"

"Eoin!" shouted a teenage boy who ducked under a woman's arm to get to the front. "Eoin, can I get an autograph?"

"Your autograph?" I asked the man called Eoin with a confused frown. "Why does he want your autograph?"

But Eoin didn't answer me as he stopped the approaching boy with a massive paw of a hand extended out in front of him.

"Later, lad," he said. "I have something very important to do right now."

Before I could ask him what exactly that was, Eoin pulled

me into a massive hug that crushed my lungs and stole my breath. He rocked us back and forth there on the ice as I remained helpless with my arms pinned to my side. He finally released me, but only to hold me by the shoulders so he could lean back to get a better view of me.

Attempting to push away his iron grip, I said, "Okay, so, one, are you famous? And two, please tell me that you didn't just say soul—"

"Fuck, darling dearest! You must be freezing!"

Eoin immediately began stripping off his coat and then his sweater and then, I'm shitting you not, his t-shirt, leaving his very impressively chiselled chest naked save his snow-dotted scarf.

Around me the crowd grew as whispers became louder and concern changed to excitement. A buzz took over as I heard his name on every lip.

"Yeah, yeah, it's him. It's Eoin O'Sullivan."

"I told you! You called me a goddamn liar and I told you. Eoin O'Sullivan, Eoin Fucking O'Sullivan."

"Eoin O'Sullivan... Eoin O'Sullivan... Eoin O'Sullivan... Eoin, Eoin, Eoin O'Sullivan."

Dumbfounded, I could only stare as "Eoin Fucking O'Sullivan" piled his clothes on me like a shivering coat rack. My head tilted to the side as I studied him. Shite...this man wasn't a stranger after all. I'd seen him before. I'd seen his face on a rugby poster in Andy's office. His dark hair was hidden beneath his hat, but his green eyes, wide and boyish and sweet, were more than enough to recognise him by. Eoin O'Sullivan was a rising star for the All Ireland rugby team. And if I wasn't mistaken, he had just pronounced his love for me.

Christ.

Shoving aside the arm of his wool coat so I could breathe, I lifted a finger and said, "Thanks, but, um, I'd like to go back to what you just said a second ago, if you don't mind. Did you say soul—"

"Shite! Are you guys alright?" Through the circle of people watching us and whispering excitedly to one another, a man burst through, hands digging anxiously through his hair. "I just lost control, fuck, I—are you alright? Hey, you're Eoin O'Sullivan. Fuck, I almost killed Eoin O'Sullivan. You were brilliant in the Six Nations finals last year against England, you know? Jaysus, are you alright?"

I held up my hands to calm down the mounting situation. "We're fine," I said. "Everyone is just fi—"

"We are not fucking fine!"

My eyes widened in confusion at the emotional outburst from the rugby star on the ice with me. The still growing crowd fell into a startled hush as Eoin pushed himself indignantly to his feet and threw his scarf back over his broad shoulders. "We are far from fine, my friend," he boomed. "*Far* from fine, you hear?"

Scrambling to my feet, I stepped in front of Eoin. "No, no," I assured the driver, who stared at Eoin behind me with worry in his eyes. "We're both fine. No harm, no foul. You can all go. We are fine, just fi—"

"Wrong!" Eoin interrupted.

Gloved hands reached into coat pockets and purses for cell phones that began to blink red lights, which meant, to my horror, that they were recording all of this. Flashes snapped from all directions so it was impossible to cover my face from all of them.

"Should we call the police?" a woman in the crowd asked, phone already in her hand. "An ambulance?"

"Call everyone," Eoin ordered, circling his hand over his head. "Call every authority there is. Get everyone here right away. Call the goddamn prime minister."

I blindly reached behind me to cover this lunatic's mouth as I desperately waved a hand at the woman. "Please, do not call anyone," I begged. "Really, we're just fine."

"Ladies and gentlemen!" Eoin called out so everyone in all of Cork could hear. "This stunning woman before you has clearly lost her mind."

Before I could reply, he twisted me around to face him, slid my hand to the searing hot skin over his heart, and kneeled in front of me.

"Wait, what are you doing?" I hissed.

He ignored me as he held my hand firmly affixed to his pounding heart, snow falling on his dark hair. "This woman just saved my life."

The buzz from the crowd was attracting even more attention from the local bars and pubs. I looked longingly at my car past a sea of winter hats and ear muffs—so close and yet so, so far.

"Ladies and gentlemen," Eoin continued. "This gorgeous, stunning, beautiful woman before you clearly must have hit her head when she bravely dragged me back from the brink of certain death, because she keeps insisting that we are fine."

I looked imploringly at the crowd. "We are fi—"

"We are *not* fine," Eoin interrupted. "Not me, at least."

I leaned down and whispered, "Maybe we don't make a big deal about this?"

Eoin reached up, cupped my cheek, and shouted to the crowd, "How can I be just 'fine' when I've found the love of my life, my forever, my soul— No, no, wait!"

I sighed in relief. Good, I thought. He wasn't going to say it.

"No, no," he shook his head emphatically. "I didn't find her. No, my soulmate found *me*."

Like a goddamn movie scene, the crowd, probably fuelled by a pint, *maybe* two, clapped and cheered as Eoin stood and swept me up into his arms, my elf ears tumbling to the ice.

"I love this woman!" he shouted. "I love her!" He then looked down at me, his green eyes crinkling with more happiness than I thought was possible in one human. I had to admit it was quite infectious. "Come get a drink with me."

"Oh, I don't know…"

Eoin again addressed the crowd as I hung suspended in his arms. "Should she come get a drink with me or what, folks?"

A raucous "yes" drowned out the pounding music from Dooley's. I was about to make up some excuse when I noticed Andy, thankfully clothed once more, wedging his sizeable belly out of the back alley exit. Our eyes met and I saw his widen in surprise before narrowing in anger. Shite. Agreeing meant avoiding a confrontation with Andy.

So agree I did.

"Alright," I said with as much enthusiasm as I could muster given the situation.

"Yeah?" Eoin asked, his excitement admittedly helping a bit.

I smiled, his boyish charm too much to resist, and nodded. "Yeah."

Eoin grinned and tightened his hold on me. "I want you to know that I'm going to treat you like a proper lady," he started, looking down at me with such earnestness. "You deserve to be treated right and right you will be treated."

"Great." I smiled.

"I promise you to be the most perfect gentleman to you."

"Emhmm." I nodded along to Eoin's passionate, soul-baring, not-quite-Shakespearean monologue while craning my neck to see past his broad shoulder. I almost yelped at the sight of Andy now barrelling toward us, only slowed down by the ice and his drunken double vision.

"…and I vow to buy you all the flowers in Cork and Dublin and all of fecking Ireland and all of Eur—"

"Right, right." I tapped Eoin's shoulder impatiently. "How 'bout we just start with that drink, yeah?"

Eoin grinned down at me and winked. "Off we go then." He took a massive step forward.

I couldn't help a tiny smile as I watched Andy stumble to his knees. *Serves him right*, I thought as Eoin carried me through the crowd.

"You bitch!" Andy called from the ice. "You're fired, you bitch!"

Ducking my head into the safety of Eoin's shoulder, I sighed in relief as he took me farther and farther away from that surely nasty encounter.

"Did you hear something?" Eoin asked.

I shook my head emphatically. "Nope."

We continued down a quiet alley, me still in his arms as the snow swirled in the light of the street lamp above us. It was actually a little romantic. And if his pile of clothes weren't warm enough, his bare chest felt like fresh logs on the fire. Maybe a drink with Eoin "the love of my life, my forever, my soulmate" O'Sullivan, wouldn't be so terrible after all.

"We're going to have a wonderful life together, darling," he said, his green eyes finding mine in the sparkling light.

I nodded politely like my mother taught me.

Eoin paused no more than a second or two. "So, eh, what's your name then?"

3

DARREN

*T*he sharp click-clack of heels on the grease-covered floors of my garage were an unfamiliar sound. It took a woman calling out a tentative "hello" for me to finally realise the source.

Rolling out from beneath the undercarriage of my mother's car, I found my date for the night clutching her black velvet purse tight to the chest of her black mink coat as she surveyed my work space with an upturned nose. Outside the open large bay door, night had fallen and a few flurries of snow fell on a pile of rusted motorcycle parts next to the sign for Kelly's Garage. I hadn't meant for it to get so late, but it was Ma's car so it had to be done, and it had to be done tonight.

"Over here, Trish," I said with a hasty wave. "Thanks for meeting me here. I'm just finishing up."

Without waiting for a response, I returned into the darkness beneath the car. Some people felt safe and comforted with a blanket by the fire or in the arms of a lover in bed or submerged in bubbles with a glass of wine. My place was down here with dirty coveralls and a wrench in my hand.

Hidden beneath the undercarriage, I watched Trish's five-inch heels tiptoe around the splotches of oil toward me.

"Darren?" she asked, sounding confused.

Pausing with my wrench halfway cranked, I dragged myself back out from under the car just enough to reach out a hand. "Nice to meet you."

After an awkward moment of silence, I saw Trish's hand, covered in bejewelled rings and with fire-engine red nail polish on her fingernails, extend toward mine before hesitating and pulling back slightly. "Umm..."

It was only then that I realised I was still wearing my filthy work gloves. Clenching the index finger between my teeth, I tugged the glove off and tried again. "Sorry about that."

Trish didn't seem to find my bare hand any more appealing to touch and shook my hand with the enthusiasm of shaking a dead trout down at the Dublin fish market. Maybe they were a little greasy.

"Nice to meet you," Trish said as if her mom was going to flick her ear for being impolite if she didn't say it.

"I just need a couple more minutes and then we can go to the restaurant," I said, returning to my work. "Grab yourself a beer while you wait, if you'd like. They're over in the cooler by that big red toolbox."

Trish's pointy heels did not move. "The restaurant takes last orders at ten, you know."

I switched on my head lamp and nodded. "We'll make it," I assured her.

"It's 9:15," Trish added. "And the place is twenty minutes away."

"No problem. Almost done."

The front axle of my ma's car snapped earlier that morning when she hit an unexpected pothole on the way to the store to grab groceries for Sunday lunch tomorrow. Knowing about my date tonight, she insisted there was no rush in getting it fixed when the tow truck had dropped it off around noon. In not so many words, I told her that was goddamn bullshite—family came first over everything.

Especially Tinder.

"There's a chair over there in the corner, Trish, if you want to take a seat," I said, my voice echoing back to me in the tight, cramped space. "Just toss that gas tank to the side." I grunted as I struggled to keep the new axle in place.

"Umm, I'm okay," Trish finally said. "So, umm, how long have you worked here?"

I took a moment to swipe a bead of sweat from my forehead despite the frigid temperatures outside. "Since I was fifteen," I answered. "So...nine years about." I didn't bother telling her I owned the place; I didn't bother telling anyone.

"You worked here through college then?" Trish asked.

Hidden beneath the car, I twisted my arm around in the shallow space to scratch at the back of my neck. "Actually, I didn't go to college," I admitted.

"Oh."

I sneaked a peek from my work to see Trish's heels fidgeting back and forth on the concrete. I reminded myself to act interested.

Clearing my throat, I asked, "So did you go to college then?"

"Trinity."

I blinked up at the grease- and salt-covered undercarriage. "Oh. Well you know what they say, Trinners are winners." I winced as my lame joke fell flat.

My mind searched for something else to ask her, but the more I focused on the wrench and the axle and the work, the more I couldn't seem to recall a single detail from Trish's Tinder profile.

"So, umm, it's snowing pretty good out there, eh?"

"Darren," Trish's tone of voice reminded me a bit of my constantly disappointed teachers right before I dropped out of school, "perhaps you could finish this work tomorrow? It really is getting quite late."

"Alllllmost finished," I replied, scooting around to get a better view.

Trish's toe began to tap. It sounded like a snare drum for a firing line down here.

"I know you're really going to love this little place," I lied. "It's one of my favourites."

I didn't have "favourites". You can't have "favourites" when you don't ever go out. I had a "favourite" chair in my garage, a "favourite" drawer in my "favourite" toolbox, and a "favourite" beer cooler with my "favourite" beer.

"It's nearing 9:25," was all Trish said in response.

"Just need a minute or two more. Sure you don't want a beer?"

Trish was silent.

I paused my work beneath Ma's car and stared up into the darkness as the silence grew and grew.

I'd had good intentions of making this date, just like all the others. It had even been a family affair. I bought a new tie Ma said would look nice, asked Michael for a recommendation for the restaurant, and even practised some small talk with Noah. Eoin, the little snot, offered to teach me how to kiss and I, unsurprisingly, did not take him up on that.

But just like all the other failed dates, I got unlucky.

It was bad luck that Ma's car broke down. Bad luck that I had to spend half the day tracking down the part when it should have been stocked everywhere. Bad luck that traffic was bad because of the snow and ice. That was all before I even got my hands on the car itself.

Then I stripped a lug: bad luck. I misplaced the right

wrench: bad luck. The batteries on my work lamp died and I was all out of AAAs: bad luck.

That's all it was: good ol', nothing-to-be-done-about-it, shitty bad luck.

"Um, Darren, do you have a backup plan if we miss the restaurant?" Trish asked.

"We won't miss the restaurant," I called out beneath the undercarriage. "We're going to have a lovely date, I promise."

Again there was no reply.

"We're going to sit in a dark, cosy corner booth," I said as I twisted the wrench, getting back to work again. "There's going to be candles lit when we sit down and we won't leave till they've burnt out, their wax dripping down over the crisp white tablecloth."

I tried to imagine myself there with Trish, with someone kind and sweet and warm beside me. I tried and all I saw was the dark smear of grease inches from my nose.

I went on. "There's going to be live music at the restaurant, violins and saxophones and guitars even, but we're not going to hear any of it, because our ears will be filled with each other's whispers of tiny, insignificant things that are each more wonderful than the last."

I tried to hear a perfumed whisper in the empty, silent space beneath the car. I tried to hear little secrets and favourite songs and silly dreams and hopes she'd never dared to say aloud before. I tried to hear anything, even the band in that candlelit restaurant.

I heard nothing but the metallic screech as I tightened a rusted bolt.

"Don't worry, Trish, we're leaving soon," I continued as a familiar claustrophobia that had nothing to do with the hot, dim tightness of the space beneath the car quickened my heart rate and made the wrench slip in my suddenly sweaty palms.

"When we're there at the restaurant, we'll start a little way away in that intimate corner booth, a little tentative at first. But then our knees will brush up against one another's. My fingers will find yours on your thigh and I'll interlace mine with yours. I'll scoot closer and then you will, too. Maybe it's me who says we should go back to your place. Maybe it's you. But we'll be together, close...closer..."

I could have that with someone again, I told myself as I worked, intense and focused. I could have that with Trish even.

But I couldn't feel her sheets against my back, only hard metal. I couldn't sense her calm breathing next to me, only the stillness of rubber and concrete. The only warmth I could grasp in that moment was not the warmth of waking up with someone in my arms, but my own harsh, shallow breath against the cold axle.

I worked and worked and worked, because it was all I could do to keep myself from panicking. I stayed down there under the car, because it was bright compared to the darkness I would face out there. I only stopped when my hand slipped and blood ran down my wrist from a fresh cut.

"Damn it," I hissed, using my heels to pull myself from beneath the car. "Let me just put a bandage on this and then just a minute or two more."

I blinked in the light of my garage. Trish was no longer standing by the car. I stood and craned my head around the empty space. Outside, her car was gone. With a frown, I wandered over to the little office at the back of the garage and shifted aside an old carburettor to see the dusty analogue clock blinking harsh red numbers.

Eleven forty-eight.

With a tired sigh, I covered back up the clock, put the tie waiting on the back of my chair back in its store packaging, and returned to work.

4

DARREN

*T*he couch in the little makeshift office at the back of my garage wasn't meant to serve as a bed. The puke-green fabric, pilled and torn, a relic of the '70s, was covered in grease and beer stains. It sagged low enough in the middle that most times it was more comfortable to just sit on the stacks of invoices and receipts littering the floor. So when I woke up on the couch the next morning to the blare of my cell phone alarm after only an hour or two of sleep, it was with a crick in my neck and an ache in my back.

Groggy and craving a cup of coffee, I stumbled back bleary-eyed to my ma's car. I winced at my joints groaning with stiffness as I rolled back into the dark of the undercarriage and got back to work.

Three hours later I drove the now functioning car into Ma's drive, hastily tugged on a clean shirt, and grabbed the tub of store-bought mashed potatoes from the backseat. The front door was unlocked, like always. I kicked off my boots, adding them to the mountain of shoes beneath the overburdened coat rack. Like always, the aroma of fresh herbs, butter, and a roasting bird wafted toward me through the narrow hallway, made even more narrow by a massive gallery of family photos framed with Ma's flea market finds. Like always, in stark comparison to the tranquillity of my garage, the place was so damn noisy: the commentators of a rugby match on the television in the living room tried to outshout the radio in the dining room reporting on the weather trying to be heard over the never-ending kitchen melody of people laughing and shouting and pans clanging and clattering.

Ma's place was warm and cosy and loving, everything my garage was not. And yet I couldn't help that constant nagging feeling in the back of my mind that I'd rather be there than here. I took a moment around the corner from the good-natured chaos to close my eyes, suck in a steadying breath, and remind myself to smile—Ma would worry if I didn't, like always.

My fingers grazed over the well-worn indentations in the column next to me. I could feel the marks for heights and years along five lines. I avoided touching the one that stopped just a little bit shorter than all the rest. I knew it best of all, even better than my own, and wished every day the jagged line across my heart would fade like the one there on the wall.

I rounded the corner into the cramped, busy kitchen stuffed with my family. I first found Ma by the stove, where she stirred a pot of mulled wine with cinnamon sticks, orange slices and spices. I kissed her cheek and dropped her car keys on the hooks by the stove.

"How was your date, love?" Ma smiled at me, pushing aside a strand of her long silver hair that had slipped from a bun atop her head.

"Must have been damn good since he's so late to Sunday lunch," Noah said, swinging his legs back and forth from the kitchen island as he munched on some roasted Brussels sprouts still steaming from the oven. With his long sandy-blond hair tousled, his scruffy jawline sharpened, and his blue eyes glinting, he grinned like he was in a toothpaste commercial. I knew plenty of women would line up to buy whatever he was selling, even if it was Brussels sprouts.

"Leave him be," Aubrey, his American fiancée and the big sister I never had, said from across the kitchen where she stood in one of Ma's pink aprons icing a chocolate cake not nearly as sweet or dark as her eyes.

Noah shrugged, feigning innocence even as his eyes betrayed his mischievousness. "I'm just saying Darren here is never late for Sunday lunch."

I ignored him and gave Aubrey a wink when she sighed in exasperation. I lifted the tub of mashed potatoes, cold from the drive over. "I didn't have time to cook, Ma. I'll put them in a casserole dish and warm them up in the oven."

"*And* he didn't have time to cook," Noah announced to Michael over by the sink, who also wore a pink apron over his Italian suit that cost more than my monthly rent, and to Eoin, the youngest of the O'Sullivan clan, who sat hunched over his phone at one of the barstools. "Who, I mean, *what* were you so busy doing that you didn't have time to cook like the rest of us, Daz?"

Eoin looked up from the video highlights of his most recent rugby match playing on his cell phone to howl like a junkyard dog.

Michael, grabbing another dirty dish to clean, shook his head while somehow managing to not disrupt a single strand of his immaculately styled, freshly cut dark hair, ready as always for a corporate boardroom. "The maturity of this family never fails to astound me," he grumbled.

Noah tried to send me a sneaky wink but earned an elbow in the rib from Aubrey. I whacked Ma's knee with a cabinet door while trying to find a clean casserole dish.

"Just put it here, dear," she said. "I'll take care of it. You just focus on cleaning those filthy hands."

"Very filthy, Darren," Noah grinned from the island. "Absolutely nasty."

This elicited another howl from Eoin, who still hadn't bothered to look up.

"I was working on a car this morning, you ass," I told Noah after tossing a spare cinnamon stick at his face.

Noah teased and joked, revelling in pushing a button or two on occasion, but his was the number I would dial first if I ever needed anything. It meant more than I could say to know he would answer before the second ring.

"A car," I repeated, a finger pointed at him as I tried to hold back a small grin.

"Oh, yeah?" Noah plopped another Brussels sprout into his mouth even after Ma smacked his hand with her wooden spoon stained by the aromatic mulled wine. "Did you make that engine purr?"

Eoin, nose still buried in his phone, meowed obnoxiously before cheering at his own try.

"Boys," Ma warned, lifting the lid of a pot on the back burner to check the stuffing. "Darren. Hands. Now."

But as I tried to get through to the sink to wash the grease and car oil off my hands, Aubrey, now armed with kitchen mitts, blocked my path to retrieve the roast as the egg timer went off and rattled itself right off the counter. I went to snatch it up, only to bang my head against Noah's knee.

"Feck, Darren," he yelped. "Get down on your knees for your lady friend, not for me."

"*Noah!*" Ma snapped.

"No, no," Michael said, looking over his shoulder from the sink as it filled it up with sudsy water. "You can't go down on the first date."

Aubrey crossed her kitchen mitts over her chest. "What kind of nonsense advice is that?"

Eoin, zooming in on an image on his cell phone, let out a grunt. "Why hasn't *Sports Illustrated* called me yet? Have you seen my glutes? I mean have you *seen* these babies?"

"There was no lady friend to get or not to get down on my knees for," I insisted, making another attempt to get to the sink before Michael irritably shooed me away as he scrubbed at a large dish. "There was only a car."

"Hey, we're family," Noah grinned with his hands held up. "We don't judge."

"I'm washing my hands upstairs," I said, shoving away Noah's massive bear hug as I passed by him.

"You love me, right?" Noah called after me.

"Yeah, yeah." I waved a hand behind me before turning the corner back to the hallway.

As I climbed the narrow, creaking stairs (avoiding the broken step eight up from the bottom like every sober-ish O'Sullivan always knew to do), Aubrey pressed Michael about any other policies on when to go down on a woman, Ma lectured Noah about eating the Brussels sprouts, and Eoin continued to marvel at the beauty of his ass muscles. I loved them more than anything in the world, but the smile their fading voices brought to my lips was always accompanied by a heaviness in my heart. Because I could hear the silence loudest in moments like these: happy, cheerful, light, innocent, and bright moments. I could hear it as loud as twisting, screeching metal that one voice was missing. And it killed me. It killed me because I knew that one voice would always be missing.

At the top of the stairs, alone and in silence, I felt what I always felt alone and in silence at the top of the stairs: guilt. Guilt because I felt safer here. Guilt because I felt relief here.

Guilt because I didn't want to return back downstairs, back down to them, my family, my life blood, my heart and soul.

Dragging a hand over my eyes already stinging with weariness, I sighed and moved by memory down the upstairs hallway. I knew the planks of warm wood beneath my wool socks better than the veins along the back of my hands. I reached blindly for the door to the bathroom between the one with a sign saying "Michael + Eoin. Stay Out Losers" still hanging from a nail and the one with nothing on it all, the one that we now always kept shut.

Wanting a splash of cold water to the face even more than a bar of soap, I twisted the knob and pushed it open. One step inside, I dropped my hand and froze at the sound of a surprised inhale.

Normally when you accidentally walk in on a person stepping naked from the shower, you cover your eyes, hastily apologise, slam the door shut behind you, and beg for your life to end as your cheeks turn every shade of red.

Normally you don't freeze like a stone gargoyle, lose not just the ability, but the drive to move, and stand there staring like you've been transfixed.

But then again, you don't normally open the door to see a woman like her.

No, that's wrong. You don't *ever* open the door, this door, a door, any door, to see a woman like her.

Her long, wet hair, tucked to one side, cascaded past her shoulders and gave her the appearance of a nymph who would flit away if I dared to breathe. Long bangs tangled like wild vines in her long eyelashes as she blinked slowly. Her green eyes were wide and her sweet pink lips were parted just slightly in surprise, but she did not speak.

When my eyes followed the trail of her hair down her slender neck to her delicate collarbone, she did not move.

Even the beads of water from the shower seemed to freeze on her pale skin like diamonds or morning dewdrops. Even in the steam-filled bathroom, they sparkled like glass down her long bare legs, along the arch of her foot held suspended as if to run, on the tip of her big toe that grazed the floor with such gentleness that even if the tile was the surface of a quiet forest pool I wouldn't expect even a single ripple. The beads of water clung to her narrow shoulders, her goose bumped arms, slender like the bones in a sparrow's wing, and her graceful fingers that skimmed her sumptuous hips, her full breasts moving with her steady breath, the only movement in that silent, sacred space.

The beauty of her naked body and the curiosity of her wide green eyes focused intently on me stunned me. Excited me. Terrified me all at once. I wanted to run to her and I wanted to run from her and I wanted all of her and none of her and only her, her, her.

"I'm sorry," I muttered, averting my eyes from heaven, from hell.

And slammed the door.

5

KAYLEIGH

*T*he door slammed. It was like a hypnotist's fingers snapping inches from my nose.

A blush seared like wildfire across my cheeks as I lunged for the towel on the bathroom counter and draped it hastily over my naked body despite the fact that I was now alone. With trembling fingers, I wrapped it tight around my chest, heaving as if I'd just sprinted three miles, as if I'd narrowly escaped being hit by a car on an icy road.

As if I'd just made passionate, hungry, *needy* love.

Hurrying to the door, I fumbled with the lock, requiring more tries than my rattled brain could count to finally turn it. With a shuddering breath, I sagged to the floor with my back sliding against the door and dropped my head between my knees.

I had just stood there when he'd burst in. I didn't reach for a towel to cover myself. I didn't run back into the shower. I didn't open my mouth to yelp, to scream, to curse, to breathe.

It wasn't because I couldn't. I knew deep in my heart that if I'd moved my hand, it wouldn't be toward the counter where the towel sat at the edge of the sink. It would have been toward him.

If my legs moved at all, they would wobble because I'd never seen steel-blue eyes like his. If I opened my mouth, I knew for certain the only sound to fall from my lips would be a sigh, a gasp, a plea.

Something more had just happened than a man opening a door on a naked woman. That was something ordinary. That was something that probably happened every day, somewhere around the world. That was something unremarkable.

This was not that.

He was not that.

A laugh escaped my lips and filled the silent bathroom where before the only noise had been blood rushing past my ears. I was being ridiculous. Of course I was.

It was Eoin I had feelings for, not a stranger who walked in on me and barely said a word. I think I believed this by the time I dragged myself up from the floor, dried off, got dressed in an old sweater and cheap jeans from Penneys, and went downstairs to meet the family, stumbling on a broken step near the bottom.

I vaguely recalled the way to the kitchen from Eoin's whispered tour late last night when we'd arrived, but the sound of voices easily guided my way. As I approached down the narrow hallway lined with a multitude of family photos, I quickly realised the conversation was about *me*.

"Soulmate?" someone hissed. "What do you mean soulmate? How long have you known this girl?"

"Love, let's not turn this into an interrogation." It was the voice of an older woman.

"Ma, how do we know she's not using him for his money or his fame?"

Pressing my back against the mismatched frames, I bit my lip and tucked under the sleeve of my sweater to hide the ever-growing hole as I continued to listen. Eoin's voice was easy to pick out.

"I've known her my entire life," he said, his voice indignant. "Every night I closed my eyes, I saw her, I talked to her, I touched her. She and I have known each other since the existence of the universe, Darren."

I heard a groan. "How long, Eoin?" the first voice repeated, sounding tired but tense. "How long?"

Eoin sighed. I knew it was Eoin because he'd sighed just like that and given me those irresistible puppy dog eyes when I'd tried to argue that maybe it was a little soon to go meet his whole family after forty-eight hours give or take. I'd obviously lost.

"Just meet her, Darren," he said. "You'll see. You'll probably fall for her, too, you know. I'm telling you, you won't believe her eyes."

"I already saw her," the voice said.

So it was *Darren* who had stumbled into the shower upstairs.

"And?" Eoin prodded.

It surprised me when I realised my fingernails were digging into my palms. My pulse was beating faster and my head was craned closer to the corner. It was an unavoidable fact that my body was eagerly waiting for Darren's response. I leaned in so not to miss a single word. I held my breath so something as silly as an inhale of oxygen didn't muffle the sound. My heart quickened in anticipation. I swear I didn't tell it to.

Darren paused only for a moment before answering, "They're just eyes. Nothing worth throwing your life away for."

His words hurt more than I wished to admit.

I forced a smile, slid backwards a few steps, and walked loudly enough that they would all hear me coming into the kitchen.

"Um, hi," I said with a shy wave, my hand tucked into the sleeve of my sweater.

My eyes skimmed over the family gathered in the tight but

cosy and delicious-smelling kitchen, careful not to seek out Darren's face. Eoin leapt off a barstool and barrelled toward me. His affection felt like getting blindsided by an eighteen-wheeler as he flung his massive paw over my shoulders, nearly making my knees buckle. His body, tight to mine, radiated more heat than the stove just past the island laden with food for not seven, but seventy.

"Everyone, everyone, listen up!" Eoin shouted despite the fact that his family was politely waiting in silence. "It is my greatest pleasure to introduce the incredibly stunning, magical creature that is Kayleigh...Fi..." Eoin paused and I felt my cheeks warm as he glanced down at me with questioning eyes.

"Scott," I whispered with a nervous smile.

"Right, right." Eoin snapped his fingers, the sound like a tree trunk breaking in two. "The one, the only, Kayleigh Scott!" Eoin held out his arms like he expected a round of applause; there was only the proverbial crickets.

I nearly cried in relief when Eoin's mom untied her apron, stepped forward, and flicked Eoin's ear.

"Jaysus Christ, Eoin," she chastised. "She's a beautiful woman, not a bear in a tutu at the circus." Holding each of my shoulders, Eoin's mom smiled radiantly at me. "Welcome to our home, love," she said. "I don't know any name other than Ma in this place, so you might as well call me that too if you ever want to get my attention."

I tried to extend a hand as I told her it was nice to meet her, but she swatted it away like a pesky fly and pulled me into a tight embrace, her arms wrapped firmly around my back. I didn't know what to do for a moment; this wasn't even something I experienced with my own mother, let alone the mother of the man I met two days ago.

"Don't overthink it, dear," she whispered in my ear. "Just squeeze."

I squeezed and it was everything I ever imagined of a normal mother-daughter relationship: apple pie with ice cream, tea parties in sunlit attics, matching pyjamas on Christmas morning. I almost didn't want it to end as she pulled away and wrapped my hand in hers, patting it gently.

"Now here we have Noah," she explained, pointing to a distractingly handsome man with a mischievous pinkie dipped into the icing of a chocolate cake. "He's my oldest, though you wouldn't always know it."

I nodded. "Nice to meet you."

"And his lovely fiancée, Aubrey, a gift from the States."

"A delicious gift," Noah amended before plopping some icing on Aubrey's nose.

"I'd have married her if Noah hadn't beat me to it," Eoin added behind me with a chuckle.

Aubrey paused with her finger in her mouth and raised an eyebrow. "You know I would never have said 'yes', right?"

While Eoin stuck out his tongue at Aubrey, Ma O'Sullivan directed my attention to a slick-looking man in a pink apron.

"The one with his nose buried in his work phone despite being told several times not to bring it to lunch is Michael," she explained.

Michael lifted his blue eyes momentarily and muttered a quick "hello".

"That means he likes you," Eoin whispered over my shoulder, following like a directionless puppy. His excitement over me meeting his family was infectious; I wanted to meet his chaotic, wonderful, loving family, too. Hell, I even wanted to be a part of it.

Of course, all that changed when Ma turned me around in the crammed kitchen and I came face-to-face with *him*.

"This is Darren."

I wasn't sure how I didn't notice it before. His kind of coldness surely should have formed icicles on the condensation-streaked bathroom mirror. The churning storm in his grey-blue eyes should have brought with them gusts of brutal wind that turned my naked skin blue despite the swirling steam. How could I not have noticed the chill of his gaze that threatened to turn the tiles beneath my feet to ice.

"I've got to wash my hands," was all he said by way of introduction.

He turned, and even though Michael shouted after him that he could use the sink now, Darren disappeared around the corner. I winced at each pounding step up the stairs.

"Don't mind him," Eoin said, his arm again feeling like a stack of bricks slung over my shoulders. "He doesn't like anything. Or anyone."

"Come, come," Ma said, and I realised I already liked calling her Ma in my mind far too much. "Let's get the table set to eat."

Setting the table as a child with my own family meant laying out three plates in an icy dining room, even though we all knew only two would be needed. Shivering across from one another, my mother and I would stare down at the congealing gravy on our slices of dry turkey as the whistle of a referee from the television in the dark living room cut through the tense silence. My fingertips were always blue by the time my mother shifted uncomfortably in her chair, swallowed nervously, and had to clear her throat twice to squeak out, "Lunch is on the table, dear."

"Don't nag me," my father would bark from his lounge chair positioned next to the only heater in the house before cursing at either the rugby match or my mother. "I heard you the first time. Just bring my plate out here."

If my mother made noise pushing out her chair, she would get yelled at, so she moved slowly, carefully, robotically. Sometimes I would watch her tiptoe to the microwave to reheat the food she'd spent two and half hours preparing. I would continue to stare at the greyish-brown film spreading across my cooling gravy, because I feared I'd scream if I saw my mother wince one more time at the noise each button made before the whirl of the microwave started.

"Are you coming or what?" my father would holler angrily from the living room.

If my mother made it to him before we heard the creak of springs, we were safe. If we heard the creak of springs, no one was eating Sunday lunch—my father would storm off to the pub for "some goddamn food", my mother would clean the mess off the floor, and I would climb the stairs to my room so at least she didn't have to hear the hungry growls of my stomach.

In the bustle of the O'Sullivan's kitchen, Ma noticed me delicately placing each plate to avoid making unnecessary noise. She grabbed my shoulders to whisper in my ear, "Darling, we'll never eat at this rate."

She grabbed the next plate from my hands and tossed it haphazardly onto the table. Clanging about the whole time, the plate wobbled as it lurched this way and that and got dangerously close to toppling right over the edge.

"I just don't want to break anything," I said with a wince.

She squeezed my shoulders. "Break all of them, it doesn't matter, love," she said before adding with a wink, "I suspect my boys wouldn't mind at all stuffing their mouths straight from the pot like the little piggies they are anyway."

I smiled and nodded. "Alright."

Ma patted my back. "Good woman."

I had been hesitant about agreeing to come here in the first place, but as we all sat down to Sunday lunch, I found myself falling. But it wasn't Eoin that I toppled helplessly head over heels for—it was his family.

The cacophony of mismatched wooden chairs graffitied

with crayon scuffing against the well-worn hardwood floors as we bellied up to a table about to buckle beneath the weight of a cornucopia of food sent tingles down my spine. My heart fluttered as unabashed laughter and clattering knives and forks and playful teasing and the clink of glasses filled the room warmed not by the oven, but by the overwhelming sense of love. The buttered roll Noah lobbed to Michael over the steaming roast and the already half-empty decanter of mulled wine might as well have been a shooting star in my hazy, happy vision. If the question "Kayleigh, can you pass the potatoes?" was a proposal, my answer was "Yes, yes, a thousand times yes."

The only dark cloud in my sky was Darren.

Seated as far as possible from me, he did not even glance in my direction. In fact, he didn't even look up from his plate as he pushed around his Brussels sprouts and carved rivers of gravy through his mashed potatoes. He did not engage in the lively conversation that bounced around the table. He did not laugh at Noah's jokes, smile at Aubrey's "Drunk of the Week" story from The Jar, a Dublin bar they ran together, or even groan with the rest of his family when Eoin burped a table-rattling burp.

So when Darren abruptly shoved back his chair and stood, everyone glanced up at him in surprise. Noah paused mid-sentence to stare at Darren with the rest of us.

"We need pie," he announced.

Eoin laughed, leaning back to balance on the back two legs of his chair. "Pie?" he shook his head. "We've got enough cookies to feed all of Santa's elves."

"I baked a chocolate cake," Aubrey added.

"And Ma just put a rum raisin pudding in the oven," Noah nodded toward the kitchen and its merry pile of dirty dishes stacked high near the sink.

Darren, still staring down at his plate, straightened his unused knife. "I want pie," he said. "So I'm going to go get pie."

Ma laid a gentle hand on Darren's. "Alright, dear," she smiled. "After lunch, I'll go wi—"

"We need pie now," he interrupted. "And I think Kayleigh should go with me."

6

DARREN

*R*eason #16 To Really, Really Dislike Kayleigh Scott: she laughed far too loud.

Even with Michael on one side of me arguing with Noah all the way across the kitchen table about that year's taxes for The Jar, Aubrey on the other side smacking her lips after every bite of Ma's Sunday roast, and Eoin's rugby match blaring behind me, I could still hear her laughter over all of it. It was far too loud, far too happy, far too bell-like and sweet for my liking. I glared at my potatoes as Eoin said something to make her giggle over her glass of mulled wine.

Reason #31 To Really, Really Dislike Kayleigh Scott: her giggle was even worse.

I hadn't touched a bite of my lunch because I'd been too busy drafting my list in my mind. I clung to each reason not to like her, not to get swept up in her smile, not to drown in the waves of her fiery red hair as if each one was a foothold on a sheer cliff face.

Because I couldn't fall.

I couldn't.

When all I could come up with for Reason #19 To Really, Really Dislike Kayleigh Scott was "green eyes *too* green", I knew I was in trouble. Unable to hold myself back any longer, I shoved back my chair, declared we were in desperate need of pie, and said, without explanation, that Kayleigh was the one who needed to come on this urgent errand with me.

When I finally looked over at her across the table, I found her eyes wide and staring at me, and I realised again why I'd tried to avoid them during all of Sunday lunch. Reason #4 To Really, Really Dislike Kayleigh Scott: because tearing my gaze away from her eyes was like dragging myself out of a pit of quicksand with my arms tied behind my back and my ankles weighed down with a car tyre.

I watched Kayleigh glance around the table before holding a delicate hand up to her chest with an eyebrow raised at me. "Me?" she asked, incredulous.

I crossed my arms indignantly over my chest. "You don't like pie?"

She shook her head. "No, of course I do, but—"

"Then let's go."

Damn, I thought as I turned without another word and walked toward Ma's front door. That would have been the best reason I could think of so far to *actually* not like the girl.

Behind me I heard Eoin tell Kayleigh to get cherry, cherry, cherry. She then asked what flavour he wanted because she didn't get it the first ten times, and I bit back a grin as oblivious Eoin sighed and answered again, "Cherry."

Reason #45 To Really, Really Dislike Kayleigh Scott: *not* funny.

"Don't be an idiot," Michael grumbled back in the kitchen. "It's pumpkin or nothing at all."

"Just don't let him get pecan!" Noah shouted after her as

padded footsteps hurried down the hallway behind me. "That would be nuts!"

Aubrey's groan quickly followed. I imagined her playfully smacking his chest as she always did, and a pang of envy for that kind of closeness with someone tugged at my heart. I comforted myself the way I always did: I reminded myself I didn't deserve it.

I was pulling on my coat when Kayleigh ran up beside me.

"Do you really need me just to go grab a pie?" she asked.

I slung my scarf over my shoulder and fished my keys out of my pocket. "I'll be in the car," I said, opening the door and stepping out into the blast of icy air.

I welcomed the biting wind that stung my cheeks as I sucked in a deep, steadying breath of fresh air. It was as close as I could come to a splash of cold water in my face, and I drank it in till it burned my lungs and made my eyes water.

In the driver's seat, I waited as the engine idled without even glancing at the heater. My eyes were focused on the windshield lined with frost, and I was determined to keep it that way as the passenger door opened and Kayleigh hopped in.

"Brrr," she said, shivering next to me. "Should I turn on the heater?"

Reason #43 To Really, Really Dislike Kayleigh Scott: very high maintenance.

Reason #18 To Really, Really Dislike Kayleigh Scott: not environmentally conscious at all.

"No," I grumbled as I shifted the car into gear. "I'm not cold."

Ice crunched beneath the wheels as I pulled out of the sleepy little neighbourhood of puffing chimneys and sparkling Christmas lights and onto the busy highway, and still there wasn't a peep next to me.

Daring a glance over at her, I found her face half buried in her lavender wool scarf. Her white beanie with a fluffy ball on top was pulled down to her eyebrows and she had her mittened hands tucked under her armpits. Her cheeks glowed a cheery pink. I immediately wished I hadn't looked.

"You're not cold either then?" I asked, trying not to let my teeth chatter as my own fingers developed hypothermia while gripping the frozen wheel.

She turned to me, green eyes bright and sparkling, and shook her head. "Nope," she smiled. "I'm all nice and toasty over here myself."

Reason #21 To Really, Really Dislike Kayleigh Scott: only thinks of herself. It was quite inconsiderate to ignore the red of my nose, just because *she* was "all nice and toasty" over there.

"Do you want to listen to some music?" she asked after a quiet moment between us.

"I prefer silence."

"Yeah," Kayleigh nodded. "Me, too. Fuck Christmas carols."

Reason #3 To Really, Really Dislike Kayleigh Scott: doesn't like Christmas carols.

My little brother was dating a monster.

I pulled into the nearly empty parking lot of the local supermarket, got out, stuffed my freezing hands into my coat pockets, and stalked toward the glass sliding doors without making sure that Kayleigh was following. I only knew she was by her little puffs of condensed breath beside me as she slipped on the icy footpath while trying to keep up in her beat-up Converse with a piece of duct tape over the left toe.

"So what do you do for a living?" she asked as a blast of warm air hit us along with the smell of fresh baked bread.

Reason #23 To Really, Really Dislike Kayleigh Scott: nosy.

"I think we should just focus on getting the pie," I said just before turning onto the first aisle.

Kayleigh's sneakers squeaked on the linoleum floor as she hurried after me through the dead store.

"Why did you bring me along if you didn't want to talk to me?" she pressed, practically jogging to keep up with my long stride.

Add tiny legs to the list.

We passed a row of brightly coloured cereal boxes, and as we rounded the corner onto the condiment aisle, I answered simply, "To hold the pie."

In response to this, Kayleigh reached out, grabbed my arm, and stopped us smack dab in front of the mustards. "You really don't like me, do you?" Her green eyes seemed even bigger than before with half her face hidden behind her bundle of winter clothes.

I stared down at her, waited for a moment, and then replied, "No."

My arm slipped easily enough from her mittened hand, and I continued down the aisle and onto the next, leaving Kayleigh where she stood.

"You aren't going to tell me *why* you don't like me?" she called from behind the pickle jars.

I paused next to the tiny onions and bit my lips. *Because you make me nervous when you're around. Because I feel like I'm not in control when you're looking into my eyes. Because there's a promise I haven't broken in ten years, and it only took you a morning to make me want to shatter it.*

"Because you're using my brother for his money or his fame," I shouted over the top shelf stocked with pickle jars. "Or both."

I didn't believe it, not really, but it was better than the truth.

I continued down to the end of the aisle only to find Kayleigh waiting for me in the next one. She stood buried under her scarf with her arms folded over her peacoat. "I don't like you either, you know," she said with an aggravated huff.

Shrugging with a nonchalant smile, all I replied with was a causal "Okay" before slipping by her. Meandering down the next empty aisle alone, I managed to make it past the bags of ground coffee, past the boxes of teas—chamomile, peppermint, chai, blackberry, green and black and white—past the energy drinks and juices and hot chocolate concentrates. I only managed to make it halfway past the rainbow of Gatorades before giving in.

"Why?" I asked in the general direction of where Kayleigh had been last.

At first there was only silence and then an announcement for a deal on Swiss and then silence again. I thought she wasn't going to answer, but then I heard her voice from the soda aisle one over.

"Because you make snap judgements about people that aren't true at all and then base your whole opinion of them on that to justify treating them poorly when really you just want a reason to be moody all the time for heaven knows why."

This took me by such surprise that I found myself liking her grit and honesty and spunk before realising that was the opposite of what I was supposed to be doing.

"Well, bollocks," I shouted over to her as I moved over two aisles to the canned vegetables. "You could have just said that you didn't like my hair."

Kayleigh laughed. "Oh, that too."

I tried to listen for her squeaky footsteps, but couldn't figure out where in the grocery store she was as I ran my fingertips over the row of canned green beans.

"I don't like you because you look at someone like you know them," I said. "Like you can see straight through into them."

I didn't see Kayleigh in the pasta and sauce aisle, but I heard her. "I don't like you because you regard basic human empathy and compassion as an invasion."

That wasn't true, I reassured myself as I passed the capellini and then the farfalle. That wasn't true at all.

I cupped my hands over my mouth to make sure she could hear me as my pulse quickened in irritation. "Well...well...I don't like *you* because you don't even know how to lock a bathroom door so people don't walk in on you naked!"

I rounded the corner and came face-to-face with an elderly woman with a frozen pizza in her pink gloves.

"Excuse me, ma'am," I quickly said, squeezing her shoulders, narrow even under her navy puffer coat.

Avoiding her disapproving frown, I hurried around the corner to the frozen foods to find Kayleigh at the other end, hands on her hips, cheeks red.

"Don't even get me started on how much I don't like you because you aren't even polite enough to *knock*!" She took an angry step toward me.

I took an angry step toward her and before we knew it, we were storming toward each other from each end of the aisle.

"You just stood there!" I shouted.

"No, *you* just stood there!" she shouted right back.

My hands were balled into fists at my side as I stormed past the fridge full of ice cream. "You could have covered up."

Kayleigh shoved up her white beanie, which was falling over her eyes, and then pointed her mitten at me as we drew nearer and nearer to one another. "You could have turned around."

Neapolitan.

"You could have closed the door."

"You could have closed your eyes."

Cherry Garcia. Vanilla Bean. Salted Caramel Brownie.

"You could have done *something*," I growled, not three feet away from her.

"You could have done *anything*," she snapped.

At the exact damn time, we stopped in front of one another, chests heaving, eyes flashing with what I hoped was anger and what I feared was arousal and said, "But you didn't."

With the hum of the fridges and the rasp of our breaths as the only sound between us, we stared at one another. I wondered if she was thinking of me standing there at the bathroom door, looking at her naked. Because I certainly was. I wondered if it was stirring something deep inside of her. Because there was no denying it did for me.

We stood there until another announcement blasted over the intercom for the same Swiss deal.

Kayleigh rubbed at her eyes and nodded toward the fridge to her left. "Pies are there," she said.

I turned on my heel and started walking back toward the car. I never wanted feckin' pie.

The car ride back home was filled with a tense silence that threatened to choke off my air supply, blacken my vision, and send me careening off the icy road. We got out of the car in silence, we walked up the driveway in silence, we stepped inside Ma's house in silence.

As we were hanging our coats, Eoin came crashing down the hallway, a huge smile on his face. Kayleigh gasped when he swept her up into his arms without warning and pressed his lips to hers. Wedged into the tight corner, I was forced to watch him kiss her.

Worse, I was forced to watch her kiss him back.

It felt like an eternity before Eoin eased Kayleigh back to the floor. I avoided her eyes as she straightened her beanie on her dishevelled hair.

"So, where's the pie then?" Eoin asked, eyes searching my empty gloves, then Kayleigh's empty mittens.

I ignored him as I slipped past her still held in his arms. I didn't even take the time to unlace my boots, instead tracking muddy prints all over the hardwood floors.

"Darren," Eoin called after me nonetheless. "Darren, did you get cherry?"

Reason #1 To Really, Really, Fucking *Really* Dislike Kayleigh Scott: she wasn't mine.

7

KAYLEIGH

I thought about *him* as I scrubbed the dishes, elbow deep in sudsy water that could cut through the toughest grease but somehow not through the image of his eyes on me. When I ran out of dishes to clean, I thought about him as I listened to Michael ramble on about the intricacies of corporate law, nodding along as if I wasn't listening out for someone else's voice. I thought about him while wandering the cosily cluttered house, trying to convince myself I wasn't searching for one face in particular in each family picture I stumbled upon.

Because that face wasn't Eoin's.

That voice wasn't Eoin's either.

He was Darren.

He infuriated me, frustrated me, annoyed me, irritated me, boiled my blood and wiggled his way beneath my skin. I found his melancholy unapproachable, his moodiness unlikeable, and his grumblings nearly incomprehensible. He pushed buttons I didn't know I had, and based on the gargoyle-like rigidity of his features, he seemingly didn't have any for me to press in return. I did not like his attitude, I did not like his standoffishness, I did not like his perpetual frown, I did not like his broad shoulders that cast a wide shadow over the bright little living room, and I certainly did not like his grey eyes.

Or were they blue?

Darren O'Sullivan was, without exception, an entirely disagreeable man with no redeeming qualities in sight, and I had nothing but negative things to say about him for anyone unlucky enough to ask.

But for his younger brother, Eoin, I had nothing at all to say.

When I returned from the store with Darren, I'd almost forgotten I was here with *Eoin* visiting *his* family till his lips were smashed against mine.

So it came as even more of a shock than it should have when Eoin suddenly dropped down to one knee in front of me before I'd even finished my first bite of rum raisin pudding later that evening.

Maybe if I hadn't been brooding about how rude Darren was, I would have noticed Eoin pacing back and forth in agitation as he chewed at his nails in front of the flickering fireplace.

Maybe if I'd been listening to anything but my blood rushing in my ears, I would have heard Ma pause her crocheting on the couch and ask him with a raised eyebrow, "What in the world is wrong with you, boy?"

Maybe if I wasn't too busy formulating in my mind a put-Darren-in-his-place, make-him-feel-guilty, give-out-to-him speech (one I'd never in a million years deliver), I would have seen Aubrey, legs crisscrossed on a rug where she played checkers with Noah, snatch up her spiked hot chocolate to keep it safe from Eoin's thundering steps as he marched toward me with determination in his eyes.

Maybe if Darren hadn't consumed my world, I could have had a tiny bit of a warning for what was about to happen.

But none of that mattered anymore, because there I was

sitting petrified in a tufted leather chair with a fork full of crumbling pudding suspended halfway to my mouth, thinking about his older brother when Eoin dropped to one knee.

My fork clattered to my plate. If Eoin's present position hadn't already stolen the rest of the family's attention, the noise certainly did the job.

"What are you doing?" I whispered. I may as well have yelled it out, given every pair of eyes in the living room was already fixed on us.

Eoin tried to grab the blue and white dessert plate from my fingers so he could take my hands into his, but I resisted, squeezing onto the porcelain edges as if my last name depended on it.

"Eoin..." I laughed nervously, glancing to Ma, who had paused mid-stitch. "Eoin, very funny."

One by one Eoin peeled back my fingers, pulled my plate out of reach and laid it on the floor next to his bent knee. *Maybe his shoelace is untied*, I thought, only to have another wave of desperation crash over me when I saw he was wearing very shoelace-less slippers a few sizes too small.

I leaned forward in my chair, and this time it was a plea when I whispered, "Eoin."

Even the snap of the flames in the stone fireplace seemed to hold their breath as Eoin squeezed my fingers, closed his eyes, and opened his mouth. "Kayleigh Scott..."

"Oh, no," Aubrey gasped, looking over at us between parted fingers like this was a scene from a horror movie.

Noah pushed himself to his feet, perhaps to intervene, but Michael stuck his arm out to stop him. Michael had been reading the *Financial Times* with a glass of sherry next to Ma on the couch. Now he stared at Eoin's back in the same way you stare at a crash on the highway.

Darren was in the chair in the farthest corner of the living room near the fireplace, reading by the light of a lamp. He hadn't even bothered to put down his book.

"Kayleigh Scott, you are the moon to the chaotic waves of my soul," Eoin started, eyes still closed. "You are the sunlight to the budding of my heart."

Well, that was surprisingly beautiful. At least I'd have those lines to hold onto for the rest of my "till death do they part".

"The gravity to my rugby ball."

Bit of a slip there... Aubrey barely contained her groan.

Eoin's hands clung to mine. "You've completely turned my life around. I'm a new man because of you. You've made me want things I never thought I'd want before."

I winced as Eoin sucked in a deep, wobbling breath.

"So...Kayleigh Scott..." *Oh God. Oh God.* "...would you do me the great honour..." He paused again, his eyes moving behind his eyelids. "The greatest honour, really," he added, "...the honour of all honours...the MVP of honours...the Rugby World Cup Champion of honours...the—"

"Jesus Christ," Aubrey cried. "Spit it out already."

Eoin opened his eyes and smiled up at me. "Kayleigh Scott, will you be my...will you be my Dublin gal?"

I stared down at him in confusion. "Huh?"

Eoin leapt to his feet, unable to contain his excitement any longer. "Move to Dublin, Kayleigh! I want you to move to Dublin."

A collective sigh circled the living room. I sagged against the well-worn back of the leather chair in relief.

"Oh, thank goodness," Aubrey groaned, collapsing onto the checkerboard and sending black and red pieces scattering across the rug.

I caught Darren's eyes glancing at us from over the top of his book to which he immediately returned, once again hiding his face from me.

"I need a drink," Michael said, folding up his newspaper.

Noah offered him a hand up from the couch and added, "Something strong, eh?" They left the living room together.

Ma just chuckled under her breath and returned to her crocheting.

Eoin frowned in confusion at everyone over his shoulder. "What?" he asked. "What? What's wrong?"

Gently, I placed my hands on either side of his face and turned his head back toward me. "Eoin," I said as patiently as possible. "Eoin, I like you, I do, but I don't have a place here and—"

"Move in with me," Eoin blurted out.

I almost burst out laughing, the idea was so ridiculous. "Eoin, I... I..."

His puppy dog eyes searched mine as my lips searched for the words. "What?" he asked. "You don't want to?"

"No, it's just that...umm..."

"Candace needs a roommate," Aubrey interjected.

I leaned around Eoin's muscular thighs to see her. "What's that?"

She glanced up at Eoin, who was watching her, and very diplomatically said, "*If* moving in with Eoin is a *teeny* tiny bit too big of a leap after a weekend together, you could move in with Candace. She lives above a dive bar not far from The Jar, and if you don't mind a little late-night noise, she has an extra room right now."

Eoin grinned over at me excitedly. "It was meant to be, Kayleigh. Written in the stars." He swept his arm over his head. "So you'll say yes then?"

"Eoin, I can't just—I mean, I don't even have a job."

I thought for sure this was my saving grace. I thought for sure there was no way he could snap his fingers and have a job for me right then and there. I thought I'd avoided disaster.

Turns out I was barrelling right toward it.

"Darren will give you a job."

In the far corner, I heard Darren's book snap closed. Both he and I responded with an immediate and firm, "No."

In my mind I added a "fuck, no", and I wouldn't have been surprised if Darren added one of his own as well.

"What?" Eoin threw up his hands. "Why not? It's perfect."

Darren crossed his arms over his chest. His features were dark even in the light of the reading lamp, his eyes cold despite the warmth of the fireplace no more than an arm's length away.

"I don't need anybody at the garage," he said. "It's just me and that's the way I like it."

Eoin frowned. "Weren't you just telling me how badly you needed a receptionist to help you get organised and stuff?" he asked.

Aubrey craned her head around to look at Darren as well, who shifted uncomfortably in his chair. He scratched at the back of his neck. "I filled the position," he tried.

It sounded even to me like a shot in the dark.

"Filled the position?" Aubrey's eyes narrowed suspiciously. "Filled the position you just said you have no need for?"

Before Darren could respond to this, I leapt in. "It's fine," I said. "It's really fine. I'd be a terrible receptionist anyway. I'm no good with...umm...phones."

Eoin dismissed me with a wave of his big paw of a hand. "Darren will teach you."

Darren set aside his book on top of the already wobbly stack of books next to the reading chair and pushed himself to his feet.

Our eyes met across the living room and time froze.

The ceiling was no longer striped with wooden rafters but dotted with a multitude of stars. The walls transformed into a thick forest of windless pines on either side of us, and the chill of midnight doused the red and yellow and orange flames of the fireplace. Beneath our feet the softness of the rug hardened to asphalt, a thick yellow stripe streaking between us. My lungs seized as an invisible seatbelt tugged against my chest as I stomped on my failing brakes. In the flash of the blinding headlights I could see him and he could see me and we each knew: we were on a collision course.

Working together meant more time together when what we needed was less. Working together meant hours without Eoin, which would be disastrous since I managed to forget all about Eoin in a fifteen-minute trip with Darren to the store for pie. Working together meant lingering gazes, tense silences, brushing fingers. Working together meant day after day of temptation.

Working together meant wrenched metal, shattered glass, fire and smoke.

As we looked into each other's eyes, we both knew neither of us would survive the crash.

I blinked and in an instant the living room was back, Darren's eyes were gone, and he was stepping toward Eoin.

But the panic was still there. In him. In me.

"I'm just a mechanic." Darren sounded as if he was almost pleading. "I'm buried in oil and grease all day. All I know how to do is turn a wrench and twist a screwdriver. I don't know how to train a receptionist."

Aubrey threw a red checker piece against Darren's chest from her place on the rug. "Don't be silly," she laughed, because she couldn't smell the burning tyres as Darren and I tried to stop the inevitable collision. "You don't have to train her at all— Kayleigh's perfectly capable of using a phone."

"You really don't want me anywhere near an office," I said, standing as well. "I'm messy and unorganised and I'm really just scatter-brained when it comes to numbers."

Eoin moved over and knocked the wind out of me with his arm around my shoulders. "Trust me," he grinned. "That office at the shop can't get messier than it already is."

My heart raced with desperation as I slipped from underneath his arm. "I actually have a bit of savings I could dip into and—"

"And the shop is really quiet around the holidays and..." Darren was closer. Too close. "...and—"

"And I'd need time off to visit my mom," I said. "And—"

"—and there's all that software Michael keeps talking about that could keep me organised and—"

"Do you two have a secret history I don't know about which is the real reason why you're making such a big stink about a silly job in a silly shop?" Both Darren and I turned to look at Eoin, who had crossed his big arms over his wide chest. My stomach flipped when his puppy dog green eyes narrowed as he frowned from me to Darren, who I didn't dare look over to.

Had it been that obvious? Had everyone else felt the same electricity that I felt? Had they all felt the same thrill I had, like a child rubbing their socks under the sheets and then ducking under in the dark to see the sparks? Had he caught me glancing over at Darren, secretly hoping that I'd catch him glancing over at me, too?

Eoin uncrossed his arms and whacked both of us on the back as he let his head fall back in big, hearty laughter. "The thought of you two together," he cackled. "Hilarious!"

Darren and I eyed each other nervously before each half-heartedly joined in with Eoin's obvious merriment.

"Ridiculous," I added, watching for Darren's reaction.

But he wasn't looking at me any longer. He patted Eoin on the arm and said, "Of course Kayleigh can come work at the shop if she wants."

He grabbed his book from the pile next to the fire and kissed

Ma on the cheek before slipping silently out of the living room. I was watching him go when Noah and Michael returned with a bottle of whiskey.

"What'd we miss?" Noah asked, wrapping Aubrey in his arms on the floor.

"Kayleigh was just saying how she'd say yes to Darren's job offer," Eoin said. "Right, Kayleigh?"

Eoin craned his neck so that he could see my face. Nervously, I glanced around the room and found his family all smiling encouragingly up at me. I usually couldn't say no to even one person. So saying no to Eoin *plus* his wonderful family who had been nothing but kind and warm and welcoming to me...well, that was never going to happen.

Just like a mangled car was never going to drive again.

Just like the shattered pieces of glass strewn across the highway were never going to weave themselves back together.

Just like the black smoke hanging over the fiery crash was never going to do anything but choke your lungs and bring water to your eyes.

I managed a tentative smile as I looked up into Eoin's expectant wide eyes.

"Yes?"

8

KAYLEIGH

*O*ne advantage of living above a college dive bar that I
didn't expect was the free and *eager* moving service.

"Thanks a million, fellas."

From the couch, surrounded by stacks of boxes, I watched
with awe as Candace leaned out the cracked open door to give
each of the three muscular jocks crammed in the narrow spiral
staircase leading up from the bar to our apartment a bright red
kiss on their stubbled cheeks.

"Sure you don't need any more help?" the one with the
rugby jersey on asked, craning his neck into the apartment.

"Toot-a-loo, Stuart." Candace, at not a hair over five foot no
matter what she tried to argue to the contrary, reached up to
press her hand firmly against the big man's chest. She flicked
him on the nose when he tried to kiss the length of her
petite arm.

"Don't miss me too much," she called cheerfully in her
charming Brazilian accent as she closed the door after a little
seductive wiggle of her fingers under her chin despite the boys'
desperate protests outside.

Turning to lean against the door, my new roommate crossed

her arms over her chest and lifted a dark eyebrow. "Not bad, eh?"

I laughed as I checked my wristwatch.

"You managed to get me moved in in less than fifteen minutes," I said. "I'd say 'not bad' is an understatement."

Candace flicked her mane of long, curly raven hair over her shoulder and grinned. "I know, I know." She gave me a wink as she twirled toward the fridge covered in stickers from around the world. "*Sou incrível.*"

As she pulled a bottle of champagne from the freezer, I frowned. "What does that mean?"

Candace tucked the bottle under her arm, snatched two chipped mugs from mismatched hooks under a wonky cabinet, and sambaed toward me. She leapt onto the couch next to me and handed me a mug. "It means..." She grimaced as she struggled with the cork. "It means, 'I'm incredible.'"

She cheered when the cork finally exploded from the bottle and careened across the apartment just as the front door opened. The cork whizzed past Aubrey's head to crash harmlessly against the metal rail of the staircase.

"Jesus Christ, Candace!" Aubrey kicked the door closed behind her as she balanced two boxes of pizza, a bag of breadsticks, three containers of marinara, and a bottle of ranch dressing in her arms. "America brings a delicious peace offering and Brazil declares war?"

Candace leapt off the couch just as quickly as she had leapt onto it and galloped toward Aubrey with her tiny hands in the shape of guns. "That all depends on whether you got extra jalapeños the way I like, Aubrey dearest..."

Sending the ranch and the breadsticks toppling to the floor, Candace lifted the lid of the first pizza box and stretched her head back to yell at the ceiling. "World peace!"

Aubrey shook her head at me as she set down her food haul,

including the fallen breadsticks and ranch, on the makeshift coffee table crafted out of two old trunks and a faded surfboard. She joined me on the couch as she finished the task of pouring the champagne that Candace abandoned.

"So," she said, handing me a nearly overflowing mug that claimed "Put some whiskey in my coffee because it's Ireland somewhere", "what do you think?"

"She obviously loves it!" Candace shouted over a mouthful of pizza before grabbing the champagne to take a swig straight from the bottle.

Aubrey tossed a glistening breadstick at Candace, who was sitting cross-legged on a tasselled pillow on one of many clashing rugs that covered the wooden floors. The breadstick smelled intoxicatingly of garlic and butter.

"I asked Kayleigh," Aubrey laughed. "*Quieto!*"

Candace grabbed another slice and grumbled, "Your Portuguese accent is terrible."

Chuckling, I sipped my champagne to keep it from running down the sides and splashing onto my jeans. "I do love it," I admitted to Aubrey truthfully.

The floors pulsed and vibrated from the pounding music downstairs, nothing inside the apartment matched anything else, giving it an undeniable sense of chaos, the Brazilian flag stretched across the exposed bricks to my left couldn't possibly be bigger or brighter, but I did—I loved it.

Strings of lights, some white, some multicoloured, some shaped like tigers or snowflakes or roses, seemed to be strung from anywhere and everywhere. Old bossa nova music playing from a record player filled the room with an irresistible cheerfulness, and even I, with two left feet, couldn't resist tapping a toe or two along. The vaulted ceilings made it feel spacious and the rugs and cushions and pillows and blankets scattered everywhere made it feel cosy. It was a hectic, disordered, messy Bohemian paradise. I really wasn't sure whether I just moved into a new apartment or joined a cult, but either way I was wearing fuzzy socks, smiling and eating pizza.

"Don't let her put that stuff on your slice," Candace warned, nodding her head toward Aubrey.

"It's called ranch," Aubrey said as she squirted a pool of it onto her plate. "And Kayleigh, you should only try it if you're ready for your mind to explode."

"American slop." Candace shuddered.

I reached over to dip the tip of my slice into the ranch. Both girls watched my reaction as I tasted it.

Candace groaned when I smiled. "That's it!" she shouted. "I'm kicking you out!"

Aubrey raised her This Girl Runs on Coffee mug to me. "You have excellent taste, Kayleigh," she said with a grin.

Candace swigged champagne before pointing the bottle at me. "Maybe not in food," she said and then winked. "But your taste in sets of abs is superb." She kissed the fingertips of her free hand. "Eoin is *esplêndido*." She pressed her hand dramatically to her forehead. "Which in English means scrumptious, scrumptious, goddamn *scrumptious*."

I picked at an olive on my pizza slice and smiled awkwardly. "Yeah," was all I managed to spit out. "He's very...muscular." My cheeks reddened slightly as I stared at my plate. Thankfully Candace didn't seem to notice as she continued.

"So Aubrey snatched the beautiful Noah from me," she said, causing Aubrey to choke on her champagne.

"*Snatched?*" Aubrey's eyebrows raised in incredulity.

Candace nodded. "Snatched," she repeated. "Noah was moments from sweeping me off my feet and carrying me away in his strong, tanned arms when you ruined my fairy tale ending."

Aubrey laughed. "I think the only thing that was going to sweep you off your feet was a strong gust of wind."

Candace leapt to her feet, her champagne spilling. She pointed a fiery finger at Aubrey. "I'm five-two!"

Aubrey nodded. "Yeah, and I'm six-five."

Candace whipped around to face me. "You believe I'm five-two, right, Kayleigh?"

Fearing for my life, I nodded.

"*Porra…*" Candace cursed as she returned to the floor, pushing her dark curls out of her face.

Aubrey winked at me and took another massive bite of ranch-covered pizza.

"So, as I was saying," Candace said, calming down. "Calm", I was beginning to realise, was relative for her. "Aubrey *snatched* the Greek god O'Sullivan and you scooped up Sporty Spice O'Sullivan."

Aubrey snorted.

Candace sighed and consoled herself with the champagne bottle. "So I guess I'm left with Wall Street O'Sullivan," she said. "He'd fall for me for sure if I could just get him to look up from that *maldito* phone."

Still playing around with my food, I cleared my throat and asked as casually as I could manage, "Um, what about the other one?"

"Who, Darren?" Candace wrinkled her nose and shook her head. "Darren's impossible to love," she said and then added, "even with those grey-blue eyes of his."

I caught myself before scooting to the edge of the couch, my interest peaked. "Umm," I forced myself not to blurt out the words. "What do you mean?"

Candace shrugged. "All men are like eggs, you know?"

I had no clue, but I agreed nonetheless because I wanted to

hear what she had to say about the withdrawn, moody O'Sullivan brother, the one who I was very much *not* dating.

Candance tapped her nails on the champagne bottle and continued, "The goal is to crack them, you know? To get to the soft, yummy, good stuff inside."

"Right." I nodded.

"Well, some guys are harder to crack than others. Some are really tricky, really, really tricky," Candace said. "But I'm convinced there's nothing to crack with Darren: he's solid all the way through. So unless you like knocking your head on brick walls over and over again..." Candace shrugged again and then shook her head as if to clear Darren's very name from her head. She winked at me. "Just be happy it's Eoin who likes you," she concluded.

Aubrey elbowed me. "Seems a bit more than 'likes', eh?"

I blushed and tried to hide it behind another sip of champagne. Was I blushing because I was embarrassed how much Eoin obviously adored me? Or was I blushing because Eoin obviously adored me and all I wanted to do was steer the conversation back to Darren?

"Are Darren and Eoin close?" I asked once my cheeks had cooled.

Aubrey glanced over at Candace and hesitated. "Darren's not exactly 'close' with anyone in the family," she explained. "I mean, maybe I should let you ask Eoin about this—"

"No, no, go on," I insisted.

When both Aubrey and Candace raised their eyebrows at me, I realised I'd been too enthusiastic. I had to come up with a reason to cover my stupid, reckless ass. Stat.

"Umm, it's just that I want to know about Eoin's family, obviously," I paused as my mind screamed *since he's the one you're actually dating!*, "but, umm, we're so early in the dating stage that I'm not sure I'll get an honest answer from him, you know?"

Aubrey and Candace both nodded.

"You're still in the 'say anything to get laid' phase," Candace offered.

I snapped my fingers. "Exactly."

Aubrey grinned. "The 'keep the family skeletons in the closet' phase."

I nodded.

Candace reached for another breadstick and added with a mischievous smile, "The 'no, my family definitely doesn't wear matching sweaters and go pumpkin picking each year' phase."

Aubrey's mouth opened wide in shock. "I told you that in confidence!" she shouted indignantly.

Candace just laughed. "You told me that in drunkenness."

"They're one and the same," Aubrey said, grabbing the breadstick before Candace could take a bite and adding when she whined in protest, "You've lost your breadstick privileges."

"Right, right," I said, more than eager to hear more about Darren. "I just want an honest perspective, that's all."

Aubrey leaned back against the cushions on the couch and munched on her breadstick contemplatively. "Darren loves his family," she finally said. "He never misses any time with them: holidays, events, Sunday lunches. He's always there..."

I waited as Aubrey paused, searching for words.

"...but he's also not there in a way, not really. He..."

"He comes to The Jar sometimes," Candace jumped in when Aubrey trailed off. "But he doesn't talk to anyone except for Noah and Aubrey. And he always looks like he'd rather be anywhere else in the world. Girls go up to him, even send him drinks sometimes, but he refuses them all."

Aubrey nodded along as Candace spoke.

"He says he's happy to be there though," Candace finished with a shrug. "Happy to support Noah and Aubrey."

"He says he's happy to be with the family, too," Aubrey continued. "But his face always says something different."

"That's it," Candace agreed. "His face gives him away."

I drummed my fingers against the side of my mug, thinking. "What does his face say then?" I finally asked.

Aubrey and Candace looked at each other, as if confirming answers. Finally, Aubrey met my eyes. "Honestly?"

I nodded.

She sighed. "That he's being tortured."

Her words shocked me and I turned to Candace for confirmation. She just nodded. "Like he's being tortured and he wants more."

A sombre silence settled over the three of us despite the up-tempo Latin music playing from the vintage record player in the far corner. It was finally Candace who hopped to her feet and raced toward the freezer to fetch another bottle of champagne.

"Okay, enough downer stuff, Kayleigh," she grinned. "Let's get down to the nitty gritty, the juicy details, the yummy, yummy stuff."

I frowned.

She rolled her eyes at me as she struggled again with the cork. "Eoin's *galo*, chicka! Spill the beans."

I laughed and shook my head as the cork exploded from the bottle like the next two after it would. Or was it three?

"I'm so sorry," I winked up at my new crazy roommate. "I'm afraid I don't speak Portuguese."

9

DARREN

I didn't pray much anymore.

I didn't even open the Bible Ma placed in the bottom drawer of my filing cabinet when she thought I wasn't looking.

I couldn't remember the last time the multicoloured light from a stained-glass window coloured my cheek.

So my mornings alone in my garage were the closest I ever got to a confessional. The hazy first light of dawn cast growing shadows from my toolboxes and spare parts scattered across the cold concrete floors; those shadows weren't all that different from pews lining the floors of the church. Silence hung over my workspace just as heavily as it hung over the shoulders of boys and girls who waited with hushed breaths for the priest to enter so they could recite, "Bless me, Father, for I have sinned..." No one could convince me there was any difference in the tight, unmoving air of a wooden confessional booth and the dark undercarriage beneath a car.

One I needed like a drug, one I avoided like the plague, but they were both the same thing: goddamn coffins.

As I drove my motorcycle up to my shop early that morning to be absolved from the same sin I confessed day in and day out, I found my church ruined. The garage door was already raised, a ritual only I performed. The floors were swept clean, the stiff, stale air disturbed by the wafting scent of fresh coffee, the silence violated by blasphemous pop-diva music in my sacred space.

There, in the middle of it all, stood my greatest temptation.

"How'd you get in?" I barked after tugging my motorcycle helmet off my head.

Kayleigh paused mid-sweep and looked over her shoulder in surprise. I slipped on the fine layer of frost coating the asphalt, but continued to stalk toward her in irritation.

"Did you break in?"

Kayleigh's only response was to shove the broom handle into my hands and walk away. I stared at the broom and then at her in confusion. She returned with a steaming cup of coffee.

"Do you take sugar?" she asked.

"No."

She nodded. "Milk?"

I shook my head.

"Surprise, surprise, he takes it black. Like his heart," she mumbled as she took back the broom and handed over the coffee. "Drink."

Still fuming about the invasion to my shop, I nonetheless lowered my lips to the hot cup and took a sip, breathing in deeply the strong, invigorating aroma. When I looked back over at Kayleigh, she was smiling sweetly. "Good morning."

I stared at her unflinching smile before muttering a reluctant "mornin'" of my own. She folded her hands over the top of the broom handle and rested her chin on them, blinking up at me with those wide, green eyes. When I finally realised she was waiting for something, I rolled my eyes and sighed. "Thank you."

She lifted an eyebrow, which disappeared under her soft red bangs. "'Thank you' for the coffee? Or 'thank you' for taking the initiative as your new employee to get the spare keys from Michael, get here early, sweep, brew coffee, and make it inviting for you when you came in?"

A tiny grin tugged at the corner of her pink lips. She wasn't even smiling and already church-inappropriate thoughts were flooding my mind. I had to get away from her.

"For the coffee," I answered and tried to shoulder right past her.

She ran with her broom to move back in front of me. "Okay, okay, okay," she said, holding her free hand up against my chest to stop my retreat to the office before realising how intimately she was touching me and then dropping her hand like I was on fire. "Okay," she said again. "I wanted to come in early and do something nice on my first day as a sort of...as a sort of apology, I guess." She lifted her eyes hesitantly to mine.

"An apology?"

She nodded, biting her lip. I wanted to tell her not to do that. I wanted to tell her we wouldn't make it through the workday if she kept doing that. I bit the inside of my own cheek to keep my bleedin' traitorous mouth shut.

"Listen," she said. "I think maybe we got off on the wrong foot the other day when we, umm, when we met."

I watched a baby-pink blush creep across her freckled cheeks, because we both knew exactly what "met" meant. Her eyes ducked to her feet as she fidgeted with the broom handle.

"I don't know what got into me at the grocery store," she continued, clearing her tight voice. "That's not like me at all to argue or even raise my voice. It's just that, you...you..." She paused, watching me through a curtain of long, fluttering eyelashes, her lips parted like she was about to finish her sentence, but there was nothing. Her green eyes searched mine as if the words were somewhere in their depths. But I knew she wouldn't find any answers she would like in there.

It's just that you...have eyes that I wanted to study like the rarest of emeralds.

You caught me by surprise and it scared me. I'd been walking a tightrope over an endless canyon and you were a sudden gust of wind and I'm falling and I'm reaching for safety and I'm angry because I know it's already far too late.

It's just that you...will never—can never—*be mine.*

I wasn't sure how long we stood there, silent and staring into each other's eyes.

Kayleigh suddenly shook her head. "Anyway," she smiled and extended her hand out to me, "let's start over. I'm Kayleigh."

I didn't even glance down at her hand. There was no way I could bear to touch her. "I'm busy and you know my name."

This time she didn't stop me as I manoeuvred around her and continued my path toward my office. When I heard her pitter-patter steps behind me, I sighed and pleaded with the dusty ceiling fans overhead in lieu of a crucifix hanging high above an altar.

I shoved the door to my office, not bothering to hold it open for her, hoping that would send the message I wanted to be alone. There was no rattle of blinds as it slammed closed behind me, so I knew I had only succeeded in trapping us in an even tighter space together. *Great.*

"I'm trying to be nice here, and, well, I don't want to be rude or disrespectful, especially seeing as you're my boss now and all, but—"

"Just spit it out," I interrupted as I tossed my motorcycle

helmet onto a stack of invoices I had yet to send out despite the stack of red-stamped bills right next to it I had yet to pay. Or rather, I had yet to have the necessary funds to pay.

Kayleigh sighed behind me. "It's just that maybe you don't have to make this so difficult, is all."

I had a feeling that was not what she had wanted to say at all. Not even close. I had a feeling there was a string of curses flying through her pretty head, each more accurate than the last. I found myself wanting to hear them, the way I heard them in the grocery store when she'd apparently had no problem at all speaking her mind freely and uncensored.

Her patience holding strong, Kayleigh tried again when I remained silent. "I'm not exactly sure what you want me to do."

Oh, what a dangerous question.

I shrugged off my black leather jacket and slung it over the back of my beat-up office chair that was missing a wheel and leaned heavily to the right.

"Maybe that's because I don't want you here," I said to my ancient brick of a computer.

Her loud scoff was enough to make me glance over my shoulder at her. She crossed her arms over her chest as she leaned against the door frame.

"You could have refused to hire me," she argued, clearly trying to keep her tone of voice civil.

I mindlessly arranged a messy stack of papers to give the appearance I wasn't hanging onto her every word.

"And you could have offered to find a job elsewhere," I countered.

I looked over at her again and found her silently watching me. I wondered if she was thinking the same thing as me.

"You could have closed the door..." "You could have closed your eyes..."

"You could have covered up..." "You could have turned around..."

"You could have done something..." "You could have done anything..."

"But you didn't..."

Finally, Kayleigh shook her head.

"It doesn't matter," she insisted. "When does everyone else get here?"

I frowned. "You mean customers?"

"No, I don't mean customers," she grumbled in frustration. "I mean everyone else who works here."

This brought a genuine smile to my lips as I spread my arms out wide. "Here I am, darling."

Kayleigh stared at me with wide eyes, which narrowed as my words sank in. "What about the other mechanics?"

I sat on the edge of my already overburdened desk and counted out on my fingers. "Well, there's me and then there's..." I paused. She waited. "... and then there's me and, um, yeah, *me*."

Her stern face was clearly not amused. "Alright, who's the boss?"

"Me."

She rolled her eyes. "Yeah, yeah, you're a boss, Darren. I meant who is your superior?"

"No one."

She huffed, her hands balled at her sides. "Who signs your pay cheques?"

"I sign my own cheques."

Kayleigh stomped her foot, seemingly one step away from tugging at her hair. "Who owns the place, assho—" Kayleigh stopped herself by biting at her lower lip as if needing to physically prevent herself from calling me what she was in her perfect right to call me: an asshole. She steadied herself by closing her eyes for a moment and then tugged a smile onto her face. "Darren," she started again, her voice tender and quiet, "would you mind kindly telling me who owns Kelly's Garage?"

Instead of answering, I just stared at her.

Realisation dawned on her pretty face slowly, then reluctantly, then unbelievingly. "You?"

I remained silent as Kayleigh's face remained suspicious.

"Eoin didn't say you *owned* the place."

Not surprising, I thought. I wasn't sure Eoin even knew himself that I bought the place, despite it happening over a year ago. Kayleigh's frown deepened as she pointed a finger at me.

"*You* didn't say that you owned it."

She was entering uncomfortable territory for me so I averted my eyes from hers and slipped past her. "I've got to get to work."

As I strode toward my toolbox, I again heard her behind me —my little, noisy, unwanted shadow. "Did you just buy the place then?" she asked.

I opened a random drawer with no clue what I wanted to grab. I wasn't sure which vehicle I was working on or what was wrong with it. Hell, I didn't even know where it was. All I knew was that Kayleigh was behind me.

That she smelled like peppermint.

That her hair looked nice braided down her back like that.

That her freckles reminded me of the powdered sugar dusted on the Christmas pastries in the golden window displays along Grafton Street.

"I bought it a year ago," I grumbled under my breath. "Now I have to get to work."

I grabbed a random wrench just so I could move away from her; there was only so long I could maintain the self-control required to not fall headlong into those green eyes, softer than a cashmere scarf, deeper than the midnight sky on the winter solstice.

"Wait, you bought this place a year ago?" Kayleigh exclaimed, unbelieving. "A whole year?"

I found myself opening the hood of the closest car. I stared down at the engine in the dim light as if I'd never seen any of these parts before, as if I hadn't been working on them for the last ten years. With Kayleigh so close, leaning her head beneath the hood to stare incredulously at me, I couldn't tell the spark plug from the windshield fluid valve even if you had a gun to my head.

"Why haven't you changed the name?" she asked, searching my eyes.

My mind was a muddled mess. I shook my head, but even that failed to clear it. "The name?"

She crossed her arms over her chest when I closed the hood and tried to escape from her by hurrying to the other car already up on the lift.

"Are you a Kelly?" she pressed, close at my heels.

"What?" I glanced back at her, feeling irritable. "No, but—"

"But you had a year to change it."

I balled my hands into fists at my sides and let my head fall back to stare at the ceiling. "Kayleigh, let the name go," I said through clenched teeth. "It doesn't matter."

"But it's your shop," Kayleigh insisted. "It should have *your* name."

"It's not my name!"

I wasn't able to keep my cool any longer. Like an overworked engine, the steam had to go somewhere at some point. When I saw the shock on Kayleigh's face from my outburst, I sighed and dragged a hand over my face.

"I just mean that it's not mine to change." I tried to recover as best as possible. "I bought it from a friend, a mentor, and it's his name, alright?"

I saw the debate raging behind Kayleigh's eyes as she bit her lip and stared at me.

"Just let it go, yeah?" I said.

Without waiting for an answer, I lowered myself to my rolling creeper and wheeled myself under the car, still with my worthless wrench in hand. I sucked in a steadying breath as the dim light of the confined, tight space welcomed me like an old friend. From beneath the undercarriage, I craned my neck to see Kayleigh's boots still standing next to the car. Silence sank again over the garage as I heard only my harsh breath against the cold, hard metal. I stared at her boots and waited, waited, waited.

If this was the same girl who made my blood boil and my heart race at the grocery store, she would have bent down, grabbed the edge of my creeper, and dragged me back out from beneath the car. If this was the same woman who spoke the truth, the painful, painful truth I alone knew in my heart, she would have lowered her face to mine, jabbed a finger at my chest, and called me out on my bullshite excuse for not changing the shop's name to mine. If she was the same fiery soul who had shaken mine without us even touching, she would have pissed me off, sent me past my limit, driven me crazy because she knew I *needed* that push.

After waiting for what could have been a few seconds or minutes or bleedin' days, Kayleigh's voice echoed down to mine, sweet and calm and lacking any trace of anger. "Anything you want me to get started on first then?"

I stared up at the undercarriage of the car for a moment before replying. "Just make yourself useful," I grumbled.

"Sounds good," Kayleigh said without hesitation.

Part of me was relieved. Part of me exhaled against the metal frame because we hadn't clashed again like before. Part of me was thankful that I could be left alone to work, to not be bothered, to not fear slipping up and falling, falling, falling.

Part of me wished I could see that girl from the frozen food aisle of the grocery store again. Part of me wondered where she went...and why...why was she suddenly gone?

Kayleigh's boots moved away from the car with quiet, tentative steps. Even though I had the wrong tool for the wrong car, I remained there in my place in the dark.

As it should be, I thought. *As it should be.*

10

KAYLEIGH

I smiled and he scowled and the week came and went. Earlier and earlier I dragged myself out of the loft to tiptoe past the drunk passed out at the front of the downstairs bar and drive toward the faint glow of dawn along the foggy horizon and beat Darren to the shop so I could greet him with a cheerful "Good morning" and a steaming cup of black coffee. Each morning he received it in his gloved hand with his motor-cycle helmet tucked under his arm, dark hair a messy tangle atop his head as he brushed past me to stalk to the office without even a glance in my direction. I made sure to keep a skip in my step as I followed after him each morning.

"Anything you need me to do today?" I'd ask, chipper as the birds whose song Darren would soon drown out with his welder.

Each morning, despite the office door slamming in my face harder and harder till it rattled on its hinges, I forced my lips into a smile and gave a big thumbs up to the white peeling paint inches from my nose. "Roger that, boss."

I was determined as hell to keep a positive attitude, maintain a pleasant demeanour, grin till my cheeks ached and I had to ice them with a bag of frozen peas after work on the couch while Candace shook her head and called me "*Louca*". *Crazy.*

Because I wasn't the girl at the grocery store. I wasn't the girl who stomped her foot by the instant mac and cheese, leaned her head back, and just shouted exactly what was on her mind to the long phosphorescent lights overhead. I wasn't the girl who was brutally honest, who didn't care what you thought about her. The girl who let herself lose her temper in the frozen foods section because a man managed to get under her skin.

Because that girl would listen to her body when it told her that she liked it, that she wanted him under her skin, that she wanted him under her hands and under her covers. Because that girl wouldn't try to convince herself that there was nothing between her and that man with the grey-blue eyes. Because that girl would break another man's heart for the sake of being honest.

And I wasn't that girl. I couldn't be that girl.

So when Darren picked up his lunch and moved away from me when I tried to join him, I smiled and called after him, "Maybe next time then."

When he grumbled that he couldn't find anything he needed with my new filing system, I smiled and redid it.

And when he erased a new, friendlier voicemail message I recorded on the phone, I smiled and nodded, "Yeah, that's better. It adds a bit of mystery when you have no idea where you've called. Fun."

Any and all of my efforts to update, reorganise, modernise, clean up, decorate, or just change the shop in the slightest were met with irritation and a gruff command to "put it back the way it was". I'm fairly certain he even switched the toilet paper roll after I added a new one in the bathroom.

But when a package arrived that dull Thursday morning, I knew, just knew, that he couldn't possibly dislike this change.

When the delivery truck arrived, Darren was on his back, flashlight held between his teeth as he frowned at the underside of a motorcycle a customer had dropped off earlier with the vague complaint that "it didn't sound right". The headlights swept across the garage as the truck pulled up the drive, and I leapt up from the now clean desk in the office, tugged on my beanie and mittens, and ran out to meet the delivery man. Darren didn't even bother glancing up from his work, which didn't surprise me.

When he worked on a vehicle, he sort of disappeared. It was like he wasn't even there in the shop anymore. I had to call his name several times before he'd mumble an aggravated, "What now?"

I met the delivery man at the back of the truck where he was struggling with a large, narrow cardboard box. Drizzle caught in my eyelashes as I hurried to help him ease it down to the icy drive.

"What have you got in this big ol' thing?" the man asked, wiping at his brow with the back of his bright orange utility gloves.

I patted the top of the box and grinned. "A smile," I said.

The delivery man eyed me as he handed over a pen atop a thick clipboard with a receipt for me to sign.

"Yeah, sure. Whatever you say," he said somewhat warily as I scribbled my name at the bottom. "Have a nice day then."

He disappeared around the side of the truck, exhaust swirling in the cold air as he started the ignition and backed away down the drive. Rubbing my hands in excitement, I lowered my shoulder and heaved against the box to slide it into the warmth of the garage. My boots slipped and I caught myself before my knees crashed to the slippery ground. Gritting my teeth in determination, I turned around and lowered my back to press against the edge of the box, heaving and ho-ing to shove it backwards.

By the time I managed to get the massive box into the garage, the blast of hot air was oppressive on my sweaty face. I peeled off my beanie and tugged my mittens off with my teeth to fling them on the floor. Only after I had sagged against the damp side of the box did I see Darren leaning against the motorcycle with his arms crossed over his chest as he watched me with an amused grin, or at least the closest thing Darren was ever going to get to what us humans would call a "grin".

"Need any help?" he asked, his voice husky as he raised a questioning dark eyebrow over at me.

My heart rate leapt as a bolt of anger flashed through me like it had at the grocery store. I resisted the urge to ball my sweaty hands into fists, narrow my eyes till they squished against my rosy cheeks, and open my mouth to tell him exactly what I thought about him.

"You're an asshole, Darren."

"I'm not sure I've seen anything hotter than you up against that motorcycle with those low-slung jeans, that tight grey Henley, and that smudge of engine grease just below your eyes that are part frozen lake, part coal."

"I think you're acting like this because you feel the same way that I do and just like me, you have no fucking clue what the hell to do about it."

Instead, I tugged up the corner of my frozen lips as mechanically as if I'd used a winch and said, "Good. I'm glad I've got your attention. There's something I want you to see."

I pushed myself to my feet and glanced at the box. "I just need to go grab some scissors," I said. "Wait just a second."

"I'm really busy," Darren called after me as I hurried toward the office.

I rolled my eyes as I grabbed them from the desk drawer. "It'll be worth it," I called out. "Trust me."

Maybe it was because I'd piqued his interest or maybe he felt just the teeniest bit bad about not helping me, but Darren remained where he was as I cut through the tape around the big box and stepped back to let the side fall to the shop's concrete floor. I pulled back the shipping material and then looked over quickly to catch Darren's reaction. I frowned in slight confusion when his expression remained unchanged, scowl still firmly in place.

I double-checked that he could see everything alright. I scooted aside a few more packing peanuts from the bottom corner before again looking over at Darren. This time I found him already looking at me—he was not happy.

"What is that?" he asked.

Any trace of playfulness, as infinitesimal as it may have been before, was now without a doubt good and gone as he glared at me across the shop.

I swallowed heavily and answered, "Umm, a sign."

"I can see it's a sign," Darren snapped. "A sign for what?"

My eyes darted nervously from the box back to Darren. Well, this wasn't going according to plan at all. In fact, I wasn't sure it could be going any worse.

"A sign for what, Kayleigh?" Darren growled.

He was still leaning against the motorcycle, but I could see that his shoulders were tense. He seemed to be trying to keep his chest from heaving with ire, but it was plain as day from the way his fingers dug deep into the muscles along his arms.

"A sign for what?" His voice shook.

"A sign for the shop," I answered, my voice small, hesitant, weak.

Darren seemed to be restraining himself by the motorcycle. I could almost hear the rattle of the invisible chains wrapped around his broad, strong chest; they were held taut against the bike like the chain on a pit bull chomping at the bit in a junkyard.

"A sign for what shop?" he shouted.

My eyes moved again to the sign just beside me. I'd designed it myself on Darren's ancient brick of a computer in his back office. As he disappeared into his work on this motorcycle or that car, I'd fumbled my way around a slow as treacle program, waiting for hours it seemed just for the stupid mouse to move, in order to make something I thought he'd like, something he'd be proud to put outside his shop instead of the old faded sign that didn't even say his name.

I made the background the colour of his ma's kitchen, the place where they all gathered for Sunday lunches. I made the font the same as the street name carefully hand-painted on the mailbox outside their home. And I made sure to print "O'Sullivan's Garage" as big and as loud as the O'Sullivans themselves.

For me the answer to Darren's question couldn't have been more obvious: it was the sign for his shop. It couldn't be a sign for anything or anyone else in the entire world.

"Darren," I said softly, looking back toward him, "it should have your name outside."

Either the invisible chains around him were released or he finally managed to burst through them, but regardless, Darren stepped forward and paced angrily back and forth in front of me and the sign.

"Did you not hear me?" he asked, eyes more churning grey skies than calm blue waters when they darted over to me.

"What?"

"When I said the name was the name," he said, looking at me but refusing to look at the sign. "Did you not hear me?"

I stared at him as he paced.

"Did you not hear me when I said that I didn't want to

change the name of the shop?" he continued, if anything just growing more and more angry as he turned on his heel to march the other direction. "Is that the problem here?"

Standing there in the suddenly roasting heat of the shop, I reminded myself that I had promised I was going to keep my cool. I told myself I had promised to always keep a smile, always keep the tone of my voice even, and never, never raise my voice. I repeated again and again, as fast as I could in my mind, that I wasn't, I wasn't, I *wasn't* going to let Darren get under my skin. Again.

In the blink of an eye, I promptly forgot it all, every fecking word of it.

"I heard you," I hissed, my voice still quiet but no longer small, no longer weak.

At the sound of my voice, Darren stopped his manic pacing. He stopped and he stared at me and he crossed his arms over his chest. "What's that?"

It was me who surged forward this time. I didn't care that we'd just replaced frozen pies with spare tyres and greasy wrenches. I didn't care that the only thing that had changed from before was that it was the hum of a generator and not the hum of a freezer that competed with our ragged, angry breaths. I didn't give a fuck that we were falling into the same hole we fell into before and the only difference was that the bottom was grey concrete and not white linoleum.

I was mad and I wanted to be mad. I wanted to be mad at Darren. I wanted to mad *with* Darren.

"I said, 'I heard you'," I said darkly, narrowing my eyes at him. "I heard you just fine, actually. The only 'problem' here is that you are wrong."

Darren's cheeks reddened at my words. Unluckily for him, I was just getting started.

In a tone of voice that would make my mother gasp before

hurriedly doing the sign of the cross with her spindly fingers, I moved even closer to Darren, punctuating each word with a step. "Dead. Ass. Wrong."

I didn't wait for him to open his mouth to counter or argue. I dove right back in.

"If you want something, you take it," I whispered angrily. "If something is yours, you claim it. If you love it, if you truly love it, you don't let anyone else put their bleeding name on it. No one."

I was shaking from head to toe when I turned in a huff and marched to the office, slamming the door behind me. I reached out for the chair and collapsed into it just before my knees gave out. I buried my face in my hands as I shook my head back and forth.

What in the hell was that? *Who* in the hell was that?

My mother had taught me more self-control than that. She'd beaten it into me since I was a young girl. Night after night she drilled the importance of not raising my voice, not speaking my mind, not making anyone mad into my impressionable head so I soaked it all up like a sponge.

And then one mysterious man with grey-blue eyes and a bad attitude comes along and it all goes out the window?

As my heart thudded erratically in the confines of that small office, I knew the problem wasn't that I didn't believe what I'd said to Darren. I'd believed every word of it. The problem was that I hadn't been talking about some stupid mechanic's shop sign.

And I think he knew it.

11

DARREN

*B*ehind the shop was a narrow alley with a graffitied dumpster, a stack of pallets covered in fallen leaves, and more than its fair share of rats. This is where I intended to toss the sign Kayleigh had ordered and purchased for the shop without my consent—with the rest of the trash.

The door to my office in the back had barely finished rattling on its rusty hinges after Kayleigh stormed off and I was already gripping the top of the sign and dragging it across the concrete floors. Even the horrible shrieking of metal against metal wasn't as unbearable as the very sight of my family's name on the goddamn thing. I kicked the alley door open and cursed under my breath as I manoeuvred the giant sign into the narrow space lined in crumbling bricks. In the gently falling drizzle, it clattered noisily against the dumpster, disturbing a few rats from their greasy pizza box homes.

Without another glance back at it, I hurried back inside the shop, puffing warm air back into my frigid fingers and shaking off the cold from my shoulders. I told myself it would be picked up with the rest of the rusted cans and sticky beer bottles and mountains of snot-filled tissues the next morning. I reassured myself that I had seen that the very last of O'Sullivan's Garage. I comforted myself with the knowledge that I was in Kelly's Garage, where everything was quiet, everything was safe, and nothing was mine.

Throughout the day, as I crossed the shop to retrieve this screwdriver or that bolt, this wrench or that sealant, this hammer or that cable, I found my eyes drifting involuntarily toward the door leading to the alley. I tried to focus on my work, to get dragged under into that world of mechanics where everything had its place, reason, role, where everything made sense. But my mind wouldn't stop drifting back to that goddamn sign.

When Kayleigh left at exactly 5 p.m. without a word or glance in my direction, I stopped pretending to work on replacing a motorcycle's brake pads and hurried yet again toward the alley door at the back of my shop. I cursed under my breath again as I manoeuvred the bulky, heavy sign through the door to get it back inside.

I wiped my sweaty brow after letting the sign fall with an echoing ring against my workbench and stepped back to look at it.

"I don't want to change the name to O'Sullivan's Garage because I'm respecting my friend, Stephen Kelly." I said the words aloud, hoping that if I heard them, I'd believe them.

I'd told this excuse to Kayleigh and expected her to believe it, but that was difficult even for me. The first thing Stephen had asked me after we signed the papers and shook hands was what I was going to change the name of the shop to. Stephen himself would probably be surprised to see that same old shabby sign with his name on it still outside.

"I don't want to change the name to O'Sullivan's Garage because it's just too much of a hassle," I tried next.

This excuse wasn't much better. Even knowing I would never change it, I'd tortured myself one night by researching the steps it would take. The hardest part would be getting a new sign in, and well, here one was right in front of me.

"I don't want to change the name to O'Sullivan's Garage because I don't feel that I deserve to use the family name," I finally said after staring at the sign for what felt like hours.

These words didn't echo around the empty garage like the last ones. They hung around my neck, heavy and true.

And yet, I couldn't do it. I couldn't throw out the sign, even though it was like a stab in the heart every time I looked at it.

It took half the evening to hide it in the office. I dragged out every filing cabinet, every box of old invoices, every accordion folder of receipts, every knickknack and poster and ten-year-old calendar still pinned to the wall. The damn thing just barely fit, but it fit. I arranged everything back in front of it, and when I finally closed the door to the office for the night, I was certain that even I wouldn't be able to see it in the morning.

My alarm clock rang and rattled off my nightstand a full thirty minutes earlier than usual so I could beat Kayleigh into the shop. I knew uttering the words "I'm sorry" would be difficult for me, so I figured making the coffee would have to do as a sort of peace offering. She couldn't have possibly known the heavy baggage I weighed on the O'Sullivan name, and I shouldn't have taken my anger out on her.

But there ended up being no need to rush around in the dark, because 7:30 rolled around and then 8...9...9:30...

By the time Kayleigh's car pulled into the shop's drive, the pot of freshly brewed coffee was ice cold. From my stool next to the motorcycle I didn't fix the day before, I watched her march straight to the office, eyes fixed ahead, and close the door promptly behind her. Drumming my fingers on my knee, I glanced over at the coffee pot. I could microwave a cup. Everyone knew women loved microwaved cups of coffee...

I could try again tomorrow morning. And if she came in

early the next morning and I missed her, I could try the next day or the next or the next. Eventually I would get her a hot cup of coffee and we would be square.

The ridiculousness of it all was obvious to even me. I exhaled loudly while pressing my fingers against my eyes. I had to do it. I had to face Kayleigh and apologise face-to-face.

With a deep breath, the kind you hastily suck in before leaping off the high diving board as a kid, I called out in the quiet shop. "Kayleigh, can you come out here for a minute?"

I winced at the sound of my voice as I stared anxiously at the office door; even I thought I sounded like a chain-smoking robot. For a moment I thought she wasn't going to come out. For a moment I thanked my lucky stars. But then the door creaked and Kayleigh peeked her head out. "Did you say something?" she asked.

She had yet to step a foot outside the office, but at least she was talking to me. That was a first step, I supposed.

"Umm," I cleared my throat, "would you mind coming over here?"

She eyed me warily, but finally came when I dragged over another stool for her to sit on. She scooted it farther away before lowering herself to sit on the very edge of it. The message was clear: she was ready to bolt at any misstep. With her green eyes fixed on me and the smell of her peppermint shampoo just teasing my nostrils, I considered returning to the microwaved coffee plan.

"Did you need something?" Kayleigh asked, impatiently tapping the toe of her boot.

"Umm, yes, I..." My sentence trailed off as I scratched at the back of my neck.

"Well?" Kayleigh lifted an eyebrow.

"Umm..." Why was I suddenly sweating? I reminded myself to check the heater as I fumbled for the right words to say.

Kayleigh shook her head and started to push herself to her feet, saying, "Look, if you don't need anything, I'm going to go back to my off—"

"That," I blurted out.

Kayleigh, paused halfway between standing and sitting, going and staying, glanced in confusion over her shoulder to where I was vaguely pointing. "What?"

Eyeing my toolbox, I quickly improvised. "The screwdriver."

When Kayleigh looked toward where I was indicating, I took the opportunity to slip the perfectly capable screwdriver I had been using to work on the motorcycle into the side pocket of my work pants.

"A screwdriver?" Kayleigh's suspicious eyes returned to me. "You called me out here so that I could fetch you a screwdriver?"

Mission Apology was off to a rough start, it seemed. But what was I going to do at this point? Just open my mouth and tell her exactly how I felt? That I felt bad about getting angry at her, but I struggled with expressing my emotions, like guilt (especially like fecking guilt) aloud? No. Hell no. *That* was even more ridiculous than microwaved coffee. I was left with only one option.

Nodding my head, I said, "Yeah, would you mind grabbing it for me?"

Kayleigh hesitated, eyes searching mine, but then she walked over to the large toolbox and held up a screwdriver. "This one?"

I squinted to see if it was the right gage.

"You know you could just come over here and look and I could go get back to work in the office," Kayleigh grumbled, drumming the tip of the screwdriver against the toolbox.

"No, no," I said before she decided to leave. "That should work just fine."

Kayleigh rolled her eyes and I held back a grin, because it

was real. When she smiled she was beautiful, but I often couldn't help but think that it was a beautiful mask. I'd take the rolled eyes, the exaggerated sighs, the cheeks flushed in anger any day.

Kayleigh stopped just close enough that if I stretched my arm out as far as I could, the tips of my fingers could just barely grip the tip of the screwdriver. She didn't even wait for me to grab proper hold of it before letting go, turning on her heel, and taking a determined step back toward the office.

"Wait, wait," I called to her, fumbling to catch the screwdriver.

Kayleigh stopped, glancing back at me over her shoulder. "You need something else?" she asked.

Her shoulders were relaxed, her hands held loosely at her sides, her lips parted just slightly. Everything about her body language was casual, nonchalant, easy, like I was a stranger on the street who just asked her if she knew where the nearest coffee shop was. Everything but her eyes.

She couldn't hide the interest, the curiosity, the searching from her eyes.

I didn't need anything from her, but I *wanted* so much. And I think she wanted me to need something from her, too.

"Can you help me really quick?" I asked.

Kayleigh glanced at the office. "I've got quite a bit of work to do," she said.

She resisted because she had to. It was a rule of this dangerous game we were both playing, whether we knew it or not. She had to resist because she was mad at me. She had to resist because I was her boyfriend's asshole brother. She had to resist because if she didn't resist, the game was over and we all would lose: me, her, Eoin, my entire family.

"It will just take a minute or two."

Biting her lip, Kayleigh looked at the stool next to me like it was covered with rusted nails. She shook her head. "I shouldn't."

"I'm sorry." The words that slipped from my lips startled even me.

Kayleigh recoiled like I just blurted out the most heinous, foul curse words known to man. She turned to face me. "For what?"

I opened my mouth to reply with the answer that I at first thought was obvious: for yesterday. But the look in Kayleigh's eyes made me pause. Maybe she knew before I did. Maybe she could hear the whispers of my mind that I'd pushed away, ignored, deafened with the electric saw or the pounding hammer or the roar of this or that engine. Maybe she could see in the way I looked at her that I had much more than just yesterday to confess.

My work stool wasn't a pew and Kayleigh wasn't a priest, but in the silence of the shop, I looked up at her and finally let the guilt wash over me.

I'm sorry that I saw my brother's girl naked and didn't turn away.

I'm sorry that I think about my brother's girl when I go to sleep.

I'm sorry that I want to kiss my brother's girl, hold my brother's girl, laugh with, scream with, ride with, make love with, tangle sheets with my brother's girl.

I'm sorry that I want my brother's girl to be my *girl.*

"Darren?" Kayleigh whispered.

With a defeated sigh, I dragged my hand over my face. I scratched at the back of my neck before finally saying, "I just wanted to say that I'm sorry about yesterday."

Kayleigh watched me, eyes darting between mine. But I couldn't admit the truths of my heart. Not aloud. Never aloud.

"I shouldn't have reacted like that to the sign. I'm..." I shrugged lamely. "I'm sorry for yesterday."

Kayleigh held her arms tight against her chest and shuffled the toe of her boot against the concrete floor. "Thanks," she said and then added under her breath almost too quietly for me to hear, like a silent admission to herself, as if the shop wasn't a confessional booth for just me, "I'm sorry, too."

We remained in silence for a moment or two. I expected Kayleigh to return to the office when I returned my attention to the motorcycle, but when she finally took a step it was toward me. I looked at her out of the corner of my eye as she took a seat on the stool next to mine.

"I have a minute or two to help," she said softly.

The wheels of her stool scuffed against the concrete floor as she moved a little closer to me and the motorcycle. I never thought such a simple sound, one I heard day in and day out as I worked, could send lightning through my body like that. Kayleigh's knee brushed against mine and I nearly dropped the screwdriver.

"Okay," I said, swallowing heavily. "So this right here is the camshaft..."

For Kayleigh, the day was spent learning about the brake system on a '79 Triumph Bonneville motorcycle. For me, the day was spent ripping my heart open and exposing it piece by piece to her. My work at the shop was often the only thing keeping me together. Just as often it was the very thing tearing me apart. It was my torture chamber; it was a still, quiet pool of healing. I wanted to escape it; I wanted to lock myself in, board up the exits, and never leave.

On the days where it was just small adjustments, cosmetic changes, or simple maintenance checks, I got lost in the work and it was a brief respite from the constant war in my mind. When a totalled vehicle came in, the struggle waged more than ever, because it was an undeserved chance at redemption and it was a deserved reminder of the mistake I could never make right.

My work and my shop were held in the most intimate parts of me, and sharing them with Kayleigh made me feel vulnerable and exposed, but also, for the first time in a long time, *seen*.

"Have you been on one?" I asked as the street lamps outside flickered on in the early light of dusk.

Kayleigh brushed a strand of long red hair out of her face with the back of her hand because her fingers were covered in grease. I didn't have the heart to tell her that she'd had a streak on her cheek since the morning. Besides, it was too damn cute. "A motorcycle?" she asked.

I nodded.

"Never."

I hesitated, pretending to be busy adjusting a bolt along the brake pad I showed Kayleigh how to replace. "You know, I could take you for a spin sometime," I said. "I mean, if you're going to help with the bikes you should at least see what the big fuss is about."

I glanced over at Kayleigh nervously and found her smiling at me. "Tonight?" she asked excitedly.

"Tonight?"

She grinned. "Why not tonight?"

I laughed. I wasn't sure when the last time was that I laughed within these four protective, confining brick walls.

"Umm, alright," I said, feeling a buzz from Kayleigh's infectious energy. "Once we finish up these brakes we can go around the block."

Kayleigh's eyes held mine and her pinkie brushed against mine as I held the wrench against the motorcycle. "Or farther," she whispered.

My eyes drifted from the green of her eyes to the pink of her lips, full and soft and delicate. They were so out of place amongst the dark metals and sharp edges. I couldn't help but feel that her lips would be just out of place against my own: a rose petal against a chainsaw.

"Kayleigh, I—"

A series of three loud, blaring honks shattered through the hushed communion of the shop. I winced at the harsh glare from a pair of headlights. A car door opened, pounding rock music thundered out, and a pair of feet crunched on the gravel.

"Kayleigh Bear!"

Kayleigh's hand pulled away from mine and she stood, moving quickly away from me as Eoin, dressed in a sharp suit and carrying a massive bouquet of red roses, strode confidently into the shop. I averted my eyes and focused back on the bolt. In my periphery, Eoin swept Kayleigh into his arms and kissed her, spinning her around and around.

"Eoin, what are you doing here?" Kayleigh asked with a nervous laugh as he set her back down.

"Your prince is here with your chariot to sweep you off to a romantic date," Eoin announced, shaking Kayleigh's shoulders with the energy of a puppy playing with a new chew toy. "Champagne and rooftop bars and caviar— Hey, do you like caviar?"

"I, umm—"

"You'll love it, trust me," Eoin interjected. "It's very fancy stuff. Very expensive. Very romantic."

Out of the corner of my eye, I sneaked a glance to see Kayleigh smiling up at Eoin. But her smile didn't crinkle the corners of her eyes. There was no way he could tell the difference between that and the real thing. There was no way anyone could, probably. Except me. I could.

"We're going to a five-star hotel in Dublin and they'll valet the car and give us fancy mints and call us Mr and Ms," Eoin continued. "I'm going to wine and dine you till you feel like an absolute princess."

Eoin didn't squeeze his teddy bears as tightly as a child as he did just then to Kayleigh. She laughed and patted his arm, almost like a boxer tapping out in the ring.

"Alright, alright," she grinned. "Eoin, that all sounds lovely, but I have work to finish and Darren was going to take me—"

"I can finish up," I cut her off before she could finish. I looked up from the motorcycle.

"Oh, hey there, Darren," Eoin said with a wave. "Didn't see you back there."

"Go have fun on your date," I said to Kayleigh.

"But the ri—"

"Really, I've got it."

I smiled when she hesitated, eyes searching my face for the crack in my happy mask. "Okay..." she said slowly, not finding any.

She wasn't the only one who'd mastered the mask.

"Alrighty then!" Eoin clapped his hands together. "See you Sunday, Daz. I've got a beautiful lady to please."

Kayleigh stepped toward me. "Darren, I—"

Eoin grabbed her around the waist and tossed her easily over his muscular shoulders. He whisked her out of the garage while loudly singing "That's Amore" off key over the sound of Led Zeppelin on the radio in his car. I watched him lower her into the passenger seat and then stuff the two dozen roses in after her so her face was hidden entirely by the flowers. And like that she was gone, disappearing around the corner with nothing more than the screech of tyres.

I sighed and finished fixing the Bonneville's brakes in less than ten minutes. It was easy work, after all. I had just dragged it out because I liked the excuse of having Kayleigh by my side.

When I was done, I leaned against the bike, crossed my arms over my chest, and stared out into the dark.

"I'm sorry that I let it get this far," I whispered. "I'm sorry that I want it to go much, much farther."

Her voice echoed in my head.

"Or farther."

12

KAYLEIGH

I was terrified to ask for the mashed potatoes.

Because if I asked for the mashed potatoes, Ma would smile, say, "Why, of course," and lift the dish. Ma would pass them to Michael next to her, who would lean across the table to bypass Noah, who was busy refilling Aubrey's glass as they discussed The Jar's finances, to pass the steaming dish to Eoin. If I asked for the mashed potatoes, Michael would shout at Eoin to hand them over to me as he held the dish suspended over the roast, but Eoin would hold up a finger to him as he leaned back in his chair till the front legs lifted off the floor, because England was only two-and-a-half meters or so from scoring a try against France. If I asked for the mashed potatoes, Michael would curse irritably under his breath, glance around the table as his arms grew tired holding the heavy potatoes, and finally he would shove them toward Darren across from me.

"Here," he would grumble. "You take them." Darren would hesitate, but Michael would insist. "I can't hold them forever, Daz."

Darren would grab the mashed potatoes and he would turn

toward me. Our eyes would meet. His fingers would brush mine as he handed over the dish. Noah would freeze as he poured the wine, not even noticing when the deep red cascaded over the lip of Aubrey's glass and onto her lap as she also stared across the table at Darren and me, mouth still open from where she cut off her argument about The Jar's overheads mid-sentence. Eoin's chair would crash back to the floor, the rugby try entirely forgotten, Ma's forkful of cabbage and bacon would hang halfway between her mouth and her plate, and Michael would be staring at me instead of his suit sleeve that he'd just dragged through the gravy.

And they would know, they would all know right then and there.

They would all know that there was something between Darren and me.

Something electric and undeniable and *wrong*.

If I asked for the mashed potatoes, I'd destroy this perfect family, and that was something I couldn't allow myself to ever do.

Dramatic, much?

Maybe.

Maybe not.

So at Sunday lunch that afternoon at the O'Sullivan's, I resigned myself to a potato-less plate, refused another glass of wine, and made sure to laugh extra hard at Eoin's locker room jokes. I was well aware that these tactics were all just duct tape on a leaking, splintering dam, but it was either duct tape or a goddamn truckload of C-4.

I was in trouble and I knew it.

Every glance in Darren's direction felt like a betrayal to Eoin, because the mere feeling of Darren's eyes on me excited me more than any of Eoin's hugs.

Every chuckle at Darren's dry humour made my stomach

churn with guilt, because all I could think was how easy and natural it was compared to forcing laughter for Eoin.

Every word from Darren's lips was a lure to the rocks, because before I even realised it, I was leaning away from Eoin and toward that husky, low voice that called to me like a siren.

Eoin pounded his fist next to the bread basket in frustration, and I jumped along with everyone else at the table.

"Unbelievable," he grumbled as he swatted a hand in disgust at the television in the living room. "Just unbelievable."

"Eoin, if you break my table, you're buying me a new one," Ma warned, pointing her fork across the table at him.

"I'll send the bill to the queen herself," Eoin grumbled. He returned all four legs of the chair to the floor and then turned to me. "Did you see that, babe?"

"Oh, yeah. Definitely."

What? Was I supposed to admit that I had spent the last ten minutes staring at the mashed potatoes from across the table?

"Those boys are a disgrace, aren't they?" Eoin shook his head.

I nodded. "A real disgrace."

Eoin smiled widely and patted my back so roughly I almost coughed back up my last bite of roast. "She's perfect," he announced to his family as I counted my broken ribs. "She even loves rugby just like me. I mean, how did I get so goddamn lucky? It's like a real-life fairy tale, you know?"

The family all smiled as Eoin leaned over and planted a kiss on my mouth. The family minus Darren, that is. He was too busy stabbing his green beans as if they were personally offending him. Guilt flooded my chest as all I could think to do in response was pat Eoin's hand.

"Did everyone see the necklace I got Kayleigh?" Eoin asked between mouthfuls of Greek yogurt-smothered sweet potatoes sprinkled with unflavoured protein powder. "Babe, babe, show them."

"Oh, um..." I stopped mid-bite and set my buttered roll on the edge of my plate. "Okay."

I noticed Darren's eyes on me as I slipped my hand beneath my turtleneck and pulled out a delicate gold chain from which hung a stunning two-carat diamond. The momentary flash of pain on Darren's face at the sight of it made me want to rip it off and throw it away, shatter it with a hammer and let the wind carry the pieces to the sea. But then there was Ma and Aubrey and Michael and Noah, and they were asking for me to lean closer, to come show them, to hold it up to the light so they could see it sparkle.

"Beautiful, Eoin," Ma said, squeezing his boyish cheeks after walking around from the other side of the table to get a closer look.

"You did good." Aubrey elbowed Noah. "I'm assuming my diamond necklace got lost in the mail, Noah."

"I can't even imagine the financing on a rock like that," Michael grumbled under his breath while shaking his head. "Does nobody use my Excel spreadsheets for budgeting?"

Ma flicked the side of Michael's head as she passed him on her way back to her chair. "It's beautiful, honey," she repeated to me. "Very beautiful."

"It is," I said, forcing a smile as I looked at Eoin, who just beamed.

I didn't have to lie; the necklace was undeniably stunning. But that didn't change the equally undeniable fact that when I ran my finger along the delicate gold chain, I would gladly exchange it for the heaviness of a wrench. The diamond caught the light and dazzled, but I would have traded it in in a heartbeat for the dullness of a grease-covered screwdriver. The way the necklace hung from my neck was beautiful, but I still preferred the smudge of grease on my cheek that Eoin had pointed out on our way to that fancy restaurant the other day even as I longed to be back in the shop.

With the dirty tools.

With the oil-covered car parts.

With the concrete and soft whispers and guiding hands and stolen glances.

With Darren.

"Come on now, boys," Eoin shouted next to me.

He was again leaning back dangerously on his chair to see through to the living room where England and France were back after halftime. Aubrey had returned to talking with Noah, this time describing her ideal diamond necklace as he nodded along and mimed taking notes. Ma was patiently listening to Michael complain about the family member's irresponsible personal finances.

And that left Darren and me.

I needed to think of something to say to him, because the way we were each staring at our plates and yet not eating wasn't exactly normal. In the O'Sullivan household it seemed like nothing drew more curious attention than silence. A casual conversation, that's all I needed. Weather. Sports. Food. Hell, even politics. Anything. I could talk about anything so we wouldn't stick out.

But as the lunch continued, I remained silent, because none of the things I wanted to say to him were things I could say to him.

"I dreamed of you when I got home from my date with Eoin. I dreamed that I stayed like I wanted to and that you took me on the ride you promised me."

I wanted to tell him that I was still thinking of it. The words pressed against my lips, threatening to spill out every time I took a sip of water to cool myself off. I wanted to tell him that it felt so real, my arms around his waist as I held on tight. I wanted to tell him I'd never gone faster, but never felt safer than when I rested my cheek against his back. I wanted to tell him that in my dream, he stopped and I told him, *"Farther, farther, farther."*

I wanted to tell him I could still feel the rumble of the engine between my legs, the sway of the bike as we leaned into the dark bends, the wind in my hair as we disappeared together into the night.

"Kayleigh, darling," Ma smiled at me from the other end of the table. "Would you like some mashed potatoes?"

"No!" I blurted the word out before I could stop myself. I blushed as my outburst drew the attention of everyone at the table. I smiled nervously as I tucked a loose strand of hair behind my ear. "I mean, no, thank you," I said, forcing a calmness I didn't feel. When the confused looks remained, I laughed and gestured toward the television. "Rugby's got me riled up, I guess."

The family finally nodded and joined in my awkward, tense laughter.

"Thank you," I repeated to Ma as everyone returned to their conversations. "Thank you, but no."

I glanced over at Darren, who alone was still staring at me. His grey-blue eyes searching mine. I tugged my attention away from him and focused again on my plate.

"No," I whispered. "No."

13

DARREN

*I*f there was a computer in all of Dublin older than the one at my shop, it was the one sitting in front of me atop the little wooden desk in Ma's tiny study. We boys had tried to convince her to get a new one, even going as far as buying one as a Christmas gift a few years ago, but each time she insisted hers was just fine and the money could be put to better use, namely in the kitchen.

So each year for Sunday lunches the roasts came out juicier, the pies crumblier, the breads fluffier, and the Google searches slower...slower...slower...

Amongst stacks of childhood books, overflowing picture albums, and more cookbooks than I could count, I rocked back and forth in the old faded leather office chair and I waited for the Dublin Chamber of Commerce website to load.

My family's laughter from the living room next to the warm crackling fire barrelled down the narrow hallway and crashed into me like a sledge hammer to the chest. In the cold blue light of the computer screen, it hurt more than usual because I could make out Kayleigh's giggles, sweet and infectious, amongst the rest.

I had offered to do the dishes, all the dishes if that's what it took, just so I could escape that sound. When Ma shooed me away and insisted she would do it, I tried talking with Michael, but the moment he sat down on the couch he received one of his quintessential "I have to take this" calls. I suggested I could do a check-up on Aubrey's car out in the garage, but she thought it was a joke because I looked it over two weeks ago.

"Go keep Kayleigh company in the living room." She shoved at my arm. "I'll bring hot chocolates."

At the very sight of Kayleigh in the dancing glow of the flames, I knew I couldn't be alone with her. Her hair cascaded over her shoulders like liquid amber and her green eyes caught specks of gold as she watched the mesmerising fire. Maybe I could have handled her beauty. Maybe I could have sat there and *not* stared greedily at her profile, stealing the sight away like a jewel thief to admire later. Maybe.

What ultimately turned me away was the reflection of light off of the necklace Eoin gifted her.

So I found myself alone in the study, where I decided to take the opportunity to research again what it took to change the shop's name. A part of me foolishly believed that if I used the new sign, if I cleaned up the garage, if I worked on branding and marketing and social media like Kayleigh suggested, that maybe the shop could one day be successful enough so it'd be me who could afford to buy her diamond necklaces. Foolish, I know.

It was still a tantalising enough dream to wait a near lifetime for Ma's computer to pull up the information. I was scrolling through the list of requirements when the door to the study swung open and Noah, followed by Michael and then Eoin, crammed inside.

"Daz, you've been hiding in here while I've been dragging England up all by myself!" Eoin complained.

Startled by the intrusion, my fingers fumbled for the mouse

to hastily, and not so subtly, close out the window. I didn't want to admit it, but I was embarrassed for my brothers to see. I much preferred them thinking I didn't have ambitions for the place. Or, even better, I preferred them not even remembering that I owned it in the first place.

"Ma, Darren's watching porn!" Noah cupped a hand over his mouth to shout back into the hallway, a bottle of whiskey held in his other hand.

Sighing, I spun around in the creaky office chair as Michael grabbed the cushioned footrest and Eoin pushed aside some framed grade school photos of us to sit on the edge of window sill.

"I wasn't watching porn," I said, my voice emotionless and monotone as always.

Noah came over and leaned against the desk, crossing his ankles over one another as he rested his elbow on my shoulder. "I know you weren't watching porn." Noah grinned. "You were pining."

Noah raised his eyebrows up and down as I stared up at him.

"Pining?"

He nodded and jabbed a finger at my chest. "Pining."

"Don't think we haven't noticed that something is up," Michael said, looking ridiculous as he sipped his expensive sherry in his expensive suit while sitting cross-legged on a fringed floral footrest. He took a thoughtful sip and regarded me in the dim light of the standing lamp. "Spill the beans. Who is she?"

"The juicy details," Eoin said next as he struggled to pop the cap off the first of two beers he brought in against the edge of the bookshelves. "Bra size, favourite position, any interesting tattoos. You know, the usual." With a grunt, the cap tumbled to the floor along with a cascade of white foam. I shook my head as Eoin busied himself trying to catch as much as he could before it hit Ma's rug.

"I have no fecking clue what you all are talking about," I said with a shrug of my shoulders.

"A secret romance then," Michael said. "Perhaps it's a little taboo as well? I didn't think you had it in you, little brother."

"Maybe she's famous?" Eoin offered. "A celebrity?"

"Or rich?" Michael asked.

Noah snapped his fingers. "Is it someone we all know?" he prodded. "Is that why you're not telling us?"

"No!"

Ah, shite. Judging by my brothers' wide eyes fixed on me, I said that way too damn quickly. I forced my shoulders to relax as I brushed my fingers through my hair.

"I mean, no, she's not famous or a celebrity or rich," I said as casually as possible. "And no, you don't know her. Because there is no 'her'."

Noah eased a rather healthy glass of whiskey into my fingers and nudged it toward my mouth. "Here you go." He nodded at the glass as he spoke. "This might help loosen those lips. Drink, drink."

"Look, guys, I hate to disappoint, but there really is no one." I set the glass aside next to the keyboard.

Michael immediately shook his head in disbelief. "No, no, no," he said, pointing at me with his glass of sherry. "All the signs are there. You didn't say a word during lunch. You barely looked up."

I tried to laugh this off. "I never say much."

"But you usually try," Noah argued. "You didn't even try today. And that's because you were thinking about someone, I'm sure of it."

I prayed that the light in the study was dim enough that none of my brothers could see the warmth that flooded my cheeks. Because I was thinking about someone. But revealing her name would be like lighting a stick of dynamite and tossing it to our feet.

"Daz, you offered to do the dishes," Eoin mumbled around the neck of his beer bottle.

"Excellent point, Eoin," Noah nodded before returning to his interrogation of me. "You'd have to be drunk or high to offer to do the dishes after Sunday lunch. So do you have a hidden alcohol problem or were you drunk in love?"

Eoin made obnoxious kissy noises, and I groaned.

"I was just trying to be a good son," I tried, only to be showered with a volley of bollocks, bullshites and an in-me-hoop-you-were.

"We all have our lovers," Noah said. "I have Aubrey, Eoin has Kayleigh, and Michael has his Blackberry."

"Hey," Michael warned.

Noah ignored him and grabbed my chin. "We don't keep secrets, brother."

If he knew the real answer to all these nosy questions, Noah would think differently. If he heard the name that was on the tip of my tongue, he would tell me to swallow it and never speak it aloud. If he knew the face behind my lids every time I closed my eyes, he would tell me that some secrets should be kept, even from brothers. Some secrets, if revealed, wouldn't strengthen a brotherhood, but destroy it.

I let Noah's eyes search my face and clung to the only truth I could: this was for the best. He'd see if I was lying if I tried to convince myself I wasn't falling for Kayleigh. He'd see something off if I told myself there was nothing going on between me and Eoin's girlfriend. He'd call my bluff if I lied and said again there was no one.

But as his eyes darted between mine, I repeated the only

truths I clung to: it would hurt Eoin to find out, it was better if I kept it secret, this was for the best.

Grinning, I shrugged my shoulders and looked innocently up at my older brother. "Satisfied?" I asked.

Noah tried for a few more silent moments to unlock the truth behind my steady smile. But what he didn't know was that that key was long gone; I tossed it over my shoulder and it sank down, down, down into the depths of the sea one night almost ten years ago. With a sigh, Noah sagged back against the edge of the desk and asked one last time. "There's no one?"

I held back a laugh, because he had no clue just how accurate that was, how accurate it had been for nearly as long as I could remember. For this answer I was able to look Noah straight in the eye and say without any deceit in my heart, "No one."

My brothers were all disappointed that I had no "bra sizes" or "favourite positions" to share, but in the end they all believed me. The conversation in Ma's little study turned to the upcoming holidays, Eoin's rugby team, parties at The Jar, ways Michael found to reinvest our savings, plans to fix up Ma's porch in the spring. I was thankful as always that none of it had to do with me.

I'd been reckless.

I'd let myself go too far with Kayleigh. Stolen glances weren't free, and it was Eoin who was going to pay. Fingers just brushing against each other in the shop were like brushing against fire: it didn't take the whole hand to get burned. It hadn't gone past thoughts in my mind, but that didn't mean that my thoughts were innocent. Not by a fecking long shot.

In my mind, I was stealing Kayleigh's breath. My lips on hers. Hers, sweet and soft, on mine. I was stealing her kisses, her time, her love. In my mind, the only thing "just brushing" against us and our naked bodies were bed sheets. Our legs were intertwined, our fingers locked with one another's, my chest pressed against hers as the bed frame ruined the dry wall in my apartment. In my mind, I didn't want to be guilt-free. I didn't want to do the "right thing". I didn't want to be innocent.

I hadn't *touched* Kayleigh in real life, but I had in my mind and that was too far. I had to be more careful. I had to watch myself. I had to remember those green eyes were not mine.

I would talk more with the family, with Kayleigh, even. Avoiding her would be suspicious, after all. I would smile more; I'd practice again in the mirror if I had to. I would pretend better.

The old grandfather clock in the hallway outside the study chimed out midnight and Michael squinted at his bottle of sherry as he held it up to the light of the lamp.

"Well, boys, I'm out," he said. "So I think I'm out." He stood up from the footrest, wobbling just a little, and patted me on the shoulder before saying goodnight to Noah and Eoin.

"Who's up for the bar, eh?" Eoin asked, fingers already on his phone to order an Uber before Michael's footsteps disappeared up the stairs.

"Oh, to be twenty-two again," Noah lamented.

Eoin paused in the doorway and glanced back at me, his lifted eyebrows the unspoken question. I just shook my head. Eoin pouted for a moment, but then hurried out to pile on his coat and gloves and scarf and pat his back pocket to see if his wallet was still there and call up his rugby buddies and check his breath against his own palm and maybe say goodnight to Kayleigh. Maybe not.

I pushed back the office chair to head off to bed myself but paused when I noticed Noah lingering in his spot next to me against the desk, scratching at the back of his neck.

"What?" I asked, knowing it was definitely something when

Noah kept his gaze averted from mine, focusing instead on the old rug.

"Look, Darren," he said, still not looking at me in the dim light of the study. "I just want to say that if you want to ta—"

"Talk about what?"

I hadn't even let him finish his sentence; I hadn't needed to. You didn't need to see the head of a rattlesnake to hear it hidden in the tall grasses. My tone was suddenly dark, threatening.

Noah glanced over at me, shifting uncomfortably where he sat. "Daz, it's just that I know this time of year is hard on you and—"

"Talk about what?"

I could already sense Noah moving away from me at the sharp whip of my voice.

Good.

Noah ran a hand through his hair. His head fell back and he stared up at the ceiling. "Eoin and Michael said it had to be a girl, the reason you've been withdrawn...different," he said, each word seemingly harder to get out than the last as if each were a tooth he was pulling from his own mouth. "But I thought that maybe you were struggling with—"

"Talk about what, Noah?"

Noah's head fell to his chest in defeat.

My own chest beat so violently, I wasn't sure I was the only one who could hear my pulse loud and erratic in my ears. I glared at Noah, who stared at his fingers in his lap. "Talk about what?" I asked once more, struggling to keep my voice from quivering in anger.

"Nothing," Noah finally sighed, his voice nothing more than a whisper. "Never mind."

His words were a pardon. But they were also another turn of the key in the prison of my heart, locked good and tight.

"I'm going to bed." I stood and left without another word, without a glance back at Noah alone in the study.

As I was hurrying up the stairs, I ran into Kayleigh on her way down. I sensed her eyes searching for mine; I focused on the steps, one after the other.

"Goodnight, Darren," she whispered after I'd shouldered past her.

My name on her lips sent goose bumps up and down my arms. I cursed my ears as I pulled my bedroom door closed behind me. The Darren who used to live here would have said, "Goodnight, Kayleigh." He would have lain awake thinking about her, seeing her eyes out his bedroom window instead of the Little Dipper. He would have finally rolled out of bed, slipped into the hallway, and knocked at her door as silently as tiny pebbles thrown at Juliet's window.

"Good morning, Kayleigh," he would have said.

But the Darren who used to live here did not live here any longer, so I tugged the covers up over my head and prayed for the small mercy that I'd at least fall asleep quickly.

It had been a long time since my prayers had been answered.

It was no different that long, cold night.

14

KAYLEIGH

*P*erhaps Darren assumed that I was hard at work Monday morning in the little office at the back of the shop because of the constant click-clack of the keyboard at the ancient computer. The truth was I was only typing two letters in caps lock again and again.

"Y" and "N".

"Y" I go out there.

"N" I stay in here.

"Y" I go ask Darren if I can help him again on the vehicles.

"N" I do my job, focus on the task of finding tax software compatible with a dinosaur, and making sure the thing doesn't catch on fire while trying to install it.

I stopped typing for only long enough to stretch out my fingers, roll my wrists, and plant my palms firmly over my mouth so Darren wouldn't hear me screaming as I squeezed my eyes shut.

"Y" I wanted to go out there because I found the work interesting and wanted to learn more about engine mechanics from an engine mechanics expert.

"N" I wanted to go out there because I found *Darren* interesting and wanted to learn more about Darren from a Darren expert.

I wasn't exactly sure what my plan was. Type as fast and furiously as I could till the computer started to smoke and freeze and the last letter would be my choice? Type as fast and furiously as I could till my hand cramped and I had to take workers' comp and go home and therefore avoid any choice at all? Either way I was pretty sure I was going insane in that office.

"Y" I push down my emotions, keep things professional here at work, and stick it out with Eoin, because it was obviously the path of least resistance.

"N" Fuck it all to hell, because I wanted *him*.

When I heard Darren mutter an irritated "bollocks" out in the shop, I took it as an excuse to finally push myself back from the desk. Although I wasn't entirely sure that I needed it.

"Need any help?" I asked, leaning my head out the door.

Darren was hidden beneath the hood of a car and he remained hidden when he responded as usual with a gruff, "I'm grand."

Shite.

With my "excuse" having just flown straight out the window, I was left searching for another one, fingers now drumming against the door frame instead of the yellowed "Y" and "N" keys.

After coming up empty while Darren cursed away under the hood, I came to the conclusion that I didn't have an excuse, despite how terribly I wanted one. If I stepped out from behind the safety and security of the office door, it was because I wanted to do so. If I crossed the stretch of grey concrete to stand by his side, it would be because I alone told my feet to move. And if I asked if I could help, there was no way of escaping the words that weren't spoken aloud: "*I* want to help."

Knowing full well it was probably a mistake I would surely

regret, I sucked in a deep breath, tugged open the door, and marched straight over to Darren.

"Show me what you're doing."

Darren started and banged his head on the hood. Well, things were off to a smashingly good start, weren't they?

I almost turned and ran back to the little office as his expletives echoed around the garage. With a scowl and an incoming knot on the back of his head, Darren pulled himself from beneath the hood and glared at me. "What?"

I released the lip I had been biting nervously to smile nervously. "Umm, I'd like to learn." I rocked back and forth on my heels.

Darren stared at me in confusion. He rubbed the spot he'd hit on the hood like it was the reason for not understanding the words coming from my lips. "What?" he repeated.

I pointed vaguely at the engine he had been working on and shrugged. "I could help you," I tried, "if you, you know, show me...and stuff."

I was suddenly a schoolgirl again on the playground with my crush—just as nervous, just as awkward.

Darren wiped his hands on the towel he had tucked in the waistband of his jeans. "You want to work on the cars?"

I nodded and then added a *totally* nonchalant, "I mean, sure. Why not."

Darren's stormy blue eyes narrowed. "I can't afford to pay you more for it."

"It's not about the money," I said.

"Then what?" Darren asked. He didn't bother waiting for my answer. "I mean it's hard work, Kayleigh. It's dirty manual labour. My hands are always greasy and usually bleeding. At the end of the day your back will ache, your knees will be bruised and you'll still have no idea what that funny noise coming from the engine is. At its very best it's frustrating, at its very worst it's deadly."

With those eyes of his fixed intently on mine, I couldn't help but be honest. "It's just that I've bounced around from...job to job and, well, I haven't found one that I'm passionate about. A job, I mean."

Darren flinched so slightly that I wasn't sure if I had just imagined it. I wanted him to hear me. I wanted him to know what I was really saying. I wanted him to understand because the unspoken words of my heart were the unspoken words of his own.

"And, well," I continued, "I was thinking that maybe this could be the job I've been searching for."

Darren stepped back and crossed his arms over his toned chest. "You already have a job."

I tried to read the tone of his voice. Tried to read the expression on his blank face. Tried to read the pace of his chest rising and falling, the steadiness of his blinking, the colour of his cheeks. But it was all a foreign language. Or worse, I could read him just fine and just didn't want to accept what was right there in front of me.

Darren was going to tell me to go back to my office. He was going to ask about the tax software. Or say, "We can't do this. You know we can't do this. Ever."

But after moments of tense silence, he asked, "Are you sure?"

Are you sure?

"Y" I know what I'm getting into.

"N" I have no fucking clue what I'm getting into.

"Y" I don't care.

My eyes remained locked on Darren's as I slowly, oh so slowly, nodded my chin. "I'm sure," I whispered.

Darren hesitated, still searching my eyes. Then he extended his hand to me slowly, oh so slowly. My eyes drifted down to see it hanging in the open space between us. I blinked and saw the deep lines etched across his palm, black rivers of grease and oil. I blinked again and saw a half-healed cut along his thumb. I blinked once more and this time I saw nothing of Darren's hand, because mine was covering it as I laid it gently in his.

I was surprised to find the concrete beneath me after taking that first step toward Darren, because to me it felt like stepping off the ledge of a cliff.

Darren's voice—as he explained the various components of the engine, the different processes for it to run, and the common issues he has to deal with—made me feel drunk. Bending under the hood, my neck ached and I'd quickly lost all hope of ever having clean nails again, but I wanted to keep listening to him forever in that dim, intimate light.

"Do you understand?" he asked, voice thick as honey, smooth as a forty-year barrel-aged Scotch.

"Y"

"Does that make sense?"

"Y"

"Do you want me to show you how this works next?"

"Y"

"Y"

"Y"

When my cell phone beeped in the office, dusk was already casting long shadows across the shop.

I wiped at the sweat on my brow with the back of my hand after tightening a lug nut on the intake pipe and gave Darren a buzzed smile. "Just a minute."

If Darren was my alcohol, the text I received from Eoin was a cold shower, a hot cup of coffee, and a slap in the face.

Can't wait for our date tonight, Kayleigh Bear. You've made my life complete. Be at your place at 8 to pick you up.

My pulse spiked. I tossed my phone back into my purse because I couldn't bear to look at it.

"N" I'd have to face Eoin. I'd have to break his heart. I'd have to see the pain right there on his face.

"N" I'd have to destroy Eoin and Darren's relationship. Who knew if they could ever recover from a betrayal like that?

"N" I'd have to ruin the perfect O'Sullivan family.

I could maybe handle the other two. Maybe. But the last thing? Never.

The tips of my fingers felt numb as I went back out into the shop. Darren smiled as I took my place next to him. I couldn't manage the same.

"Alright, so you remember the cylinder head here?" he asked, jumping back into my lessons.

I shook my head. "No."

He looked slightly surprised, but he recovered quickly. "That's alright," he said. "So it's right here next to the fuel rail and—"

"I don't remember that either," I interrupted.

Darren straightened next to me. "Kayleigh?"

"I think you're right," I said.

Darren frowned, concern darkening his eyes.

"This is too hard," I admitted, swallowing heavily. "My body already hurts and I'm dirty and I can't remember anything you just said and I'm...I'm just not right for this job."

Darren responded in a low voice, "You just started."

I shook my head and rested my chin on my chest, staring at the grease beneath my fingernails. "I know," I said, "but if it was what I was meant to do it would be easy, you know?"

I glanced up and looked at Darren through my eyelashes.

"And it's just not," I whispered. "It's not easy for me."

"Maybe it's not supposed to be easy," Darren said. He reached out his hand for me, but I pulled back.

"I think I'm going to go back to my job," I said, trying to keep the emotion from my voice. "Working on cars...with you, it just isn't right." I turned and walked toward the office.

"Kayleigh!" Darren called after me. "How can you know if it's not right if you only just started?"

At the door, I glanced over my shoulder at Darren. He looked mad and hurt and confused all at once.

"But I didn't really get started at all, did I?" I said sadly. "All I did was get my fingers dirty."

Inside the office, I sagged against the door and sank to the floor, tugging my knees up tight against my chest.

Are you sure?

"N" I can't reveal the truth to Eoin.

"N" I can't do that to him.

"N" I can't do that to his family.

So why did I hit "Y"?

And why was I so terrified that I was going to hit "Y" again and again till it wasn't the computer catching fire, but the O'Sullivan family?

15

KAYLEIGH

*I*t turns out that if you let them sit long enough untouched, the bubbles of a 1984 Dom Perignon in a hand-blown Swarovski crystal flute sitting on a pressed white tablecloth fizzle out almost as quickly as the bubbles from the cheapest bottle of sparkling wine bought from the local corner store (that also sells Cheese and Onion Taytos and Cadbury Starbars) and served in a "Doolin Cave Rocks!" souvenir mug.

I'd dreamed of fancy restaurants with waistcoated maître d's, crystal chandeliers, polished steak knives and decadent chocolate souffles that melt the very second they touch the tip of your tongue. But in reality, a fancy restaurant meant pinched toes. It meant salad instead of pasta because you're still wearing the tag of your exorbitantly priced dress, and if you stuff your stomach with sage and butter gnocchi you'll bust the zipper in the back and, well, you can't exactly return that, now can you?

Turns out a light bulb is just a light bulb, a steak knife is just a sharp knife, and a souffle is just expensive cotton candy without the fun colours.

I had just finished ordering my fifth salad seated stiffly in my fifth waist-pinching gown in the fifth restaurant whose name I couldn't pronounce when Eoin reached across the white table-cloth to push yet another glass of '84 Dom Perignon toward me beneath the dazzling light of yet another chandelier.

"Should I have ordered the '83?" he asked.

I shook my head (careful not to shake it *too* hard so that my tedious up-do didn't come undone). Then smiled as I carefully placed my fingers around the delicate stem to take a sip.

"No, no," I insisted, squeezing his hand. "It's lovely. Thank you, Eoin."

He beamed from ear to ear and a pang of guilt stabbed at my chest. It was obvious that he was in love, "head over heels", "stars in his eyes", "wrapped around my little finger" love. He was blinded, stricken, obsessed by it. There was no doubt that Eoin O'Sullivan's heart pounded out faster and faster, over and over these four letters: L - O - V - E- L - O - V - E- L - O - V - E!

Those letters were beautiful, but they weren't K - A - Y- L - E - I - G - H.

Did Eoin love me or did he love romantic dates in nice restaurants with the snow falling gently outside the candlelit windows? Did Eoin love me or did he love the fairy tale story of his soulmate saving his life and then falling into a lifetime romance? Did Eoin love me or did he love...love?

Or was this my way of feeling better about the letters *my* heart beat out?

"What do you think of the restaurant?" Eoin asked, glancing around the spacious room. "Do you like it?"

I nodded without taking my eyes off of the golden bread in the basket that the tag digging into my right shoulder blade reminded me not to touch.

"It's wonderful," I said, trying to smile. "It's really lovely."

In reality, I wasn't even quite sure whether we'd been here before or not. All the expensive restaurants Eoin took me to for our seemingly endless dates ran together at some point. Shining, cold marble floors. Grand gold-framed paintings. Red velvet couches in the waiting areas you weren't sure whether you could sit on or not.

I shifted uncomfortably in my itchy sequin dress I desperately wanted to rip off in favour of leggings and fuzzy socks and smiled over at Eoin, who looked equally out of place in his stuffy black suit instead of his grey sweats and sleeveless training hoodie.

"Thank you," I repeated.

It was all I could think of to say to him. He brushed his thumb along my hand. "You're my soulmate, Kayleigh Bear." He grinned. "How could I not give you the whole world?"

What if I didn't want the whole world? What if I just wanted one quiet, solemn corner of it where broken things go to get fixed by a broken soul?

I shoved aside those thoughts and instead said once more, "Thank you."

I winced because I sounded just about as genuine as a politician repeating it for the ten-thousandth time as she shook the ten-thousandth hand with the ten-thousandth pearly white, shite-eating smile. But Eoin's grin widened nonetheless and we held hands in silence and watched the bubbles in our champagne fizzle out one by one, trapped equally by the necklines of our uncomfortable clothes and the expectation of decorum in the fancy restaurant (whatever the hell this one was called).

We were halfway through our meals when Eoin glanced up from his steak, which he was pretending wasn't bite size for him. "You're quiet tonight," he said.

My fork paused halfway to my mouth, pieces of unfilling and unsatisfying lettuce hanging suspended over a plate full of yet more unfilling and unsatisfying lettuce. His words surprised me because it was the first time I could remember when Eoin seemed to see me as I was and not me as he wanted to see me:

perfect, lovely, *loving* soulmate. I put down my fork and looked over at him. "Oh, umm..."

I hadn't expected to need an excuse, a reason, a lie, so my mind whirled trying to find one. In the end, I decided to give Eoin as much truth as I could.

"I'm actually thinking about work," I said finally.

The expression on Eoin's face was less interest and much more confusion. "Work?"

I nodded and reminded him gently, "Yeah, umm, at the shop...with Darren?"

Eoin snapped his fingers and immediately glanced around apologetically at the other restaurant patrons for his disturbance. "Right, right," he lowered his voice, leaning forward so only I could hear him. "Is it Darren? He must be terrible to work for."

I laughed the first genuine laugh of the night. "He is actually terrible to work for. But that wasn't what I was thinking about."

Eoin sliced another tiny bite of his tiny steak, and I imagined him already thinking about his McDonald's order after we finished our date.

"Maybe I could get your opinion about it, actually?" I asked, thankful for *something* to talk about at last...even if it was dangerously close to the one thing I shouldn't, couldn't talk about.

Eoin nodded while pretending that he needed to even chew that bite.

I grabbed my glass of now not-so-sparkling sparkling wine. "Today I worked with Darren on the bikes instead of my normal stuff in the office," I explained. "But just a few minutes in and I was lost. My mind was all twisted around and I had no idea what he was talking about."

Eoin nodded along as I went on, telling him everything that had happened in the shop that afternoon. I'd made it through my glass of champagne by the time I was finished, having said more, with more passion than any conversation with Eoin before that.

"So Darren says I can't give up because it's hard, but I say that if it was something I was meant to do, I would have a knack for it, right? It'd be easier. Why fight it, you know?" I said, leaning back in my chair, not caring anymore about the expected posture in a fancy restaurant. "So what do you think?"

Eoin had long ago finished his plate and started in on the bread basket. He tapped his finger against the crust of the last piece. "I think, Kayleigh Bear," he said, "that you are one thousand and one percent..."

I grinned when he paused for dramatic effect.

"...one thousand and one percent correct!"

"Thank you!" I smacked the table with my palm and an older couple next to us gasped.

"You're either good at something or you're not," Eoin added, pointing a beefy finger at me.

"Exactly," I said excitedly. "That's exactly what I was trying to tell him."

"Like take me, for instance." Eoin laid his hands on his crisp white shirt, and I was too pumped up to worry that he might leave buttered finger marks. "From the very start I was shite at math, just shite. Numbers were like Chinese to me. But rugby? Fuck, I got that from the very second I stepped onto the pitch."

I nodded along emphatically after lifting a finger to request more champagne from the maître d'.

"I was a natural. That's what everyone said. A goddamn natural," Eoin continued. "Why would I struggle with math when I could dominate with rugby? That makes no sense at all."

"Exactly." I waved my hands for emphasis. "That's it *exactly*, Eoin."

Eoin blushed and wiggled in his fancy chair like a puppy

who'd just been praised for doing a trick. The maître d' returned with a bottle of champagne, and I leaned across the table as he poured.

"Like I'm good at answering the phones," I said.

"No," Eoin interrupted, leaning across the table to mimic my enthusiasm. "No, Kayleigh Bear. You're the *best* at answering phones. The absolute best."

I hesitated, because despite Eoin's overwhelming and flattering confidence in me, that wasn't *entirely* true. I hadn't quite nailed transferring calls from the office to the little cordless by Darren's toolbox. I did find myself missing calls sometimes because my mind was out in the shop with Darren. But those were just insignificant details, I assured myself as I took a swig of champagne. The point was I could (mostly) use a phone while I definitely couldn't manage a voltage meter.

"And the coffee," I pointed out while pointing my glass at Eoin. "I've never struggled making the pot of coffee in the morning. First try on my first day, I nailed it."

Eoin reached across the table and squeezed my shoulder with his beefy hand. "Because you're a natural at making coffee, Kayleigh Bear. A natural!"

"Exactly!"

I didn't bother waiting for the maître d' this time as I grabbed the bottle of champagne to refill my own glass. "So I was right then?" I asked. "I was right that I just wasn't meant to be a mechanic, right? I mean, what was I thinking? Who did I think I was?"

The kind of girl who chases after what she wants no matter the hurdles? The kind of girl who sees a challenge and runs toward it instead of away from it? The kind of girl who stokes the flames of passion in her heart so they became an uncontrollable wildfire?

"No," I gripped my champagne glass as I stared down at my

fancy gown. "No, making coffee is easy. Writing sticky notes is easy. Answering the phones is easy."

"Maybe some things aren't supposed to be easy."

Darren's words echoed in my mind even as I tried to push them away.

"And someone will always have to answer the phones," Eoin assured me, winking and pointing a beefy finger at me across the table. "Talk about job security. You can answer the phones for the rest of your life."

I looked up at Eoin, and this time I was aware of every muscle it took to raise a smile. Maybe it wasn't a great sign when expressing happiness felt like weightlifting.

"Exactly," I said, enthusiasm dying as quickly as the bubbles in that exorbitantly expensive bottle of champagne.

I could answer the phones for the rest of my life.

I could curl my eyelashes and swipe on red lipstick and wiggle into tight dresses for the rest of my life.

I could drink champagne and smile and rely on the crystal chandeliers for the glow in my cheeks for the rest of my life.

I could stay with Eoin for the rest of my life.

Because it was easy.

"Maybe some things aren't supposed to be easy."

"Hey, Kayleigh Bear." Eoin's hand snaked around the bread basket and between my glass and the flickering candle to hold my fingers. I looked across at him as he rubbed his thumb along the back of my hand. "What do you think about taking our dessert to go?"

I shrugged, suddenly feeling deflated. "Yeah, sure," I said. "Should I ask for the dessert menu?"

As I shifted in my chair to find the maître d', Eoin squeezed my fingers and cleared his throat. "No, no, um." He leaned forward and lowered his voice, eyes darting conspiratorially back and forth. "No, I, um, I meant..." He blushed slightly and again cleared his throat. "I meant maybe we taste each other's tiramisu back at my place."

My body went rigid. It was my turn to duck my eyes with red cheeks. "Oh, um..."

"We could make a *cake* together back at my place," Eoin added, leaning in even closer.

I frowned, a tad confused by that particular metaphor.

Eoin's eyes travelled down to my chest as he whispered, "Like we could mix up a pudding back at my pl—"

"Eoin," I interrupted. "I got it. I got it."

"I'm talking about sex," Eoin needlessly clarified. "Back at my place."

I slipped my hand from his and patted it with kindness that felt more motherly than romantic. "Eoin, honey, I knew what you were talking about."

Eoin sighed loudly and sagged into his chair in a dramatic show of relief. "Good," he exhaled. "I've been struggling with how to bring it up, you know? We have been dating for almost twelve days now."

I smiled. "I know, I know," I said. "It's just that I'm feeling kind of tired right now."

Eoin did his best to hide his disappointment, but I saw his pout before he forced the corners of his lips back up into a smile. "No problem, Kayleigh Bear."

"Thanks, Eoin," I said. "You're a good man."

And I meant it. I really did. It was part of what was making all of this so damn difficult.

"We're soulmates, after all," Eoin added, sipping his champagne. "We have forever for...that."

Forever for nice restaurants and simple conversations and no fighting.

Forever for chairs held out for me, doors opened for me, bills paid for me.

Forever for easy.

"Ready to go then?" Eoin asked, raising his hand to signal the maître d' for the bill.

I nodded. "Yeah."

Yeah, I was ready to go.

I just had no clue how to tell Eoin.

16

DARREN

*T*here was no wafting smell of black coffee in the shop when I tucked my motorcycle helmet under my arm and stepped inside, brushing a few stray raindrops from my hair. On top of the toolbox closest to the garage door I found a size twelve wrench, a grease-smudged yellow invoice, and an old copy of *Bike Buyers' Guide*, but the normal neon pink stickies with a list of missed calls in Kayleigh's curly cursive were nowhere in sight. The office door was still shut, the lights were still off, and the phone was ringing with no one to answer. Where was Kayleigh?

I heard a muffled, "Motherfucker."

My wet boots squeaked on the concrete floor as I followed the quiet cursing and the *ting-ting* sound of metal against metal. I stepped past a motorcycle stripped of its back wheel, around another with dismantled handlebars, and behind a beat-up old junker Volkswagen Polo whose missing tail light was the least of its problems.

From my place near the rear bumper, I leaned around the side to see a pair of skinny legs jutting out from beneath the car. Next to the flat front tyre and its dented hubcap was a wobbly stack of old manuals that nearly towered past the rusted hood. I watched silently as Kayleigh's feet squirmed this way and that while she muttered to herself in escalating frustration. I winced myself when I heard her bang her forehead against the under-carriage, having done it at least a million and a half times myself.

With a sigh, I followed the bumper around the side of the car and stood between Kayleigh's outstretched legs. Crossing my arms over my chest, I placed the toe of my boot on the edge of the creeper and rolled her out from beneath the car. I kept my lips fixed in a stern line as Kayleigh blinked in the sudden flood of light, but damn, was it a struggle with the way she looked beneath me.

Her long red hair was twisted into two messy knots on the top of her head to keep it out of the way of my head lamp. She blew her ruffled bangs out of her eyes. There was already a smudge of grease on her cheek, and I wanted nothing more than to reach down and brush my thumb along her soft freckled skin. I'd never found her sexier than she was right then as she held a wrench the wrong way in work gloves at least two sizes too big for her with a manual incompatible with the car she was working on opened across her chest. It nearly sent me over the edge when she smiled up at me on top of all of that.

"Good, you're here!" she said as she struggled to sit up on the creeper. "You can show me how to take off the inner socket assembly."

She flopped the '80s car manual on the concrete floor next to her and ran her gloved finger across the black-and-white diagram.

"I've been at it for an hour. I mean, damn, time goes by quickly under there, and I can't seem to figure out where this pinion bushing is." She was talking so quickly, so excitedly that I could barely understand her. "I found the control arm, or at least I *think* it was the control arm, but maybe it was the centre link. It's so dark down there! Anyway, I was trying to repair the spool valve, which I read could be the problem, but then I couldn't reach it because the control arm was in the way. But then again, maybe the control arm was the pinion bushing?"

I thought she was finished, but it turned out that she was just pausing long enough to suck in a breath.

"And after that I want your help figuring out what this weird sound from the engine is, because I've been trying to read and I read in one of those manuals there that it might be the air intake, but I tightened and cleaned everything around that and the sound was still there and—hey, where are you going?"

I walked away because if I didn't walk away, I was going to drop to my knees right there in front of her, take her face in my hands, and kiss the shite out of her.

"Darren?" Kayleigh called after me. "Hello? Darren?"

I breathed in a steadying breath as I pulled open the first drawer of my toolbox. I was safe here. Things made sense here. The head of this screwdriver fit with that nail, the gage of this wrench could turn that bolt, the width of this wire could connect with that bulb. I understood things here.

"Darren?" she called, her voice breaking through to my safe place. "Are you coming back? Darren?"

"Go do your job, Kayleigh."

It had been a mistake to agree to show Kayleigh how to work on the vehicles with me. It meant too much proximity, too much intimacy, too much time alone with our breaths hot against one another's beneath the hood of a car. I was relieved when Kayleigh realised it was a mistake and returned to the office.

I'd almost managed to make myself believe that last part. *Relieved. I was relieved.* I'd repeated it on my drive home yesterday. I'd repeated it while heating up a can of soup for dinner. I'd repeated it while brushing my teeth, while trying to fall asleep, while waiting for my alarm clock to go off in the morning because I hadn't fallen asleep. I could almost say it in my head without hearing the other words I banished: disappointed, hurt, stung, discouraged, devastated.

"Kayleigh," I craned my head back to call across the shop, "the phone's ringing."

There was no answer from her as the last harsh rattle of the old wall-mounted phone died in the dark office. I should have just focused on finding the right part to switch out the handles on the Davidson.

"Kayleigh, are you going to go get the phone?"

There was no hesitation this time: "No."

My fingers curled and my nails sank into my palms as my head dropped down between my shoulders.

"I'm going to fix this spool valve," she said stubbornly. "Whether you come back and help me or not."

I sighed in frustration as I heard the wheels of the creeper on the concrete floors. I glanced over toward the Volkswagen.

No. I wouldn't go. I couldn't go.

Turning my head back toward the toolbox felt like turning a wrench on a rusted ancient bolt that was practically welded to the metal. I had a better chance of reading a piece of classic French literature than comprehending the motorcycle specifications on the worksheet for my first job as the sound of Kayleigh working filled my ears. I stared at the row of wrenches and suddenly none of them seemed to fit anywhere.

I was rubbing my eyes, trying to clear my vision, when I heard a pipe rattle loudly to the floor and Kayleigh hiss in pain before cursing. With a sigh I grabbed the first aid kit from the side of the toolbox and walked back to the car just as Kayleigh was rolling herself out from underneath it.

She frowned up at me as she held her hand over her left eyebrow, the manual still spread across her chest, the head lamp askew over her messy knots. "I don't need you," she grumbled.

"No?" I asked, lifting a curious eyebrow as I stood nonchalantly with the first aid kit at my side.

"No," Kayleigh said.

"The rack unit didn't fall when you loosened it because you didn't support it with a winch?"

She averted her eyes from mine. "Nope."

"And there's not a nice cut right there above your eye and a nasty bruise on its way?" I asked, rocking on my heels.

Kayleigh started to shake her head, only to quickly think better of it. "No," she said. "You can go back to work now, thank you very much."

I finally threw off my "I don't care" persona as she tried to push herself up.

"Hey, hey," I said softly, hurrying to her side and dropping to my knees next to her. "Take it easy, alright?"

With one hand supporting the small of her back and one gently holding her shoulder, I eased her up to sitting, watching her face as she squeezed shut the eye I could see.

"Easy," I repeated as her skin paled slightly. "Easy now."

Kayleigh sucked in a breath and opened her eye to stare at me. "I really don't need you. I want you to know I was doing just fine without you."

I nodded as I wrapped my fingers around the wrist of her hand that was covering her left eye. "Yes, yes," I said. "You don't need me, I get it. Now let me see."

Kayleigh ducked her head as I pulled her hand away from her face. There was a small cut across her eyebrow. She watched me through a curtain of long eyelashes as I prodded gently at the purpling skin around the cut. She hissed when I got too close.

"Sorry," I whispered.

"How'd you know?" Kayleigh asked in a small voice as I reached behind me and opened the first aid kit.

I was grinning when I shifted back around to face her with two small butterfly bandages and a disinfectant wipe.

"Because I made the exact same mistake when I was first learning," I explained. "And I was rewarded with the exact same cut."

Kayleigh tenderly touched the area around her eye as she looked at me. "Really?"

I nodded. "Hurt like a fucker, right?"

Kayleigh at last smiled and a tiny laugh escaped her pink, sweet lips. "A real motherfucker."

Our eyes met and for just a moment we were just two people smiling, just two people enjoying each other's company, just two people with their futures wide open, their hearts free, their possibilities together endless. My smile faltered and my eyes dropped to the grey concrete floor when I remembered that Kayleigh was with Eoin and my heart had not been free for a long, long time.

"This might sting a little bit," I mumbled as I ripped open the disinfectant wipe.

When I looked back up at Kayleigh, her eyes hadn't left mine, although she was no longer smiling. Up this close I could see her irises were delicate patterns of dark and light greens and streaks of a green so pale that it almost looked silver. Kayleigh's eyes weren't just a forest of pines; they were a forest of pines whose leaves sparkled with fresh snow. I imagined getting lost amongst them, the crunch of untouched snow beneath my feet, the smell of the pine under my nose. I imagined the whisper of the wind through the quivering branches, and that was all without closing my eyes.

I swallowed as I forced my attention to her cut. Kayleigh

flinched when I touched the disinfectant wipe to the open skin along her eyebrow, but she did not pull away.

"So, umm, what happened to giving up?" I asked.

My eyes darted to hers. They were already waiting for me. She blinked and her long eyelashes swept across her cheek, but she remained quiet.

"I thought it was too hard," I whispered, "...this new job."

I set aside the disinfectant wipe and grabbed the butterfly bandages as the silence in the shop grew louder and louder. It seemed to me as if the rest of the world outside of my brick-lined shop was falling away, turning into darkness. My little repair shop drifted on a shoreless sea, and all that existed was Kayleigh and me and the wind and the water.

I glanced down at her as I placed the first butterfly bandage on the cut. My voice was low and soft as I said, "I thought you said it wasn't meant to be."

I added the second and sank back to the floor in front of Kayleigh. She fidgeted with the corners of the car manual and bit her lip. Finally, she looked over at me.

"Someone maybe changed my mind," she said quietly with a little grin tugging at the corner of her lips.

I lifted an eyebrow. "Someone?"

Kayleigh nodded. "Someone with a very bad attitude problem," she said, eyes searching mine. "Someone grumpy and irritable and often very rude."

I rested my hands on the floor and leaned back. "Hmm. Someone dark and handsome?"

Kayleigh tilted her head from side to side and tapped her finger against her lip. "Someone who could bother to smile every once in a while," she said. "Because when this someone smiles, this someone is actually very nice to look at."

I resisted grinning at Kayleigh.

She frowned, leaned back against the passenger door of the car, and crossed her arms over her chest, still seated on the creeper. "Someone who is the most stubborn ass I've ever encountered in my entire life," she added, levelling her eyes at me.

I shrugged. "I must not know who this someone is," I teased.

Kayleigh studied me with tender eyes and said with empathy in her tone instead of humour, "I'm not entirely sure you know this someone either."

Silence fell back around us and again I got the sensation that we were the only people remaining on the planet.

Finally Kayleigh whispered, "I want to try again."

From the motion of the open car manual, I could tell her chest was rising and falling faster than before.

"This job," she continued, eyes fixed on mine. "I want to try again."

I scratched at the back of my neck. "You know it will be difficult?"

Kayleigh nodded.

"And painful?"

Kayleigh smiled and grazed her fingers along the butterfly bandages over her eyebrow, but I could tell from her eyes that she knew I wasn't talking about a cut in her skin. I wished that was the kind of pain I was talking about. I wished the worst that could happen if the two of us took a step down this path was some blood and a few stitches. My lips would have been on hers right then and there if that was the pain I was talking about.

"You know it will be easier in the office," I said at last. "You won't get hurt in the office...no one will."

Kayleigh flinched at these words, just like she flinched when the disinfectant wipe burned her open wound.

"I can't keep answering phones just because it's easy," she said. "Or that's all I'll ever do in life: answer phones." She looked across at me earnestly as she clutched the manual to her now heaving chest. "I want to try again, Darren," she whispered passionately. "I *have* to try again... I have to see if we—*I* can do it."

I hesitated, knowing I was about to make the wrong decision and knowing I didn't care. I exhaled shakily. "Alright."

Kayleigh's eyes filled with hope as she leaned forward slightly. "You'll show me?"

I nodded. "Lesson one: using a winch."

17

KAYLEIGH

*A*t the back of the little office at the back of the shop there was a little bathroom with a dingy mirror above a chipped porcelain sink and a single halogen light bulb hanging from the ceiling that flickered like a horror movie. This is where I was forced to get ready for that night's date with Eoin. Needless to say, it wasn't going well.

Every time I raised my arms to curl another strand of my red hair, I bumped my elbows against the faded tiles. The light in the mirror was so dim that I had to check in my phone camera every time I swiped my mascara over my eyelashes to make sure I hadn't gotten it all over my eyelids. I banged my forehead against the wall when I bent down to tug up my burgundy gown. I had to sit on the toilet, which was missing its seat, to strap up my heels. So when I finally slipped out past the door plastered in motorcycle brand stickers, I had no idea whether I looked like a lady or a lady of the night.

I was craning my neck around to make sure I wasn't trailing a snake of toilet paper behind me when I heard a loud clang. I turned around, searching for the source of the noise, and found Darren rubbing at the back of his head while he put the stand for the hood of the Volkswagen back in place. He busied himself with the exhaust valves.

"Darren?" I asked.

He responded with a low grumble.

I sauntered over to him. "Darren," I said with an uncontrollable smile, "Darren, did you just smack your head looking over at me in this dress?" I leaned against the driver's side door, not caring at all about the dust getting on the velvet bow at the bottom of the backless dress.

Darren glanced over at me from under the hood and frowned. "I have no idea what you're talking about," he said. "I'm far too busy to take notice of what you're wearing."

I bit back a laugh and nodded. "So I just imagined the sound of a skull hitting the metal of a Volkswagen Polo hood?"

Darren, focused back on his work, shrugged. "I don't know what to tell you, Kayleigh. I'd recommend getting your ears checked."

I narrowed my eyes at him. "So if I felt the back of your head, I wouldn't feel a bump?"

Darren shook his head, gritting his teeth with the same effort as turning his wrench. "Flat as a pancake."

"Maybe I should check then," I said.

His eyes darted to mine, looking at me through that curtain of dark eyelashes. "Maybe you should."

His words sent a bolt of electricity from my heart all the way to my fingertips, which twitched toward him. Before I could remind myself what a terrible idea touching him was, I was reaching my hand toward his hair. Our eyes held one another, fear and excitement and guilt reflected back, as I carded my fingers through his thick, soft, unruly hair, still messy as it always was from his motorcycle helmet. I licked my lips as Darren leaned just the tiniest bit into my touch. I moved my hand to the back of his head and ran my fingernails along the nape of his neck.

My chest was rising and falling harshly when my cell phone buzzed from within the office. I pulled my hand from Darren's hair as if I'd been burned and cleared my throat. "I should get that," I said, voice rough.

Darren nodded as I turned toward the office. My heels rasped on the concrete floors of the shop. I tried to bite my lip but I couldn't stop myself from saying, "If I turned around right now, there's no way I would find your eyes on me, right Darren?"

"Absolutely not, Ms. Scott."

I managed to hold back a lustful sigh till I was in the safety in the office. The mental image of Darren watching me walk away did more for me than Eoin's lips pressed hot and tight against my own.

I reached for my cell phone with both reluctance and guilt.

EOIN: *Kayleigh Bear, my own true love, my soulmate, my one and only, I shall cover your bedroom with a million and two roses to make up for this, but I have to cancel our date tonight. Coach is having us stay late at practice after last week's loss. Can you possibly ever forgive me, my princess?*

MY RESPONSE back only took a couple clicks: *No problem!*

The contrast of my text to Eoin's was obvious and terrible. Before I tossed my cell phone back into my purse I added: *Have a great practice, hon.*

I leaned against the door frame of the office, sighing as I looked across the shop at Darren still ducked under the hood of the Volkswagen. The sleeves of his charcoal-grey Henley were pushed past his elbows, and I could see the long, lean muscles along his forearms strain as he worked. After pulling a rag from the waistband of his dark jeans, he stretched toward the back of the engine. I caught a glimpse of his defined abs and the patch of dark hair that disappeared down to a region of Eoin's brother I definitely should *not* have been thinking about.

"Um, Eoin had to cancel," I said almost timidly into the quiet space.

Darren stood and wiped his grease-covered hands on the rag. "What's that?"

I should have said this: "Eoin has rugby practice so he cancelled our date, so I'm going to go head home."

It was the right thing to say. I knew that. But when I opened my mouth, I just couldn't quite get my lips to move that way.

"Eoin has rugby practice so he cancelled our date so...so I don't have plans tonight."

Darren slowly finished wiping off his hands, one agonising finger at a time. When he finally looked over at me, he swallowed heavily. "You should go out with Candace and Aubrey," he said. "You look... I mean, you got all dressed up and...and someone should take you someplace nice."

I hesitated.

Could he not see that I didn't want to go someplace nice? Could he not see that I was tired of chandeliers and '84 Dom Perignon and hushed, polite whispers? Could he not see that all I wanted was a smudge of grease on my cheek and his hands on my body?

"Or..." I said slowly, stepping carefully toward him. "Or you could take me on that motorcycle ride you promised me."

Darren searched my eyes when I stopped a few feet away from him.

"It'll be cold," he said.

"I know."

"Your hair will get ruined."

"I know."

"You might get dirty."

I smiled. "Good."

Darren paused a moment longer, seemingly thinking, pondering, weighing. Finally he nodded.

"Alright."

"WHAT DO I NEED TO DO?" I asked as Darren leaned down to adjust the straps of my helmet.

His eyes briefly met mine, a comet here then gone. "Just hold on."

My fingers brushed against his as he helped me onto the back of his motorcycle, the engine rumbling beneath me. He got on. I wrapped my arms tentatively around his waist, unsure of myself, unsure of how close I could get before I'd gone too far.

Darren twisted his head around so I could hear him. "Tighter."

I adjusted myself on the seat and snuggled in closer, squeezing my arms more firmly around him. My chest pressed against his back and my heart skipped. His leather jacket smelled faintly of oil and pine as I rested my head against it.

"We have to lean as one," he shouted back at me as he turned on the headlight. "It might feel like you're falling when I take a tight curve and your body might want to fight against it. But don't fight it." His eyes again met mine, a strike of lightning, here then gone.

"Don't fight it."

I managed only a nod and we were off.

The glare of city lights soon turned into the twinkle of stars, the shimmer of moonlight off a stream, and the magical illumination of fresh snow atop firs as we followed the signs for the Dublin Mountains. The wind whipped cruelly at my cheeks just like Darren promised it would. My fingers were frozen just like he said they would be. And I was quite certain that my coat was splattered with mud kicked up by the back tyre just like he warned it might.

But I never wanted it to end.

The asphalt was like an icy black river that disappeared beneath us as Darren revved the engine and we flew faster and faster into the night. With my arms around him and the motorcycle rumbling beneath me and my breath hot against Darren's leather jacket, I felt powerful and wild and free.

When Darren finally pulled off to an overlook of Dublin, my heart was racing and my eyes were wide and clear. Darren killed the engine and climbed off the bike before reaching out a hand to help me.

My legs were shaky and I stumbled into his arms.

"Woah, woah," Darren cooed, tugging off his helmet so he could see me better. "You alright?"

"Yes," I answered immediately, holding onto his strong biceps to steady myself as I grinned. "Yes, I'm fantastic. I'm incredible. I'm—I'm—"

I leaned my head back suddenly and shouted over the city in the distance, "I'm alive!"

Darren laughed and the sound was glorious.

My mother would have scolded me for making such an unnecessary ruckus. "You'll disturb your father," she would have chastised in a low hiss with her thin, bony finger wagging at me. "You must keep quiet, Kayleigh. You must always keep quiet no matter what."

"I'm alive and *loud*!" I shouted again, grinning from ear to ear.

Darren surprised me by also leaning back his head and shouting, "And very dirty!"

I chuckled as I swatted playfully at Darren's chest. "Hey!"

Darren's only response was to removed my helmet and gently wipe his glove over my cheek and show me the smear of mud as evidence. I looked down at my clothes and chuckled when I realised I was filthy.

Shouting as loud as I could to the sea of stars up above me, I added with joy in my thundering heart, "I am alive and loud and *very* dirty!"

Darren craned his neck and shouted at the top of his lungs, "And very, *very* beautiful!"

Darren waited with his eyes facing the stars till the echo of his dangerous, dangerous words faded over the rolling hills illuminated in the moonlight. Then he slowly turned to look at me, his blue-grey eyes the colour of icicles under a full moon. There was dirt on his own cheeks that matched mine. I swallowed heavily, the silence between us filled with only the sound of the wind through the trees, and then tugged my mittens off one by one, dropping each to the cold earth beneath my boots.

The icy night nipped at my fingertips, but I didn't care as I stretched my hand up to wipe a thumb across the mud splattering the skin beneath Darren's eyes. "You have a bit of dirt right here."

Despite the bone-chilling cold, his skin felt warm beneath my touch as I continued to trace the sharp line of his cheekbone. Those stormy eyes stayed on mine. I ran my fingers across the mud on his cheek. "And here." The stubble of his dark beard pricked my fingertips as I moved them along his strong jaw. "And..." My breath came in stuttering gasps as my fingers found their way to Darren's lips.

He shifted closer when I smeared my thumb over them then felt them supple and soft beneath my quivering fingers. I wanted to write my name in the mud. I wanted to see my name on Darren, all over Darren. I wanted to unzip his dirtied leather jacket and write my name along his chest. I wanted to strip him naked right there on that mountain and write my name with mud over and over again on his thighs, his chest, the soles of each of his feet.

Darren's hands ghosted along the sleeves of my coat so softly I wasn't sure at first whether it was him or a swirling gust of wind. He moved his hand slowly to my cheek and I shivered.

"And you have a little bit of dirt right here," he said.

My eyes fluttered closed and goose bumps travelled down my spine as Darren's thumb ran along my cheekbone, as gently as if he was using a feather. I feared that all of this was just some fantastical dream. But I opened my lids and the trees were there and the lights of Dublin were there and Darren, complicated, sensitive, intriguing Darren was there.

"And?" I whispered.

Darren swallowed hard. "You have some on the tip of your nose."

He traced his fingers along my face to my nose. "Got it," Darren said, eyes finding mine.

"And?" I asked, doing everything in my power to keep my voice from shaking.

There in the cold our hearts each beat erratically, but together they created a rhythm that pounded faster and faster and faster.

Darren hesitated. "And...you might have a little near your mouth."

I stepped a little closer to Darren, my knees feeling like they were going to buckle right there beneath me.

"Um, do you want to maybe get it for me?" I asked, my voice barely audible over the wind.

He lifted his hand and pressed his thumb to the corner of

my lips. Slowly, ever so slowly, he dragged it across my bottom lip. I heard his sharp intake of breath over the thundering of my heart.

Then he was lowering his head closer and closer to mine. My eyes fluttered closed as I laid a hand against the beating of his heart, wanting this more than anything I'd ever wanted before in life.

But at the first taste of mud on his lips, I recoiled back. *What was I doing?*

Horror immediately painted Darren's face. "Kayleigh, I'm—"

"No, no, it's fine. It's fine."

My cheeks immediately flared red as I stepped away and dragged a hand through my hair with a shaky exhale. I pointed toward Dublin in the distance as I tried to catch my breath. "Um, the view, the view here is—it's, um, amazing, isn't it?" I stammered.

Behind me Darren's voice was husky and thick. "It's getting late. Maybe we should get you back?"

I nodded and avoided eye contact as Darren helped me back into my helmet.

I had the rest of the ride home to convince myself that I had done the right thing, that kissing Darren would have been a mistake, that cutting things off before they went too far was the only thing to do, the only way.

But by the time Darren turned onto my street, all I wanted was to go back to that moment atop the Dublin Mountains.

All I wanted was to taste the mud on his lips.

All I wanted to do was get dirty.

18

DARREN

Christmas shoppers hurried this way and that around us in the busy Blanchardstown shopping centre. I stood silently next to Kayleigh with my hands stuffed in my pockets as she held up one pair of socks, frowned, and then held up the other. "I'll Be Home For Christmas" played forlornly over the store's speakers. She then gave a curt nod, her white beanie slipping farther toward her eyes, and moved to put the first pair of socks back on the shelf only to hesitate, hold them back up, and then let her head flop back as she moaned in frustration.

"I can't get Eoin socks for Christmas," she grumbled irritably before shoving both pairs back into the messy pile.

Like a pack of vultures, five or six shoppers swooped into the sock section when Kayleigh marched off. I followed her out of the store and almost ran straight into her when she whirled around and threw her mittened hands up into the air.

"Why is this so difficult?" she asked in exasperation.

My continued silence as I stared down at her wide, searching eyes only made her more frustrated. Her hands balled into fists and she spun on her heel, stomping through the crowd laden with winter coats and red and green shopping bags. I easily kept up with the white fluffy ball bobbing atop Kayleigh's head as I weaved in and out of the plastic trees sprayed with fake snow.

Kayleigh stopped at a kiosk of gift cards for everything from music and restaurants to shoe stores and sporting events.

"You're the one who asked to come along," she grumbled when she sensed me again beside her, still silent, my hands still stuffed into my pockets. "The least you could do is help."

I watched her fingers skim over a row of brightly coloured pieces of plastic before plucking one up seemingly at random. She disappeared around the corner of the kiosk and I followed her to the register.

"Is this a good gift for a...?" she started to ask the woman before pausing. Kayleigh checked my distance from her and lowered her voice as she continued, "Is this a good gift for someone that you're casually dating who is *not* your boyfriend, but who definitely thinks it's more?"

I couldn't help but grin at the fact that Kayleigh specified quite clearly that Eoin was *not* her boyfriend. Not even close.

The bored woman at the register glanced up momentarily from her cell phone to see the gift card. "He likes the opera?"

Kayleigh frowned. "Huh?"

The woman nodded toward the gift card in Kayleigh's hand. "That's for The Gaiety Theatre, hon."

Kayleigh shouldered past me on her way to return the gift card to its place. We continued down through the mall, me following a pace or two behind and Kayleigh hurrying along as her head swivelled from side to side, searching store after store window.

She stopped next to a silver and gold tinsel-covered Christmas tree whose massive gold star stretched toward a glass-domed ceiling three stories up. Her wind-chapped cheeks speckled with freckles were as red as her vibrant braids when she turned around and crossed her still empty arms over her chest. "I'm supposed to be dating your brother, you know that, right?"

People mumbled irritably as they were forced to step around us smack dab in the middle of the flow of traffic, but neither of us seemed to care. I kept my face passive and undisturbed as Kayleigh glared up at me.

"Are you going to say anything, Darren?" she pressed, moving one step closer before realising this only brought her closer to me and instead taking two considerably larger steps backward. Her green eyes flashed with anger, yes. But with something more. And it was that something more that I wanted to see more of.

"Hello? Earth to Darren."

Kayleigh seemed ready to burst. I not only didn't say a word, but grinned just the teeniest, tiniest bit. She glanced to either side of her, and when she noticed the curious stares over steaming cups of hot cocoa and hushed whispers behind bags overflowing with tissue paper, she forced her voice to a harsh whisper as she leaned in toward me.

"Darren, what happened," she stopped and then corrected herself, "*almost* happened, the other night on the mountain... that, that can't hap—"

"Let's go ice skating."

My words caught her with her mouth open, eyes wide. She stammered for a moment and then shook her head. "What?"

"Ice skating," I said with a smile while pointing to a sign with an arrow for a rink next to me. "Let's go ice skating."

Before Kayleigh had time to respond, I grabbed her mittened hand and pulled her along beside me through the crowd.

"Darren," she hissed as I guided her to the small ticket

counter outside the rink. "Darren, we really need to talk about—"

"Two for ice skating, please," I said to a teenager with a black hoodie pulled over his head.

I fished my wallet out of my back pocket and handed my card over.

"Shoe sizes?" the kid asked as he ran my card.

"Kayleigh?" I glanced down at her to ask.

Kayleigh tried to tug me away from the counter, but I was as immovable as one of those firs in the Dublin Mountains. I turned my attention back to the teenager behind the counter. "We'll need a size twelve and a size six, pl—"

"Five."

I looked back down at Kayleigh. "What's that?"

She ducked her eyes and kicked one toe of her boot against the other. "I'm a size five," she mumbled into her scarf.

I bit back a grin. I took our skates and led Kayleigh into the rink with a hand at the small of her back. Inside, a peaked white roof sparkled with hundreds of strings of lights hung from wooden rafters. Lush green wreaths dotted with cranberries and pine cones and weaved with silver beads lined the walls. And in the centre of the rink, a grand tree stood, its trunk circled by a burgundy velvet couch.

I happened to catch the look of awe in Kayleigh's sparkling eyes just before she noticed me watching and reaffixed a scowl to her soft pink lips. "Darren, we have to put a stop to all of th—"

"Sit."

Not caring about the ice cold of the concrete around the rink, I knelt and patted my palm on the metal seat of a folding chair. Kayleigh remained unmoving as she looked down at me hesitantly.

"Sit, sit," I insisted.

Kayleigh eyed me before lowering herself to the very edge of the seat with stiff shoulders and a tense back. Bing Crosby's "White Christmas" started to play, mixing with the soundtrack of laughing children and skates scuffing on the ice. I unlaced Kayleigh's petite white skates and then gently slipped off her boots. Her gaze on me softened just slightly as I tenderly held her ankle to guide her foot into the skate.

I felt her eyes on me as I tied the laces and then moved to put on my own skates. Wobbling slightly, I stood and held out a hand for Kayleigh.

"Ready?" I asked.

Kayleigh shook her head and answered, "No."

And yet she laid her mittened hand in mine, squeezed her thumb around my palm, and followed me when I led. I opened the gate to the rink for her. Kayleigh pushed off on the ice and glided under the twinkling lights as effortlessly as if she were flying. It took her a moment or two to realise that I hadn't managed to leave the safety of the railing. Kayleigh's eyebrows disappeared into her red bangs when she finally saw my shaking knees, slipping skates, and white-knuckle grip as I struggled not to fall. Her skates scraped against the ice as she hurried back to me.

"What's wrong?" she asked. "Why aren't you coming?"

I leaned more heavily against the railing as my skates wobbled. "I, er, don't know how to skate."

Kayleigh's mouth dropped. "You don't know how to skate?" she asked incredulously. "Are you serious?"

I nodded, trying to find my balance as I watched children surely no older than five twirling and racing around the tree in the centre of the rink.

"You really don't know how to skate?" Kayleigh's eyes looked quizzically over my trembling body as if trying to find the punchline to my lame joke.

"I really don't know how," I insisted. "I don't think I'm very good at it."

Kayleigh struggled to hold back laughter as she stared at me. "Darren, why in the world would you want to go ice skating if you don't know how to skate?"

I managed something sort of resembling a shrug while my skates persisted in slipping and sliding outside my control. "Because I'm happy," I said.

My answer clearly wasn't what Kayleigh had been expecting, because for a long time she couldn't find a reply. Lovers skated hand in hand past us as Bing sang the final chorus of "White Christmas".

In the weighty silence before the next song, Kayleigh reached out her hand to me. "Come on," she said softly. "I'll help you."

It was my turn to lay my hand in hers, squeeze my thumb tightly around her palm, and follow, stumbling and cursing silently as she led. Just that simple touch of hers consumed me so wholly that I couldn't recall the next song no matter how hard I tried. The only sound in my entire world was her gently spoken instructions as we made our way slowly around the rink.

"Am I leaning too heavily on you?" I asked as we started our second turn round the circle.

Kayleigh's eyes found mine. "No," she said. "I think I can handle it if you lean on me."

She was clearly trying to communicate more, to say more. But in that instant, with my focus not fixed on my feet, my skates bumped into one another and I slipped backwards, dragging Kayleigh down with me. I landed on the ice. She landed on my chest. I blinked up at the strings of colourful lights as my head throbbed and the cold of the ice seeped through my coat and jeans.

"Are you alright?" Kayleigh asked, hands holding each side of my face in concern.

Grinning from ear to ear, I laid my hands over hers. "What are you going to get me for Christmas?" I asked.

Kayleigh laughed, and I realised I was never happier than when I was making her laugh.

"I think you hit your head pretty hard," she said, eyes searching mine, probably for signs of a concussion.

"Do you know?"

Kayleigh smiled down at me and did not move her hands away from my face. "Know what?" she asked.

"Know what you're getting me as a gift for Christmas?" I repeated with a grin.

Her eyes flashed mischievously. "No idea," she said.

I raised an eyebrow, ass frozen, head aching. "No?"

Kayleigh tried to hold back her grin. "Nope."

"Not even the faintest idea?" I prodded as I started to run my fingers softly over hers, still warm against my cheeks.

Kayleigh shrugged on top of me. "I haven't even started thinking about what I am getting you for Christmas," she said, not able to entirely hide her playful smile. "Haven't even given it the tiniest thought, Darren O'Sullivan."

Without thinking, I reached up, brushing her fiery red bangs out of her soft eyelashes. "I do."

Kayleigh frowned. "You do?"

I met her gaze and smiled. "I know exactly what I'm getting you for Christmas, Kayleigh Scott."

Neither of us moved as we stared into each other's eyes there on the ice, our skates intertwined, our lips just inches from one another's.

The little white lights draped over the large tree behind her outlined Kayleigh's sweet face as she blinked as slowly as drifting snowflakes, and I imagined a constellation of her in the night sky. I imagined tracing, star by star, her image. I imagined wishing on them, one by one, as they disappeared into a golden dawn. Sometimes Kayleigh felt as far away, just as out of reach, as those glowing heavenly bodies.

But with her there in my arms, she wasn't like the distant stars on a cold night, but drops of dew glistening in the morning light. With her heart beating against mine, she felt as close as those tiny beads of water clinging to the delicate petals of the wildflowers that grew in the cracks of the sidewalk outside my garage—the ones I only started noticing when Kayleigh walked into my life.

With her mittened hand soft against my cheek as she smiled down at me, I thought maybe I could reach her. Maybe she was closer than I thought.

Maybe she could be mine.

19

KAYLEIGH

*C*locking into work at the motorcycle shop the next morning was like starting a ticking time bomb. The air in the garage hung heavy and still as if even the wind itself was holding its breath as it waited. As we moved amongst the vehicles, Darren and I looked with increasing frequency at the dusty clock hanging above the toolbox as if we could somehow escape the inevitable explosion if the big hand simply hit five. We barely spoke to one another as the tense minutes and then hours ticked by, but when I was forced to ask what oil a Harley needed, or when he needed to find a customer's invoice in the office, we whispered as if our very voices might set off the charge.

Every time Darren's hand brushed my arm as he reached across me to grab a wrench or screwdriver, it was as if the seconds remaining on the bomb jumped forward thirty seconds. Every time our eyes accidentally met across the garage where we were trying our best to avoid one another, we both froze as if we'd accidentally triggered a trip wire tied between two hubcaps. And whenever Darren called my name, whether it was to answer the phone or to show me something he was working on beneath the hood of an old Mercedes, I was certain the display flashed red double zeros, because it was more than I could stand.

I was going to fuck up.

I was going to fuck up and kiss Darren.

I *wanted* to fuck up and kiss Darren.

I wanted to fuck up and *fuck* Darren.

The bomb on my life, on his life, on the O'Sullivan family's perfect life was ticking, ticking, ticking.

But noon came and went and we held ourselves back.

One, then two, then three o'clock all passed by and everything was still in one piece: the cars, the sign outside, the brotherly relationship between Darren and Eoin.

I watched the big hand hit 4 p.m. and I started to think that maybe I was wrong. Maybe there was no unstoppable timer counting down. Maybe there was no bomb. Maybe we weren't destined to destroy everything.

At 4:15 Darren spoke with a customer who brought in his Kawasaki with a flat back tyre, and I was safe till 4:21. I busied myself with sweeping the shop floor to avoid having to ask Darren about a carburettor I was struggling with. Because I knew he would have come close to me and if he came close to me and I smelled his perfume and saw the different colours in his eyes and watched his supple, sexy lips as he described the problem to me, it was over.

Over.

Sweeping bought me till 4:29.

Organising the mail chewed up another three or four minutes.

I splashed cold water in my face to cool myself off in the bathroom till a quarter to; it didn't help much with the dirty images that kept popping up in my mind every time I even thought of Darren.

At 4:55 I asked if I could leave a bit early—something about getting to the grocery store before all the good bread was gone. I wasn't even sure what I was saying at this point.

At 4:56 Darren, kneeling by the Kawasaki, said that was "grand".

At 4:57 I went into the small office at the back of the shop to grab my coat from the back of the wonky rolling chair in front of the old computer.

At 4:58 I was pulling my white fluffy beanie over my head and starting to wrap my scarf around my neck.

At 4:59 I turned around at a noise at the door.

At 4:59 I saw Darren with his hands pressed so tightly against the doorway that the muscles along his biceps shook.

At 4:59 I noticed I could no longer tell whether his eyes were more blue or more grey, because his eyes were dominated by his pupils so wide and so dark that I could see in them the reflection of my heaving chest.

At 4:59 Darren, his voice raw, said, "I'm sorry."

And at 5:00 the timer hit 0:00.

At 5:00 the bomb went off.

Like a summer storm rolling in fast and hard across the horizon, Darren closed the distance between us in three long steps, backing me up against the wall. My shoulders collided against the outdated motorcycle calendar, which fell to the floor when Darren's lips finally, *finally* crashed onto mine.

I wasn't sure if it was his tall, muscular body crushed against mine or the searing heat of his lips that stole the air from my lungs, but I was quite certain that I never wanted it back. As Darren kissed me hungrily, greedily, needily, his strong hands gripped my waist. He easily lifted me and pinned me against the wall. I locked my ankles around his ass and dug my fingers into the nape of his neck.

With a groan, I arched my head back as Darren kissed a trail along my jaw and down my neck. Our hands collided with one another's when we each at the same time tried to tug at my scarf with eager fingers. I clawed my fingernails down Darren's back when he finally pulled the scarf away enough to suckle at my collarbone.

Darren moved back to my lips, his teeth catching my lower lip and biting just enough to make me roll my hips against his crotch. With a growl, Darren yanked off my beanie and ran his fingers through my hair. His tongue flicked against mine and I struggled to slip my coat off, still pinned deliciously against the wall.

Our frantic, lust-filled pants filled the small space of the little back office. Blood rushed past my ears and my heart thundered louder and louder in my chest. I'm guessing it was the same for Darren.

As we fell deeper and deeper into the kiss, we couldn't have heard the roar of his motorcycle engine, even if it rumbled just outside the office door. We couldn't have heard the ring of the telephone, the buzzer of the doorbell, the shout of a customer hoping to catch someone before the garage closed. We couldn't have even heard our own voices begging the other for *more, more, more*, the sound of our breaths and blood and hearts was so deafening.

So we definitely didn't hear the squeal of tyres as an SUV turned onto the street where Kelly's Garage was located.

There was no way we heard the crunch of gravel beneath its tyres as it passed the old faded sign out front.

And there wasn't a chance in hell that we heard it pull into the drive just outside the big, open garage door.

Maybe it would prove to be luck or maybe it would end up being a curse that the glare of headlights against my closed eyelids drew my attention as a car door opened outside.

"Darren, Darren," I exhaled, pushing away his shoulders. "Someone's here."

Darren's head immediately swivelled to the half-closed blinds of the window overlooking the shop as I slid back to the floor.

"Who is it?" I asked, catching my breath and wiping a hand across my lips as I sagged against the wall, knees still weak.

Panic filled Darren's eyes when he looked at me.

"Eoin."

20

DARREN

*O*f all the things my little brother could shout out into the empty, echo-y as hell garage moments after I dragged my lips away from the girl—*his girl*—who I wanted nothing more than to strip naked right then and there in my office, this was by far the goddamn worst: "Kayleigh Bear, my soulmate, the love of my life, where are you?"

Next to me, Kayleigh muttered a breathless "fuck" as she bent over to grab her scarf and beanie.

"Hey, Eoin," she called out, sucking in a shaky breath as she adjusted the coat she had been seconds from pulling from her shoulders. "I'm in here with Darren."

Kayleigh's eyes avoided mine as she smoothed down her hair and slipped past me so she was in the middle of rearranging a stack of invoices when Eoin appeared in the doorway of the office with a massive grin on his boyish face.

"Hard at work as always, now aren't you?" he said. "How's it going, Darren?"

I was still frozen, petrified, horrified. I wanted to turn away from the sight of Eoin in the doorway, but I couldn't. That was where I had stood, hands pressed against the doorframe just like his were. It was my brother who should have pushed Kayleigh against the wall. It should have been his tongue hot against her skin. It should have been him who, in the heat and passion of the moment, wanted more, more, more.

But it had been me. There was no taking that back.

"Hey, your calendar fell down," Eoin said, pointing to the floor.

Dropping her stack of invoices, Kayleigh scurried to pick up the calendar as if it were an incriminating pair of black undies and not an outdated collection of motorcycle pictures. She muttered some excuse about the heating fan or the draught from the garage, which only made things worse as Eoin stared curiously at her with a lifted eyebrow.

Could he see her back had slammed into it when I pushed her against the wall?

Could he see that it ripped from the rusted tack when she flung her arms around my neck?

Could he see that it was her boot print on the stack of invoices from where she tried to get closer to me?

Because that's all I could see.

"No worries." Eoin laughed as Kayleigh failed again and again to desperately hang back up the calendar.

But there was already a tear that she couldn't repair and she wasn't ready or willing to stab a new hole.

Eoin walked over to Kayleigh and stopped her anxious efforts with an arm slung over her shoulders.

"Kayleigh Bear, your amazing, hot, famous, super-athletic boyfriend is here with early Christmas presents," he joked. "Forget about the calendar."

Kayleigh blushed. She finally let the calendar flutter back to the carpeted office floor. I was certain she hadn't forgotten about the calendar. I would have bet good money that she wouldn't forget about that calendar for a long time.

Neither would I.

I looked over at Kayleigh, who was still avoiding my eyes as she stared unblinkingly at the dusty blank computer screen.

"Well?" Eoin blurted out impatiently, waving his hand in front of Kayleigh's face before snapping in my direction.

I dragged my attention to my brother, who looked moments away from stomping his foot.

"What's that?" I asked. It felt like I hadn't used my voice in years; every syllable tore at my throat and the words fell from my lips rough and hoarse.

Eoin sighed dramatically and loudly. "Don't you want to know what your early Christmas presents are?"

I blinked at him stupidly like he hadn't been standing there for the last three minutes and instead just magically appeared. "Presents?"

Eoin groaned. "You two are no fun at all," he grumbled, reaching into his big coat pocket. His annoyance immediately disappeared though when he pulled out two tickets and grinned from ear to ear while waving them between Kayleigh and me. "Eh? Eh?" Eoin prodded, searching her and my reaction. "Are you excited or what?"

Kayleigh had to clear her throat before asking in a tiny, almost inaudible voice, "What are they?"

Both of Eoin's eyebrows flew up. "'What are they?'" His voice boomed through the crowded office space. "Is that really what you just asked, Kayleigh Bear? *These* just happen to be two of the best tickets for the hottest, most anticipated rivalry game of the season, Leinster v Munster. That's what these are, baby."

Eoin clearly expected us to either leap into the air or cheer uncontrollably or shout "ah, shhhtop!" or some combination of the aforementioned. Maybe he expected a little sampling of all of them. What he got was crickets.

"Who are they for?" I finally asked, glancing nervously at Kayleigh.

"Jaysus, what did you two take?" Eoin asked, his frustration obvious. "They're for you two."

"I can't go," I immediately blurted out the second Eoin confirmed my fear.

Eoin laughed. "I haven't even told you when the game is, Daz. How do you know you can't go?"

"I'm just really busy with the shop," I answered, scratching awkwardly at the back of my neck. "Sorry. But Kayleigh can take off whenever she wan—"

"No, no, brother." Eoin pulled his arm from Kayleigh and hurried over to me. He grabbed my shoulders with those massive bear paws of his and shook me as he looked imploringly into my eyes. "You *have* to go. I *need* you to go."

I frowned as I asked a slow and tentative, "Why?"

I wasn't sure I wanted to know the answer. My stomach churned as Eoin leaned in closer like he was about to tell me a very important secret I wouldn't be able to unhear.

"Because, Daz," he whispered, likely unaware it was plenty loud enough for Kayleigh to hear in the tight confines of the small back office, "the guys who come to the rugby matches are absolute pigs, and you know it."

Eoin glanced over his shoulder at Kayleigh, whose red cheeks had been drained of colour. She knew where this was going, too.

"I don't want their grimy, greasy, beer-sticky hands all over her if she's stuck with them up in the stands," Eoin continued, squeezing my shoulders and lowering his voice uselessly.

I resisted the urge to hide my oil-stained hands in the pockets of my jeans. Because my grimy, greasy hands had been all over her. And I wanted my hands to be all over her again.

And again.

And again.

And again.

Eoin leaned in conspiratorially as he whispered, "I don't want them staring at her body and thinking all those dirty thoughts, you know?"

What a fucking relief that Eoin couldn't read my mind; what a fucking goddamn relief. Because I could guarantee you that for every dirty thought a stranger in the packed, ruckus stands might have, I had five thoughts ten times dirtier.

"They're animals," Eoin shook his head in disgust. "Just animals."

He was talking about me; *I* was the animal.

"Eoin, listen," I said, glancing over at Kayleigh's horrified face over my brother's wide shoulder, "I'm sure one of your buddies can go along with—"

"I don't trust them," Eoin interrupted.

I'd made a mistake. A terrible mistake, a horrible mis-turn, an uncorrectable misstep. I'd pointed the handle bars of the motorcycle straight off the cliffs and I was plummeting toward the jagged rocks below. All that was left to do was wait for the pain, the hurt, the *agony*.

Eoin smiled innocently, completely innocently, and said with utter confidence, "I trust *you*, Darren. I know family is the most important thing in the world to you."

Those few, simple words were worse than if Eoin had walked in on Kayleigh and me kissing; I was quite certain of that. They were the words I dreaded hearing above all others. It was the one sentiment that managed to break my heart, flood it with shame, and choke it with so much guilt that I stopped breathing.

Eoin smacked his hand against my arm the way a brother smacks his hand against his flesh and blood. He laughed the way a brother laughs with someone he's known for his entire life. And he said the words any brother should be able to say to his brother without a trace of doubt. "I mean, there's no way you're going to touch her, right?"

I tried to laugh like a brother should laugh.

I tried to force a smile that looked like a brotherly smile.

I tried to keep my voice even, because a brother, a true brother, wouldn't have to lie when he said, "Of course, Eoin."

In that moment the last thing I felt like was a brother. I didn't deserve that title. And worse, I didn't want that title.

Because I wanted *her*.

"So you'll go with my adorable little Kayleigh Bear then?" Eoin asked as he went over to ruffle Kayleigh's hair.

"Sure," I managed to croak.

Eoin lifted Kayleigh's chin and smiled down at her. "Darren's the best guy I know," he said. "You'll be safe."

Kayleigh nodded as she managed a small smile that didn't even begin to reach her eyes.

"Great!" Eoin clapped his hands together and slapped the tickets onto the stack of invoices on the office desk. "Ready for dinner then, babe?"

Kayleigh nodded and grabbed the white beanie I'd ripped off. Her fingers shook just slightly, so slightly that Eoin would never notice. But I did.

I didn't move as Eoin guided Kayleigh out of the office and out through the garage. I was still standing there when Kayleigh checked back over her shoulder toward the office. Our eyes met through the open blinds, and I saw fear in that soft green as she looked at me.

It was the fear that coursed through your blood every time you revved the engine of a motorcycle.

It was the fear that rumbled in your chest as the tyres spun on that icy black asphalt.

It was the fear that you were going too fast, too fast, way too fast. It was the fear that you wouldn't be able to slow down, that you didn't want to slow down. That you were about to lose complete control.

Eoin said Kayleigh was safe, but she wasn't. Not even close to it.

Because I was going to crash us both.

21

KAYLEIGH

*E*ven layered under a tank, two sweaters, a puffy vest, a jacket, and the largest, fluffiest scarf Dublin sold, just the slightest brush of my shoulder against Darren's felt like a sin. It made my body tingle as if he'd brushed his palms across my naked breasts. It made my breath catch in my throat as if he'd exhaled against my mouth before he kissed me. It made my eyelids flutter shut for just the briefest moment as if my fingers were intertwining with his just before he entered me.

I forced myself to keep my eyes forward as Darren and I followed a security guard down a long concrete hall beneath Aviva Stadium, because if I thought my shoulder bumping into his in the tight, bustling stands was bad, a single glance into those grey-blue storms was ten times worse.

"So, did you two enjoy the match?" the security in his big black jacket looked back over his shoulder to ask.

He was taking us to the team locker room to see Eoin to celebrate the victory. He had to nearly shout to be heard over the rattling rafters above us as fans stomped their frozen feet.

"Yes," Darren answered stiffly next to me, his voice as frigid as the brutal wind had been during the match.

The security guard's eyes found mine. I managed a smile even with my ice-cold cheeks.

"Emhmm," I said. "Great craic."

In reality it was ninety minutes of torture in the freezing cold. I clapped numbly when the crowd cheered, but other than that I couldn't recall a single thing from the match. I remembered Darren's musk amongst the stench of beer and popcorn. I remembered his knee always an inch from mine. I remembered his hands resting unmoving on his knees, and I remembered wondering if his pinkie twitched toward me or if it was only my imagination. I remembered the curl of his breath against the black sky next to me. I remembered thinking that he was like a shadow: I could see him, but I could not touch.

I remembered it drove me fucking insane.

Darren and I kept the same safe distance between us as we turned the corner as the security guard's walkie-talkie crackled and popped.

An awkward silence fell back over the three of us as the noise of the fans faded.

The security guard winked at me over his shoulder and, of all the things he could say, he just *had* to say, "It must be something being Eoin O'Sullivan's girlfriend, eh?"

My eyes darted over to Darren, who seemed entirely unaffected as he stared forward, save for maybe a slight paling of his wind-chapped cheeks.

"Oh, I'm not sure we've really defined things at this point and—"

Before I could finish stammering through my explanation that I wasn't Eoin's girlfriend, the security guard pushed open the double doors to the home team's locker rooms and a blast of shouting, laughing and pounding music interrupted me.

I ducked under the security guard's arm and into a chaotic swarm of half-naked men. Some whipped each other with towels, others chased down a teammate to give him a nuggie, and a few stood butt-ass naked with a foot up on a bench intently discussing the match. Just as I was about to turn around and ask if I should really be in here, I heard my nickname called from across the locker room.

"Kayleigh Bear!"

Through a sea of hairy thighs and shoulders the size of semi-trucks, I caught sight of Eoin sitting next to his locker, bare chested and wearing only a towel around his waist. I gave him a small wave before weaving my way through the waves of testosterone.

"Sorry," I mumbled, "sorry, sorry."

"Hey, O'Connor, you asshole," Eoin cupped his hands over his mouth to shout. "Get out of the way of my soulmate, you fucker!"

"We're just dating," I muttered to a scowling bald man with a bristly black beard, "...I mean, sort of."

After dodging a Gatorade hurled across the locker room as another rock song blasted on the stereo, I stood before Eoin, wincing when he threw his arms up into the air in excitement.

"A dream come true!" he shouted. "My girlfriend coming to see me after an epic victory. Three tries, babe. Three! Can you believe it?"

"Yeah, it was great, Eoin." I leaned in, whispering in a hushed voice so none of his teammates could hear. "Hey, listen, I think we really need to talk about where we are togeth—"

"I know right where we are," Eoin interrupted with a wide, beaming smile.

Before I realised what was happening, Eoin's hands found my waist and he tugged me onto his lap. I was mid-yelp from the suddenness of it all when his lips smashed into mine. My eyes went wide as his tongue darted into mine like a bait in a rough stream bobbing along with the current.

I wanted to shove Eoin back and bark, "What the *hell* are you doing?" My hands were already squirming to get free from where they were pinned against my sides by Eoin's iron grasp. But then I heard the cheers of his teammates. I saw their reactions if I reprimanded Eoin in front of all of them. I saw Eoin's embarrassment and I suddenly froze because I just couldn't bear to cause a scene.

So I let Eoin kiss me.

When he finally let me come up for air, he proceeded to cut off my lungs by crushing me against his chest in the tightest bear hug I've ever experienced in my life.

"Isn't she just the most beautiful thing in the world?" Eoin said to his teammates, who whistled and slapped each other on the shoulders as they eyed me. Feeling like a piece of meat, I blushed and couldn't imagine the moment possibly getting any worse than it already was.

But, of course, I hadn't seen Darren's face yet.

He stood all the way across the locker room not more than a foot inside the set of entrance doors. He was staring at me with a look of horror like it hadn't been two lips colliding in front of him, but two vehicles head-on on the highway and he couldn't look away from the carnage.

Embarrassed and ashamed, I wanted nothing more than to explain that I hadn't wanted to kiss Eoin back. I tried to wriggle off Eoin's lap to put some distance between the two of us, but Eoin held me tight with one arm. He, too, noticed Darren and waved him over.

"Daz, three tries." Eoin grinned. "*Three!* Can you believe it?"

Darren walked up with his hands stuffed into the pockets of his coat, back stiff, and managed a nod of his chin. "Congrats, Eoin."

I squirmed uncomfortably in Eoin's lap as Darren's eyes seemed to take in everything I wanted to hide: Eoin's palm on my upper thigh, his arm around my waist, his nose buried in my wind-tangled red locks.

"Nobody messed with my little Kayleigh Bear, did they?" Eoin asked, rubbing his nose against my cheeks playfully as I tried to hide a grimace.

Darren shook his head, his movement robotic like he was in auto drive.

"I knew I could count on you," Eoin grinned. "You're coming out to celebrate with us and the guys, right?"

It took me a moment to realise that "us" meant Eoin and me. My stomach sank.

Eyes fixed on the floor at his oil-stained boots, Darren again shook his head. "I've got some work I've got to get to at the shop."

"Can't it wait, Daz?" Eoin pleaded. "Come on, we'll help you find a nice little lady at the bars, like Kayleigh Bear here."

Darren's eyes lifted to find mine and all the blue was gone: they were the steel grey of the knife that stabbed through my heart. "I've got to work," he said.

"I could come with you and help," I blurted out before I could stop myself, my eyes reaching out to beg in a way my words could not. "At the shop, I mean. I could come hel—"

"No." Darren's voice cut through the chatter and laughter of the locker room like the grim reaper's scythe.

He did not shout. He did not yell. If anything, the single word from his lips was closest to a whisper. But it brought a chill over the room and ice to my heart.

"No," he repeated. "You two go out and have fun." His eyes met mine before he turned to leave. There was no anger or betrayal or hurt in them. Our eyes met like two strangers on a bus, a passing glance of coincidence and nothing more. There was no disdain. Barely any recognition. It was as if Darren had wiped me from his memory.

That hurt worse than any amount of anger could.

Darren disappeared into the crowd of Eoin's teammates, who were now dancing together between the lockers, oblivious to what had just happened.

Eoin himself didn't even seem to notice as he again squeezed me tight. "Ready to party till dawn, Kayleigh Bear?"

I was ready to run after Darren.

I was ready to slap him.

I was ready to get up into his face and shout, "I know it's an act. I know you haven't forgotten me. I know you haven't forgotten our kiss."

I was ready to fight!

But, no.

I was the polite, respectful, ruffle-no-feathers, make-not-a-peep girl my mother raised me so diligently to be. Tugging up the corners of my lips into a smile was like cranking that rusted wrench in Darren's garage that always got stuck. I managed. Because I always managed. I smiled at Eoin and nodded.

"Sure."

22

DARREN

*T*oday was the hardest day of the year. Every year on this day, I tried every trick in the book to try to get through it. My first attempt, of course, was to get blackout drunk. That had been rather effective, but it made Ma worry, and I didn't want her to worry. So I keep myself to a few fingers of whiskey instead of the whole goddamn bottle.

Drugs were never really my thing, so that was out. I gave meditation a shot, positive affirmations, mantras and deep, mindful breathing and all that shite. It *was* shite.

Hell, I even considered the military once to have a legitimate reason to be absent from family for the holidays. But I don't do too well with orders.

No, the best way I'd found to deal with the anniversary of my twin brother's death was to wear an oversized hoodie, stuff my hands into the pocket pouch, and squeeze my thumb and forefinger into the skin of my palm till the pain was all I felt.

Till I didn't hear the crackle of the fire in the living room as my brothers went around retelling the same stories about Jaime they did every year.

Till I didn't hear their laughter at this story that died off slowly and sink, sink, sink into a heavy silence filled with incurable sadness.

Till I didn't hear the creak of the recliner or the crack of the couch cushions or the moan of a wooden floorboard as each of my brothers shifted uncomfortably once all the happy stories had been exhausted and there was only the sad ending left unspoken.

Forever left unspoken.

As long as I kept pinching and as long as the hoodie was black or dark navy or some shade of maroon to hide the blood from my punctured palms, this method worked alright.

This year my oversized hoodie was a charcoal grey so dark, it looked black in the light of the fire burning low in the living room. Michael, Noah, and Eoin were currently recalling stories of Jaime as a baby, and I had yet to break through the callused old scars on my left palm; that would come later when the silence grew louder, when the silence grew unbearable.

"Ma told the local seamstress that she had twins and that she wanted something 'spooky' for their Halloween costumes," Noah was saying, already clutching at his chest in laughter. "Next thing you know the neighbours are whispering about two little boys trick-or-treating and dressed up in frilly dresses as the creepy twins from *The Shining*."

Eoin's booming laugh, despite the fact that we'd all heard the story countless times, drowned out Michael's chuckle and Noah's gasps for air. I just pinched my palm and smiled.

We went through mishaps of Jaime and my elementary school years, the mischief of our pre-teen years, and the embarrassments of our adolescences, and they laughed and laughed and laughed because laughter was easier than tears, or worse, silence.

None of my brothers wanted to get to the point of the night where we ran out of stories. None of my brothers wanted to acknowledge that there would never *be* more stories. None of my brothers wanted to feel the distance between our lives—with plans the next morning, appointments the next week, New Year's celebrations marked on the calendar—and the life that stopped with a squeal of tyres and a crunch of metal.

I sensed the lull in the remembrance and glanced around the living room from my place in the single, high-backed wooden chair in the darkest corner. Michael crossed and uncross his legs, Noah glanced at his wristwatch, and Eoin got up from his place on the couch to stoke the fire that didn't need stoking at all. I felt the wetness of blood on my palm as I pinched harder and harder, but the sting of pain was more welcome than the sting of tears at my eyes.

Eoin returned to his place next to Noah on the couch, and Michael practically sighed in relief when Eoin opened his mouth. Unfortunately, his words brought my troubled soul no semblance of ease.

"You know, I bet that Jaime would really like Kayleigh." Eoin smiled at each of us in turn.

He smiled at Noah last, because we'd had this same discussion when Noah had finally made things official with Aubrey. It was a way of dragging Jaime's memory along with the progress of our lives, a way of pretending like he was still a part of our joys and triumphs, our failures and disappointments, our once-in-a-lifetime engagements and everyday mundane to-do lists. But it was all a façade. It was all a way to make us feel better. No, it was all a way to make *me* feel better.

Because whether they would admit it or not, my brothers had moved on from Jaime's death. They had processed their grief healthily, mourned respectfully, and remembered happily.

I was the one who refused to speak of my brother. I was the one who was haunted by his ghost. I was the one who had a rainy night almost ten years ago stuck on loop every time I closed my eyes.

Because I was the one who knew the truth.

"I bet Jaime would have just loved her to pieces," Noah said, reaching over to pat Eoin on the hand.

"He definitely would have thought that she was the most beautiful girl in the world," Michael added with a gentle smile. "Along with Aubrey, of course."

I should have just nodded when Eoin glanced over at me and asked, "What do you think, Daz? Do you think Jaime would have liked Kayleigh if he could have met her?"

I should have just nodded and pinched harder and gotten through my hell night, just like every other hell night before it. But I just couldn't. I just fucking couldn't.

My brother's all shifted in surprise when I stood and marched across the living room rug, past the crackling fireplace, and out into the darkness and the cold of the hall.

"Darren?"

Eoin started to shout after me before I heard Noah lean over to him and say, "Just let him go."

In the hallway I bit down on my lip to keep from shouting and resisted the urge to bang the back of my head against the row of picture frames again and again. Why didn't I just keep my cool? Why didn't I just sit there and give Eoin one single goddamn nod? Why couldn't I just keep up the guise for thirty more seconds that I was fine, just fucking *fine*?

But I knew. Of course, I knew.

It was her.

I was just about to head upstairs when I heard Michael, eager to reassure Eoin that everything was fine, say, "Tell us how it's going with Kayleigh."

I shouldn't have stayed.

I stayed.

"She's the cutest, most adorable creature ever," Eoin started as I listened in from the hallway. "She's smokin' hot and I love just squeezing her, you know?"

Michael chuckled and Noah remained silent.

"And don't even get me started on the sex..." Eoin then said.

The boys let out little wolf whistles.

I stayed.

I shouldn't have stayed.

"Go on then. Bra size, favourite position, any interesting tattoos. You know, the usual." That was Michael quoting Eoin's own words.

Eoin let out a snort. "As if I'd tell you any of that."

"But you always—"

"She's not some wan I picked up in a bar. She's my fecking soulmate."

There was no reason that it should have come as a shock to me that Kayleigh and Eoin had been intimate. They had been dating for long enough by today's standard. But it came as a shock nonetheless.

I felt hurt.

Then I felt stupid.

And, finally, I felt angry.

Angry at Eoin. Angry at Kayleigh. Angry at myself. Most of all, angry at Jaime.

Because Jaime would have liked Kayleigh. He would have really liked Kayleigh. But not for any of the reasons that Eoin listed to my brothers. Jaime would have liked her because she was thoughtful. He would have liked her because she listened better than anyone I knew. He would have liked her because she called me out on my bullshite.

Jaime would have loved Kayleigh.

But Jaime wasn't here.

Kayleigh wasn't mine.

And my hoodie was wet with blood.

23

KAYLEIGH

*W*hen Eoin asked if I wanted to come along with him for a family thing, I expected it to be something Christmas-related. I wore an extra layer in case it involved carolling or hanging Christmas lights. I decided on comfy pants so I was ready for a day of baking Christmas cookies or snuggling up with Aubrey and Ma on the couch for an afternoon of *It's a Wonderful Life* and *The Grinch*. I fully expected to drag in a pine from the Christmas tree lot, string freshly popped popcorn, and listen to Michael play the piano as we hung childhood ornaments.

So it came as quite a surprise when I got into Eoin's car parked outside my apartment and he revealed that the family thing was visiting his brother's grave.

I reached over and turned off the local Dublin radio station whose DJ was merrily, and suddenly wildly inappropriately, listing the results for that year's Christmas light display competition. I pushed my sunglasses up onto my white beanie because it was a gorgeous, bright blue sky, glistening sunshine, gentle breeze soft as silk kind of day.

It was not the kind of day for graves.

"Wait, what did you just say?" I asked Eoin, eyes wide as I tugged at my seatbelt so I could turn fully to face him in the passenger seat.

Eoin shifted uncomfortably and busied himself with read-justing the rear-view mirror he'd just checked moments ago. "Um, yeah, the cemetery isn't too far and it won't take too long, I prom—"

"Eoin," I interrupted, laying a hand on his forearm. "Eoin, that's not what I meant. I just, I just had no idea you had a brother who..."

Eoin nodded as his hands fidgeted on the wheel. "We, um, we don't talk about Jaime much," he explained. "It happened nine years ago, but I think it still hurts Darren. He was his twin."

"Darren had a twin?" I blurted out, blushing when I realised how insensitive it sounded in the tight confines of the car.

Eoin remained silent.

I sank back into my seat and pulled off my beanie to drag my fingers through my hair, still shocked by all of this. "He never told me..."

I muttered this more to myself than to Eoin, but he none-theless glanced over at me with a pitying smile.

"Don't take it personally, Kayleigh Bear," he said. "Darren locked that vault and threw away the key a long, long time ago." Eoin patted my leg with his big bear paw before he pulled the car out onto the street.

I stared at the road rolling away beneath us, not seeing a single yellow stripe. I wasn't seeing anything but the little lines on the corner outside the kitchen in Ma's house marking five heights for four brothers—I hadn't thought anything of it until now. I wasn't seeing anything but the little macaroni and crayon signs with the brothers' names on every bedroom door, save one. I wasn't seeing anything but Darren in the shadow of the fireplace in the living room, half present with his family. Half not. Like something was missing. Like *someone* was missing.

"It's a wound that's still healing for all of us," Eoin said quietly, his voice sombre for the first time. "But for Darren it's like the wound is just getting longer and deeper and more painful. And we don't know why."

I looked over at Eoin, who sighed.

"Darren tries to hide it," he continued. "He thinks he's convinced us that he's fine, but I see the truth because I'm his brother. I just don't know how to help him."

I reached across the centre console and intertwined my fingers with Eoin's and squeezed. It had nothing to do with romantic love or the fact that we were still technically dating. It was just one heart reaching out to another heart to try to simply say, "I'm here."

We rode the rest of the way to the cemetery in contemplative silence. I found a new respect for Eoin. Under all that flirty banter and confidence bordering on arrogance, he was thoughtful and sweet and, above all else, cared for his brother.

We walked hand in hand toward Noah and Aubrey as the dead leaves crunched beneath our boots. Eoin's other hand held a bouquet of lilies that he gripped so tightly, I could hear the stems snapping. But I understood he needed to hold on tight, so I said nothing.

Michael and Ma soon joined us at a simple white headstone engraved with Jaime's name, the years of his life, and these words:

Little Brother, Big Brother, Twin Brother.

A FEW OF the last remaining withered leaves tumbled from the limbs above Jaime's grave in the slight breeze as the family took turns laying their flowers at the base of the headstone. We silently regarded the words engraved in stone. I glanced over my shoulder at the small parking lot at the edge of the cemetery. My eyes skimmed the line of grey and blue cars for any sign of a motorcycle but saw none.

Tears streamed down Ma's eyes as she held her black shawl tight around her shoulders. "Jaime, honey, I'm going to add an extra stick of butter to the mashed potatoes for Christmas this year. Just the way you always liked them."

The O'Sullivan brothers all chuckled amongst sniffles and swipes of the sleeves of their wool coats over their red eyes. I couldn't help but search behind me to see if Darren was hurrying through the gravestones toward us. But the labyrinth of stone and weeds and shrivelled flowers behind me was empty, save the wind and brilliant sunshine.

Where was Darren? Where was more important than being here with his family and his twin this morning? Was he caught in traffic? Had his motorcycle broken down on the highway? Run out of gas? Did he get a flat after hitting a stray piece of glass?

Was he calling one of his brothers for help? Was he trying to fix it himself? Had he run home to change and clean the grease off of his hands and fingernails before coming?

Was that why he wasn't here?

As the family went around saying sweet little things to their lost brother and son, I realised that wasn't the most pressing question. The question that really needed answering was why didn't anyone seem to notice that it was not one, but two members of the family who were absent?

Leaning over to Aubrey next to me, I whispered, "Aren't we going to wait for Darren to start?"

Aubrey dabbed at her eyes and whispered back, "Darren never comes to these."

I frowned in confusion. "What do you mean?"

Aubrey shook her head and answered, "I don't know. Noah won't tell me much about it either. All he has told me is just that Darren doesn't come to visit his twin's grave with his family. He never has, apparently."

I nodded and whispered a "thanks" before turning my attention back to Jaime's gravestone along with the rest of the family. Despite Aubrey's answer I still glanced once more over my shoulder.

It should have come as no surprise that the only other human I saw was the gardener lazily snipping at a row of shrubs along the fence line with a rusted pair of shears.

Where was Darren then? Was he in the dim light beneath the undercarriage of that Honda? What was he trying to find down there? Or...what was he trying to hide from down there, alone in the dark?

We walked back to the little parking lot together in a sombre silence. Ma moved over toward me. I fidgeted with my gloved hands, unsure of what exactly to say to a grieving mother on the anniversary of her son's death.

"What did Eoin tell you?" Ma asked before I could stumble over my own words.

"He...told me in the car on the way over here that we were visiting his brother's grave."

Ma nodded. She linked her arm around mine as we walked together. "Jaime was in a car accident. We were all lucky enough to be able to say our goodbyes before he passed," Ma explained. "But Darren got to the hospital ten minutes too late."

My heart sank. Fresh tears pricked at my eyes as sadness threatened to drag me under.

"Eoin won't tell you that because it's not something that is ever spoken by anyone in the family," Ma went on. "As if guilt can be healed by silence."

I nodded. My fingers felt numb and it had nothing to do with the cold.

"It's impossible for most people to understand why someone wouldn't come to his brother's gravestone with the rest of his family on the anniversary of his death," she said, "let alone when those brothers were twins."

I glanced over to find Ma's eyes waiting for mine. Her sharp blue eyes held my gaze like she desperately wanted to communicate something to me.

"I don't believe you're most, Kayleigh," she finally whispered. "I think you understand Darren."

Throat tight, I nodded.

Ma squeezed my arm before following after Michael, who held open the passenger door for her to slip inside his Mercedes.

I found Eoin already at his car. "Do you want to go get lunch with us, Kayleigh Bear?"

As I climbed into the car, I shook my head. "Could you actually drop me off somewhere?" I asked. "I've got something I've got to do."

"Sure." Eoin smiled, leaning over to kiss my cheek. "Anything you want."

But it wasn't what I wanted. It was what I needed.

I *needed* to find Darren.

I had a hunch I knew right where to look.

"Where should I take you?" Eoin asked.

"The garage."

24

DARREN

*E*very year when my family went to visit Jaime's gravestone for the anniversary of his death, I dragged in the oldest, most beat-up piece of shite clunker I could find with no hope in hell of ever running again and crawled beneath it for the day. It didn't take a psychologist to point out the distressing similarities between that dark, confined space and the dark, confined space where my brother would remain forever, but they could shove their diplomas right up their ass.

Because it was where I wanted to be.

Where I needed to be.

It was where I *deserved* to be.

That morning I kept the door of the garage pulled down because I didn't want to see the fecking sunshine. The chirping of birds made me want to gag.

All I wanted to do was disappear beneath the undercarriage and squeeze the wrench with my bandaged palms till blood soaked through and made my grip slippery. I wanted to emerge from darkness into darkness and drive my motorcycle home late at night, clinging onto the useless hope that I might actually be able to get to sleep.

I heard the garage door clank and clatter nosily as it rolled up on the metal tracks.

Pulling myself out from beneath the undercarriage with the heels of my boots, I winced in the sudden sunlight and held my hand over my eyes to see Kayleigh, of all people, walking toward the toolbox at the back of the garage. She stalked right past me.

I frowned in confusion as I watched her pull off her white beanie, her scarf, and her coat before tossing them haphazardly onto a Kawasaki motorcycle that still needed fixing.

My mouth fell openly dumbly to ask her what the fuck was going on, but I couldn't manage to form the words as Kayleigh rolled up the sleeves of her nice blouse, tugged on a dirty pair of work gloves, and grabbed an extra creeper from the side of the toolbox.

Without a word she came over to the other side of the rusted junker I had been working on, got down on her back, and rolled underneath.

"What are we working with here?" she asked, her voice muffled by the tight space of the undercarriage.

When I remained dumbfounded and silent, Kayleigh whistled and added, "Jaysus, this is a piece of shite."

I leaned my head down to see her click on her headlamp and whack her wrench against a pipe, which rained specks of rust and dirt down on her. She coughed but did not move to wipe the mess from her fancy shirt.

"Kayleigh, what are you doing?" I finally asked.

Kayleigh's only response was to bite her lip in concentration, test the stabilizer link, and shake her head. "How in the world is this thing still in one piece?"

"Kayleigh?"

"I mean, the ball joint is worn down to almost nothing and this bit here is pure rust," she continued, oblivious that my neck was aching craning down to look at her. "I'm afraid if I touch it, the whole thing will disintegrate."

"Kayleigh?"

"Can you come hold the centre link for me?" she asked, still ignoring my question. "I forgot to bring a winch under with me."

With a sigh, I leaned back down onto the creeper and with my heels, rolled myself beneath the undercarriage next to Kayleigh. I rested my cheek against the grease-covered plastic and looked over at her in the dark, but her eyes were focused up on the car.

"Right here," Kayleigh said, reaching down for my wrist.

I relented and let her guide my hand to the centre link, a bar that stretched across the width of the undercarriage above us.

Kayleigh's gaze remained fixed on the car, but I caught the sharp rise and fall of her chest as she sucked in a ragged breath in the small space. She licked her lips and exhaled shakily as she placed my hand on the centre link.

"Um, over this way just a bit," she whispered and I could almost feel the heat of her breath next to me.

The rough leather of her work glove skimmed over the back of my hand as she guided it gently toward her along the centre link. I gripped my other hand over the edge of the creeper to keep myself from screaming.

"Yeah," Kayleigh said, her voice reaching straight through my chest right into my heart. "Yeah, right there."

Kayleigh's hand was holding mine as I held the centre link, and she did not move it to begin work. Instead she turned her head, rested her cheek on her creeper, and searched my eyes, blinking slowly, like time itself moved slower down here in the dark.

"What are you doing, Kayleigh?" I asked.

Kayleigh's breath came in little gasps as she continued to

stare at me. Beneath the undercarriage of the car, her lips seemed impossibly close. I watched as they parted just slightly.

"I want to help you," she whispered, her voice barely audible.

Her fingers pushed mine apart so hers could intertwine with mine as we continued to both hold onto the centre link. I wanted to resist; fuck, I wanted to. But I didn't. I couldn't.

"This thing is never going to run," I said, keeping my eyes on Kayleigh's. "There's no point in helping. It's useless. It's a waste of time."

Kayleigh's eyelashes were dusted with specks of rust from the ball joint. Those eyelashes were meant for catching snowflakes or raindrops in a sun shower. They were meant for tangling with pieces of confetti and champagne as someone deserving held her tight on New Year's Eve.

"I don't want it to run," Kayleigh whispered. "And I don't need it to be fixed. I just want it to..." Kayleigh squeezed my hand and the look in her eyes intensified, the green somehow burning brighter even in the dark. "I just want to be here for you, Darren," she whispered. "I just want to be here *with* you."

Either I could hear both of our hearts pounding in the confinement of concrete and metal or mine was beating so quickly and so erratically that it sounded to my ears like two instead of just one. It was the first time either of us had dropped the pretext between us. Kayleigh was no longer hiding behind metaphor, innuendo, allusion. Gone was the subtlety of a sneaked glance over the shoulder or a passing glance of pinkies at the family dinner table or a whiff of her perfume caught up and carried to me on the winter wind. This was out in the open, in plain language, stripped down and laid bare honesty.

It scared the hell out of me.

Because it was what I wanted. Of course it was what I wanted.

"Your ma told me what happened with Jaime that night."

Lost in the hurricane of my own thoughts, I almost missed what she said at first. But when I caught it, it was as if the whole weight of the iron and aluminium junker collapsed onto my chest, crushing my lungs and stealing even the hope of a breath.

"What?" I asked, voice thin as dark spots flashed in my field of vision. "What did my ma tell you?"

It was as if I suddenly developed a debilitating case of claustrophobia as the worst panic I'd ever experienced flooded my chest. Did Ma know? *How* did Ma know? I'd kept my secret locked up tight since that night. Every breath where I managed to not scream the truth to anyone around was agony, but I'd managed. And I'd promised to keep managing till the day I died.

How did Ma find out?

"Darren?" Kayleigh reached over to me as my breath grew ragged in the tight, and only growing tighter and tighter, space beneath the undercarriage. "Darren, what's wrong?"

"I have to get out of here," I gasped. "I— I— I have to—"

My boots couldn't find purchase on the concrete floor as I scrambled to pull myself out from beneath the rusted car. I clawed at the metal pipes and covers above me, now entirely unable to see it as anything but the top of a coffin.

"Darren..." Kayleigh's voice shook with concern as I finally managed to escape the tomb beneath the car.

I staggered to my feet and stumbled away, Kayleigh's voice echoing in my ears. I sagged against the toolbox in the back of the shop, turning my head away from the car because even just the sight of it constricted my lungs in a vice grip.

"Darren." Kayleigh's hands, rough from the leather of the work gloves, were on my cheeks as her wide eyes searched mine. "Darren, please talk to me."

"What did she say?" I held my throbbing chest as I sucked in shallow breaths of air. "What does my ma know?"

Kayleigh's eyebrows furrowed together, but she quickly answered, "She said you didn't make it. She said you were too late to say goodbye to Jaime."

I turned my head toward Kayleigh. "That's it?"

The confusion in her green eyes only grew. "What?"

I swallowed heavily and leaned further on the toolbox. "That's all my ma told you?"

She nodded. "That's all she said. Darren, are you alright?"

I exhaled in relief. I expected the tightness in my chest and the pain in my heart to lessen. But they didn't. They only got worse.

Because my secret was still a secret. The infection in my heart still festered. The disease in my soul still stank like blackened tar. The sin I committed that night was still dragging me to hell.

I missed the one and only chance to say goodbye to my most beloved brother because I put myself first. Here on the anniversary of his death, I wanted to do the same exact thing.

I wanted to put my desire for Kayleigh above Eoin. I wanted to throw away my commitment to my family for another woman. I wanted to hurt my brother just so I could have what I wanted.

What the fuck was wrong with me?

One of Kayleigh's hands moved to the back of my neck and the other moved to rest over my thundering heart. Just looking into her eyes felt like a betrayal of the worst kind.

Kayleigh's sweet pink lips parted. "Darren, I know you're hurting and—"

"I'm not."

Kayleigh's head jerked back a little at the abruptness of my tone. "What do you mean?"

"I've moved on," I said darkly, as I pulled her hands from my body. "Why else do you think I didn't go to the grave?" I shouldered past her and opened a random drawer in the toolbox.

"Darren, don't do this," Kayleigh warned, sadness tinging her voice. Her hand reached out for me.

I brushed it off and then glared at her over my shoulder. "Shouldn't you be with Eoin right now?"

Kayleigh froze, her hand suspended in the heavy, unmoving space between the two of us.

"You're with him, right?" I spat venom with each word. "What kind of girlfriend isn't with her boyfriend when he's grieving?"

Kayleigh's hand dropped limply to her side, her cheeks reddening as if I'd slapped her with each violent word.

Her voice was low when she next spoke. "You can try to mask your pain in anger and coldness and rudeness, but I see you, Darren," she hissed. "I see you."

Rage so hot and so fast that I could barely stand still flooded my veins as Kayleigh laid her coat over her arm and turned to leave.

"Why don't you go heal Eoin's pain, Kayleigh?" I shouted after her. "He's the one you're fucking, after all."

Kayleigh did not turn back to face me when she spoke. "I've never had sex with Eoin."

I stood against the toolbox and watched the darkness coming for me as the door lowered noisily behind her after she left. The inky black covered my grease-stained boots first, then my dirty jeans, then my black t-shirt. I sucked in one last gulp of air as if the darkness I was plunged into was bone-chilling black water I couldn't escape.

And I drowned in it.

25

KAYLEIGH

I figured maybe a night or two of wall-shaking music, eardrum shattering karaoke, and a brain-piercing headache might drown out any and every thought of Darren from my mind.

Turns out the thoughts of him were louder.

After I fought with Darren in his shop, I texted Aubrey and asked if I could pick up a shift or two at The Jar for some extra cash; I didn't bother telling her right away that by "extra cash" I meant rent and food costs and utilities and anything else I needed to stay alive, because I wasn't going to go back to work with Darren.

Thankfully Aubrey didn't ask any questions and said yes right away. The roughest part of the whole process was listening to Candace scream for three minutes straight when I told her I'd be working with her that night.

We walked over to The Jar together for our shift. With her normal exuberance, Candace showed me where the kegs were located in case they needed replacing during the night, how to load up dirty pint glasses into the dishwasher, and who to call in case someone got just a smidge too rowdy. I nodded along politely and tried to show enthusiasm for what she was showing me, but truthfully, it was nothing new.

If you've worked in one bar, you've worked in every bar.

Ten minutes into the shift, I'd learned everything there was to learn, and there were still seven hours and fifty minutes left. At least the single clock on the wall was covered with a splatter of neon silly string so I wouldn't be tempted to check the time every thirty seconds or so.

"Are you just loving it?" Candace shouted over the music that rattled the floors beneath us after returning from the back with a clean rack of pint glasses. "Isn't it just the best job in the world, Kay?"

I started to help her stack up the glasses and nodded. "Yeah, it's alright craic, I guess."

It was the fifth rack of pint glasses we'd unloaded that night, and we were only halfway through at that point.

"Way better than that dingy, dirty garage, right?" Candace nudged me with a wink for good measure. Her tactics in trying to convince me to work here full-time weren't exactly subtle. But then again, Candace didn't exactly *do* subtle. Ever.

"Emhmm," I managed to eke out half-heartedly without pointing out the obvious fact that the soles of both of our pairs of sneakers were sticky with spilled liquor and that the bar top was coated in a layer of cheese and onion Tayto crisp crumbs.

"I mean, here you have great music." Candace waved her arm in the air above her head to the lively rhythm of Beoga's contemporary trad hit, "Dolan's 6am", as she poured a Guinness for a customer. "Is music even allowed in that place? Or do you have to whisper like it's a boring old library?"

"What?" I shouted over at her while running another customer's card.

"Don't you like the music here?"

"Oh. Yeah. Sure."

Really, I found myself missing the silence of the shop. When it was silent I could hear Darren's calm, steady voice next to me under the hood as he showed me how to change something or fix something. When it was silent I could catch a little tune he hummed every once in a while, probably without realising. Then again when it was silent, I could hear my heart pounding out the letters of his name again and again and again.

"Plus, you're making people happy here." Candace pointed to a group of girls laughing as they attempted to Irish dance in heels.

I didn't have the heart to tell Candace that I wasn't quite sure they were going to be so happy tomorrow morning.

"It's great here," I told her, forcing a smile. "I like it, I really do."

Candace had to stretch up to sling her arm around my shoulders. She grinned up at me between a curtain of raven curls. "And there really is no better co-worker than me, isn't that the goddamn truth, amiga?"

I laughed and put my arm around her as well. "You're alright, I guess."

"Alright?" Candace leaned back and stared at me with her jaw dropped in mock horror. "*Alright?*"

I grinned and pulled her back close to me. "You're the most wonderful, most beautiful, most funny, most amazing co-worker *ever*, Candace."

Candace winked and patted my butt. "That's right."

I chuckled, shaking my head as I started an order for two vodka tonics with lemons.

"So you'll leave that grumpy hermit and come have the best job here with the most wonderful, most beautiful, most funny, most amazing co-worker *ever*, right?" Candace asked while counting out change. When I didn't answer, she elbowed me again in the side. "Think about it, okay?" she said with a smile. "I'm going to go get more pint glasses."

She disappeared into the crowd on her way to the kitchen as I stood before a sea of expectant, bleary-eyed faces. In that moment, I wanted to pull up a hood and watch them all disappear. I wanted to replace the bottles of whiskey with cylinders, the keg taps with engine valves, the dishrag soaked with Jägermeister with an old torn t-shirt stained with oil and grease. I wanted the music to die and the voices to all fade but one.

The one who wasn't here.

The one who I left.

The one who pushed me away.

"Hey, can we get a pint or something?" a college-age kid shouted at me from the end of the bar.

"Yeah, in a sec," I replied. "We're out of pint glasses."

Candace returned hidden by a rack of freshly cleaned pint glasses. "Never fear, fellas, we have pint glasses!" she announced to a roar of cheers and applause. "We'll always have pint glasses and we'll always have beer!"

Candace beamed when the man she handed the overflowing beer to leaned across the bar and planted a wet kiss on her candied-apple cheek.

"Now, what's *your* name, cutie?" Candace purred after playfully grabbing his chin.

I smiled and left her to her new "friend" to serve the throngs of parched patrons farther down the bar. It was all the same for the rest of the night: take order, pour drink, tap card, avoid getting hit on, repeat.

Repeat.

Repeat.

Repeat.

At the end of the night with eyes half closed, I pushed a mop across the beer-soaked, broad wooden planks back and forth, back and forth, back and forth. Candace was right: there would always be more pint glasses. Dirty pint glasses, clean pint glasses, almost-empty, half-full, lipstick-stained pint glasses. There would always be beer. Ale, red ale, stout, larger, IPA. Any kind of beer you could think of, we'd have it. There would always be people. There would always be laughter and the craic, music and more craic, and more pint glasses to fill with beer.

But there wouldn't be him.

"So," Candace drew the word out long and slow in her thick Brazilian accent as she counted cash for the end of the night at the register behind the bar, "will you be back tomorrow night, my darling *amiga*?"

I glanced over at her from where I stood with the mop in the centre of the sticky floor.

There wouldn't be him.

"Umm..."

"*Não, não, não.*"

Coins clattered the ground as Candace ran to me, swept my hands up into hers and clutched them dramatically against her chest. "Don't break my heart like this, Kayleigh," she moaned. "Please, please, please."

There wouldn't be him.

Maybe that was for the best. The best for both of us.

I squeezed Candace's hands and smiled. "Count me in."

I barely had time to pull my hands from hers and slap them over my ears before my undyingly passionate roommate leaned her head back and gave half of Dublin a very unwelcome 1:30 a.m. wake-up call.

I wish I could have said I felt even an ounce of her enthusiasm. Instead I was silent.

Silent yet again.

26

DARREN

I'd driven past the graveyard where my twin brother lay more times than I could possibly count, but I'd never stopped. Each time the wind would tear the tears from my eyes as I twisted the accelerator on my motorcycle instead of reaching for the brake. My headlight would cut through the fine mist and I'd wonder if it was his tombstone that the harsh yellow beam illuminated amongst the weeds and dying leaves, but I never paused long enough to check. Every time I passed the marbled hills of the dead, my chest ached as if the tether between Jaime and my heart still existed through the veil and I was ripping it apart again and again and again as I drove faster and faster and faster away.

Always away.

Tonight was the first time I stopped. The engine of my motorcycle sputtered and died in the small parking lot at the edge of the wrought iron fence, rusted and claimed by tangles of thorny ivy. I cut out the headlight and felt the cold of the asphalt creep into the soles of my boots. I stuffed my frozen fingers into the pockets of my leather jacket and sat there on the frigid leather seat, watching my breath unfurl like tendrils of a cigarette against the black night. I suddenly craved the burn of nicotine in my lungs. Or whiskey. Or lighter fluid. Anything, please, anything to warm my soul.

My fingers, numb from the drive, twitched toward the key still in the ignition. I wasn't here for the right reasons. My family came to remember Jaime, to celebrate his life, to feel closer to him. I was here that night because I was selfish. I was here for selfish reasons. I was here because *I* needed something.

Chewing on the inside of my mouth, I stared out over the hundreds of tombstones dotting the plot of land. I still couldn't quite believe my brother was one of them. I remembered when we were kids and we would hold our breaths whenever Ma drove past a cemetery. Huffing and puffing, red in the face and clutching at our throats, we'd laugh and laugh once we were finally past, because for us death was an impossibility. It would never be our names carved in marble. It would never be us that a gardener moved grass above with a bored sigh, squinting in the sunlight we no longer saw. We would forever have an empty space after the dash following our birth year.

Turns out the impossible is entirely possible: all it takes is a little bit of ice, a blink of an eye, and a traffic light pole.

I waited for the headlights of a passing car to plunge me back into darkness before swinging my leg stiffly over my motorcycle. It was as if I'd forgotten how to walk as I approached the cemetery fence, my feet stumbling and my knees threatening to buckle. I weaved across the parking lot like I was drunk. Hopping the shoulder-high fence would normally be no problem, but I was sweating and panting by the time I managed to drop down into the wet leaves on the other side.

An inky black hung like a curtain over the graveyard. I didn't bring a flashlight or my cell phone. Maybe I just forgot. Maybe I was hoping that I would wander around in the dark, tracing the carved names on random gravestones before I gave up, went home, and honestly said I tried to find him. Or maybe it was just too fecking cold to think properly.

I lifted the collar of my coat against the bitter wind as my boots crunched the brittle leaves beneath me. It was the only noise around me save for a passing car now and then, here and gone.

I remembered the burial plot pamphlets on the funeral home director's desk two days after Jaime died. I remembered not listening to anything the long-faced man was saying as I stared at his pale, bony fingers stretched flat across the desk; I was too busy wondering whose job it was to make those bleedin' pamphlets with their morbid "selling points". I remembered Ma asking in a broken voice, "Are there any trees?"

In this graveyard, there were five large oaks. I moved toward the smallest and thinnest—we were poor when Jaime died and I had no doubt that a piece of dirt beneath a fine, stately oak cost more, just like an apartment with a view cost more.

When I finally found Jaime, I walked right past him. I was halfway back to my motorcycle when I sighed, stared up at the shifting grey clouds, and dragged a hand over my weary face. My boots grew heavier and heavier with each step back toward him. I stopped at the edge of the branches, their bare fingers reminding me of the funeral director's as they swayed above me in the wind. I couldn't look at his gravestone, as if the grey marble had eyes and I was ashamed to meet them.

"Um, hi," I mumbled, scratching at the back of my neck.

People always talked aloud to headstones in the movies and I always found it ridiculous. But here I was, speaking aloud to my dead twin brother.

It suddenly didn't feel so ridiculous.

I cleared my throat and swallowed heavily. "I'm sorry that it's taken me so long to, um, well...to, you know, come see you...or whatever."

I glanced over, half expecting to see Jaime sitting on his gravestone, arms crossed over his chest, dark eyebrow lifted as he smirked at me. But there was, of course, just the cold marble, the tufts of browned grass, and the flowers from Ma and my brothers now withering.

Turning my face away, I sighed before saying, "Maybe you wouldn't even want me here, Jay. Maybe you're rolling over in your grave right now."

I chuckled, because I knew goddamn well that Jaime would have chuckled, too. But as my soft laughter died in the still graveyard, I was left feeling only colder and terribly alone.

"We didn't exactly end things on good terms, now did we?" I asked my brother while staring at a random lopsided Celtic cross half buried by tall, untrimmed grasses. "I suppose I have a knack for making a mess of things, don't I?"

How I wished I could take back the things I said the night I left. How I wished I had looked back one last time before peeling out of the driveway. How I wished I had stayed.

These were things I couldn't say aloud. These were things I needed most to say aloud. But these were the things locked away in my stony heart, harder than the ice-cold marble with Jaime's name less than ten feet away.

"I, um, I came here because there was nowhere else to go," I said, my voice half carried away by the wind.

Not that it mattered how loud I spoke. I could scream at the top of my lungs and there was no chance in hell of Jaime ever, ever hearing me. *Never* again.

"I guess that hasn't changed, has it?" I said as guilt again flooded my tight chest. "I'm still a selfish asshole with a penchant for making horrible, devastating decisions."

Again I glanced over my shoulder, and I could almost see Jaime shrugging. *"You said it,"* he'd say. *"Not me."*

A tiny grin tugged at my lips as I imagined him huffing and

patting the space next to him on the gravestone. *"What's her name, Daz?"*

I hesitated for a moment and then turned around so I was facing Jaime's gravestone. At first it was too much: face-to-face with the empty reality of the stone. That Jaime was nothing more than a lifeless body rotting beneath the frozen earth. I squeezed my eyes shut so I couldn't see the truth, the mean, hard truth.

"Her name is Kayleigh," I said, voice shaking, "and she's Eoin's girl."

It was certainly just the whistle of the wind through the leaf-less oak limbs, but with my eyes closed I could pretend it was Jaime whistling in disbelief as he leaned back and shook his head. I laughed darkly.

"I guess you understand why you were the only person I could talk to about this."

I dared to peek one eye open, and Jaime was smiling. *"No shit, dumbass."*

I opened the other. "I tried my hardest not to fall for her," I explained, more earnestly than I had expected. "Jay, you have no idea how fecking hard I tried."

The wind through the naked limbs was my brother's only response. I dragged my hand through my hair and sighed.

"It just feels like everything I tried only ended up shoving us closer and closer together," I continued, moving so I stood directly beside Jaime's gravestone. "It feels like I can't avoid colliding with her."

It feels like I don't want to…

My fingertips skimmed the cold marble of my brother's tombstone as gently as a falling leaf, but the sensation struck my chest like a ton of bricks. Sinking to my knees in the damp grass, I gasped for air as emotions I'd shoved down for years filled my throat. I pressed my palm against my brother's etched name and leaned forward to rest my forehead against the year that was wrong, wrong, wrong.

I sobbed, unable to do anything more than that as the earth chilled my body and my tears seared my cheeks. I felt like I still had rivers to cry, lakes and seas and oceans to cry, but I found myself suddenly laughing, because I imagined Jaime seeing me now.

"Are you going to tell me about her boobs or should I go ask Eoin?"

Sagging against his gravestone, I shook my head, because the image was ridiculous. But it wouldn't leave my thoughts. I kept trying to return to my grief, my pain, my sorrow, but the memory of Jaime—light-hearted and carefree and funny as hell Jaime—wouldn't let me. Finally, I wiped at my eyes, shifting over so my back was against the frigid stone, and sniffled. "You're a real ass, you know that, don't you, Jaime?"

Jaime would have smirked and tilted his head. *"You always were an ass man, brother."*

I choked on something halfway between a laugh and a sob filled with more pain than I could bear.

"Her name is Kayleigh," I said, starting over as I imagined Jaime's shoulder brushing against mine as he slid down next to me. "And her freckles look like a dusting of cinnamon..."

27

KAYLEIGH

*I*t was Christmas Eve and there was no peace on earth.

With everyone piled inside the snug and cosy O'Sullivan house, it would seem easy enough to avoid one-on-one contact with Darren, but at every turn I quite literally ran into him.

With a cup of hot chocolate and a cinnamon roll from the kitchen, I went to hide in Eoin's room during breakfast only to collide with Darren leaving his to sneak back food of his own; I didn't risk going back downstairs for another mug. Instead I sat on the edge of Eoin's bed and stared grumpily at my marshmallow-stained sweater in the hamper.

Later I slipped inside the empty study, thinking it would be safe, only to have the door slam against my ass two seconds later when Darren opened the door with a book under his arm.

We bumped into each other in the hall, in the kitchen, on the porch, and in the living room so we each had bruises on our skin to match the ones on our hearts.

The only place I didn't run into Darren was getting out of the shower earlier that morning, and maybe that was because we'd already been there, done that. Or maybe it was because I got up at 5 a.m. to make sure it didn't happen.

After all, Darren and I hadn't seen each other since fighting in his garage after the family visited Jaime's grave earlier that morning. To say that things were tense would be an understatement. And nothing made things more tense than trying not to be tense. It was the equivalent of someone telling you to "relax" when you were stressed: all that accomplished was the further grinding of teeth and clenching of fists.

I was alone in the kitchen when I ducked down to pull out a sheet of sugar cookies from the oven. I stood and collided with Darren. He yelped, grabbing at his arm as metal clattered to the floor and hot cookies scattered on the kitchen floor.

"Watch it!" we each hissed at the same time before banging our heads together as we bent over at the same time to pick up the mess.

I knelt across from Darren as we each rubbed our heads and sent angry glares across the confectionary calamity.

"You burnt me," Darren hissed, flinging cookies over my head into the garbage bin behind me.

"*You* ruined my cookies," I said back irritably.

"You should have been more careful." Darren's stormy grey-blue eyes glared at me.

I leaned forward and jabbed a finger at his chest. "*You're* the one making a mess of things," I whispered.

Our breaths were hot against one another's as our eyes locked with anger and something more that I dared not dwell on.

"Is everyone alright in here?"

As if shot out from a cannon, Darren and I both popped up immediately from behind the island with wide smiles, wide, *fake* smiles for Darren's ma.

"Everything is great," I said, voice dripping with cheerfulness. "Just fantastic."

"Merry Christmas Eve, Ma," Darren said next to me.

Ma's eyes narrowed slightly as she eyed a cookie that had rolled all the way to the fridge. "I thought I heard something crash in here," she said suspiciously.

"Oh, that was all my fault," Darren jumped in before I could. "I accidentally knocked Kayleigh here as she was taking a pan of cookies out of the oven."

"No, no," I insisted, laying an arm on Darren's before realising my mistake and yanking it back like it was the edge of the cookie sheet and not just flannel. "I should have seen you coming and—"

"Don't be silly," Darren interrupted, not so gently pushing me away. "It's all on me."

"No," I said through gritted teeth as I turned to face Darren, frustration threatening to boil over. "I insist, it was *my* mis—"

"What's going on?"

Noah, followed by Aubrey in matching black and red plaid pyjamas, entered the kitchen and stood next to Ma. He frowned as he spotted the disaster of cookies on the floor. "What happened here?"

"It seems," Ma started before Darren or I could manage to open our mouths, "that either Darren ran into Kayleigh or Kayleigh ran into Darren. Either way there has clearly been quite the collision."

"A collision?" Michael wandered into the kitchen next, his face buried in his work phone. "What colli—ugh!"

I winced as a cookie crushed under Michael's leather loafers.

"Why are there cookies on the floor?" he asked, balancing to flick crumbs off of the sole of his shoe.

I felt my cheeks redden as Ma's sharp blue eyes looked

between the Darren and me. Noah and Aubrey each lifted an eyebrow. I was stammering, unsure what to say, when someone stampeded down the stairs. It could only be Eoin.

"Are the cookies ready yet, Kayleigh Bear?" Eoin asked, his voice booming with childlike excitement before noticing Michael. "Mikey, why'd you step on the cookies?"

"They were on the floor," Michael grumbled. "It wasn't my fault."

"It was their fault," Noah pointed to Darren and me.

Barely unable to stand it any longer, I forced a smile and a laugh and said, "I'm going to go get a broom to sweep all of this mess up so we are done with it."

I sensed Darren tense next to me as Ma told me that I could find a broom in the garage. I didn't even bother grabbing a coat before slipping out the back door, and I thanked the blast of icy air in the grey morning for helping to clear my mind. As I was rounding the corner of the small house, someone caught my wrist and whipped me around. I came face-to-face with a storm infinitely darker than the clouds above us.

"We can't keep on going like this," Darren said, placing a hand on either side of my head against the brick façade and looming over me. His long dark eyelashes were too close, his full, sensual lips were too close, his throat, the same one I traced with my lips, was far, far too close.

Ducking my eyes, I easily slipped out from under the snare of his arms, stepped away from him, and crossed my arms. "I agree," I said, daring a glance at him, which I immediately knew was a mistake.

Darren was looking at me with an intensity I'd yet to see in him. He wasn't looking at me like he wanted me, longed for me, yearned for me. He was looking at me like I was *his*, his and his alone. He was looking at me like Eoin didn't exist, like his family didn't exist, like nothing existed but him and me.

Swallowing heavily, I started to whisper, "We need to stop whatever this is between us and—"

"No."

That one single word from his lips somehow managed to terrify me, thrill me, anger me; I was turned on as hell.

"No?" I repeated, lifting an eyebrow as I took a step toward him.

"No," Darren said, his eyes focused intently on mine. "What we need to do, Kayleigh Scott, is to stop pretending like there isn't something between us."

"There isn't," I said out of instinct, out of protection, out of fear.

"Bullshite."

"There isn't," I insisted, my chest now just inches from Darren's, whose heaved just as heavily as mine.

"There is," he said, leaning down to hiss against my lips. "There is something intoxicating and magnetic and unstoppable."

My heart pulsed to the rhythm of his every word, but nevertheless I shook my head stubbornly.

"There can't be something between us," I whispered, glancing over my shoulder to make sure that we were alone, "all we do is fight. That's not lo—that's not what you do with someone you have feelings for. Eoin and I never fight."

"You have feelings for Eoin?"

I paused too long. Darren's question caught me off guard.

I cursed at the dark flint in his eyes when he knew the answer as clearly as if I had shouted it into his face: *no, I don't.* But him reading me so easily filled me with bristling frustration.

"Yes," I lied. "Yes, I do."

"No, you don't," Darren said, searching my eyes.

My chest pressed against Darren's as I jutted my chin defiantly up at him. "I'm done fighting with you," I hissed.

A devilish grin tugged up at both the corner of his mouth and the strings of my heart. "I'm not done fighting with you," he said, lowering his lips so they were as close as possible without touching.

I spit out a laugh. "You *want* to fight with me?"

"Yes," Darren said immediately. "It's all I want to do."

I stared at him, dumbfounded. "Why?" I asked, genuine confusion momentarily taking the place of my anger at him.

His blue-grey eyes trapped mine just like his arms had done with his hands on either side of my face, but this time I couldn't escape so easily.

Darren whispered, "Because it means there's something here worth fighting for."

My heart pounded against his as our icy breaths twisted together in the cold. Finally, I stepped back and cleared my throat. "I have to get back inside," I said, slipping past him toward the garage to retrieve the broom. "Eoin will be wondering where I am."

Darren was wrong.

It was a good sign that Eoin and I never fought. That's what a healthy relationship was like. That's what love was supposed to look like: harmony, peace, quiet.

Darren was wrong.

Darren was wrong.

Darren was wrong...

28

DARREN

*W*as it childish?
Probably.
Was it misdirected?
I suppose so.
Was there any way in hell I wasn't going to goad Eoin into a fight?
Nope.
The honest truth was that I was mad and I was frustrated and I needed to punch someone but didn't have the nerve to give myself an upper cut so swift that I tasted the tang of copper between my teeth. Kayleigh left me outside alone in that cruel wind, and I'd been nearing my boiling point ever since. It was near fecking inevitable that I was going to lose it; it was just a matter of time.
"What the fuck, Daz!"
Eoin threw his hands up into the air when I flopped down on the couch with a book and switched off the television right in the middle of a try during the rugby match he'd had on. I craned my neck over my shoulder to look back at him, ignoring Kayleigh perched awkwardly on his lap.

"Oh, were you watching that?" I asked, feigning innocence. I felt her darkening eyes on me as I shrugged. "Sorry about that, man," I said, clicking the television back on.

"Fecking hell, Darren!" Eoin called after me as I moved to the study. "I can't go back in time, you asshole."

Well, I couldn't go back in time either. I couldn't go back to find Kayleigh before Eoin did, and unfortunately Eoin had to pay for that.

I already told you it was childish. I already told you I didn't care.

"Hey, Darren, hand me that oven mitt," Eoin asked later, bent over the oven and struggling with a massive steaming casserole.

I ignored him.

Kayleigh hurried over to help him after shooting me a glare of daggers. I ignored her, too.

"Ow! Fuck, Darren!"

I accidentally wedged Eoin's fingers against his chair when I scooted mine in for dinner, and the red in his cheeks was a good sign that I was getting close. Eoin was renowned for being hot tempered on the rugby pitch, and I knew exactly which buttons to push. Head ducked over my plate, I heard Kayleigh whispering sweetly on the other side of Eoin, "Here, here let me see", as she cupped his fingers in hers; this only made me madder.

I managed to bite my lip when Eoin's fingers intertwined with Kayleigh's on the table while Ma said grace before all of us began our Christmas Eve dinner. My own fingers pinched the sensitive skin of my wrist as I clenched my eyes shut.

"Hey, Daz, pass the spuds, will ye?" Eoin asked, nudging me in the ribs.

I scooted my chair away from him without a word and instead reached for my whiskey glass. Brimming over like a whistling teapot, Eoin grabbed his chair by the seat and hopped it over toward mine.

He pressed his mouth to my ear and shouted, "Hey, *Darren*, pass the spuds, will ye?"

My hands clenched into fists beneath the table. I resisted the urge to shove Eoin back; he needed to take the first shot. Next to me, Noah winced at Eoin's shouting and grabbed the potatoes.

"Here, just take these, alright, Daz?"

Noah held the white casserole dish of scalloped potatoes and waited for me to take it from him to pass to Eoin.

"Eoin can reach it," I mumbled, stabbing a slice of turkey so aggressively that I feared I might have cracked the porcelain plate underneath.

Noah rolled his eyes and held it out closer to Eoin. "Here you go."

Eoin sat back in his chair and crossed his arms over his chest. "No. I asked *Darren* to pass me the spuds, not you. So *Darren's* going to pass the spuds."

I kept my eyes fixed on my plate, silent.

"My arms are getting tired here, fellas," Noah said.

There was the sudden screech of a chair and then Kayleigh was moving behind me, grabbing the potatoes, and setting them squarely in front of Eoin.

"There," she said with a curt nod of her chin. "No need to fight."

Oh, how wrong she was...

I was plotting more ways to irritate Eoin when he proceeded to push the casserole dish back across the table, knocking over the butter tray and spilling Aubrey's wine glass.

"Hey!"

As half the table scurried to soak up the red wine before it soaked through the napkin on her hunter-green dress, the other half shouted at Eoin to stop. But Eoin was just getting started.

Perfect.

"Hey, brother," he glared at me, chest rising and falling angrily (all he was missing was the steam unfurling from his ears), "pass the potatoes, will ye?"

Out of the corner of my eye, I noticed Kayleigh's hand on my brother's arm as she started to say, "Eoin, it isn't worth..."

Her voice trailed off when I picked up the potatoes. Aubrey stopped patting frantically at her lap, Ma paused halfway up to get a towel, Michael looked up from checking to make sure the spilled wine hadn't fried the work phone he'd sneaked onto the dinner table.

This was the point where I should have seen the impact my actions were having on my family. This was the moment where I should have realised that these relationships were more important than a relationship with a girl I hadn't even been on a proper date with yet. This was the moment where I should have said enough.

Instead, I said, *Fuck it.*

With Eoin boiling next to me and the rest of the family watching my every move, I lifted the dish above my plate and slowly scooped out a spoonful of potatoes onto my own plate before returning the dish to right where it had been beside Noah.

"Oh, fuck," Noah whispered, hiding his face in his hands a half second before Eoin's massive palms slammed into my chest, sending my chair crashing back to the floor.

"Eoin!" Ma shouted.

I scurried to my feet, my vision red and pulsing, and buried my shoulders into Eoin's stomach.

"Darren!"

I heard Ma's voice. But I also heard my inner voice of anger and frustration and lust and hurt and they were all louder. Much, much louder.

Eoin stumbled back a few steps before I drove him into straight into the cabinets, sending stacks of plates and rows of glasses rattling. I was barely aware of chairs screeching on the tiled floor as Eoin's tree trunk arms slammed down on my back. I fell to the floor. Down but not out. I yanked Eoin's feet from underneath him and scrambled on top of him.

I was lifting a fist to swing down when Noah caught my wrist —this stopped me from hitting Eoin, but it did not stop Eoin from hitting me. His knuckles, hardened by cold nights and rough turf, connected with my eye socket. Then Eoin was on top of me and the back of my head was smacking against the hard tile before I could even register the radiating pain. I thrashed beneath him even as Michael and Noah tried to yank him off of me.

Things should have been over when they finally succeeded, panting and grunting as Eoin kept swinging at the air. I should have laid on the ground, patted my fingers gingerly over my swollen eye, and wobbled to my feet toward the pack of frozen peas in the fridge. I should have come to my senses and *stopped*.

Fuck that.

With a growl of rage I barely recognised as coming out of my own throat, I lunged at Eoin, tackling him out of Michael and Noah's arms and back to the ground. His fist caught my ribs. Mine caught his jaw and his head whipped back. My knees pinned his arms at his sides and I lifted my arm again to strike his face when I caught sight of Ma standing with the broken shards of a glass from the cabinet in her hands.

Her eyes were on mine. They struck me with more pain than the full weight of Eoin's fist. In her eyes I saw the thing I never wanted to see in them: worry, hurt, *fear*.

"I'm sorry," I whispered, glancing down at Eoin.

But I meant it for her.

My fist fell limply to my side. Eoin pushed me roughly off of him. He scrambled to his feet, ready for more, before Michael jumped between us.

"Woah, woah, it's over," Michael said, hands out to separate us. He glanced over his shoulder at me. "It is over, right?"

I nodded as I pushed myself wearily to my feet.

"What the fuck was that, Darren?" Eoin asked, rubbing at his jaw where a black and blue bruise was already forming.

I was certain I had a matching one myself.

"I'm sorry," I repeated. "I'm just—it's just the shop."

My eyes moved to Kayleigh, who kept her attention focused on her napkin, which had fallen to the floor.

"I'm worried about the shop," I said. "I'm worried I could lose the shop."

Noah broke the awkward, tense silence with a hearty laugh. He patted me on the shoulder and squeezed, a silent communication between brothers. "Nice try," he said in an easy-going, friendly way. "You can't convince me that it's not a girl making you a little...*on edge* recently."

"Yeah," Aubrey said with a hesitant smile, "Noah was the exact same way before he and I got together."

Eoin nodded. "If it was you who had Kayleigh and I was all alone pining after a lady, I'd maybe blow up like that, too. I get it, I get it."

There was a round of forced laughter in the terribly silent kitchen, an attempt to shove things under the rug, to salvage the dinner, to pretend I didn't just ruin everything. But three people in the kitchen did not laugh along with the others: Ma, myself, and Kayleigh.

"I think I just need to get some air," I finally said.

"Right." Noah patted my shoulder again, winking at the rest of the family. "Some 'air'."

"Tell 'Air' we say hello," Michael added.

I wished they wouldn't act like this. I wished they wouldn't try to laugh it off, joke about it, pretend it was anything but inexcusable. I wished they would stop always trying to make it better.

It wasn't better.

It was worse. Before I met Kayleigh, I could smile with them all. It felt like agony, yanking up the corners of my lips, but I could do it. Before I met Kayleigh, I could play along just fine: I could sing the songs, drink the mulled wine, eat the Christmas cookies. I could keep it all in, all the hurt and pain and regret, till I was finally alone. Before I met Kayleigh, before I *fell for* Kayleigh, it was better.

I was numb.

With Kayleigh I felt everything: love, joy, happiness, irritation, sure, but also hope and peace and something almost resembling forgiveness. It also meant that I felt pain, and in that moment with Ma's eyes on me like that and Kayleigh's on the ground like that, I couldn't stand it.

"I'll be back," was all I could say before hurrying away.

My shoulder brushed against Kayleigh, but she didn't seem to notice. Her eyes remained on the floor as I stepped outside the kitchen and down the hall.

"Let's get you an ice pack," I heard Aubrey say to Eoin.

"Let's get him a Scotch!" Noah said to another, less tense, less awkward series of laughs.

Good, I thought as I grabbed my motorcycle helmet and keys from beside the front door. They deserve to enjoy their Christmas Eve.

I revved the engine and took off into the icy dark, knowing I wouldn't be able to outrun the memory of Ma's eyes on my raised fist.

29

KAYLEIGH

*M*aybe it was Eoin's snores that kept me tossing and turning late that cold Christmas Eve night. After we'd said our goodnights to the family (minus Darren, who was nowhere to be found) and headed upstairs, he'd "called" the top bunk, practically shoving me through the hallway wall to be the first to leap up onto the spaceship-and-alien-covered bed with a loud "Yippee!" Like a little kid tuckered out after a day of playing in the snow, Eoin was asleep in less than thirty seconds.

And snoring like a drunk walrus in forty-five.

So maybe it was Eoin's snores that kept me awake, staring hour after hour at the warped planks above my head. Or maybe it was because I felt cold without a pair of strong, grease-covered arms wrapped around me. Maybe it was because I missed the sear of a muddy kiss against my lips as my eyes fluttered closed. Maybe it was because I couldn't shake the uncomfortable, inescapable, unfixable feeling that I was in the wrong room.

But no.

No, no, it wasn't that. It wasn't any of that. It was the unbearable noise coming from Eoin above me and the fact that it shook the wobbly wooden frame of the bunk bed so I lived in constant fear that it (and the 200+ pounds of muscle along with it) would collapse on me. That was it. That was the reason I couldn't sleep.

With a sigh, I yanked back the cowboy-and-cactus sheets and tiptoed out of the little room still crammed with a rocking horse and a shelf of Eoin's rugby trophies and Michael's Mathlete awards side by side. Easing the door closed behind me, I made my way down the hallway, hands held out in front of me as I squinted in the dark. I managed to not break my neck on the stairs. On the ground floor, as I was heading toward the kitchen to get a glass of water (and maybe something a little more adult), I noticed the fire in the living room was still on. So were the lights of the Christmas tree.

There, sitting alone cross-legged on the floor beneath it, was Darren.

I was going to turn around right then and there and slip back upstairs when the floorboard under my left heel betrayed me. The low moan might as well have been an air horn in the silence. Darren turned around and our eyes met in the soft glow of the Christmas lights.

My cheeks warmed and it had nothing to do with the roar of the fire as I started to stammer.

"Sorry, I was—I—"

"Do you like hot chocolate?"

I frowned. "Huh?"

Darren continued to watch me as I fidgeted uncomfortably with the hem of my pink and white plaid pyjama shirt.

"Whipped cream? Chocolate shavings?" Darren asked. "Cinnamon? How do you feel about cinnamon?"

My jaw hung open in confusion and an amused grin played at Darren's lips.

"Are you smiling?" I finally asked, finding a grin of my own growing just at the sight of his.

"I asked you several questions first that are yet to be answered," Darren countered.

I narrowed my eyes at him and then crossed my arms, sighed, and ran through the list. "Hot chocolate, yes. Whipped cream, yes. Chocolate shavings, double yes." I paused and tapped my chin. "What was the last one?"

"Cinnamon."

I nodded. "Cinnamon, yes," I said. "Now, you have to answer my question."

Darren pushed himself to his feet and walked toward me. "What was your question?" He passed me on his way to the kitchen.

I followed after him, completely forgetting that moments ago I was intending to run back upstairs and hide.

As Darren disappeared behind the open refrigerator door, I said, "I asked, are you smiling?"

Armed with whipped cream and milk, Darren kicked the fridge closed behind him and shook his head. "Definitely not," he answered. "I am definitely not smiling."

I groaned as he fished cocoa powder, cinnamon, and chocolate shavings out of the cabinet.

"*Were* you smiling?"

Darren clicked his tongue as he put the saucer on the stovetop. "That's another question entirely," he said. "That wasn't part of the deal."

With a little huff, I placed my hands on my hips. "But I answered like five of your questions," I protested in a not-so-hushed whisper.

Darren scooped cocoa powder into the warming milk and lifted an eyebrow as he held another spoonful suspended over the sauce pan. "More?"

I raised an eyebrow. "*That's* another question."

Darren shrugged and tipped over the spoon. I watched him scoop up more cocoa powder and again suspend it over the already chocolatey mix. "More?"

I remained resolute, determined to get my answer. This time Darren poured in that spoonful, then another and another and another until, unable to stop myself from laughing, I grabbed his wrist.

"You win, you win," I chuckled. "No more, no more."

Darren smiled over at me.

My eyes went wide. "That? Was *that* a smile?"

It disappeared behind a frown as he stirred the hot chocolate. "I have no idea what in the world you're talking about, Kayleigh," he grumbled. "Perhaps you're dreaming."

I grinned as I hopped up onto the counter next to the stove and wiggled my fuzzy socks back and forth. I knew I wasn't dreaming, because if I was dreaming I could lean across the hot chocolate that filled the kitchen with the most delicious aroma and give Darren a kiss. If I was dreaming I could part my legs a little wider when Darren walked over to me. If I was dreaming he would know just what I wanted, just what I needed.

If I was dreaming the hot chocolate would burn in the saucepan and neither of us would give a damn.

A few minutes later we found ourselves sitting beneath the Christmas tree side by side armed with steaming mugs of hot chocolate.

"So...I'm glad you pulled a Cindy Lou Who tonight," Darren said, referring to my coming downstairs in the middle of the night.

I turned to see his face lit softly as he stared up at the angel atop the tree. "You know that makes you the Grinch, right?"

Darren looked over at me, and there was a twinkle in his eye. "I know. Trust me, I know," he said. "Appropriate, eh?"

I nodded. "Pretty spot on."

Darren laughed. I thought he might return his gaze to the tree and the pretty little lights, but he didn't. He continued to stare at me as his eyes softened and his smile faded. "I wanted to apologise," he said, his voice barely above a whisper. "I wanted to apologise for letting things get this far."

I immediately shook my head. "Darren, I—"

"Kayleigh, I pushed too hard," he interrupted. "I crossed the line that I never should have crossed."

"Darren, plea—"

"I love my family and somewhere along the line I stopped putting them first and started putting my wants, my needs, my... desires first," he continued, the passion clear despite the hush of his whisper. "I can't hurt Eoin. I can't hurt my family."

I reached out my hand to grab his, but Darren pulled it away from me before I could. I looked up into his waiting eyes.

"I wanted you to know that you were right," he whispered. "And I wanted you to know that I'm going to back off. I'm going to let you and Eoin be happy together." Darren smiled again, but it wasn't like the smiles before.

A sadness tugged at my chest, because I wasted those few, honest, *real* smiles. I should have held on to them. I would have, if I knew they were all I would get.

This time Darren did return his gaze to the Christmas tree above us. He sipped his mug with a casualness like he hadn't just ripped something away from me without warning. Darren looked at the tree. I continued to look at him.

I wanted to tell him that he was wrong. He didn't let things get too far, *we* did. If he pushed too far, then I pulled too far. If there was a line crossed, it was crossed hand in hand, heart in heart, soul in soul, *together*.

I wanted to him that *I* was wrong. I wanted to tell him that what I said in the backyard was out of fear, not truth. I wanted to tell him I didn't want him to back off. I wanted more, more, more.

Not of Eoin.

Of him.

I opened my mouth to spill all of this to him, like cutting open my very heart and watching it bleed across the rug, when Darren spoke first.

"I got you something," he said. "Something for Christmas."

I remembered back to the ice-skating rink: Darren beneath me, his eyes bright in the cocoon of my hair around his face as he looked up at me. I'd told him I had no clue what I was getting him for Christmas. I'd told him I hadn't even thought about it, not in the slightest.

"I do."

That's what he'd said. I remembered being certain he was lying.

"You do?" I had asked.

He had smiled before saying, *"I know exactly what I'm getting you for Christmas, Kayleigh Scott."*

And I had believed him. I had believed him more than I had believed anything else before that.

I set aside my mug as Darren crawled beneath the ornament-laden branches and pulled out from the very back a simple box wrapped in butcher's paper and twine. He placed it in my hands and then kissed me on the cheek.

"Wait, where are you going?" I asked as he stood and brushed some needles from his hair. "Don't you want to watch me open it?"

Darren winked down at me. "I already know what it is."

He turned to leave as I stared down at the little bow tie, brushing my thumb over the butcher's paper.

"Oh, and Kayleigh?"

I glanced over my shoulder at him.

"Yes," was all he said.

I frowned in confusion. "Yes?"

Darren nodded with his hands stuffed into the pockets of his dark hoodie. "The answer to your question," he explained. "Yes."

And without a word more he disappeared into the dark of the hallway. I heard his boots on the stairs and then I was plunged into a silence broken only by the rapid beating of my heart in my ears. I couldn't remember being this excited for a gift in years.

My fingers tugged at the twine and I carefully peeled back the butcher's paper. I peeked inside and tried to fight back the feeling of disappointment at the sight of an A/C condenser box. Hey, it was at least a very practical gift. I opened the lid.

But inside was not an A/C condenser at all. Inside was a beautiful new leather tool belt. I pulled it out and laid it across my lap, fingers tracing along all the hooks and pockets. I laughed at myself when I found my eyes watering over Darren's gift. I wasn't crying because it was a tool belt; I was crying because it was more than that.

It was someone's belief in me.

It was a future.

It was a passion I'd struggled all my life to find.

I almost didn't notice that it was embossed. If I hadn't been crying before, I was then:

Kayleigh Scott: Mechanic.

It was an identity.

I hugged the tool belt to my chest and found my tears shifting to tears of heartache. Darren gave me everything I could have wanted for Christmas, except for the one thing he could not give, the one thing he could never give: himself.

And it was all I wanted. In that moment beneath the tree, I knew it—Darren was all I wanted.

Were you smiling? I'd asked.

Yes.

30

KAYLEIGH

I woke up Christmas morning to the pounding of Eoin's feet on the stairs, the clatter of pots and pans in the kitchen amongst laughter, and the faint sound of carols from the old record player tucked behind the oversized fir in the living room. I couldn't help but grin like a child again.

It was the Christmas morning I'd always dreamed of, year after disappointed year, when I was young.

When I was as child, running down the stairs to see what Santa left me "might wake up your father, Kayleigh." There was no fresh batch of cinnamon rolls steaming from the oven. It was cold cereal and even colder "hot chocolate". We hadn't even owned a record player. There was no music, no Christmas carols. There was just silence and nervous twitches at anything and everything that broke that silence.

But the O'Sullivan house on Christmas morning was loud and chaotic and I loved it.

Still in his reindeer pyjamas that seemed about two sizes too small for him, Eoin was rummaging underneath the Christmas tree, tossing present after present behind him like a terrier digging for a bone. Aubrey in a pink fluffy sweater and even fluffier pink slippers was biting her nails and giving nervous instructions as Noah assured her again and again that he "had it" while attempting to flip a massive omelette in the cast iron skillet on the stove. Michael hurried out of the way, phone tucked protectively against his chest, as the yellow omelette flipped end over end in the air. Ma popped a bottle of champagne to celebrate the omelette not splatting on the kitchen floor, and before I could even say "good morning" I was handed an overflowing mimosa from Michael, a mug of hot chocolate with a mountain of whipped cream from Aubrey, and when I quickly ran out of hands, Ma prompted me to open my mouth for a heaping bite of cinnamon roll.

I grinned as sweet cream, butter, or both trailed down my chin, and I didn't even bother to wipe it off before getting whipped cream on the tip of my nose from a sip of hot chocolate.

"Kayleigh Scott, how unladylike!" my mother would have chastised, reaching immediately for a napkin or bottle of bleach.

No one in the O'Sullivan family pointed out my messy face or tried to offer anything to clean myself up with because they all had messes of their own. Messes and smiles and noise: the way life should be.

"Presents, presents!" Eoin shouted impatiently from the living room.

I glanced over my shoulder and couldn't stop myself from laughing at the sight of Eoin cross-legged on the floor with a bottle of champagne in his lap and the presents for everyone organised in small clusters along the furniture.

"Are children supposed to have alcohol?" Michael joked, heading toward the living room nonetheless.

Aubrey and Noah each kissed my cheek and wished me "Merry Christmas" before following after Michael. I moved to put my mimosa and hot chocolate on the counter, but Ma stopped me.

"Oh, but I wouldn't want to spill on the rug," I said.

Ma chuckled as she lifted the huge tray that nearly sagged under the weight of the fresh cinnamon rolls.

"Don't worry, dear," she smiled at me. "I'm sure one of the boys will beat you to the punch."

Eoin and Noah bellowed in the living room and threw up their hands.

"Michael, you idiot!" Noah shouted.

"I was reaching for my phone," Michael said as he patted at the spilled mimosa with a holly-printed napkin.

Ma turned back to wink at me before carrying the cinnamon rolls into the living room. Casting away the image of my own mother's bony finger wagging, I scooped up into my arms champagne, hot chocolate, a can of whipped cream, and snowflake sprinkles, because why the hell not!

I paused just outside the living room and took in the merry sight of the family joking, laughing, smiling, snuggling, smearing whipped cream on each other's faces. In my eyes they were perfect, simply perfect.

Yet a sadness tugged at my heart, because it was Darren's absence that crafted this happy little picture. It hurt to think that when he arrived, he would come like a rain cloud, a cold wind, a flurry of snowflakes. Like the solemn Ghost of Christmas Past.

I ached because I felt like there was nothing I could do to help him. And I wanted to. I wanted to help him...

"Hey, is Darren still asleep?" I asked Ma as I joined her on the couch next to my small pile of presents.

"Oh, no, no," Ma answered, leaning in close to me to whisper. "He got called into the shop."

I frowned. "The shop?"

"A family's car broke down just as they were on their way to visit grandparents," Ma explained. "Darren agreed to help them. He left early this morning before everyone woke up."

I nodded, sinking back into the couch and sipping quietly on my mimosa. Darren's "shop emergency" was pretty easy to see through: the shop didn't have an on-call system, so there was no way at all that this so-called family could have reached him. I glanced over at Ma, who was chatting with Aubrey about The Jar. Did she know it was a lie? With those sharp blue eyes, she must have known.

Why didn't she call him out on his bullshit?

Why didn't she insist that he stay with the family on Christmas morning?

Why did she let him be alone?

The warm fire crackled as a log shifted, but it suddenly didn't feel so warm knowing Darren was by himself in that cold garage. The Christmas lights on the tree twinkled, but I couldn't enjoy them quite as much as before when I imagined that the glare of the head lamp beneath the undercarriage of a car was Darren's only light.

I was lost in thought when Eoin's loud voice burst through.

"My Kayleigh Bear first! Shut it, everyone. I'm giving Kayleigh my present."

Blinking, I watched Eoin manoeuvre over the cinnamon rolls and around the maze of drinks to kneel in front of me on the couch.

"Merry Christmas, my Kayleigh Bear, my soulmate, my fairy tale princess," he said, grinning ear to ear.

From behind his back he produced a small box wrapped messily in green and red paper topped with a sparkly silver bow bigger than the box itself. The sight of it made my stomach drop.

The living room dropped into a much more familiar silence as I reached out my hand to take the box.

"What is it?" I asked with a nervous laugh.

Eoin's big paws shook my knees as he bounced up and down excitedly. "You have to open it up to see, silly."

"Yeah, but what is it?" I repeated, this time not succeeding in keeping my voice light.

Eoin rolled his eyes and sighed dramatically before saying, "Here, I'll help you."

Frozen in place, I did little more than hold the box as Eoin tore at the wrapping paper and flung the bow over his shoulder.

"There," he announced, pushing my hands and the black *velvet* box in them, toward me.

My heart started to race. I leaned forward, wishfully thinking that only Eoin could hear me as I whispered, "Eoin, is that a..." I lifted a pointed eyebrow, but Eoin was too busy smiling excitedly at the velvet box to notice. I leaned forward a little more. "Eoin, I really think we should talk first about—"

"Open it! Open it!" Eoin burst out.

Not able to wait any longer, Eoin lifted the lid on the box, which faced everyone but me. Aubrey gasped and covered her mouth. Michael whistled. Noah sent Eoin, who was searching the room for approval, a big thumbs-up.

No, no, no. This cannot be happening. Not like this.

Not with him.

"They're lovely, Eoin, honey," Ma said, smiling softly as she cupped her mug of hot chocolate.

"They were the most expensive in the whole entire store," Eoin announced, beaming with pride in front of me. "The whole entire store! And it was a really fancy store, too."

The utter panic in my mind paused momentarily for a brief interjection of logic: "they". Ma and Eoin said "they".

Twisting the box around, I did my best to hold back the

biggest sigh of relief at the sight of a sparkling pair of diamond earrings.

"Oh, thank God," I muttered under my breath, running a hand over my sweaty forehead.

"What's that, Kayleigh Bear?" Eoin asked.

I smiled and reached out to cup Eoin's cheek. "They're beautiful. Thank you, Eoin."

In reality, I had barely even seen them. They glistened in the soft sunlight, but not in my eyes. They were rare and beautiful, but not in my mind. They would be the envy of every woman I passed, but in my heart the only thing I wanted on my ears was car grease.

"Put them on, put them on," Eoin cheered, getting his entire family in on it.

"Alright, alright," I said, forcing a good-natured laugh.

I eased the diamonds from the backing and slipped them through each ear, tucking back my long red hair so Eoin and the family could see.

"Gorgeous," Aubrey said, before grinning mischievously at Noah. "Please tell me the store was having a buy one, get one free sale."

Noah ruffled Aubrey's hair and tugged her into his lap. "You're getting socks and you know it."

Eoin gave me a quick kiss on the mouth, but apparently his attention span was all used up, because he crawled back across the maze of Christmas treats and lifted the first present he could reach. "My turn!"

I patted Ma's hand and said softly, "I'm going to go see how they look, alright?"

"Of course."

I hurried quickly up the stairs and closed Eoin's door behind me before going to the bed and lifting my pillow beneath which I'd hidden Darren's gift. I buckled it around my waist before slipping back into the hall and ducking into the bathroom.

Inside the bathroom, I stood in front of the mirror and saw the two women before me. There was Eoin's girl: diamond earrings, fancy restaurants and blisters from toe-pinching stilettos. Then there was Darren's girl: hard-working, tough, simple and, yeah, a bit messy.

I had to decide which girl I wanted to be.

The answer was right there in front of me.

It'd been right there in front of me the whole time.

31

DARREN

I added "lying to Ma on Christmas morning" to the long, long list of sins I needed to confess to the priest the next time I made it back to church, if ever. Funny, it wasn't even the worst of my sins and even funnier that it wasn't even close.

Since there was actually no desperate family trying to get to grandma's, I busied myself with cleaning and repairing my own motorcycle. I was lost in the black sheen of the gas tank when the back door swung open.

A burst of cold air barrelled into the garage, dousing any trace of heat that sputtered out of the dusty heater in the corner by the back office. But it wasn't this assault of wintry freeze that sent goose bumps along my bare forearms, my charcoal-grey Henley pushed up to my elbows.

It was the fire burning and pulsing and snapping in Kayleigh's eyes. It was the fire that gave me chills.

She stood in the doorway, outlined by an inky-black night as if she'd travelled to me from the very far reaches of the universe. The wind tugged at strands of her long red hair as she pulled off her white beanie and let it drop by her side, uncaring that it was dirtied by dirt or oil.

Her cheeks were flushed, her pupils wide as her eyes fell on me like a judge's gavel falling in the courtroom, its sharp echo ringing endlessly in my head; the sentence was pronounced, the verdict sealed, my fate doomed:

I was hers.

I was hers.

I was *hers*.

Even though she could never be mine.

Stuffing my grease-covered rag into the back pocket of my jeans, I stood from where I was kneeling beside my motorcycle and dragged my fingers through my hair with a tired sigh. "Look, Kayleigh, I'm sorry that I wasn't there at home with everyone today. But I meant what I said last night."

Kayleigh did not move to close the alleyway door. She did not shiver in the icy blasts of wind from outside. She did not even part her sweet pink lips.

She took a step forward, a step closer to me.

Watching her with curious eyes, I scratched at the back of my neck awkwardly. "I intend to do just what I said I would do," I continued, "I'm going to step back. I'm going to give you and Eoin your chance. I'm going to do the right thing."

Kayleigh did not acknowledge that words were coming out of my mouth as she walked along the '67 Mustang at the back of the garage. Her eyes remained on mine, unflinching, unwavering, undeterred.

"It's just that I'm afraid that doing the right thing is going to be harder than I thought," I said, pausing before adding, "much harder than I thought."

It's why I fled to my garage this morning. It's why I lied to Ma in order to get away. It's why I considered taking a trip somewhere, anywhere. To drive my motorbike as far as it would go and then farther. Just for a little while. Just long enough to get Kayleigh out of my mind, my heart, my soul.

I almost managed to convince myself it would just take a few weeks, a month at most. I almost managed to believe it wouldn't take a fecking eternity.

"It's just that I don't have as much self-control as I thought I had," I said, eyes fixed on Kayleigh as she placed one foot in front of the other on the dirty grey concrete. "Kayleigh, when you're around it's like I don't have any self-control at all and I..."

The rest of my thought trailed off because how could I possibly think of any other words than "beautiful", "seductive", and "irresistible" when Kayleigh was looking into my eyes like that. She had yet to open her mouth as she continued to stride toward me, unaware of what her growing proximity was doing to my heart.

"Kayleigh...you don't know what you do to me." Desperation entered my voice. Desperation because if she kept walking toward me like that, I feared I wouldn't be able to stop myself. Desperation because if she kept walking toward me like that, I feared I wouldn't *want* to stop myself.

"We need to stay away from one another," I said, licking my suddenly dry lips as Kayleigh's fingers traced the long, sleek line of the hood of the car in front of my motorcycle.

Step back, I told myself. Step back before you make a mistake you'll regret, a mistake you won't be able to take back. I knew all about those kinds of mistakes. I knew the pain they brought, the agony they burned into your heart like a brand.

"Kayleigh, I don't think it's a good idea that we work together anymore." My words were half an assertion, half a plea.

Kayleigh did not open her mouth to agree, nor did she open her mouth to disagree. She did not open her mouth at all. Her eyes remained fixed on mine, one foot in front of the other.

She was walking the plank and I was the rough, choppy seas

beneath the safety of the ship. Didn't she know I would drag her under? Didn't she know she would drown in me? Didn't she see that the sparkling sun was far, far, far away from my dark depths?

"Really we shouldn't be alone together at all," I said, then well past desperation.

Step back, my mind screamed. Step away. Run away.

But my feet did not move and Kayleigh's did not stop.

My voice was tight, strained as I said, "I can stay away from the house till the holidays are over and then we can figure out what to do after that."

Now she was close enough that I could smell the scent of her shampoo, fresh cream and strawberries.

I did not step back.

I could make out each distinct freckle along her cheeks, along the tip of her nose, like the lens of a telescope focusing on the night sky.

But I did not step back.

Kayleigh was close enough to me that I could hear her tiny exhales as she breathed, ragged and uneven and breathless.

Still I did not step back.

"Kayleigh, I can't be around you," I said, chest tight, fingers numb at my sides. "I can't be around you because I can't stop myself."

Was she even hearing me? Could she not hear the truth pulsing like a heartbeat through my every word? Could she not see that I was a half-step away from grabbing her, pushing her up against the hood of the Mustang, and tearing at her clothes?

The toe of Kayleigh's boots brushed against mine as she stopped in front of me. She looked up at me through a curtain of eyelashes and all I needed to do was step back, just one step. One step back and I could breathe. I could think straight. I could gain back an ounce of self-control. I could. I could...

"Kayleigh," I whispered, "please, I can't stop myself around you. I can't hold myself back. I—"

Kayleigh's arms reached up to lock around my neck, dragging me down to her, our lips crashing. This was us colliding. We were going to sink together and we'd never need the sun ever again, together in the dark. Her fingers tugged greedily at the hair at the nape of my neck as she pressed herself up against me.

Her lips tasted of mulled wine: hot and spiced and sweet. One sip and I wanted to get drunk on her, her and her alone. No whiskey would ever give me a buzz ever again. A keg of beer wouldn't do a thing for me. Vodka, scotch, bourbon, it was all worthless now.

With an uncontrollable growl, I wrapped my arms around her waist and grabbed handfuls of her coat, eager to have my hands on her hips, her ass, her tits. We kissed hard, desperately, only parting for ragged breaths of air before colliding again.

I wanted her and she wanted me and we were done pretending that it was a choice. There was no decision here: she was mine and I was hers.

Tools clattered to the concrete floor as Kayleigh pushed me roughly against the toolbox behind my motorcycle. She dragged her nails down my back before slipping her fingers beneath my Henley. Her hands were ice and fire against my skin, and I prayed that each graze of her fingertip left a permanent mark on me.

I never wanted her to leave me. I wanted to smell her scent on my skin, I wanted to feel the burn of her lips against mine. I wanted to hear her every ragged breath in my ear forever and forever and forever. I wanted her to claim me, every part of me.

I wanted her to know me, all of me. I wanted her to know my every thought, my every memory, my every dream and hope and fear. I wanted her to know the things I wanted no one to know—

my secrets, my skeletons, my regrets, my nightmares, the dark side of my soul.

I'd spent my whole life since my twin brother's death wanting to hide everything: my pain, my guilt, and more than anything, my happiness, what little ray of sunshine broke through my constant rainstorm. But as I kissed Kayleigh and felt her tight against me, clinging to me just like I clung to her, I no longer wanted to hide.

I wanted her to see my pain.

I wanted her to see my guilt, raw and ugly and brutal.

And I wanted, *needed* her to see why I couldn't be happy, especially not with her.

Pushing Kayleigh away from me felt like ripping away my own arm. When had she become so integral to my being? When had her heart been sewed together with mine so when hers beat faster mine did too? How had I let myself become so dependent on her, the way I was dependent on my own hot red blood pumping through my veins?

"Wait," I gasped, the air without her not filling my lungs the way it had just moments before, "wait, Kayleigh, wait."

She didn't want to stop, her teeth nipping at my lower lip almost making me lose my will.

"Kayleigh, wait," I repeated, gripping her arms. "Stop, please stop."

Kayleigh dropped from her tiptoes and looked up at me with a slightly raised eyebrow, a silent question: why can't we keep going?

Why must we always stop?

Why can't we just take what we want, what we both obviously want?

From the quickness of her breath, the pink flush of her cheeks, the dark stretch of her wide pupils like a mirror as she searched for an answer in the pained lines of my tortured face, I knew.

I knew she didn't understand. She didn't understand why two puzzle pieces that fit like a glove aren't meant to interlock. She didn't understand why instead there had to be a permanent hole: in her heart, in mine. It didn't make sense to her, but it was only because she didn't understand.

She didn't know.

With a shaky exhale, I brushed a strand of wild red hair from Kayleigh's cheek and tucked it gently behind her ear.

"I need to show you something."

32

KAYLEIGH

*W*e stopped on a dark, empty stretch of road.

The wheels of Darren's motorcycle crunched the pebbles along the shoulder of the road as he pulled alongside a rusted metal guard rail and killed the engine with a quick twist of the key. It rumbled, sputtered, then died. My arms were wrapped tightly around Darren's waist and I didn't want to move. Part of me wanted to tell him to turn the key, start the engine of his motorcycle, and drive away. Hell, it didn't matter where. Just away, away, far *away*.

Part of me didn't want Darren to show me what he wanted to show me. Part of me wanted to go back to the garage. Part of me didn't want to know.

Because part of me feared Darren brought me here to say goodbye.

I sensed the same hesitation in Darren's tense back as he remained still on his motorcycle in front of me. Was he pondering just kicking back up the kickstand and driving away? Was he considering taking me back to his place and finishing what I started? Did he want to pretend for just an hour or two more that we could have *everything*?

Because I did…

I squeezed my eyes closed and fought back a sudden swell of tears when Darren finally swung his leg over the motorcycle and climbed off. The cold of the frigid night flooded in to fill the void, and terror gripped me because I wasn't sure I would ever be warm again. Craning my neck over my shoulder, I found Darren kicking at the dirt along the guard rail, hands stuffed into his pockets. Past him the lights of Dublin twinkled in lieu of stars. I stared down the dark, tree-lined stretch of road before slipping off the motorcycle and moving to stand shivering next to Darren. Our shoulders brushed against one another's but he felt miles upon miles away.

He was somewhere colder. He was somewhere darker. Somewhere far out to sea.

"I thought maybe it might still be here," Darren finally said, his voice almost indistinguishable from the wind.

I tried to cling to it, but it slipped through my fingers and was carried out into the cold, lost forever.

"Why are we here, Darren?" I asked. I tried to keep the fear from my voice; I failed.

Darren was still staring down at the dirt and rocks, shifting both around with the toe of his grease-stained boot as I searched his unreadable face.

"It should be around here somewhere," he said.

"What?"

Darren didn't look at me as he answered, "The wrench."

I frowned in confusion, twisting around to look around my feet. It was just dirt and rocks and trash tangled amongst thorny weeds beneath the guard rail.

"A wrench?" I asked.

Darren kicked at the same patch of dirt and seemed confused to not find any glint of a wrench.

"I don't think anyone would have taken it," he said. "It was a piece of shit. I could barely hold it myself. Damn thing kept slipping in my hands. I don't know how many times I sliced myself open because of it."

I narrowed my eyes as Darren pulled his right hand from his pocket. He twisted it this way and that, studying the jagged scars along his palm as if he hadn't seen them in years. I'd always assumed he got them working on cars; I had only been working on cars for a few weeks and I already had a couple of scars in the making of my own. But I was starting to sense that Darren's scars came from one specific car, on one specific night.

"Darren, what happened here?" I asked, voice nearly trembling.

I reached over to grab his hand—half for his sake, half for mine—but he flinched away from my touch like I'd burned him somehow.

"Please," I whispered.

Darren slipped his scarred hand back into his pocket as if ashamed at the sight of it and sighed softly, tiredly.

"I thought I couldn't possibly love anyone more than I loved her," he started, still staring at his dirty boots, still not lifting his eyes to the city lights, still not lifting his eyes to me. "Her name was Sophie and I wanted her more than anything. Or at least at the time I thought I wanted her more than anything, more than anyone."

My heart rate quickened but I bit back the questions, the millions of questions, that raced into my head.

"Of course, her father didn't approve of me. He wanted his daughter to marry a lawyer or a doctor, like him. Not a dirt-poor, no-future mechanic," Darren continued. "We were going to leave. To America, we thought. I don't think I had enough money to get us across to England, let alone America, but we were going. Nothing would stop us. Because we had each other and that was enough."

Darren was silent for a long time after he said this, head bent in petition like there was a crucifix somewhere underneath the pebbles and dust.

"Jaime caught me as I was leaving," Darren finally said. "He wasn't supposed to. But that damn stair, the third one from the bottom, creaked."

I knew the one. I'd seen Darren skip it every time he climbed the stairs in Ma's house.

"We fought," Darren continued. "He couldn't believe I was choosing Sarah over my family. He couldn't believe I would put anyone over Ma, over my brothers, over him. He couldn't believe I wasn't even going to tell him. I said I was leaving and he said he was going to the bar to drown my memory in whiskey. We both left black tyre marks on Ma's driveway because we each took off so quickly, so angrily."

Darren swallowed heavily and closed his eyes. "We said terrible things to one another. Terrible, regrettable things," he whispered. "We said the kind of terrible things siblings always say to each other when they fight, because they always believe there will be time to make up, to say sorry, to hug and laugh and move on. But...but..."

Everyone says the scariest parts of a roller coaster are the dips, the falls, the hills. But they're wrong. The scariest part is when you're climbing, climbing oh, so slowly when the rails beneath the cart go click...click...click...

That's the scariest part because you know what is coming, you can see it clear as day. You know the fall is coming and yet there is nothing you can do at that point to stop it.

My stomach lurched there on the side of that dark, empty road, because I knew then where the story was going. There wasn't a goddamn thing I could do to stop it.

"At a gas station about ten or so miles down the road from here, I called Ma's house just like I planned to," Darren went on.

"I was going to just leave a voicemail explaining where I was going, assuring her that I would be fine. It was just going to be a voicemail because it was late and everyone should have been asleep...but Ma answered."

Click...click...click...

Darren shook his head just slightly, as if he was confused. "She wasn't supposed to answer. She..."

Click...click...click...

I had been wanting Darren to turn to me, to look at me, to rest his burdens on me since we arrived to this cold, desolate place, but when he finally did I suddenly wished he hadn't. It wasn't just the obvious pain in his eyes, it was the knowledge that he'd been holding onto it, all alone, for all these years. No one deserved that, least of all him.

"She wasn't supposed to answer," he repeated once more like a broken record unable to move backward, unable to move forward. "She wasn't supposed to answer. She..."

Darren looked away when the threat of tears became obvious in his stormy eyes. He blinked as he surveyed the city skyline below us.

"Do you see the lights there?" he asked me, guiding my gaze with a pointed hand that was shaking, but probably not from the cold. "Right there next to that high-rise."

I nodded; I wasn't sure I could form words even if I wanted to.

"That's where she said they took him," Darren said. "That's where she said I needed to go to, where I need to *hurry* to. That's where my Ma said I needed to go to say goodbye."

Click...click...click...

Why did I let Darren get off the motorcycle? Why did I let him stop in this godforsaken place? Why didn't we run away?

But none of that mattered, because it was too late.

Click...click...click...

"I'm still not sure what caused the tyre to pop right here on my way back," Darren said next. "A piece of glass? A rock? A vengeful God?"

I followed his eyes to the faded yellow lines along the cracked asphalt. His breath came out shaky and uneven before he continued.

"I was trying to get the spare tyre on the car when Jaime died. I'd changed a thousand tyres before that and I...I just couldn't get it on. My twin died and I was working on a fecking car."

Darren clutched his chest with his hands, but it did little to muffle the scream of his heart. He was falling and there was nothing I could do but hold on.

"I was this fucking close." Darren jabbed an angry finger at the small twinkling lights of the hospital in the distance. "I could see it. I could fucking *see* it. It was right there. Right there. And I couldn't get to him. I couldn't..."

Darren sank to his knees. I lowered myself to the ice-cold earth next to him.

"At first Ma didn't want to tell me." Darren's voice was raw. "At first she didn't want to tell me how much I'd...how much I'd missed him by."

I scooted closer to Darren, not caring that the hard ground sliced my knees like tiny daggers, and gently rested my hand on his quivering back.

"Ten minutes," he spat. "Ten fucking minutes."

Darren rocked back and forth before leaning his head back to stare at the stars above the swaying pines.

"No one asked me where I was," he said to the sky. "Even today, no one in my family has dared to ask where I was that I... that I missed him."

Finally he looked over at me. I tried not to flinch away from the agony etched across his face.

"No one knows I was here," he whispered. "No one knows I was here with blood literally on my hands."

Darren stared down at his palms held up against his knees. We both studied the scars as if they might lead to an answer, any answer. But there was none. There never would be.

"I made a vow that I would never make the same mistake I made that night," Darren said, again hiding his hands in his pockets. "I vowed to never put my heart before my family ever again. I took my chance at happiness and...and I'm not taking it again. Kayleigh, I can't."

Darren looked at me with sadness in his eyes. My fears were realised in that terrible moment: he was saying goodbye.

Click...click...click...

As it turned out I hadn't fallen yet. I hadn't even started to fall. I was still climbing higher and higher and higher. The drop was still coming and it was going to hurt like hell, like absolute hell.

"I'm sorry," he whispered, "I just can't."

Click...click...click...

33

KAYLEIGH

I clung to Darren's back as he drove us home. But the warmth of his body against mine no longer filled the void, cold and black and empty. The wind was crueller, the road longer, the night was never-ending darkness.

"Can you stop at the garage?" I asked at a swinging red light of an empty, silent intersection.

Darren twisted his head back.

"I forgot my beanie," I said, answering his question before he had to ask it. "And if I'm not going to be, um...well, it might be a while before I'm back if—"

"Alright." Darren's voice was distant as if it was just an echo and he was still back in the dust alongside the guard rail. I was holding onto a ghost. Despite the fact that I could feel his heart beating beneath my palm, I couldn't help but think it wasn't entirely untrue.

Darren switched on his turn signal. I leaned with him as he guided the motorcycle through the turn. We moved together, but it was obvious that we were being dragged apart.

If I wanted Darren, I was going to have to fight for him. But I wasn't raised to fight. I wasn't sure I knew how. I didn't know what to say. I didn't know how to change a mind that was set in tragedy, petrified with guilt.

The headlamp of Darren's motorcycle stretched across the garage door. We both sat in silence as it clanked and clattered on its way up.

"Umm, I'll be right back," I said awkwardly over the idling of the engine.

All I received in response from Darren was a curt nod of his chin in his all-encompassing helmet. As I walked across the driveway, I glanced back at Darren, but his helmet was faced away from me. My eyes avoided the crooked toolbox at the front of the garage and the mess of tools around it as I made my way to the back to retrieve my beanie.

If I looked over at the toolbox I would remember Darren's body crashing into it, mine following after. I would remember the heat of his lips against mine. I would remember how close we had been, how damn close...

After snatching up my beanie, I dusted it off by slapping it across my knee. But there were smudges of dirt from the floor and I knew the beanie was ruined. It was no longer white and pristine and beautiful. Most would throw it out, get a new one.

But I wanted this beanie. I loved this beanie.

I walked to the front of the garage but did not step outside.

"I reject your goodbye, Darren," I shouted out to him.

He pulled off his helmet and tucked it under one arm. I was waiting for his eyes when they found mine. "What?" he called out.

I cupped my hands over my mouth and shouted each word as loudly as I could, "I. Reject. Your. Goodbye!"

Darren switched off the ignition to his motorcycle and irritably waved me over toward him. "Come on, Kayleigh. It's getting late."

I shook my head. "Nope. You can take your goodbye and shove it."

Darren sighed and rubbed at his eyes. "I'm tired, Kayleigh. Let's please go."

"No."

My toes grazed the line between the garage and the driveway. I would not cross it. Darren would have to drag me kicking and screaming across it if he wanted me to leave. I wasn't going anywhere. Hell, no.

"Kayleigh, get over here or I'm leaving," Darren threatened.

I petulantly crossed my arms over my chest. "Then leave," I challenged. "But know I'll be right here whenever you come back. I'll be right here. Because I'm not saying goodbye. Not tonight. Not ever."

Anger entered Darren's voice. "Cut the shite and get over here so we can get some sleep."

"I don't accept your goodbye, Darren," I called out to him in the dead silence of the neighbourhood.

Families were enjoying hot chocolates around twinkling Christmas trees, but I no longer cared if they heard me. I didn't give a fuck if I was interrupting any "Silent Nights". If peace on earth meant letting Darren go, then for all I cared the whole fecking world could burn to ashes.

"I am not doing this right now, Kayleigh." Darren's voice shook with something that was nearing fury as he pointed at the concrete next to his motorcycle. "Get over here."

My response to this was simply to pull on my dirty grease-stained beanie and glare across the driveway at him in the harsh glow of the headlamp of his motorcycle. Darren finally threw his helmet to the concrete and stalked toward me in the garage.

His voice was a low, dangerous hiss as he said, "Which part of what I explained to you up there didn't you understand?"

I stood my ground inside the garage as he stopped in front of me just outside of it, chest heaving in anger.

"Huh?" he said, lowering his face so his nose was an inch from mine. "What part of do I need to explain again to get through your thick, stubborn skull?"

I wasn't backing down. Not this time. I pushed myself up onto my tiptoes so Darren had to lean back to avoid our lips again colliding. "You need to explain to me the part where any of what happened that night means that you no longer deserve happiness," I said, voice not wavering even in the slightest.

Darren's wide eyes flashed with anger. "We're leaving." He reached for my arm to drag me back toward the motorcycle, but I wrenched it free from him. "Jaysus fuck, Kayleigh!"

Oh, was he angry? Was he? Well that made two of us then.

"This is my garage," Darren said, following after me, tight on my heels as I marched farther inside. "This is *my* garage so you need to get out. *Now*."

I whirled around and jabbed a finger against Darren's chest. "*Your* garage?"

The surprise that widened his eyes was expected as he continued to glare at me, his chest rising and falling raggedly.

"Is that what you really believe?" I pressed, this time forcing Darren to step back as I advanced. "You really think that this is *your* garage?"

"Of course, I do," he said. "Who else would it belong to?"

Without a word, I turned on my heel and marched straight to the back office.

This time Darren did not follow after me. He remained where he was as he called after me. "What in the hell are you doing?"

I ignored his angry shouting as I kneeled and yanked open the bottom file folder drawer that I organized one of the first days of working for Darren. All his invoices had been in a haphazard, wobbling pile atop the dust-covered boom box in the corner of the office. My fingers quickly carded through the different manila folders I painstakingly labelled till I found the one I was looking for: O'Sullivan.

Making sure to speak loud enough for Darren to hear me outside the office, I read from the invoice: "Noah O'Sullivan dropped off his car on April 5th for a 'strange noise'. Result: no noise found."

I flung the invoice over my shoulder and outside the office.

"Eoin O'Sullivan dropped off his car on April 18th for 'possible flat tyre'. Result: tyres fine."

The flimsy yellow invoice wafted to the concrete floor behind me as I snatched up the next one.

"Miriam O'Sullivan dropped off her car, brand new, I might add, on April 22nd for 'weird rattle sound'. Result: brand new car is brand new and just fine."

Invoice after invoice I shouted out and tossed behind me. There was a small spread out stack on the grease-covered floor behind me, and I hadn't even put a dent in the O'Sullivan folder. It was "weird noise" after "strange sound" after "need a check-up" after "wobbly tyre": made up excuse after made up excuse after made up excuse. I was grabbing yet another invoice when I heard Darren's footsteps. Kneeling there on the floor of the back office, I glanced over my shoulder to find Darren standing in the doorway.

"Should I keep going?" I asked, no longer shouting.

The anger had drained from Darren's face as he stared down at the pile of invoices at his feet. He was left looking lost, confused, helpless. From the floor, I stretched out a hand to him. He glanced over at it, hesitated, but then slowly slipped his hand into mine. I eased him to the floor of the office next to me, pulled the file folder out of the drawer, and placed it in Darren's lap.

He didn't open the folder. He didn't card through the remaining invoices, all from his family. He didn't even touch them. But he didn't look away from the overwhelming stack.

"I know that you see this garage as your prison, Darren," I said softly.

Darren flinched at my words but did not look up from the file folder.

"Because you were working on a car when Jaime passed, you feel it is your punishment to work on cars forever," I continued, my words bolder than any before in my life. I swallowed heavily, fighting back doubt and uncertainty and went on. "You think you deserve to be trapped in dark, tight spaces. You think you deserve to have your fingers bleed daily, your body ache nightly. You keep it cold in here, barely using the heater, to torture yourself. You keep it dark because prisons are dark. You think you deserve to be locked away in a cold, grey block, separated from happiness. Separated from your family."

Darren's thumb moved just the tiniest bit to run along the very edge of the file folder in his lap. Maybe he had hoped I hadn't seen it. But I saw it. And it gave me hope.

"But Darren," I said after a long, quiet pause, "can't you see? Can't you see your family never left your side?"

The sob that escaped Darren's lips, voluntary or not, grabbed my heart with cold iron fists and wrenched it apart.

"All this time you thought you were alone," I whispered. "But you were wrong, Darren. Your family, they came to you, they came *for* you. To your darkest, loneliest, pain-filled place, they came. Again and again and again."

I reached over and tapped the thick file folder with my pointer finger. "This is proof, Darren. This is proof that they love you, that they will *always* love you."

Darren finally looked up at me and his eyes were red, his eyelashes stained with tears. He looked young, far younger than he was. He looked for just a moment like a fifteen-year-old boy again: stricken with the loss of his twin and buried under a sea of guilt when he knew well and good he couldn't swim.

"Your family loves you."

I wondered if he heard those words that terrible night; I wondered if he believed them. I wondered if he believed them now.

"Darren, your family loves you."

Tears fell across Darren's wind-chapped cheeks as he clasped the file folder tight to his chest and leaned towards me. I held my arms open for him and he sagged against my chest, nestling his head against my breast.

"Your family loves you," I whispered, leaning over him so I could reach his ear with my soft words. I wrapped my arms around him and held him as my coat soaked up his tears.

"Darren, I—"

I knew the words I wanted to say and yet my voice halted into silence in that tiny back office. I wanted to hold Darren tighter, but his heart fluttered against mine like a butterfly and I was afraid of what would happen if I held too tightly, if I tried to keep something that was never mine in the first place.

Darren, *I* love you.

That's what I wanted to say. That's what my heart longed to say. But a string of questions one after the other kept me from uttering those simple words:

Would he believe me?

Was he ready to believe me?

Would he ever be ready to believe me?

And how was I supposed to go on if the answer was "no"?

34

DARREN

*O*ur footsteps across the cracked sidewalk leading to Ma's house were silent in the still of the night. I tried to insert the key as quietly as possible and pushed open the door inch by inch despite the frigid cold outside, praying that it wouldn't creak. We slipped inside like ghosts across the threshold, careful of the loose floorboard that would moan under the pressure of any heel. The small foyer was drenched in darkness, and Kayleigh and I were forced tight together on the small doormat by the low shelf stacked with mud-covered boots on one side and on the other, the coat rack nearly sagged under the weight of winter jackets, scarves, hats, mittens and gloves.

"We should take our shoes off," I whispered as softly as possible.

In the dim glow of the street light through the narrow windows on either side of the door, I saw Kayleigh nod.

We knelt as if the welcome mat crusted with dirt beneath our knees was a smooth, cold pew in a candlelit church, our small, nervous exhales the only sound in the sleeping house. We were crammed against one another as if we together shared a confessional booth, the mahogany walls pressing tighter and tighter against us. Her hair, which curtained her face as she leaned over toward her feet, smelled of incense, thick and rich and lingering.

My fingers shook as I pulled at the laces of my boots, and I wondered if it was the same for Kayleigh. Was this a sacred moment for her like it was for me? Here on the floor in my ma's house? Silent and hushed and alone?

"Here," I whispered, closing the distance between us and laying my hand gently over hers.

My fingers were ice cold, the tips tinged blue from the freezing ride home, but Kayleigh did not flinch. She tucked her long red hair behind her ear and her green eyes flashed in the dark as she watched me gently ease off her unlaced boot. She moved her other foot so I could do the same, and I didn't dare glance up at her as I did so.

Because if Kayleigh was sitting at the end of my bed instead of just inside the doorway, I would not stop at her boots. I would slide down her wool socks, fingers grazing along her silken skin, tracing the shape of her ankle, her foot, her toes. I would take my time unbuttoning her jeans, because I would want to remember every flutter of her stomach, every flinch of her fingers resting by her sides as she tried to keep herself from touching me. I would press a trail of kisses down her thighs as I pulled off her jeans. I would whisper for her to lift her hands over her head.

In our socks, Kayleigh and I stood without speaking. She stared up at me, our chests just inches from one another, before reaching up and brushing her thumb along my cheek. Then without a word she climbed the stairs and disappeared around the corner. From the base of the stairs I heard her door creak slightly once, then twice.

I let out a shaky exhale and sagged against the front door, dragging a hand over my face. I was just about to go upstairs to my childhood bedroom to lie to myself about getting some sleep when the front door swung open, slamming into my side.

"Shite, sorry, sorry," Eoin hissed as he slipped inside, tugging off his hat. "Oh, Darren, hey. Beautiful night, am I right? Have you ever seen a more beautiful night in all of your life?"

I frowned at my brother. "Yeah, I guess it's alright."

Eoin suddenly tugged me into a breath-stealing, lung-crushing hug.

"Okay, okay." I struggled to push him away. "That's good."

"What are you doing up?" Eoin asked as he finally released me.

Avoiding Eoin's eyes, I scratched at the back of my neck and shrugged. "Work, you know?"

"Right, right," Eoin whispered as he kicked off his massive boots.

I was on the first step, hand on the railing, when I paused and looked back at my brother. "What are *you* doing up?"

Eoin's hands fidgeted in his pockets as he bit his lower lip to hold back a grin.

I turned around on the step to face him and raised an eyebrow. "Eoin?"

Eoin's eyes shone brightly as if it were Christmas morning all over again and he was about to run down the stairs to see what Santa left him underneath the tree.

"Eoin?" I repeated, stepping back off the stair as my suspicion grew. "What's the story?"

"I was going to make it a surprise for everyone tomorrow…" he said hesitantly, his fingers tapping on something solid in his coat pocket.

I frowned. "It?"

Eoin chewed at the inside of his mouth, clearly debating something in his head.

"Eoin?"

Finally Eoin looked over at me with a massive grin. Before I knew what was happening, my brother had me by the wrist and was dragging me along behind him toward the crammed little study. He pushed me inside and I stumbled into the office chair as Eoin looked up and down the clearly empty hallway several times before hurrying to close the double doors behind him. He stepped past me to switch on the floor lamp, and I stared in confusion at his huffing and puffing chest.

"Eoin, what in the world is going on?"

Practically hopping with excitement, Eoin fished a small box out of his coat pocket, flipped it open, and displayed for me a diamond ring.

Eoin tried to keep his voice as close to a whisper as he could as he said, "I'm going to propose to Kayleigh tomorrow!"

I stared at the glistening rock in the black velvet box as my mind sputtered. I shook my head. "Propose what?"

I glanced up at Eoin, who laughed and violently smacked me on the arm with his bear cub paw. "You're so funny, Daz," he grinned before sighing in relief. "Man, I'm glad that I ran into you. I've been dying to tell someone. I'm just so excited, you know?"

Again I frowned in confusion at the ring in Eoin's big palm. My mind couldn't put together what it was for, who it was for.

"Eoin," I managed to say slowly. "Are you talking about proposing marriage?"

Eoin nodded emphatically, turning around the ring so that he could see it. "Isn't that deadly?" he asked me.

But I had a question of my own, a very pressing question. "But...to who?"

Eoin pointed a beefy finger at me, shaking his head. "Brother, when did you become so funny?" he laughed. "So do you think she'll like it?"

My eyes were growing wide and I wasn't entirely sure I could feel my fingertips. "Who?"

Eoin chuckled. "Kayleigh, of course."

Eoin handed me the diamond engagement ring. I pulled it gently from its plush cushion. It felt heavy in my sweaty palm.

I thought I knew real. I thought Kayleigh's ankle in my hand as I pulled her foot free from her boot was real. I thought the brush of her thumb along my cheekbone was real. I thought the pounding of my heart as I watched her climb the stairs was real.

But all of that suddenly felt like a mist in the wind, like a drop of dew on a velvet petal that would soon fall, like a lingering dream that would be forgotten by the next night compared to the hard, cold diamond sparkling beautifully in the lamp light.

Panic flooded my chest. I quickly shoved the ring back toward Eoin, not bothering to put it back inside the box.

"Eoin, do you know what this means?" I asked him as I pushed myself up from the office chair.

I couldn't sit still, not when my world was falling apart.

Eoin just chuckled. "It means peanut butter and jelly sandwiches for a few weeks," he joked. "That's what this means. My accountant is going to be *pissed* on Monday, that's for sure."

This couldn't be happening. This could not be happening. Eoin was grinning proudly down at Kayleigh's diamond ring when I stalked over to him, grabbed him by the shoulders, and pushed him down into the chair. Leaning over, I gripped the armrests till my knuckles shone white. "Eoin, you just met her," I said, trying to keep my voice from shaking. "You don't even know her."

Eoin frowned. The ring box snapped loudly as he closed it, like the jaws of a crocodile around the neck of its doomed prey. "I know everything I need to know," Eoin defended himself. "I know that we're soulmates and that we're meant to be together."

I growled in frustration before throwing my hands up into the air. "Soulmates?! Soulmates, Eoin?" I was having a hard time keeping my voice down as the grandfather clock in the corner neared midnight. "Eoin, what does that even mean? What does soulmate even mean?"

Eoin's own frustration mirrored mine as he, too, threw his hands up into the air. "What kind of a question is that, Daz?" he demanded. "Everyone and their ma knows what a soulmate is."

"Then tell me."

"What?" Eoin stared up at me from the chair.

I crossed my arms over my chest and leaned forward slightly. "Then tell me what a soulmate is, Eoin. If it's *so* obvious and 'everyone and their ma' knows, then tell me. Tell me what the fuck is a soulmate."

Eoin was silent for a moment, lips parting and closing, parting and closing as he searched for an answer. Finally he shrugged and dismissed me with a casual wave of his hand. "Stop fucking with me, Darren," he grumbled. "I'm proposing tomorrow because Kayleigh and I are meant to be together. And that's that."

"But how do you know?" I exclaimed before realising everyone, including Kayleigh, was asleep upstairs, and I repeated in a whisper, "How do you know you're meant to be together?"

Eoin shrugged. "I don't know. You just know."

I dragged my fingers through my hair, clenching my eyes shut to try to regain some self-control. "But *how*? *How* do you know?"

Eoin just blinked up at me, clearly bewildered by my impassioned interrogation.

"Do you know you're meant to be with her because every time you see her, you're filled with heart-aching anguish because you know at some point she'll have to leave and you'll have to survive somehow till she's with you again?"

Eoin was silent.

"Do you know you're meant to be with her because you butt heads and fight and argue and you haven't cared about anything or anyone enough to butt heads or fight or argue with in such a long fucking time?"

I don't know when I started pacing back and forth wildly in front of him, but my feet suddenly couldn't stay still any longer. Eoin's eyes followed me this way, then that, like he was trapped watching a frantic tennis match.

"Do you know you're meant to be with her because she makes you feel everything so strongly, so vividly, so clearly—love and anger and passion and desire and drive and freedom and happiness—when everything before her had been numb and dull for year after year?"

My words were tumbling out so quickly, my thoughts whirling so rapidly, that I didn't even see Eoin in the office chair anymore. I didn't even see the office anymore, for that matter. I was back in the Dublin Mountains with Kayleigh in the ice cold. My lips were back on hers and they were fire.

"Do you know you're meant to be with her because she sees your mess and doesn't run from it? Do you know you're meant to be with her because she sees your past and doesn't turn away? Do you know you're meant to be with her because she sees the mud and tar and grease on your soul and isn't afraid to get her fingers dirty?"

I was panting as I came to a stop in the centre of the office. I saw the rug again instead of a forest floor of pine needles. The rows of books replaced the rows of twinkling lights of Dublin in the distance. I saw the lamp, the computer, the desk.

I saw Eoin.

I sucked in a shaky breath as he stared at me. I felt like I'd run all the way back from the Dublin Mountains: cheeks red, lungs burning, skin hot.

Eoin laughed. "Yeah, brother, something sort of like that, I guess." Eoin pushed himself up from the chair and patted me awkwardly on the shoulder. "Alright, well, I've got a big day tomorrow, so I'm going to head off to bed."

He turned toward the door, but I had to ask. I just had to. As Eoin was reaching for the door handle, I finally asked the question I feared asking above all else.

"Do you love her?"

When Eoin asked "What?" I at first thought that he hadn't heard me, my words had been spoken softly, like a prayer. But then I saw the confusion on Eoin's face as he glanced back over his shoulder at me.

I repeated, each word more fearful than the last, "Eoin, do you love Kayleigh?"

Eoin frowned slightly before quickly saying, "I already told you, Darren, we're soulmates."

I shook my head, stepping closer to my brother. "But, Eoin, do you lo—"

"I'm going to bed." Eoin opened the door, stepped out of the office, and closed it roughly without another word, leaving me alone. At least I wished he had left me alone.

I wasn't alone.

Eoin had left me with that unanswered question ringing in my ears, echoing in the small office again and again.

Do you love Kayleigh?

Do you love Kayleigh?

Do you love Kayleigh?

Eoin didn't have an answer.

But I did.

35

DARREN

*P*erhaps it went without saying that I didn't sleep that night. Perhaps it went without saying that I didn't even try.

The sheets of my childhood bed remained stiff and tucked up neatly beneath my carefully arranged pillows while my thoughts tossed and thrashed. Every time I fell just under the surface of sleep, I awoke without fail in a cold sweat as if from some terrible nightmare.

I was living my nightmare.

After Eoin went up to bed, I paced the short, narrow hallway outside the row of rooms till I feared I'd worn a hole in the carpet. I considered knocking on the door where Eoin and Kayleigh slept. I could make up some excuse why I needed to talk to Kayleigh at 1:47 in the morning. Alone.

But every time I held my fist suspended up against the door in the dark, knuckles no more than an inch or two from the peeling woodgrain, I stopped myself.

What was I going to tell her?

So what if I knocked on the door? If Kayleigh opened it just an inch or two, squinting bleary-eyed out into the hallway. If I managed to convince her to sneak out with me, got her to the kitchen where we could talk in private.

What was I going to tell her?

"Kayleigh, Eoin is offering to give you more in one day than I could ever give you in a lifetime, and it would help me out a ton if you could just say, 'No thanks'."

"Kayleigh, you have a chance at happiness and I'd like very much for you to throw that away for me."

"Kayleigh, you're about to get the possibility of a brand-new start. But maybe instead, you'd like me to drag you down with my past, my guilt, my misery? Maybe you'd like that instead? Yeah?"

So every time, I pulled my fist back from the door and pounded it instead in frustration against my forehead. I watched the hazy light of dawn crawl across the living room floor and drove myself crazy wondering what the fuck I was going to do.

My red-rimmed eyes stung and weariness tugged at my eyelids like anchors by the time Ma came down the stairs the next morning.

"Darren, honey, are you alright?"

I nodded as she leaned over to give me a kiss on the cheek. I should have given her my usual response of "Of course," my Band-Aid of choice for the last ten years, but that morning I just couldn't manage anything but a nod.

Ma cupped my face in her hands as she studied my sleep-deprived eyes. "Come help me with the pancakes?"

She slipped her hand around mine and gently but firmly pulled me out of the chair and toward the kitchen. We worked together in the silence of the early morning. I stirred the batter as she buttered the griddle.

"Should we put chocolate chips in?"

I glanced over at her. "Chocolate chips?"

She nodded, reaching up to the cabinet above her head and pulling out a bag of semi-sweet chunks.

"We haven't had chocolate chips in our pancakes in a long time," she said, smiling over at me.

She held the bag out for me to take. I stared at it, mixing spoon frozen in the bowl of pancake batter. We both knew why we hadn't had pancakes with chocolate chips in such a long time: they had been Jaime's favourite.

If a recipe called for a cup of chocolate chips, Jaime doubled it and then added another half cup "just in case". He never explained what the "just in case" was for. But as I still stared at the bag Ma hung suspended in the space between us over the stove, waiting for me to simply reach out and take them, I thought maybe I'd found an answer after all these long, painful years. Perhaps Jaime knew, or at least a little part of him knew.

He added his "just in case" chocolate chips just in case it was his last pancakes. He added those extra few morsels because he might not get any more. He enjoyed those chocolate pancakes (more chocolate fondue than pancake) because he wasn't going to take anything for granted, not even a stupid fecking pancake.

Because he had his one life. And he was going to live it happy and fulfilled and without regrets.

My breath came out shaky as I wrapped my fingers around the bag of chocolate chips, my hand brushing against Ma's. Her sharp blue eyes watched me with nothing but kindness.

"You alright?"

I gave her a small smile in the first light of dawn. "No," I answered truthfully. "But I'm working on it."

Ma simply nodded, let go of the bag of chocolate chips, and returned to pushing the melting butter around the hot griddle. I poured the chocolate chips into the batter, stopped, and then tipped the whole bag over.

Just in case.

I WAS GOING to talk to Kayleigh.

I was going to tell her what was about to happen and that I wanted her to say no. I was going to tell her that I wanted her, I wanted to be *with* her.

I just needed to get her alone before Eoin popped the question. That was proving harder to do than expected.

"Darren!" Aubrey tugged at my arm as I was trying to slip through the kitchen when I saw Kayleigh come downstairs and join Noah on the couch. "Darren, wait, wait. Can you run to the store?"

I turned back to her, trying not to look frustrated. "The store?"

"I forgot the shallots for my famous omelette."

From the couch, Noah leaned his head back and shouted, "Nobody knows about your omelette, darling."

Ignoring him, Aubrey again tugged at my arm. "Please, Darren."

I checked the busy-as-usual kitchen where everyone was preoccupied with something, even, surprisingly, Eoin.

"Can't Noah go?" I asked, one last desperate attempt to get out of going.

Noah's excuse came in the form of an empty mimosa glass raised above his head.

So I went to the store. I cut more wood outside for the fire. I loaded the tablecloth into the laundry machine so it could be dry for dinner that night. I figured out which light bulb needed to be replaced when a strand went out on the tree. I checked the air pressure in Ma's car and Eoin's car and Michael's car. And I... and I...and I...

"Hey, have you seen Kayleigh?" I asked Noah, catching him on his way back from the champagne bottle to continue his checkers game with Aubrey on the floor in the living room.

"She went up for a shower."

I nodded and took the stairs two at a time to the second floor. I'd just seen Eoin fidgeting with the ring box in the pocket of his hoodie and it'd made me nervous. If I was going to talk to Kayleigh, it had to be now.

My heart was racing as I rushed to the bathroom door and gave it two quick knocks before slipping inside.

"Just a sec—Darren!" Kayleigh's eyes went wide as she held her towel tight against her body. "Darren, what the hell?" she hissed, pointing an angry hand at the door. "Get out!"

I held up my hands and averted my eyes. "Sorry, sorry."

"I don't care," Kayleigh growled. "Get out."

I shook my head and stayed where I was. "No. I'm afraid this is my last chance."

Kayleigh's mouth was halfway open, probably ready to hiss another "Get out", but she stopped herself. "What do you mean?" she asked. "Last chance? Last chance for what?"

The words that I'd rehearsed in my mind to say to Kayleigh disappeared, and I was left stumbling for them in the steam-filled bathroom. I wanted to tell her how I felt about her. I wanted to tell her how special she was to me. I wanted to tell her that I wanted nothing else in the whole entire world but her.

But fear tightened my throat and I couldn't get those words out.

Instead, I blurted out, "Kayleigh, you need to break up with Eoin."

Kayleigh sighed and dragged a hand over her damp face. "Darren, is this really the time and is this really the *place* to discuss this?"

"You need to do it right now."

I glanced over at Kayleigh and found her staring at me in confusion. "Right now?"

I nodded.

"On Stephen's Day?" she whispered. "In front of your entire family? The day after *Christmas*?"

I looked her straight in the face and said without a trace of doubt, "Yes."

Kayleigh stared at me, dumbfounded. "What?"

It looked like she was trying to find the punchline somewhere in my grey eyes: she could keep looking if she wanted. There wasn't one.

"I need you to do it right now, actually."

Kayleigh laughed despite the fact that there was no humour in the tone of my voice. "Right now? What, here in the bathroom? With me in a towel and you standing there?"

"Kayleigh, I'm not kidding," I said. "Eoin is—"

The pounding of footsteps echoed down the hallway to the bathroom, and Kayleigh silenced me with a frantic finger to her lips. The knock at the door came mere seconds later.

"Kayleigh Bear?" Eoin called against the woodgrain of the door outside.

Kayleigh's eyes were focused on mine as she answered, "Just a second."

She jabbed a finger at the shower and mouthed, *"Get in. I'll cover for us."* I tried to whisper that I needed to tell her something, but she smacked a hand quickly over my mouth as she pushed me toward the shower.

"My little Kayleigh Bear," Eoin called again. "Can I come in?"

Kayleigh's eyes went wide as the doorknob turned. "Hold on, hold on, I'm coming," she shouted, not doing a good job of hiding the nervousness from her voice. "Just...just a second."

My calf hit against the edge of the tub and I stumbled in as

Kayleigh shoved me back. I tried to whisper, "Kayleigh, wait. Eoin is—"

She pulled back the curtain to hide me. Before I could stop her, she was opening the bathroom door.

"Hey, there," I heard Kayleigh say in a voice a little too cheerful and a little too high-pitched before the lights flipped off and the door shut behind her.

Alone in the shower I listened to her guide Eoin away from the bathroom till her voice disappeared. "Wow, it smells delicious in here. I can't wait to eat. I'm just going to change and then I'll..."

Everything around me was now silent. I wasted my chance to warn her. I wasted my chance to tell her how I felt. I wasted my chance to argue why she shouldn't say yes to a successful and wealthy rugby star who could take good care of her.

I wasted my chance to give the only argument I had for why she should choose me being simply that I loved her.

Now I would have to wait and see.

I would have to wait and see if she loved me, too.

36

KAYLEIGH

*D*arren was insane.

As I was rifling through my duffle bag in my jeans and a bra searching for a clean sweater to throw on, I shook my head in disbelief. I couldn't believe he had asked me to do that. What was he on?

There was no way in hell I was going to break up with Eoin at his mother's house with his entire family gathered round. That was unnecessarily cruel, unnecessarily embarrassing, unnecessarily unfair.

I couldn't lie: I was just as eager as Darren was to be with him, to be truly *with* him. When he burst inside the bathroom as I was stepping out of the shower, I imagined him nodding toward the tub as he grabbed at the hem of his grey Henley and yanked it over his head.

"Get back in," I heard him say in my mind.

I imagined him stripping himself naked, pulling the curtain closed after him, and taking me right then and there under the hot stream of water, my breasts pressed against the tiles, fingers digging into the back of his neck as I tried to steady myself as he fucked me, rough and desperate and fast.

But that was all impossible. At least for a little while longer.

I pulled a comb through my wet hair in front of the little mirror in Eoin's childhood bedroom. I was certain that I wanted to be with Darren, that much I knew. But I was also certain that I had to let Eoin down gently, kindly, softly. I wasn't going to just dump him like a lump of unwanted coal from a stocking on Stephen's Day, of all days. What did Darren expect, after all? That I would say "So long, pal!" between chocolate chip pancakes and eggnog round the fire?

It was ridiculous. Absolutely ridiculous.

No, no, after today I would sit down and come up with a plan for the best way to break up with Eoin. It'd have to happen progressively so as to seem natural, five stages at least. Maybe six or seven. Because I wanted to break up with Eoin, but that didn't mean I needed to break his heart or worse, break up his family.

After I peacefully, calmly, gently, *very* gently, ended things with Eoin, Darren and I would have to wait a while before starting things. How long, I wasn't sure. A couple of months? Half a year?

I laughed to myself as I quickly braided my damp hair down my back. What on earth drove Darren to stampede into the bathroom and demand just like that, as if things could happen with the snap of his fingers, that I tell Eoin it's over?

With an amused chuckle and a shake of my head, I headed downstairs where the family was gathering around the kitchen table almost buckling beneath the weight of yet another massive feast. There were platters piled a mile high with maple smoked bacon. There were bowls filled with sugar-dusted raspberries, strawberries, and pomegranate seeds. There were plates of cheesy scrambled eggs, Clonakilty sausages, and the obvious star of the show, chocolate chip pancakes. Eoin was going around and filling everyone's champagne glass as the merry sounds of chairs scooting in and lips smacking and hands rubbing hungrily together mingled with pleasant conversation and the snap and crackle of the fireplace.

I smiled because everyone was smiling. Well, everyone but Darren, of course. His head was buried in his hands, elbows on either side of his empty plate while everyone else dug in.

I wanted to tell him that he was being silly. Everything was going to be just fine. We knew that we wanted to be together and that was all that mattered. We'd figure out all the rest later; there wasn't reason at all that we had to rush, especially if we were potentially talking about the rest of our lives. I wanted to tell him to grab a pancake and relax.

It was a beautiful, perfect day.

"Kayleigh Bear," Eoin said, grabbing my attention. He stood at the end of the table, holding out the chair for me. "Come sit here."

Smiling, I made my way around the table and let Eoin help me into my chair. I reached past Michael for the bacon, expecting Eoin to take his seat next to me. So I was left awkwardly holding the platter of bacon above my plate as well as a glass of champagne when Eoin clinked his knife against his own. Frowning in confusion, I looked first at the empty floral seat cushion on Eoin's chair and then up at Eoin, who was still standing.

"If everyone could wait just a minute to eat," Eoin announced, holding his champagne glass between fidgeting fingers. "I know Ma's pancakes look great, but if I could just...this won't take long."

The family exchanged curious glances around the table, but then one by one shrugged and set down their forks, their knives. Darren was the only one to not put anything down, but that was only because he was the only one to not have picked something up in the first place.

I went to return the heavy platter of bacon to its former place but found the spot taken by a ceramic boat of maple syrup. I was going to ask Aubrey if she could scoot it out of the way but was interrupted by Eoin clearing his throat, so I was simply left holding it.

"Alright, well, I've thought a lot about what I wanted to say," Eoin started, shifting uncomfortably from foot to foot next to his chair. "So I hope I can get at least a little bit of it out the way I got it in my head."

I tried not to squirm in my chair, but the platter of bacon really was rather heavy. How long was this going to take? Those chocolate chip pancakes looked delicious.

"I think I can speak for everyone here when I say that family is everything," Eoin continued. "We are so lucky to have each other. And we're so lucky to know that we'll always, always have each other."

The muscles in my arms were starting to strain. I tried to catch Aubrey's attention to nod at the maple syrup, but she was nestling her head against Noah's shoulder and hugging his arm tight to her chest. I bit back a defeated sigh and consoled myself with the fact that I could skip arm week in my imaginary workout schedule.

Next to me Eoin was fiddling with the stem of his champagne glass as he continued, "I considered doing this atop some mountain in the Alps with a helicopter or something like that. Or at a private villa on some white beach with crystal-clear waters surrounding us. And for like a good thirty minutes or so I was set on doing it in a hot air balloon over the Grand Canyon. That would have been pretty bad-ass."

Eoin seemed to lose himself in whatever the hell he was talking about, and it took everything in me not to tap my toe impatiently against the floor. I was starving and my arms were *burning.* Finally, Eoin shook his head loose and cleared his throat again.

"Anyway, I got rid of all of those ideas, because I realised mountains and oceans and Grand Canyons would mean nothing if my family wasn't around for the biggest moment in my entire life. So far." Eoin paused, and I thought we were finally going to get to cheers to family and eat.

But then Eoin lowered himself. Not to his chair, where he was supposed to be. But to his knee.

Eoin lowered himself to one knee next to me.

Next to me.

Why was he on one knee *next* to me?

All along the table there were excited gasps from his family. I was still busy staring at that cursed empty floral-patterned seat cushion.

"Kayleigh Bear," Eoin started.

He reached for my hands, only to find them still preoccupied with the platter of bacon. He laughed slightly uncomfortably when he tried to relieve the burden from my grip and I resisted. My mind screamed ridiculously, *"You can't put a ring on a finger that's holding a platter of bacon! Don't let go. Don't let go. Don't let go!"*

Eoin wrestled the bacon away from me and after searching the laden table, settled on just putting the platter next to his bent knee. I couldn't believe what was happening as Eoin slipped my hands into his and rubbed his thumbs soothingly along the back of my suddenly clammy palms.

"Kayleigh Bear," Eoin started, sucking in a deep, steadying breath. I'd never seen him so nervous. "That night outside of Dooley's you saved me from being hit by a car, but there was nothing you could do to save me from you. From the moment I laid eyes on you I fell, I fell harder than I ever thought was possible. I knew right then and there that I'd found my soulmate."

Panic was starting to tighten my chest as I stared down in disbelief at Eoin.

"I know we haven't been together for very long," Eoin continued. "And I know that a lot of people will say that it's too fast."

I tried to force a tiny, pained smile to match even a tiny portion of Eoin's wide, beaming smile. I hoped it didn't look like a grimace, because that's what it felt like to me.

"But as far as I'm concerned, the only thing that I need to know is that you're my soulmate, and I've known that since you were on top of me on that ice. So, Kayleigh Scott..." Eoin paused as he pulled a black velvet box from his pocket and flipped it open to reveal a dazzling diamond ring that I thought only existed in movies.

Eoin smiled up at me. "Will you do me the greatest honour of letting me get to know you and all your wonderful little details for the rest of our lives?"

I stared dumbly at the diamond ring, jaw hanging open stupidly.

Eoin leaned in a bit closer and whispered, "Just in case that wasn't clear, I'm asking if you want to get hitched. I just wanted it to sound nice, you know?"

"I understood," I managed to croak out like a hoarse frog.

Of course I understood what he was asking. It was more than obvious. The answer was even more obvious: no.

No, absolutely not. No. No. No. No, I cannot marry you. No, I'm in love with your brother. No. No. No.

I opened my mouth to speak, but then I remembered Eoin and I were not alone. My eyes scanned over the O'Sullivan family: face after face of joy and excitement and anticipation. Darren was the exception—Darren's face was paled and pained as he stared at his still empty plate. He was the reason I wanted to say "no" to Eoin.

But what would happen if I did?

Eoin would be crushed, his family would be disappointed. Darren alone would be relieved. We would all spend the rest of the holiday in awkward silence, tense small talk, impatient clock watching, all begging that the minutes and seconds flew by faster and faster.

Eoin's brothers would try to console him. Michael would take a turn. Then Noah. But when it was Darren's turn, Eoin would see in Darren's eyes that he was relieved. He would think about at all the times he almost caught Darren and me together, all the hidden glances, stolen touches. He would see what had been right in front of his nose the whole time. He would see what he had been so clearly blind to.

A fight would break out.

It would be bad. Noah and Michael would pull the two apart, but then they, too, would have to take sides. A wedge would be driven between them. *I* would drive a wedge between them. Time would pass without them talking, bitterness would grow, separation would cement.

By next Stephen's Day, Ma's kitchen table would look very different. No, not different. Unrecognisable. There would be no platters of bacon, no fluffy eggs, no sausage or fruit or decadent chocolate chip pancakes. There would be no champagne glasses with sparkling bubbles, no fire with merrily snapping logs, no chairs scratching on the floor as they scoot up hungry bellies to the table.

There would be no family.

On Stephen's Day next year five different microwaves in five different dark, lonely apartments would all beep at the same time. And that would be as close as the O'Sullivan family would ever get again.

If I said "no" I would curse all these beautiful, wonderful people to the family life I had a child. That was a curse no one deserved, especially not Ma, who had shown me nothing but kindness and an open heart.

I stared at the family gathered around me, all waiting on my response to Eoin's proposal. I could no longer see Darren's pale face with the lines of pain across his forehead as he braced himself for the inevitable collision. All I could see was an empty table. A dark kitchen. A glaring red light on a glowing microwave flashing 0:00.

The word came out before I even realised it. The word slipped out of my lips and I barely even heard it. The word fell from my tongue and there was nothing I could do to take it back.

"Yes."

The O'Sullivans immediately burst into cheering and whistling and clapping that I didn't hear over the ringing in my ears. I couldn't move. Eoin, beaming from ear to ear, grabbed each side of my face and pressed a kiss to my lips. I couldn't even lift my hand from my side as Eoin pulled the diamond ring from the box; he had to hold my hand up as he slipped it onto my finger.

The weight of it felt like a betrayal as I turned my head to see Darren's reaction.

But Darren's chair was empty.

So was my heart.

37

DARREN

I went to the garage because it was the only place I knew to go. There were only things to fix in the garage: tyres to mend, cracked pipes to seal, rusted bolts to pry loose. But I didn't want to fix anything.

I wanted to destroy everything.

Throwing my motorcycle down to the concrete, I dragged it behind me, drinking in the screech of rocks against my painstakingly painted and maintained metal gas tank. My blood was boiling so hot that I couldn't even wait for the garage door to open. I hurled my helmet at it with a furious scream and enjoyed every crunch of the shattered glass beneath my boots as I dragged my motorcycle inside the garage.

It felt so fucking good to tip over my toolbox and watch my expensive equipment go scattering across the floor. Through my pulsing red vision I caught sight of a dust-covered sledge-hammer in the corner. Within seconds I was gripping it with white knuckles.

How much destruction would it take to destroy the image of that diamond ring on Kayleigh's hand? How many swings of the sledgehammer would it take before it shattered the image of her dressed in white walking down the aisle toward my brother? How much glass would I have to shatter before I couldn't hear the echo of her answer in my head: yes, yes, yes, yes, yes?

Yes.

My muscles shook, arms quivering. I raised the sledgehammer over my head and drove it again and again and again into my motorcycle. The hypnotic siren call of anger was too much to resist. I allowed myself to get dragged under those all-consuming waters. My world was reduced to physical pain as my arms ached beyond compare, but I couldn't stop because the pain in my heart was immeasurably worse.

A small hand on my sweat-soaked back snapped my trance and I was dragged, kicking and screaming, back to reality.

"Darren, I've been calling your name," Kayleigh said, her fingertips lingering on my arm as she stared up at me in concern. "Didn't you hear me?"

Her diamond caught the overhead lights and flashed like a lighthouse in the dark. A lighthouse means danger, for there are rocks ahead. Rocks to break your bones against. Rocks to sink you. Rocks to die upon. Rocks that promise a different kind of forever.

She couldn't even take off the fucking ring to come explain why she'd ripped out my heart?

My voice shook as I pointed a hand over her shoulder and said, "Get the fuck out of here." My grip tightened around the sledgehammer.

Kayleigh shook her head, green eyes locked on mine. "I know you're not going to hurt me, Darren."

I spit out a spiteful laugh and shook my head. "Hurt you?" I practically choked, it was so fecking *funny*. "Hurt you, Kayleigh? You're family now. Why in God's name would I hurt you?"

To prove my point, I tossed aside the sledgehammer. I threw my hands up into the air, laughing wildly. "What kind of brother-in-law would I be if I hurt you on the day of your very exciting engagement?"

Kayleigh's eyes were wide as they darted back and forth between mine.

I lowered my face toward hers and hissed, "Obviously, you didn't return the favour today, my dear sister-in-law to be."

Kayleigh glanced at my destroyed motorcycle beside her. She dragged her hand through her hair, only to realise it was the hand with that cursed ring. She sighed and slipped her hands into the pockets of her jeans.

"Darren, I didn't mean to hurt you. I—"

"You didn't mean to hurt me?" I shouted, practically tearing at my hair. "You didn't mean to hurt me, Kayleigh?"

I needed to get her out of there before I did something I regretted. Because I was about to lose control. I was hanging to the cliff of my sanity by the tips of my shaking fingers. The problem wasn't that I couldn't hold on a little bit longer. The problem was that I didn't fucking want to.

I was tired.

And I just wanted to let go.

"You didn't mean to fucking hurt me?" I repeated. "Is that really what you just said to me, Kayleigh?" Her name on my lips burned like acid. "Because you did a really good job of it. Damn, I can't imagine what you could do to me if you were actually trying."

Kayleigh bit her lip. "Look, can we just talk about how to fix this?"

I stared at her in shock. "Fix this?"

Kayleigh nodded. "Yeah."

"Fix this?" I started to pace back and forth in front of her because I couldn't stand still any longer without exploding. "Kayleigh, you're *engaged* to my *brother*. You said yes to marrying him. There's nothing to 'fix' but the date of the wedding."

Kayleigh shook her head. "You know I don't want to be with Eoin." She moved toward me, reaching out for me. I wrenched my hand away. She couldn't touch me. She couldn't. "I don't want to marry Eoin. I—"

"You said yes, Kayleigh," I said, my voice breaking. "You said —fuck. *Fuck*. Why did you say yes?"

Pain was seeping back into my heart.

"Kayleigh, why?" I asked quietly.

Cracks were spreading in my iron walls. Pain, terrible, terrible pain was about to come bursting in, the walls of the dam utterly destroyed.

"Why? Why did you say yes?"

I wanted anger back. Anger was easier. I grappled for fury as if it were a lifeline slipping through my fingers.

"Darren, please just listen for one minute. Just listen, alright?" Kayleigh must have taken my silence for assent, because she leaned against the hood of the Mustang and stared at her fingers cupped in her lap. "Eoin asked me and I was going to say no, I mean, of course I was going to say no," she said, shaking her head as if this was all confusing to her. "But I...I saw your whole family there and I've never had that before and I...I couldn't destroy a perfect family."

Kayleigh's eyes darted toward me. I glared at her, but I did not interrupt.

"I just couldn't." Kayleigh buried her face in her hands, the silence drawing out like a canyon between us. When she finally looked up at me there was the hint of tears in her eyes. "Darren, Eoin was right," she said. "You're so lucky to have your family. They're just...they're perfect. Trust me."

I couldn't bite back my tongue. "I don't."

My words hit Kayleigh like a punch to the gut. She momentarily ducked her head like she was catching her breath. Her voice was soft when she finally spoke. "My father was cruel to my ma. No, not cruel. Abusive. As I child I saw it all. I couldn't even escape beneath the covers of my bed because I still heard it. And hearing it is even worse somehow. Children have such vivid imaginations, you know?"

No, I didn't like this at all. This was more pain. I didn't want more pain. I wanted Kayleigh to leave. I wanted to pick back up my sledgehammer. I wanted anger back.

"My ma always just took it. Took it and never said a word," Kayleigh continued. "I thought she just needed someone to stand up for her. That's what I thought. So one day I did."

Kayleigh looked over at me. Through the haze of tears I saw that fire I loved so terribly about her.

"One day I couldn't take it anymore. I put myself right between him and my ma. I defended her, I protected her. My father left and I smiled because I thought that was it: we would be safe now, my ma and I. We would be happy now. We could finally be a family, a family like you have." Kayleigh's chin fell to rest on her chest. "I turned around to celebrate with my ma and I was greeted with a slap to the face."

I swallowed back the revolting feeling from Kayleigh's horrifying story. I hadn't known. Hell, I hadn't wanted to know.

Did you think you were the only one hiding pain in your life?

Kayleigh's voice grew small and meek. Any fire that had burned in her eyes was doused and stomped out and starved of oxygen. "She grabbed me by the collar of my shirt and shook me and told me to never, ever do that again. She said if my father left because of me she would never, ever forgive me. She said I was always to keep quiet, to not cause a fuss, to never, ever cause another fight, no matter what."

Kayleigh let her head fall back as she stared up at the ceiling of the garage. I wondered if she was trying to force the tears back into her eyes, just like she had forced that childhood pain back into her soul: afraid to let it out, afraid to let someone see, afraid to let *me* see.

"So when I saw a family like yours it was something precious to me, even though it wasn't mine." Kayleigh looked over at me again, eyes rimmed in red but dry. "Darren, your family *is* something precious, something beautiful, something rare and delicate and perfect. How could I come in and destroy it? How could I come in and destroy something that I love?"

Kayleigh was looking over at me, pleading with her eyes. In that moment I had a choice: I could choose pain or I could choose anger.

I could choose to take on more pain. I could choose to live with it, face it head on, come to terms with it like Kayleigh had shown me the night before. I could choose to feel, and in choosing to feel, I could choose to hurt, to cry, to ache. I could choose pain; I could choose Kayleigh.

Or I could choose anger.

Oh, how anger called out to me, her voice sweet and tempting. I could choose to let the ring on Kayleigh's finger harden my heart, build up my walls, light a dark fire in my soul, impossible to ever put out. I could choose to feel good because, fuck, did anger feel good. I could choose my sledgehammer, I could choose destruction, I could choose no more goddamn pain.

"Darren? Please say something."

Kayleigh's broken voice broke my heart, and I hated it. It hurt. And I was sick and tired of hurting. I was sick and tired of fecking pain.

So I chose the only thing I could: I chose anger.

"So your answer to all of this is to follow in the steps of your mother?" My voice slashed through the space between us like a dagger so sharp, you didn't even know you were cut till you saw the blood.

It took what felt like a long time in the silence of the garage, surrounded by the broken pieces of my shattered motorcycle, for Kayleigh to realise the hatefulness of my words. I saw the hurt flash in her eyes, quickly masked by confusion.

"What?" She shook her head as if she hadn't heard me right, as if she couldn't possibly have heard me right.

But she had.

"What did you say?" Her eyes narrowed at me as anger of her own darkened her irises.

She would thank me later. She would realise I was right after all: anger felt better than pain.

I was doing this for her, I was doing this for Kayleigh's sake. At least that's what I told myself. That's the excuse I used to numb the sharp pain in my heart at the sight of betrayal on her face. That's how I justified opening my mouth again: slamming down the guillotine on any chance she and I ever stood together.

"Your mother didn't cause a stir, your mother didn't want any fighting, your mother never dared to tell the truth about what she wanted," I said, scowling at Kayleigh with my arms crossed defensively over my chest. "I don't see how there is any difference between her and *you*."

Kayleigh's eyes filled with tears as she slowly shook her head.

"Do you want me to tell you to keep your mouth shut so that you can justify agreeing to marry a man you do not love? So that you can sleep at night knowing that you threw away a real chance at love?" I was starting to shout as I gave in to my anger. Oh, how it felt good. My skin was on fire and I was plunging into a deep, dark, cool lake where I could drown in peace. "Would that make you feel better, Kayleigh? Huh?"

Kayleigh's voice cracked as the first tear streamed down her cheek. She whispered, "Why are you being this way?"

I barely heard her. All I could hear was the rushing water

against my ears as I was dragged down deeper and deeper and deeper.

"Your mother was miserable and you'll be miserable, too. Is that what you want Kayleigh? Do you want to be mis—"

"I'm not miserable." The stubbornness on Kayleigh's face made me laugh.

"You will be," I said.

It was now Kayleigh who laughed. "No, Darren, I don't think I will be," she said. "Because I'll be with a man who is kind and gentle and sweet. A man who loves me and cares for me. A man whose heart beats a little blindly at times, but, fuck, at least it beats."

I stood shocked and dumbfounded. It wasn't her words that confused me, but her face. All anger had drained away. All sadness.

Instead she looked at me with something closer to pity.

"I should thank you, Darren," she said, her voice soft. "Because you've made me see very clearly what I almost threw away for..." Her eyes searched me as she searched for words. Finally she just sighed and shrugged sadly. "...for what?"

She turned to leave, but her final words to me stayed with me there in the garage. I feared they might follow me wherever I went.

"I'm going to marry Eoin and I'm going to be happy for once."

38

DARREN

*S*omehow the stark glare of the early afternoon sunshine made the trees dotted across the graveyard appear even more barren. The stone crosses seemed more weathered, and the dead leaves stirred up by the slight breeze more dry and brittle.

I leaned against the bark of the oak, its long branches moaning overhead, and squinted in the rare brilliant rays. I told myself I was here because my brother was here. If I was honest with myself, I was here because there was nowhere else to go.

Over the past few weeks I'd used every excuse to avoid participating in Eoin and Kayleigh's wedding preparations. I'd fixed my mangled, beaten-up motorcycle as slowly and tediously as possible. I'd stayed late every night and awoken early every morning to finish every work order at the garage. I'd cleaned my apartment, cooked enough food for three weeks, and organised my office for the first time ever.

I couldn't go to Noah's place because Aubrey, as Kayleigh's unofficial wedding planner, had consumed their living room with wedding design magazines, pin boards of fabric swatches and inspiration pictures, and ten different versions of possible seating charts. I couldn't go to visit Michael because the only thing he could talk about those days was the financial impracticality of a wedding and how those funds could be put to much better use toward a deposit on a house, preferably with a 30-year fixed interest rate loan. Ma's kitchen was constantly a mess as she tested different options to serve at the reception because she insisted on doing it all herself instead of catering it in.

It was all too much, all too overwhelming.

I didn't care if the silk napkins were emerald or kelly green. I didn't give a damn if the cake was two- or three-tiered. I didn't want any part in deciding which candies should be served at the dessert bar. I didn't want any part in any of it.

That day in the graveyard I was brainstorming ways to get out of going to the wedding at all, which is difficult when you're the brother of the groom, when I noticed a familiar car pull into the small parking lot just past the iron fence tangled with vines and ensnared dried leaves.

"Ma's here," I said to Jaime.

It took glancing down at the cold grey of his headstone to remember that he wasn't really there with me. I'd been talking to my dead twin like we were sitting elbow-to-elbow at a bar, as if that fateful night never happened.

"Did you know she was coming?" I asked, narrowing my eyes at his gravestone as if he'd somehow conspired against me from beyond the veil.

In my head he zipped up his lips and tossed the key over his shoulder.

"Some twin you are," I grumbled as the iron gate creaked and Ma approached, her feet crunching the leaves beneath her.

"Hey, Ma," I said, scratching awkwardly at the back of my neck. "I didn't know you were coming here today. Thought you were going dress shopping with Kayleigh and the girls."

Ma kissed me on the cheek and told me that the dress shopping had been pushed back to tomorrow because of a last-minute shift Kayleigh picked up at The Jar. I nodded and with nothing more to say on that matter, we stood in silence next to one another in front of Jaime's gravestone.

I swallowed heavily as guilt creeped back into my chest like spilled oil into the cracks of my garage floor.

Alone with Jaime I'd been feeling fine—good, even. But with Ma there I couldn't see Jaime. I couldn't hear his voice. I couldn't imagine him laughing and nudging me as he sipped a pint of Guinness at the bar in Cassidys.

All I could see was cold, hard earth. All I could see was a slab of grey granite. All I could see was his name, the last thing left of him, etched in stone.

My heart rate quickened.

All I could see was the hospital light in the distance. All I could see was that goddamn wrench as it slipped again through my bloody fingers. And my panicked breaths condensing in the cold, dark air.

My chest tightened.

All I could see was that hospital hallway with its long phosphorescent bulbs and yellow linoleum floors. All I could see was Ma surrounded by my family as I ran toward them. All I could see was her eyes when she saw me.

She didn't have to say a word.

The horrible truth was all there in her eyes.

Jamie was gone.

I couldn't breathe. There in the cemetery, I suddenly couldn't breathe. I tried to suck in freezing cold air, but nothing seemed to reach my lungs. They tightened painfully and I wheezed, desperate for relief, any blessed relief. Black spots danced in my vision as I stared at the gravestone, the shrivelled flowers, the grass grown over the hole where they lowered him into the ground.

I couldn't breathe.

And I hadn't been there.

I couldn't breathe.

I hadn't been there.

I couldn't brea—

I felt a hand on my shoulder.

When I turned and blinked, it wasn't Ma's hand. It was Jaime's. I could see his eyes again, could hear him again.

"Tell her, Darren. It's time."

I looked over at Ma, who was staring at me with concern in her bright blue eyes, Jaime's eyes.

"Darren?" she asked, taking a step closer to me. "Darren, is everything alright?"

My tears immediately stained the collar of her jacket as I slung my arms around her and buried my face against the nape of her neck like I did when I was a child.

"Ma, I was with Sophie," I said, words muffled by her thick scarf against the cold. "I was running away with her and we were in the car and it got a flat when I was rushing back and, and I couldn't fix it in time. I, I couldn't—Ma, I tried, I tried, but I couldn't fix it. I *can't* fix it."

My shoulders shook as I cried and squeezed my mother tight as she held me, hand caressing the back of my head.

I didn't cry that night my brother died.

I didn't hug Ma or Noah or Eoin or Michael.

I didn't let them hug me.

I'd dug my nails into my palm so my eyes stayed dry and shooed away any hint of a hug with an emotionless, "I'm grand."

I finally pulled away from my ma and wiped at my tear-drenched cheeks. "Ma," my voice choked with emotion, "could you ever forgive me?"

Ma reached out and cupped my cheeks, not bothering to wipe away her own tears. It was as if she was comfortable with the pain. Like she knew it would never truly go away. As if she had learned to live with it, learned to love despite it.

"Darren, I love you," she whispered, "and there is nothing to be forgiven."

I shook my head and tried to protest.

Ma stopped me by roughly grabbing the hair at the nape of my neck. Her eyes were fierce as they held mine as if in a vice grip. "Darren O'Sullivan, listen to me," she said, her voice shaking. "I love you and there is nothing—*nothing*—to be forgiven."

Fresh tears streamed down both of our faces. She pulled me back to her chest, arms wrapped tightly, protectively around me, pulling closed the open wound across my heart.

"Do you hear me?" she whispered against the crown of my head.

"Yes," I said, fingers clinging to my ma's coat. "I hear you."

39

KAYLEIGH

*I*t's difficult enough trying to hide your heartbreak when you're supposed to be elatedly, joyously, beaming in love. But it's damn near impossible standing in front of a trifold floor-to-ceiling mirror. Three opportunities to let your performance slip. Three opportunities for everyone to see your mask slip. Three opportunities for your secret to escape without a single word.

"Oh, Kayleigh, it's stunning!" Candace said, leaping to her feet and erupting into enthusiastic applause as soon as the dress shop attendant helped me up onto the pedestal. "Absolutely gorgeous, my love! *Bela, bela!*"

Well aware that my reflection was being attentively studied by Aubrey and Ma, I tugged up the corners of my lips till the muscles in my cheeks ached.

"You think so?" I asked, hoping my voice didn't sound strained.

I pretended that I enjoyed running my hands down the silk skirt, tracing the pearl beads along the bust line, counting the jewels forming a band around my waist. I pretended that I wasn't longing for the cold sting of a heavy metal wrench, wishing to feel the roar of an engine under me instead of the pinch of uncomfortable heels, wanting to use this wedding dress as nothing more than a rag to wipe off my grease-covered hands.

"Let's see it from the front," Aubrey said, drumming the fingers of one hand contemplatively across her chin as she held her champagne glass in the other.

It was clear that Aubrey was unwilling to show too much enthusiasm for the early dresses (unlike Candace, who screamed at each and every one), because then the shopping experience (and the complimentary champagne and strawberries that accompanied it) would be over. Me, on the other hand? I would have taken the first one just to end this torture. Even if it made me look like a meringue.

To comply with Aubrey's request, the dress shop attendant lifted the heavy skirt so I could wobble around on the three-foot-wide circle, three inches off the carpeted floor. It might have been a tad bit smaller than other stages I'd been on during my lifetime, but there was no doubt that it was nevertheless a stage.

Standing there in front of Ma, Candace, and Aubrey, I had to act like I was happy. I had to act that I was just as excited as they were to be there in that elegant wedding dress, twinkling with Swarovski crystals and stuffed with cloud-like puffs of pure white tulle. And when the dress shop attendant asked if I could imagine walking toward my fiancé in this dress, I had to act like I was seeing Eoin, and not Darren, at the end of the white rose-covered aisles when my eyelids fluttered closed.

"Well?" I asked, holding the skirt out on either side of me for the peanut gallery to evaluate.

I hoped that I didn't betray how exhausted I felt. Unfortunately, there wasn't concealer for the dark bags in your voice. All the wedding preparations had truly drained me. With every plate selection or DJ interview or wedding venue tour, my nights grew more and more fitful.

Because I couldn't stop seeing *him*...

"You know what," Aubrey finally said, head tilting to the side as she dutifully assessed the dress. "I think we maybe need to see it with a veil to get the whole picture, you know?"

The dress shop attendant nodded. "We can do that," she said. "Would you like to come take a look with me?"

From the plush velvet couch, Aubrey tapped her empty champagne glass and grinned mischievously. "The veils are over by the bottles of champagne, right?"

The dress shop attendant laughed and waved her hand. "I think you'll be quite impressed with our collection," she joked.

Aubrey winked at me before following after her.

Candace leapt up next and rushed over to squeeze my hand. "I'll make sure that they pick the one with the most bling," she whispered loudly. "Don't you worry."

I couldn't manage to keep up my good-natured giggling once Candace disappeared around the corner. The fitting room sank into a sombre silence like a rock tossed into the lake. Then I remembered that Ma was still sitting silently on the couch.

I bit back a tired, heart-aching sigh and smiled over at her, the perfect actress. "So what do you think?" I asked.

Ma pushed herself slowly from the couch and walked over to me on the pedestal. She lowered her glasses to her nose from where they had been tucked atop her head along with her sleek white bun. As I watched her, she quietly traced the delicate floral pattern of lace across the bodice of the dress.

"Now that we're alone for a moment," Ma started, moving to admire the back of the dress, "I wanted to thank you."

With a frown, I twisted my head around to see her, but Ma was smoothing a wrinkle in the voluminous skirt and did not meet my curious gaze.

"Thank me?" I asked.

Ma nodded.

"For what?"

Ma moved to the front of me again and held her arm as she supported her chin with her palm. She shook her head silently.

"I think the straps are a little wide for your small frame," she said, obviously not answering my question in the slightest.

She picked up a small burgundy cushion of pins the dress shop attendant left on a wooden stool next to the mirrors and raised an eyebrow. "Do you mind?"

I shook my head.

With two pins held between her lips, Ma's sharp blue eyes focused on her work as she manoeuvred the straps of the wedding dress on me. Farther on in the shop, I could just make out Candace and Aubrey's excited giggles as they were surely trying on the veils themselves.

I was actually thankful for the small bout of silence, what felt like the first in a chaotic last few weeks. I was studying Ma's quiet, diligent work when she spoke again, her voice soft. "I spoke with Darren yesterday."

I waited for Ma's eyes to move to mine, but she remained focused on pinning the dress here and there. Ma stepped back to study her work before moving in close to me again.

"I spoke with Darren yesterday and he told me the truth of what happened that night," she whispered, her voice calm and even. "The truth of where he was when Jaime passed in that hospital room."

I stared down at Ma in surprise. That was a secret Darren had held onto for almost a decade. He was terrified, absolutely terrified of his mother finding out that painful truth.

Ma's eyes finally glanced up at me and her hands slid down the dress to find mine, her fingers intertwining with mine.

"I suspect you had something to do with that," she said. "So thank you. I've been waiting years for him to finally tell me."

"You *knew*? You knew this whole time?"

Ma patted my cheek gently and said before putting two more pins between her lips, "I'm his mother. Of course I've known this whole time."

I shook my head in disbelief.

"He was a teenager in love," Ma chuckled. "Teenagers in love aren't exactly known for being subtle. I'm pretty sure I knew he was planning on leaving home before even he did."

I couldn't form words as Ma slipped another pin into the dress.

"Besides, my bed is right above that garage and mothers have very sensitive ears." She laughed a little to herself. "I saw him leave that night." Sadness entered Ma's voice as she sighed and briefly squeezed her eyes closed.

"Why'd you let him believe all this time that you didn't know?" I asked.

Ma nodded, as if she'd been expecting this very question from my lips. "I've asked myself this very question many times over the years," she started. "Every time I saw Darren in pain, every time I saw him withdraw into that garage, every time I caught him digging his nails into his palm to the point of drawing blood whenever someone mentioned Jamie's name, I doubted my decision to let Darren keep his secret."

Ma's hands paused where they were on the strap of the wedding dress. She sucked in a steadying breath as she clearly fought back tears.

"No mother ever wants to see their child in pain," she whispered. "But I couldn't take away Darren's pain if he wasn't ready to let it go, if he wasn't ready to believe that he no longer deserved it, that he never deserved it in the first place."

Ma's lower lip quivered. I reached out a hand and ran it

gently along her arm. I felt the threat of tears myself and bit my lip to try to hold them back.

One thing could not have been more obvious to me in that quiet moment in the dressing room: we both loved, and loved dearly, the same man.

"You're the reason, Kayleigh Scott," Ma said. She cleared her throat, but her voice was still thick with emotion. "You're the reason he finally let go."

Ma reached up to run the back of her hand sweetly against my cheek. "And for that I can never repay you, my dear," she whispered. "Avoiding the truth, running away from it, trying to bury it deep, deep down where no one can see it...it only leads to pain." Ma then moved on to the other strap of the dress, inserting pin after pin as she added, eyes glancing up at me, "Pain for everyone."

Our eyes held one another's for a quiet moment, and more was communicated silently than could ever be said aloud. As I looked into her intelligent, kind blue eyes, I got the strange sense that she wasn't only talking about Darren and Jamie at this point. Did she know about Darren and me? Could that be another "truth" she was subtly referring to? Could she see what was truly in my heart as I stood there in a wedding dress, set to marry one of her sons and in love with another?

I tried to find the answers in her steady gaze, but before I could, Ma ducked her eyes and stepped back to assess again the dress and her adjustments to it.

I worried that my voice might betray my own emotion as I asked, "W-what do you think?"

Ma fidgeted with the pin cushion as she frowned at the dress from head to toe.

"Better?" I asked meekly.

Ma shook her head. "Something is still off."

I glanced down at the dress myself. The way Ma had tucked

the straps made the top look more elegant, more natural. It was, beyond a doubt, a stunning dress. When I looked up, I found Ma's eyes on me.

"Something is definitely wrong here," she said.

"What? With the straps?" I asked.

Ma kept her eyes fixed pointedly on me as she shook her head. "No, Kayleigh," she said slowly so I didn't miss a single word. "*Not* with the straps."

40

KAYLEIGH

*W*hen I rang the doorbell outside of Eoin's apartment, it sounded like the microwave ringing out in the dark kitchen of my childhood. My mother was busy taking my father his food in his room, so the microwave beeped and beeped and—

"Kayleigh Bear!" Eoin's grinning face popped out of the cracked door. "Or should I say *Fiancée* Bear. What a wonderful surprise. I was just Googling whether they make rugby ball-shaped cufflinks for the wedding."

I forced a smile as I shifted from foot to foot on his front step. I was already considering turning right around and running back to my car. I swallowed and tried to still my nerves. "Um, Eoin, can I maybe come in for a minute?"

Eoin smacked himself on the forehead and moved aside to let me in. "Of course, of course," he laughed. "We're spending the rest of our lives together, *fiancée*. You can move in right now if you want."

I winced at the second use of the word fiancée as I followed Eoin into the living room of his spacious luxury townhouse. I noticed the plastic remains of a microwavable meal still on the kitchen table and felt myself chickening out as I imagined Eoin eating many more of those meals alone.

No. I clung to Ma's words: avoiding the truth ends up being painful for *everyone.*

"Aubrey sent over those bottles of wine, by the way," Eoin said as he pointed to several bottles on the coffee table. "She says we can pick any of those for the wedding. I think she may be even more excited for about than you, Kayleigh Bear." Eoin laughed as he twisted a bottle around to frown at the French on the label. "So, um, do you want to make out on the couch or something?" he asked, shrugging his shoulders. "Or we could make out in the hot tub." He thumbed over his shoulder at the porch outside.

"Um, Eoin, I think we should sit down for this," I tentatively said.

"Yeah, babe. I suggested the hot tub or the couch," he said. "Both of those are sitting down."

This was not going well.

"No, no," I said, guiding Eoin to the couch next to me with a hand on his elbow. "Eoin, we need to talk."

Eoin's eyes narrowed with growing suspicion when I removed the hand that he placed casually on my knee. I avoided his eyes as I scooted an inch or two away from him so our hips weren't touching.

"Kayleigh Bear?" Eoin asked, worry entering his voice. "What's wrong?"

As I stared down at my hands, which were clammy and fidgety in my lap, I could feel my mother's bony, hard fingers wrapped around them as she dragged me to my room.

"You brat! You little brat! You'll make him leave."

Eoin's living room was dead silent as he waited for me to

speak, but I could hear her; I could hear her as clearly as the day that she said it. *"If he leaves, I'm leaving, too. You'll be all alone. All alone forever!"*

I flinched, even though no door slammed. No door rattled on its hinges. No storming footsteps echoed away down the hallway.

I don't want to be alone, my mind screamed at me. I wanted a family. I wanted big noisy Christmas dinners and picnics by the sea in the summer. I didn't want to be alone!

Panic filled my chest at the prospect of being alone forever if I told Eoin the truth, if I caused a fight, if I didn't keep my mouth shut: silent, like I should be.

If I just buried the truth, the truth that I loved Darren and wanted to be with him, if I just pushed it down deep, deep, deep down, if I just hid it away in my heart, I would have Eoin. I wouldn't be alone. I would have his family. I loved his family. I would have packed tables, not a chair empty.

But Darren thought the same thing about his buried truth. He thought he was protecting his family. He thought he deserved his loneliness, his guilt, his pain. He thought he was making the right choice.

But he was wrong.

I would be wrong too, if I didn't open my mouth.

If I didn't tell the truth.

If I didn't fight for what I wanted.

"Eoin, I can't marry you," I blurted out before I could second-guess myself, before my lips paralysed with fear. My chest heaved as I stared down at my hands. For a second, I grew paranoid that I only imagined saying the words because Eoin had yet to say anything.

When I built up the courage to look up at Eoin, I saw, clear as day, that I had indeed finally admitted the truth. One look at

Eoin's face confirmed what I was afraid of: yes, it was going to hurt like hell.

Eoin's eyes darted between mine with a mix of confusion and the inklings of heartbreak. "Is this some kind of joke?" he asked, voice faint. "Because if it is, I'm not sure that I get it. I...I don't get it."

My heart split in two at the sight of hope still lingering in Eoin's eyes: hope that this *was* a joke, a terrible, terrible joke; hope that he misheard me, that he was dreaming and this wasn't really over.

"I should have been truthful earlier." I slipped the engagement ring, which I'd taken off right after the wedding dress appointment, from my pocket and placed it on the cushion between us. "But I was trying to convince myself I knew what love was. I was trying to convince myself that it was what I had with you, Eoin." I paused so I could steady my breathing. "But I've learned that I've had it all wrong. I've learned what love is. What love *truly* is."

Eoin's face had gone blank. It seemed he stared not at me, but through me. I wasn't sure he was still listening, but I had to say what I came here to say; I had to at least try to make him understand.

"I thought that love was never fighting," I said, my voice shaky. "But I've learned that if it's love, it's worth fighting for. It's the only thing worth fighting for."

I felt my heart racing, but I realised I wanted my heart to race. I wanted it to race and leap and throb and ache and sting and tense and hurt so terribly because it was full: full of passion and desire and lust and longing and contentment and joy and love.

And *love*.

"For so long, I was afraid of speaking up for myself, of being loud, of creating waves," I said. "But love, true love, has given me the courage to demand what I want. It has given me the strength to let the consequences be damned and seize what I want. Above all, it has made me feel heard—whether I'm screaming from the top of my lungs or whispering in the faintest voice. I've learned love can always hear me."

I remembered Darren and me bent over the engine of a car beneath the greasy hood, our voices sounding like the only voices in the world in that hot, crammed space.

I continued, my voice steady, even if my hands weren't. "I've had this fairy tale view of love, that it's easy and simple and perfect. But it's not. Pretending is easy. Pretending is simple. And perfection isn't real. Love is messy and complicated and dirty and I wouldn't want it any other way."

I tried not to fidget with my hands as I bit my lip and stared at Eoin's far-off gaze. I'd gotten through what I thought was the hard part, but it seemed the hard part was just about to begin.

At first I didn't even hear him when he spoke.

"What?" I asked, leaning in a little to catch the wafer-thin sound of his voice, as if I'd sapped everything else from him. "I didn't hear you."

"I said, is it someone I know?" Eoin blinked and his eyes found mine again. I could almost see the anxiety in my own eyes reflected back at me, his were so wide and clear.

"What?" It wasn't that I hadn't heard him this time; it was that I wasn't expecting to have to tell that truth. Not yet. Eoin's eyes moved to stare at the discarded engagement ring sitting on the couch cushion between us.

"You don't talk like that, with that much...emotion," Eoin said, "unless you've experienced this first hand. I know people think I'm thick sometimes, but even I know this." His eyes darted over to mine and he repeated his question. "So who, Kayleigh?" he asked. "Who is it that you love?"

I could have lied to Eoin. I could have told him it was no

one. I could have told him he didn't know the person. I could have told him anything to avoid this train wreck, anything but the truth.

But I had to stop running from confrontation. I had to stop sealing my lips, hiding away the truth in the silent depths of my heart. I had to open my mouth.

"Darren," I said. "It's Darren."

It was the first time I'd admitted it aloud. The words felt strange. They tumbled from my lips, half sweet like peppermint sticks, half burning like whiskey. They seemed to hang suspended in the air like frozen snowflakes I could almost reach out and touch with the tip of my tongue.

"And he loves you?"

At the sound of Eoin's question, I blinked and my confession turned to stones tied to my ankles that threatened to drag me under the dark waters.

What if I had said all of this, blown up my relationship with Eoin, and Darren didn't love me back? What if all of this was for nothing?

No.

This was my truth. And Darren's feelings didn't change that. For once in my life, I was speaking for *me*.

"I love him," I said, voice steady. "I love Darren and that's all that matters."

Eoin tried to hide it, but I could see pain in his eyes as he reached out and plucked up the engagement ring. I never wished to cause him pain. I hoped one day he would see that we weren't right for one another, though I knew that wouldn't be today. Or tomorrow. Or perhaps any time soon.

But one day, one day I hoped he would see.

"Please leave," Eoin said in a whisper, eyes ducked to avoid my gaze.

I nodded, though he didn't see it, and pushed myself up to walk as quietly as I could toward the door. I didn't look back. I couldn't look back.

I had to look forward.

41

DARREN

*O*n the desk in the little office at the back of the garage was an old crumpled yellow invoice flipped around to the blank side, smoothed out as best as possible. I had labelled it at the top: How to Apologise to Kayleigh for Severely Fucking Up.

My pen tapped nervously on the side of the desk as I sat stooped over the ideas I had so far:

I.

AFTER SEVERAL ANGUISHED minutes of pen tapping and lip biting and staring, I leaned back in my desk chair with a defeated sigh and dragged my fingers through my hair. How could I ever apologise for what I said to Kayleigh? How could I ever tell her to come back when I'd so obviously pushed her away for good? How could I ask to break off her engagement with Eoin?

It seemed hopeless. All so terribly hopeless.

I stared up at the square-tiled ceiling and tried to come up with an elaborate apology. I could buy her roses, dozens upon dozens of roses. I could take her on a romantic trip to Switzerland, to France, to Japan, even. I could find her the most perfect diamond necklace to try to win her back.

As I considered all of these ideas one by one, I couldn't help but see Ma with her hands crossed over her apron, shaking her head at me in front of the stovetop. I couldn't help but hear her ask me, "Darren, son, are you really that thick?"

The chair squeaked loudly as I sat up, snatched up the pen, and wrote just a single item on my list.

1. Tell the truth.

BLOWING OUT A STEADYING BREATH, I reached for the phone to call Kayleigh before my heart started pounding too loudly for her to even hear me on the other end. But before I could pick up the receiver, the phone rang, echoing harshly in the small back office. After an irritable sigh, I answered.

"Kelly's Garage, this is Darren."

I was reaching for a new customer information sheet to fill out when I heard her voice.

"It's Kayleigh."

My stomach lurched, jumbling with fear and nerves and anticipation. I cleared my throat and tried to remember the words that had been so clear in my mind just moments before.

"Kayleigh, hi, I, um, I was actually just going to call you. I—how are you? I mean, are you—um..." I smacked my forehead as I squeezed my eyes shut and tried to pull myself together.

"Darren, I need to tell you something," Kayleigh said.

"Wait," I blurted out. "Before you do, just please give me a chance to say something first."

"Okay, but you should know that I—"

"Please, let me go first," I insisted. If I didn't say what I needed to say now I might lose my nerve.

"Alright then," Kayleigh said. "You go first."

I tried to push back my desk chair so I could stand, pace back and forth, move about, but the wheels got caught in a run in the carpet and I was stuck. I sucked in a deep breath. I couldn't run any longer. I couldn't hide or pretend or escape on my motorcycle. I was going to sit right here and tell the truth, no matter how scary, no matter how difficult, no matter how many times the receiver slipped in my sweaty palms.

"Kayleigh, I said all those terrible things to you on Stephen's Day because I was hurt," I said, feeling uncomfortable and accepting there were some things in life more important than feeling comfortable. "I was hurt and I lashed out in anger because I was afraid of feeling more pain."

I swallowed heavily as my fingers itched to slam down the receiver, my palms ached to shove the desk away from me to free myself, my feet bouncing uncontrollably, desperate to run away from what I was saying to Kayleigh—dying to run away from the truth.

I wouldn't let years escape me like I did with Ma: wasted years of love and affection and connection.

Kayleigh remained silent on the other line as I continued. I would have thought the line had gone dead if it weren't for her quiet, unsteady exhales.

"But I want to risk more pain right now," I said, uncertain of every word and yet never more certain that I just had to keep going. "I want to risk the pain and heartache that what I say might not be enough, that *I* might not be enough."

I squeezed my eyes shut and rubbed my fingers at my temple with my head bent, as if this was a last-ditch prayer.

"Kayleigh, the truth is that I don't want you to marry Eoin," I said, heart racing. "Because the truth is, Kayleigh, that…"

Every part of my body was shouting at me to shut up, shut up, shut up! Don't risk it. Play it safe. Protect yourself, protect your heart. Walls, walls, walls; don't let them fall.

"I'm in love with you."

I hardly recognised my own voice when I confessed those words aloud. It didn't sound the voice of a man who had spent the last almost ten years shuttering up his heart. It didn't sound like the voice of a man tortured by guilt, haunted by ghosts of his own making. It didn't sound like the voice of a man who would pick anger over fear.

It sounded like a new man.

A new me.

A new me who loved and forgave. Who had let go of the past and looked toward a bright, happy future. A me I liked. A me I liked for the first time in far, far too long.

I was so awash in this warm glow that pulsed suddenly in my heart that I almost forgot about the woman who'd instilled these feelings in me in the first place. A wave of doubt and uncertainty threatened to leave my chest icy cold. Because there was nothing.

Nothing on the other line at all.

Silence.

Silence.

And more silence.

After checking the receiver to make sure that the call hadn't dropped out during my profession of love, I said a tentative, "Kayleigh?"

I cursed my decision to open up my heart over the telephone because I couldn't see her reaction at all. But I simply couldn't wait, could I? I just had to tell her. I cursed my impatience. But that was Kayleigh's fault; she did this to me. So then I cursed Kayleigh, the woman I wanted to devote my life to.

Love was confusing.

"Can I speak now?"

I tried my best to read her tone, but it was next to impossible. Maybe she found that she couldn't forgive me for how cruelly I'd treated her in the garage. Maybe she had called to get closure and my profession of love was an awkward interference. Maybe she simply didn't feel the same and she was, after all, happy with Eoin.

Maybe I was wrong.

I cleared my throat and practically croaked out a, "Sure."

"Alright then..."

Kayleigh paused. I found myself nearly at the edge of the desk chair. I'm certain it would have tipped over at some point if the back legs weren't tangled in the old fraying carpet.

"Darren..."

I almost couldn't bear it when Kayleigh again paused to suck in a deep breath. I needed her to speak. Whatever it was that she called to tell me, I needed to hear it. I was going insa—

"I broke up with Eoin."

These were the words I prayed to hear from her and yet when I heard them aloud, I simply couldn't believe them. "What?"

"I broke up with Eoin," Kayleigh repeated. I stared dumbfounded at the receiver. "I told him that I loved someone else... you. I love you, Darren."

I couldn't help the smile that tugged at the corners of my lips. I covered my mouth with my hand, because I feared if I didn't, my smile would just keep growing and growing. I squeezed my eyes shut and dropped the phone to bury my face in my hands, shaking my head in disbelief. My shoulders were practically shaking as I started to laugh, I was so happy.

It took me several moments to hear Kayleigh's voice calling out to me from the dropped receiver. I fetched it and held it again to my ear.

"Did you just say you love me?" I asked, still not certain this was real.

"Yes." Kayleigh laughed, and I could hear the tears in her own eyes as she did. "Yes. I did, you big eejit."

We laughed and cried together over the phone and it was the best moment of my entire life.

"You love me," I said, smiling so hard my cheeks hurt.

"You love me, too," Kayleigh laughed.

"I want to see you," I said. "I *need* to see you."

Kayleigh's voice caught, emotion thick in her throat, when she whispered, "I need to see you."

There only seemed one place fitting for us to meet.

"The garage," we both said at the same time.

We were laughing and crying and laughing some more when another call came in on the receiver. I glanced over, slightly annoyed at the interruption.

"Kayleigh, um, hey, hold on," I said. "Noah's calling. I'm going to take it real quick."

"Alright, alright," Kayleigh said, sniffling.

"Okay, I'll be right back."

"Promise?"

I smiled, still unable to stop myself. "Promise."

I pressed the button on the receiver to switch the call. "Hey, Noah, I'm kind of busy right—"

"Darren, it's Eoin." The sound of Noah's voice made my blood run cold. I knew immediately he wasn't calling because of the news about Kayleigh. This was something else.

Something worse.

"Darren, he's in the hospital and—"

I didn't hear the rest of what Noah said. The phone clanged against the side of the desk, but I didn't care because I already had my coat and I was out the door.

42

DARREN

*T*he elevator doors seemed to move just as slowly as they did that cold, dark night, as if they hadn't been greased in years. The screech of my boots on the yellowed linoleum was the same. The low whisper of nurses, the beeping of frightening machines, the ringing of phones and crying of babies all the same. The door was even the same: simple brown plywood with a simple silver doorknob.

I prayed the sight inside the room was far different from the one the night Jaime died.

I rushed into the room, my lungs burning and my heart racing. The door swung back and crashed into the wall. I gasped as my eyes tried to focus on something, anything. There was the array of monitors and equipment along the back wall. There were the curtains over the window, drawn tight against the glare of city lights. There was the bed with those sickeningly white sheets.

And Eoin.

There was Eoin, sitting on the side of the bed with his back to me, facing the viewless window with his head bent, his left arm in a sling. When he turned to look over his shoulder at the noise, I noticed a black eye and a small line of tidy stitches above his eyebrow.

"Eoin, thank God you're—"

I was about to say "Eoin, thank God you're okay". That was the relieved exhale on the very tip of my tongue. But the moment Eoin recognised it was me standing just inside his hospital room, his face went pale, paler than the white sheets of the bed he sat on. This only made the blue and black around his eye look more stark, more severe, more painful.

There was no way I could say that my little brother was okay. He was far from it. His body might be alright, despite a few aches and pains and a little bit of healing. But he was not okay. He was in pain, terrible, terrible pain. And there was no way I could place the blame for that on a sneaky patch of black ice or a buzz of alcohol or an iron lamp post.

It was because of me.

Me and me alone.

"Get the fuck out of here," Eoin growled under his breath, his voice quaking. "I don't want to see you right now."

I swallowed heavily and took a tentative step closer to my brother. "Eoin, please, I—"

"Get. The fuck. Out of here." Eoin's face was no longer pale, etched with deep lines of pain. With each inch I moved forward, it turned redder and redder with anger.

"I just want to make sure you're alright and then I'll go," I said.

I reached out a hand to lay it on Eoin's uninjured shoulder. He whipped around, his fist catching my jaw with a surprising amount of force. I stumbled back, holding my face as it throbbed with pain.

"Alright?!" Eoin leapt off the hospital bed with a grimace. "You want to make sure I'm *alright*?"

Eoin swung another punch that glanced off my cheek. When I stepped back to avoid the next one, I tripped on the leg of the chair beneath the old television set mounted in the corner and fell to the floor.

Eoin didn't seem to care at all that one of his arms was in a sling as he leapt onto me and drew his fist high into the air above me. My instinct was to block my face with my hands. But I fought against that surge for survival. Because I didn't want to protect myself, I didn't want to escape the pain, I didn't want to keep myself safe from my brother's attack.

As Eoin hit me, I wanted him to hit me harder. As his knuckles cracked against my cheekbone, I wanted him to hit me faster. I wanted him to pummel his strength down onto me till his breath was ragged and his lungs were screaming and he was too exhausted to even think of lifting his fist again.

I deserved it.

I deserved it all.

I didn't fight the waves of pain in my face and chest as Eoin hit me. I welcomed them. I was so lost in their agonising embrace, I didn't even hear the door open. Suddenly Noah was dragging Eoin off of me. Ma's face hoovered over me, eyes with wide concern as I blinked lethargically through swollen eyelids. She cupped my face with both her hands, but I pushed her away.

"I'm grand," I said, voice rough as I eased myself onto my elbows and sagged against the wall. "I'm grand."

"You're an asshole!" Eoin shouted at me from the edge of the bed where Noah was struggling to keep him contained. "A fucking asshole, Darren!"

He'd managed to pop loose half the stitches from above his eyebrow so blood coursed down the side of his face. Even in the sling his left arm hung strangely.

Still trying to hold Eoin back, Noah looked over at me on the floor next to Ma. "What the feck is this all about?"

Eoin spat out a spiteful laugh. "Yeah, Darren, go on and tell them then. Tell them what this is all about."

I could only hang my head, chin against chest.

"Tell them how you cheated with my fiancée, Darren." Eoin's voice was harsh and loud. "Tell them how you and Kayleigh were hooking up behind my back this whole time. Tell them how you betrayed your own brother."

I was too much of a coward to meet Noah's eyes, flooded with too much guilt to turn to look up at Ma.

"But you're not my brother, are you?" Eoin continued. "Because brothers don't hurt each other and brothers don't take from each other and brothers don't put themselves and what they want above each other."

I had nothing to say, because he was right. Of course he was right.

"Eoin, let's calm down. Alright?" Noah said. "You're going to hurt yourself."

"Calm down?" Eoin shouted. "Why the fuck should I calm down? You should be just as pissed as me, Noah. What if it had been Aubrey?"

I heard Noah sigh. "Eoin, just—"

"Why are you defending him?" Eoin growled. "Why are you on *his* side?"

"I'm not on anyone's side. I—"

"You should be on my side," Eoin barked. "He betrayed us all. You should be on my side!"

My chin was still buried in my chest so I only heard Michael walk into the hospital room and say, "I brought us coff—what the hell happened here?"

"Michael, love, would you go fetch us a nurse?" Ma asked quietly, still next to me on the floor.

"I don't need a nurse," Eoin shouted. "I need him out of here."

"Who?" Michael asked. "Darren?"

"He went behind my back with Kayleigh," Eoin explained. "She's leaving me because of him."

"No fucking way," Michael hissed under his breath. I imagined his angry eyes drilling a hole into the top of my head, still bent in shame.

"Michael, the nurse," Ma repeated.

"It can't be true," Michael insisted. "Daz? Say it's not true."

"Michael," Ma hissed. "The nurse. Now."

From there it all turned into the chaos I so feared. The fuse on a powder keg had been lit the moment I stepped into that bathroom and saw Kayleigh naked. I thought I had managed to dig my heel into it and put it out. But I was wrong.

The sparking, spitting fire continued down the fuse and there was nothing I could do to stop it. There, in that small, crammed hospital room, it exploded. It exploded because of me.

Ma, who normally kept her cool even in the most stressful situations, pushed herself to her feet and yelled at Michael about a nurse while he yelled at me to speak up. They were joined by Eoin cursing at me, and Noah yelling at Eoin to calm down before he hurt himself, the noise growing louder and louder as everyone tried to be heard over the others. From my place on the floor, I could barely make out one bellowing voice from another.

I winced in pain as I eased myself up with the aid of the wall behind me. The pain wasn't payment enough; it would never be enough for what I'd caused.

My family was so engaged with their battles, they didn't notice when I moved with a slight limp toward the door. I slipped out into the hallway and the door clicked shut behind me. It did little to dampen the noise of their fighting as I dragged my aching body toward the elevator. I was fairly certain even when the elevator doors closed, I would still hear it. When the glass sliding entrance doors slid shut and the sounds of honking cars and chattering pedestrians filled the busy city air, I was sure I would still hear it. I could get on my motorcycle and rev the engine and drive away, far, far away, and I would still hear my family fighting there in that hospital room.

I would hear it in every waking moment and every sweat-filled dream. I would never stop hearing it.

A nurse stopped me as I neared the elevator. "Jaysus, boy. What happened to you?" she asked, hands on my chest as she stared up at my bruised and blooded face. "You need to be looked at."

"I'm grand," I said, leaning past her to hit the down button. "But someone needs assistance in Room 9."

She hesitated a moment at the sight of my swollen eye, but then hurried away down the hallway.

I'd stood at an elevator just like this one after receiving the news that Jaime was gone. I remembered how empty I felt in that moment: hollow, drained, soulless. I thought I couldn't possibly feel less empty.

But now as I waited for the doors of the elevator to open, I realised that I hadn't been empty, at least not entirely, because even after my brother's death, I had something: my secret.

I had the secret of where I was that night, why I didn't make it, why I had left.

It was something to hold onto, to cling to, to clutch tightly in the darkest hour of the night. And it was a relief—at least my family didn't know.

At least my family would be alright.

But now the secret of Kayleigh and me was out in the open. I had nothing left to cling to, nothing to clutch in the darkest hour of the night. And my family was not alright.

I wasn't empty before. I wasn't at rock bottom. I couldn't have been.

Because I was there now.

43

KAYLEIGH

*W*hen I arrived at the shop and found the garage door still wide open, I didn't think anything of it. Darren was supposed to be there, after all. But as I rushed across the driveway calling his name, I heard nothing. Still, this wasn't a cause for concern.

He could be in the back office. He could be out in the alleyway taking out some trash. Hell, he could even be in the bathroom. I was far too happy to care that he hadn't come running out to greet me. We'd waited so long to have our moment, what was a few minutes more?

I wandered the empty garage, checked the bathroom, the alleyway and the back office where I replaced the phone back onto the receiver. There was no sight of Darren. It was then that I noticed that his motorcycle was gone.

I pushed away the immediate thoughts of concern that tried to worm their way into my head: he changed his mind, he didn't mean it, it was all a cruel joke that he was playing on me, that he'd been playing on me this whole time. I pushed them all away because they were ridiculous.

I'd just spoken with Darren. We'd both been happy and

relieved and excited. We agreed to meet at the garage. All of this was true.

He just went out to get flowers, I told myself. He couldn't possibly have known that I would have sped through two red lights, taken every turn too tightly, practically making my engine smoke trying to speed to him. He thought he'd have plenty of time to go out for flowers and get back before I arrived. He just went out to get flowers. And that was that.

I sent him a quick text: *I'm here.*

But my excuse for Darren's unexpected absence became less and less convincing as time passed. I chewed at my nails as I tried to convince myself the florist had just been out on an errand, making Darren late. The street lamps turned on as dusk fell over the city, and it became harder and harder to believe that maybe there was a credit card issue at the florist shop. Or a flower emergency. Or anything, really, that would explain where in the hell Darren was. My calls to his phone went straight to voicemail.

It was hours later when the glare of the motorcycle head-light finally swept across the dark garage. I shielded my eyes where I sat on the hood of an old rusted junker and then hopped off as the motorcycle engine sputtered and died. Darren tugged his helmet off as I ran across the driveway toward him.

In my mind, he would greet me with a beaming smile, sweep me up into his arms, and kiss me like I'd never been kissed before, because for the first time we each knew what love meant. In my mind, the tips of our noses would freeze out in the cold, but we wouldn't care as we held each other tight and cried, because we'd finally found one another. In my mind, this moment was the start of forever.

But my feet slowed as I approached Darren because even in the dim light of the street lamps, I could see the bruises covering his face. I stopped completely when I saw the emptiness, the defeat, the dread in his eyes.

"Darren," I whispered, eyes searching his bloodied face. "Darren, what happened?"

I tried to reach out a hand to gently brush his cheek, but he flinched away from me.

Something was wrong. Something was terribly wrong.

"Please, talk to me."

Darren couldn't even look at me. He stared down at his helmet and fidgeted with the chin straps. It didn't escape my notice that he hadn't even bothered getting off his motorcycle. It was as if he had stopped simply to make a delivery before jetting off again. I could sense his fingers twitching toward the key in the ignition.

"Please," I begged, my voice wavering just slightly as fear again wrapped icy cold fingers around my heart.

Darren lowered his chin to his chest, as if too tired to keep his head up. He briefly covered his eyes with his hand, as if he knew a car wreck was about to happen right in front of him and he didn't want to see the carnage. I tried to step a little closer to him.

"Stop." His voice was raw and it sounded painful to speak, as if he'd been screaming into the wind for all those hours he was missing.

My chin was trembling. This was not the happy reunion I expected after getting off the phone with Darren. I thought it was strange that he never got back on the line, but I figured he just forgot in his excitement. I never thought it would lead to this, whatever *this* was.

"Darren, please," I whispered. "What's going on?"

Darren shook his head and squeezed his eyes shut. I searched his shadowed face, his sagging posture, his tired sighs for any answers, but all I found was more questions.

"You're scaring me," I said.

Again I tried to lay a comforting hand on Darren's shoulder, but he yanked himself out of my reach. "I can't be with you."

"What?"

Darren simply repeated his words as if the only problem was that I hadn't heard him, as if he hadn't just pulled forever right out from underneath my feet, crushing the tiny bud of "I love you" with the heel of his boot.

"I can't be with you."

Darren immediately grabbed the key to twist in the ignition, not even giving my heart enough time to skip a beat. I lunged forward to stop him with a hand around his wrist before he rode off right down the street and out of my heart.

"Don't you dare," I whispered, words catching in my throat. "Don't you *dare*."

Darren tried to tug his hand free, but I gripped his wrist tighter. His hand was shaking. Mine was, too. I tried to catch his eyes, but he was so focused on the ignition switch, he was barely blinking.

"I can't be with you," Darren repeated, his voice small, almost childlike in its fear.

"What happened?" I begged. "Darren, please, talk to me. Just talk to me."

Tears stung my eyes. I did my best to hold them back, but every time Darren tugged at my grip around his wrist, I found it harder and harder.

"Please, look at me," I begged.

The first tear slipped down my cheek as Darren squeezed his eyes shut and shook his head.

"I can't be with you," he said.

"Yes, you can," I insisted. I felt him slipping away from me, dragged back by a tide I couldn't see, I couldn't feel, I couldn't control. "You can be with me."

"I chose wrong." Darren's words were laced with such pain that I felt the sting in my own heart. "I chose wrong again."

"What are you talking about?" I yelled. I was growing desperate. I tried to turn Darren's face toward me, but he wrenched his face away.

"Darren, please!"

He twisted his hand away. In an instant he turned the key in the ignition of his motorcycle.

"I'm sorry," was all he said.

The engine roared to life, the sound sending panic through my veins. I could not—would not—let him get away. Even as tears streamed down my face as I stood myself in front of Darren's motorcycle, blocking his path. I placed my hands on the front tyre and stared him down.

"I'm not letting you slip away again," I said. "Darren, I love you."

Darren's eyes, ringed with black and purple and traces of blue, were red and puffy. Tears clung to his long dark eyelashes as he finally met my firm gaze. His stormy eyes were wells of pain and heartbreak.

"I love you," I said again. "I love you."

Darren shook his head, tears springing to his own eyes, mirroring my own. We were the sky and the ocean, water above, water below. We were one. Why couldn't he see that? Why couldn't I *make* him see that?

"Darren, I—"

"Eoin's in the hospital."

I stared at Darren in shock. I shook my head in confusion, like I'd just fallen and wasn't sure where I was. "What?"

Darren's eyes were blank, empty and barren. "Eoin went drinking after you broke up with him. He crashed his car. He's in the hospital. He's in the hospital because of..."

Darren's words trailed off, but it wasn't hard to fill in the blanks. Because of him. Because of me.

Because of *us*.

My brain struggled to comprehend this news, to put all the pieces together: Darren being gone from the garage, his return, his insistence that *we* couldn't be. When I finally looked up at Darren, utterly dumbfounded, I found him not looking at me, but through me.

He was looking at the black asphalt behind me. He was looking into the dark twists and turns he would race through on his motorcycle alone. He was looking into a future where I was nothing but a memory, nothing but a terrible, terrible mistake. I tried to look for Darren's eyes, but he was already gone.

He was already gone.

Realising there was no hope left, I stumbled back out of the way of Darren's motorcycle. Darren slipped on his helmet, put up the kickstand with his heel, revved the engine, and accelerated past me. There was no last glance, no last words, no last kiss.

He was down the road.

He was around the corner.

He was gone.

Gone where I could not follow.

44

KAYLEIGH

"Well, well, well, look who came crawling back into Papa Claus's arms."

In the dirty, crammed office at Dooley's Bar, I tried to shake off the disgusted shiver that crept down my spine at the sight of Andy, my old pig of a boss, leaning back in his mouldy, Cheetos-stained desk chair. He stretched his arms above his head and reclined into his hands with a contented sigh of victory. His considerable belly, dotted with wiry red hairs, spilled from his two-sizes-too-small Dooley's-logoed polo and oozed over his belt that was clinging on for dear life. I avoided looking at the mustard stain in his untrimmed red moustache as he grinned at me with that yellow, toothy predatory smile I knew all too well.

Andy knew that he had all the power in this situation, and he was milking that for all it was worth. I'd returned to Cork a week ago and I was pushing the offer to crash on my friend's couch to its limit. It didn't help that all I'd been doing was lying around, surrounded by empty pints of ice cream and grease-stained pizza boxes as I moped around in my pyjamas and heartbroken misery. I had to get a job. I had to make money. I had to get my own place.

I had to move on.

"Did you miss me?" Andy asked, biting at his lower lip as his eyes scanned my body from head to toe.

I predicted this, of course, and made sure to wear my largest ill-fitting sweatpants and a giant puffer jacket for this interview.

"Did you dream about me, little Kay-Kay?"

I gripped the armrests of the flimsy plastic chair next to a disorganised filing cabinet overflowing with unpaid invoices and years-old receipts. It seemed not even a single piece of paper had been moved since I left.

Andy certainly hadn't changed, that was for sure. He was still miles past the line of appropriateness, still red-faced and balding, still a man who needed to be put in his place. The office was the same. The light in the lamp in the corner was still broken. An old bag of chips still on the edge of the desk. Even the Christmas lights lazily tacked up above his computer were still up.

It was like I hadn't even left.

"Are you going to give me the job or not, Andy?" I asked, tiring of his petty little games.

"Of course I'm going to give you the job," Andy said, his belly jiggling as he leaned forward in his chair. "How can I resist those tit—I mean, how can I resist that smile?"

I stood up from the chair. "Great," I said, tone flat with not even a hint of a smile as Andy leered at me. "Can you get me the forms I need to fill out for payroll and stuff?"

Andy dismissed me with a wave of his beefy, freckled fingers as he wiped away tears from his eyes.

"It's all still in the system, Kay-Kay the BJ Fav-Fav," Andy snorted, clearly enjoying his "joke". "I knew you'd be back. I knew you couldn't resist this."

Andy grabbed his nut sack that was half-buried beneath his belly, and I bit my tongue because I needed this job before my gracious friend kicked me out onto the street. And honestly, I needed the distraction. On the couch there was nothing to do but think about Darren. Darren, Darren, Darren. How much I missed Darren.

At least at Dooley's Bar my mind was busy worrying about which dark and dingy corner Andy and his grabby hands with those disgustingly sticky fingers were hiding behind.

"I look forward to watching that cute ass of yours behind the bar tonight on my security cameras," Andy called out after me as I quickly slipped out of the horrendous office. "Give me a little shake, would ya, Kay-Kay Queen of the Va-Jay-Jays!"

I shuddered at the sound of Andy's pig-like snorts of laughter that snuck under the crack in the office door like some sort of toxic gas following after me. Sighing in relief in the small staff changing room, I leaned against the wall and dragged a tired hand over my face. I jumped when the door opened after me. Thank God, it was only Tina and not a fat, balding monstrosity.

"Kayleigh!"

I forced a polite smile as Tina leaned in for a warm hug.

"Did you have a nice holiday?" Tina asked as she slipped off her coat to put it in one of the five or so beat-up grey lockers.

I frowned in confusion. "Holiday?"

Tina pulled off her shirt to change into the Dooley's work uniform: a tight t-shirt with a V-neck whose plunge rivalled that of Niagara Falls, selected by, of course, the boss man himself.

"Yeah, weren't you on hols?" Tina asked, adjusting her t-shirt around her red push-up bra and glancing over at me.

"I—um, well...did everyone think I was?"

Tina laughed.

"I mean, where else would you have been? What else would you have been doing?"

I nodded slowly.

No one here believed that I had left for good. No one here believed that I would ever really leave the safety and security of my job, as demeaning as it could sometimes be given not just the clientele, but the harassing boss. No one here believed that I would try to do something more, *be* something more.

"Well, I've got to get out there," Tina said, as I stood there pondering by the door. "You working tonight then?"

I smiled as she grabbed the door handle and paused. I nodded. "Yep, back at it."

Tina patted my shoulder. "Good," she said. "Grab a rack of pint glasses from the kitchen when you come, yeah?"

"Sure."

The door to the changing room clicked shut behind her, and I was left alone once more. Now curious, I made my way to the locker that used to be mine. I assumed that when I left, Andy or one of the girls would have cleared it out: given my uniforms to the new girl, tossed my magnetic nametag, and parcelled out my leftover makeup, mints, and dental floss.

I was surprised to open the locker door and find all of my stuff still inside, not an item out of place. Nothing had been moved, not even an inch, let alone dumped into the trash bin outside with the empty beer bottles and past-its-date nacho cheese sauce.

I touched my nametag still stuck to the inside of the locker and thought again—it is as if I'd never left. Nothing had changed. Nothing at all.

Nothing but me.

As if frozen in time, Dooley's remained the same during my time with Eoin and the O'Sullivans and Darren in Dublin. It had the same sticky floors, the same greasy bar tops, the same drunk passed out at the end of the bar. The staff was the same: Andy and Tina and the other girls, too, judging by the names on the same row of lockers. And the memory of the old me stayed the same as well: the remnants of the old me were all still here, right where I left them.

I would slip right back into the old me. I would pull on my skin-tight V-neck that displayed my breasts gratuitously for those horny college kids. And it would fit; it would fit like a glove. I would snap on my magnetic nametag, too. My name was still Kayleigh, after all. I would fall into the same routine again of cleaning pint glasses, changing kegs, mopping slipped beer off of dirty floors.

I couldn't help but feel like a butterfly trying to crawl back inside its cocoon.

Maybe I just tried to spread my wings too soon. Or maybe I never had wings at all; maybe I just had Darren.

With a sigh, I reached for my Dooley's Bar nametag.

45

DARREN

I'd left thirty-five voicemail messages on Eoin's cell phone.

I'd sent another forty or so texts, most consisting of either "Call me" or "Please call me".

I'd emailed him eleven times, tried to get in touch with him through his agent nine times, and harassed his rugby coach to let me into the training facility out in the parking lot of the stadium enough times that security was forced to walk me off the premises (I believe that lucky number was seven).

It had been a week since Eoin's accident and the incident in the hospital and I was desperate to find him. What I would say, I hadn't quite figured out. Thankfully I got to put all of my mental efforts into simply tracking him down.

The closest I'd gotten to him was as close as the rest of the population of Ireland: the tabloids. Just like everyone else, I'd read about Eoin's very public benders, late night partying, and hook-ups with the hottest single celebrities. I'd read about him missing practice, showing up to coaches' meetings drunk or high, and risking his future career as a rugby star with his suddenly reckless behaviour.

As a last-ditch effort, I drove over to Eoin's place on a Tuesday at 8:03 a.m. I didn't have any illusions that he would let me inside, but I didn't need him to let me inside—I had a key. All us brothers had emergency keys. If Eoin wouldn't face me and hear me out, I'd force him to by ambushing him in his bed.

I slipped the key into Eoin's door and then as quietly as possible stepped inside his swanky renovated townhouse in Ballsbridge, one of the most upmarket areas of Dublin. My attempts at silence, however, were quickly dashed when my heel crunched down on an empty energy drink can in the entry-way. I looked down to find the whole hallway littered with cans and empty bottles of Jameson. I tried to pick them up, but by the time I made my way to the living room, my arms were full. I found the recycling bin already overflowing and spilling onto the kitchen floor.

I stood in the centre of the living room, horrified to see the mess around me. There were takeout boxes scattered across the coffee table and couch, beer bottles covering the glass side tables, sticky shot glasses dotting the carpet, and women's bras and panties flung over the lampshades and door handle to the patio outside with the jacuzzi that bubbled and spit unattended even now.

The sight of it all tore at my heart—I was the reason for this.

Unable to look at it all any longer, I picked my way through discarded clothes to Eoin's bedroom door. It was cracked open. When I peeked inside I found the bed entirely empty. I tried to push the door fully open and discovered it was blocked by an entire keg. Party cups took the place of where the sheets and comforter should be on the mattress, and shattered champagne glasses shimmered with the rays of morning light coming in through the window. I checked the bathroom and then the rest of the townhouse, but it was obvious that Eoin was not there.

With a defeated sigh, I decided I would clean up the place. I knew it wasn't nearly enough to make up for what I did, but I had to start somewhere. I had to do *something*. I busied myself for nearly three and a half hours collecting trash, doing laundry, making the bed, and vacuuming. I was reaching for the door handle to carry out the last of five black trash bags to the dumpster when the door handle turned on its own.

I stepped back as Eoin swung open the door. I wasn't sure whose face revealed the most shock at the sight of the other. On the one hand, it must have been quite a surprise to see me standing in his entryway on a Tuesday morning with a bag of trash. But on the other hand, I hardly recognised the man standing in front of me.

Eoin was not just the baby of the family, but perpetually baby-faced as well: full cheeks, an infectious, non-stop grin, and bright, shining eyes that saw the world with curiosity and eternal optimism. But this was a man in front of me. A man with dark rings of exhaustion under his eyes. A man with red-rimmed, tired, defeated eyes. A man with narrow lips in a stern line. A man who looked haggard and in desperate need of a shower and a shave. He smelled like booze and looked like a bender.

I couldn't believe this man was my baby-faced baby brother.

"Eoin, I—"

"The key." Eoin held out his palm to me, but not before I caught sight of multiple club stamps scattered across the back of his hand.

"Eoin, please, can we talk? I just want to talk."

Eoin's pale face flashed red with anger, save for the purple bags beneath his eyes. He clenched the fist that still hung in the sling from his dislocated elbow and grit out between clenched teeth, "Darren, give me the fucking key."

Eoin was breathing heavily, like a bull in the arena ready to charge. I felt the key to his place in my jeans pocket but hesitated. I feared this might be the only chance I'd get to make amends with him, or at least try to.

"I can explain, if you just—"

"I'm doing everything possible to forget you and to forget *her*," Eoin growled. "And then you have the audacity to just show up at my door. Fuck you, Darren. Fuck you."

"I—"

"Give me the *fucking* key before I add to your collection," Eoin shouted, jabbing an angry finger at the ugly, healing bruises that covered half my face. "Those keys were for brothers. And as far as I'm concerned, we're no longer that."

"Eoin—"

"And don't think that you can come in here and pick up a few bottles and call us square," Eoin continued, voice shaking with rage. "Because that doesn't even start to clean up the mess you've made."

"Eoin—"

He advanced on me and I let him until my back collided with the entryway wall. He shoved his unshaven face right up close to mine, his whiskey breath hot on my cheek.

"Give me the goddamn key, Darren," he hissed, shoulders tense like a spring about to pop. "I'm not asking again."

I sighed and fished the key out of my front pocket. Eoin snatched it from me and stalked away, swaying slightly as he made his way to the living room. He collapsed on the couch.

"Now get the fuck out of here," he grumbled into the cushions. "And get the fuck out of my life while you're at it."

I took my bag of trash and left. As I walked down the sidewalk, I heard Eoin stumble back toward the door and lock it behind me. This was followed by the sound of Eoin's fist rattling the door on its hinges.

One thing was clear: he was nowhere near ready to forgive me.

The next thought that followed was terrifying: maybe he never would be.

I returned to the garage, which I had been avoiding all week. I didn't want to be there. Whenever I smelled oil, I thought of her. Whenever my hands tightened around a wrench, I thought of my arms tightening around her waist. Whenever I heard an engine roar to life, I thought of the life we could have had together, and I had to immediately kill the ignition before I fell apart completely.

But my stack of uncompleted work orders was piling up higher and higher, and the number of customer voicemails on my phone was growing longer and longer. Besides, there really wasn't anywhere I could go without thinking of Kayleigh. She was everywhere.

She was a mist, always around me, against my face, light on my lips, tangled in my eyelashes when I closed my eyes, and yet...and yet I could never grasp her, I could never manage to hold onto her, I could never cling to even a piece of her before she was carried away on the cold Irish wind.

I trudged into the little back office to grab the stack of work orders. But as I was flipping through them, a small piece of scrap paper tumbled down between my feet. I picked it up and froze at the sight of Kayleigh's swirly, delicate handwriting.

I sank into the chair, letting the work orders fall and scatter across the floor, as my eyes flew over the note:

D,

IT'S NOT REALLY fair that I never got you a Christmas present when you got me one so lovely and thoughtful. I'm sorry that it's late in getting to you, but I hope it can maybe bring you some happiness. Never forget that you deserve it.

PLEASE USE IT. For me, at least.

I WISH THINGS WERE DIFFERENT.

~ K

BELOW HER NOTE was simply an arrow that pointed to the other side of the piece of paper. I flipped it over and stared at what was written there till the sun sank low on the horizon and the street lamps flickered on one by one down the street. I stared at it till my fingers and the tip of my nose grew numb in the cold. I stared at it till it was so dark, I could no longer read it.

But by that point there was no way I could unsee it.

Kayleigh's Christmas gift to me was a telephone number.

Sophie's telephone number.

46

KAYLEIGH

*I*t wasn't the first time I'd felt Andy's grimy hands on my ass.

All of us girls at Dooley's knew full well the "team building" slaps or the "good job tonight" squeezes or the "Oops, I thought that was the door handle" gropes. I'd had him harass me in the kitchen, harass me in the changing room, harass me on the dance floor, in the bathroom, and behind the keg room. No, it certainly wasn't the first time I'd endured Andy's physical advances.

But on that cold January Saturday night, with a tray of sudsy pints in one hand and a bucket of ice in the other, I decided right then and there amongst the packed crowd at Dooley's that it would be the last.

I dropped the bucket of ice and let the tray of overflowing pint glasses crash to the floor next to me. The entire bar immediately went silent as all eyes, glossy or otherwise, looked at me. There was a time where the most noise I would make was an anonymous complaint report that was calmly and respectfully written and emailed in to a non-existent HR department.

But that was not me anymore.

This time I wanted to make a scene. I wanted to make a mess. I wanted everyone to remember that one bartender at Dooley's who let that pig have a piece of her mind.

"Did you just touch my ass?" I asked Andy, voice loud enough for the entire bar to hear it.

Andy glanced nervously at the line of bartenders and crowd of patrons all staring at him.

"What's that now, Kay-Kay love?" Andy said, laughing nervously and trying to play it off coolly.

"My name is Kay*leigh*," I said, crossing my arms over my chest. "And in case you didn't hear me properly, I asked if you just squeezed my ass in my place of work."

Andy's already red, splotchy alcoholic face turned even redder and splotchier. "No, no, of course, I didn't—"

"I think you did."

Andy eyed the crowd that was whispering excitedly to one another. No one knew they would be receiving free entertainment tonight.

"Kayleigh, maybe we can discuss this further in my office," Andy leaned forward to whisper.

He tried to grab for my wrist, but I pulled my body out of reach.

"I think we can discuss this right here," I said defiantly.

Anger flashed across Andy's piggish features. "You're making a scene, girl," he hissed.

It was my turn to lean closer to him. I grinned and said loudly and clearly, "Good. And you know what?"

He narrowed his eyes at me.

"I'm about to make an even bigger one." Snatching the most expensive bottles on the top shelf, I shouted to the packed bar. "We're drinking on our beloved boss tonight, folks."

I lined up a long row of shot glasses and messily poured

them one by one, not caring that expensive whiskey dripped down the sides of the bar.

"A shot for the time you tried to show me your cock beneath that Santa hat," I shouted. "A shot for the time you threatened to fire us if we didn't wear these slutty shirts. And a shot for each time you touched one of us inappropriately without our consent."

I kept expecting my ma's shrill, incensed voice to come hissing in my ear over the hush of the stunned bar. *"You're being extremely rude, Kayleigh Scott. You're making a mess. Who in their right mind will hire you after this? Be quiet, child! Be quiet!"*

But as the whiskey splashed over the lips of the shot glasses, I found my ma entirely absent. The harsh glare of the microwave light in a dark kitchen didn't replace the Christmas lights still hanging from the bar. The crowd didn't disappear, leaving me alone at an empty table no longer set for three. The music remained and my ma was nowhere to be found.

Instead I was surprised to find that it was Darren's voice that I heard in my head. *"Go, Kayleigh. Don't let anyone push you around. Don't let anyone take from you what is yours. Louder. Louder still."*

I saw his devilish grin, imagined him leaning against the back wall with his muscular arms crossed over his charcoal-grey Henley. My heart clenched painfully as I imagined a smear of grease across his cheek, just below those stormy blue eyes. I imagined those eyes soften as I tried to communicate to him across the room: I wouldn't be doing this if it hadn't been for you. I imagined him nodding in approval as he watched me grab the overflowing shot glass and lift it to Andy.

"Ladies and gentlemen, here's to my asshole, pig of a boss. I quit!"

As the crowd cheered, I pushed the line of shots toward the first row of people at the bar and handed the bottle of whiskey to the first person in front of me. I slipped past the other girls working at the bar and patted them on the shoulder. They all just stared at me with wide eyes.

Darren was gone. Well, of course Darren was gone. Darren was never there. But his impression on my heart was. I could feel the grooves of his fingerprints on my skin; I could trace them when I closed my eyes alone in the dark. Darren would never *be* here, but he would also never *not* be here with me.

The DJ, confused as everyone else, blasted the music to try to salvage the night while the bottle of *very* expensive whiskey worked its way through the crowd, tipped up and poured haphazardly into open mouths, spilling down cheeks and onto the beer-stained floor.

I elbowed my way to the door and stumbled outside into the cold. Gasping like I'd just run a marathon, I bent over and rested my hands on my knees while sucking in big deep breaths. There on the sidewalk, I waited for the guilt to crash over me. I waited for the regret over making a scene, anxiety about paying my bills without an income, embarrassment over raising my voice to my employer in front of a packed bar.

But none of those emotions came. None.

I guess I was just too busy smiling. I suppose it's hard to feel anxious when there is a smile so big across your face that it makes your cheeks ache. I was just too fucking happy.

I laughed as I stood and dragged my hands through my hair. Next to the crosswalk, beneath the traffic lights, I realised this was the exact spot where I'd stood after escaping Andy's advances out of the back alley. That panicked, uncertain, frightening moment was only weeks ago, but it felt like years to me.

Back then I stared at the ice-slick street stretching out in both directions with fear of the future: where was I going to go? What was I going to do? Each direction seemed a dead end. But now I sucked that frigid air into my lungs and saw nothing but opportunity. When I ran instead of confronting Andy in his office a few weeks ago, I literally collided with my future in the form of a six-foot-two giant of a man. But here, in this moment, *I* decided my future.

I decided my next step.

I decided where I was to go, what I was to do, who I was to be.

My cheeks burned rosy and hot, and my heart cartwheeled and galloped in my chest. I felt like a crazy woman there alone on the sidewalk in the middle of the night, but I'd never felt more...more *free*.

On that night I escaped from Andy, Eoin quite literally trapped me. His big, strong arms held me on top of him on the ice. And even if they hadn't, the curious eyes of the gathering crowd around us would have held me in place nonetheless. I was swept up into *his* life, carried off in *his* arms, entangled in *his* family. And I allowed all of this without a single peep.

But now it was just me. There was no one to pull me this way or that. No one to push me toward this direction or away from that. I didn't have a job to fall into, an apartment given to me, a family ready-made for me to simply insert myself into. I was all alone with the path before me entirely unclear.

And I'd never felt more alive.

If I wanted a job, I was going to have to get it. If I wanted an apartment, I was going to have to hunt one down, earn the money myself, and lug whatever futon I could find up the stairs *myself*. I was going to have to struggle and work and fall down and get back up again. If I wanted to lead the life *I* wanted, I was going to have to fight for it.

I was not going to be quiet any longer.

I was not going to let myself get dragged along with which-ever current was strongest like a piece of driftwood carried along without a choice.

I was going to fight.

I was going to be loud.

I was going to go after the life I wanted, the life I deserved.

Right there on the sidewalk with numb fingers and a burning heart, I pulled out my phone and searched for mechanic shops looking for immediate apprentices. Not caring where it was or what it paid or how messy the shop may be, I clicked on the very first want ad I found online. Within a minute, an email was sent telling the hiring manager I could be at the shop on Monday. It was only then that I even bothered to glance at the address. For all I knew, I'd just applied to a place in Louth or Belfast or Limerick.

But no.

The shop was in Dublin.

47

DARREN

*T*he bar was empty on that Tuesday afternoon, save for the drunk passed out with his hand still clinging to half a lukewarm pint of Guinness and the bored bartender who circled his dirty rag over a clean counter between exacerbated sighs and desperate glances at the clock on the wall behind me.

The wail of the jukebox drowned out the incessant tapping of my toe against the barstool as my nervous fingers peeled away the label on my bottle of beer. I wondered why I hadn't ordered something stronger. I was lifting my hand to grab the attention of the weary-faced bartender when a shaft of light from the front door spread across my face, blinding me and illuminating the dust particles that hung suspended in the air. The door swung shut, and in the dim light my eyes adjusted once more in time to see her eyes scan the empty bar and fall on me.

I swallowed nervously and winced at the shriek my barstool made as I pushed it back to stand. I greeted her with a timid kiss on the cheek.

"Sophie."

My high school love tucked a strand of her golden-blonde

hair that was still as lustrous as the day I first saw her in the sun and smiled, clearly just as nervous as I.

"I still can't believe you called," she said as she slipped into the barstool next to mine. "How'd you even find my number after all these years?"

"Um, through a friend," I answered hesitantly, hoping she wouldn't pry further.

"Well, I'm glad for your friend," Sophie said with a sweet smile as she placed her hand gently over mine, which covered the torn pieces of label.

Her hazel eyes searched mine as I tried not to flinch away from her touch. I hadn't seen Sophie since I abruptly ended things with her after Jaime's death. She came to my house in a black lace dress for the funeral. I remembered the exact pattern of the lace, delicate and intricate and fragile. There were tiny flowers, like the ones that filled the house from neighbours and friends and family. I hated those tiny flowers. I remembered her red-rimmed eyes. I remembered the way her fingers shook as she gripped her little black purse just a little too tightly.

I didn't even let her inside the house as I told her that I wouldn't be going.

I wouldn't be going to the funeral with her.

I wouldn't be going to the funeral at all.

I wouldn't be going away with her.

I wouldn't be going anywhere at all.

I wouldn't be going out with her.

I wouldn't be going out with anyone, anyone at all.

I remembered the confusion on her face. I remembered the hurt, the pain, the guilt, too. I remembered her tears. I remembered her petite, shaking fingers reaching out for me. I remembered her bottom lip quivering, because she was just as afraid as I was.

I remembered not caring.

I remembered not caring one goddamn bit.

The bartender poured Sophie a glass of white wine. I ordered a whiskey, partly because I needed something stronger and partly so that I didn't have another beer label to anxiously peel off bit by bit.

Sophie filled the empty silence between us with idle chitchat about her job in the city, her father's retirement, her vacation to the south of France over the past summer. When I'd practically worn out my neck nodding along over-emphatically to everything she said, Sophie finally sighed and slipped her fingers into mine to squeeze my hand.

"Darren," she said softly, kindly, "why did you call me here today? Today after all this time?"

This was the part I was dreading. I didn't have an answer, at least not a good one. I wasn't sure why I reached out to Sophie; I wasn't sure what I wanted from her.

"If I'm being honest, Sophie," I said while staring into my nearly empty glass of whiskey, "I don't really know. I... I..."

Sophie's thumb ran alongside the side of my hand as she waited patiently.

I swallowed heavily and wished it was more whiskey that was traveling down my tightened throat. "I guess I just—it's just...do you ever, you know...do you ever wonder?"

I was too ashamed to fully lift my face to her. I expected her to respond with a question of her own: "Do I ever wonder what?" I hadn't exactly been crystal clear.

But Sophie smiled softly and reached over to tuck a strand of my dark hair behind my ear the way she used to when we were young and in love and Jaime wasn't buried beneath a parched plot of earth.

"I did for a while," she answered, understanding exactly what I had been trying to ask her. "I think it's only natural to think what would have been, what *we* could have been if Jaime hadn't died."

She averted her eyes as she sipped her wine and stared across the empty bar. I knew that look all too well. She wasn't seeing a dust-covered row of bottles. She was seeing a long hospital corridor. She was seeing a room with an open door. She was seeing a single empty bed.

It was my turn to squeeze her hand. She took another healthy drink of wine before looking back over at me with those sweet hazel eyes.

"For a long time I was heartbroken," Sophie said. "For a long time I was angry. Angry at you. Angry at myself. But most of all —no, I hate to even admit it. No, no, no. It's almost too terrible to say aloud. I..." Sophie shook her head as her eyes grew just a little bit misty in the dim light. "I shouldn't say it."

I said it for her: "You were angry at Jaime."

Sophie's hand gripping the stem of her wine glass trembled as a tear slipped down her freckled cheek. "I hated that I felt that way. I hated myself for so long for feeling that way toward..."

Sophie tried to pull her hand from mine, as if she no longer felt she deserved the comfort of my warm skin against hers. But I only held on tighter; I wasn't going to close the door on her this time.

"Sophie," I whispered.

"I blamed him," Sophie gasped, her tear-filled eyes meeting mine, our shared pain colliding. "I blamed him for taking you from me. I blamed him for ripping my heart in two with no way to mend the pieces back together. I blamed him for ending forever, *my* forever."

As Sophie swallowed back a sob, I was flooded with bone-breaking waves of guilt for letting her, no, for making her go through this alone. The sound of the door I'd closed on her as she stood alone on the front steps of Ma's house echoed again and again in my mind. The thud of my feet on the stairs as I walked away from her forever pounded like a base drum between my ears. I wished my heart would stop pounding so terribly so that I wouldn't hear it any longer: my shame, my guilt, my embarrassment.

"But Darren," Sophie said after sucking in a shaky breath, "I know now that Jaime didn't take anything from me. It took me a long time, a long, long time, but I came to realise that there was nothing there for Jaime to take."

I glanced over at Sophie in surprise. She was clearly expecting this because she choked out a small laugh at the expression on my face and squeezed my hand. "Let's order another round, alright?"

With more liquid courage in front of us on the sticky bar top, Sophie and I sipped our drinks in silence before she sighed and continued.

"Darren, I will never regret what we had together," she said, her eyes dry once again. "You were my first for so many things and I adored you. I *adored* you. But what we had wasn't love."

I sat next to her at the bar with my fingers wrapped around my glass of whiskey, and her words sank slowly into my heart like an anchor lowered from a ship. Her words descended deeper and deeper till they buried themselves in the sands of my soul. They hit without a sound, but I could feel their weight, heavy and burdensome.

I'd always believed that Sophie and I were in love back then, terribly and wildly and madly in love. I'd always believed that we were destined to be together. The story I'd always told myself was that it was fate, and fate alone, that ripped us apart.

I'd never once considered that we weren't in love in the first place.

"What happened with Jaime," Sophie continued, her voice

soft and gentle like the first ray of sunshine after a summer rainstorm, "it terrified us. The hole he left in all of our hearts, yours especially, was filled with fear, the most horrible fear possible, I think. We were, all of us, afraid. Afraid..."

Sophie hastily grabbed her wine glass and raised it to her lips before they betrayed another emotional quiver. I couldn't blame her. I myself drank in the burn of the whiskey as it slipped down my throat.

We were afraid, all of us. Our worlds had been shaken; everything we thought we knew had been called into question. We were afraid of the future. We were afraid of a life without Jaime. We were afraid of living a *happy* life without Jaime. We were afraid of every laugh, every smile, every hug and embrace and clap on the back. We were afraid to go to a rugby match on a Friday night, we were afraid to stay up late drinking beers around the fire, we were afraid to go shopping and cook and sit in traffic and live life. We were afraid to love.

I was afraid to love.

Sophie smiled gently at me when I finally looked over at her, the beginnings of a realisation churning in my heart. She searched my face and I thought maybe she could see it. Maybe she could see that I was finally putting the pieces together.

"They say love conquers fear, right?"

Her smile turned sad and that sadness pierced my soul. "Darren, what we had didn't conquer the fear of Jaime's death. It didn't conquer the fear of the unknown without him. It didn't conquer the fear that it was somehow your fault, our fault."

"Sophie, I—"

Sophie placed a finger over my lips to stop me. I was going to try to say that wasn't true. I was going to insist she was wrong. I was going to try to manufacture some sort of reason why what she was saying wasn't the God's honest truth. But with her warm finger against my lips and her kind, sad eyes fixed on mine, I saw clear as day that there was nothing to say.

"The fear won," she whispered, voice shaking slightly. "The fear won because no matter what we wanted to believe or what we wanted to tell ourselves..." Sophie paused to steady her breathing. "Look, what we had...I'm not saying we didn't have anything." Sophie smiled. "We had feelings for each other. We had excitement and adoration and tenderness. We had something, we did."

I thought for a moment we each remembered our time together: forbidden touches in the backseat of my car, secret notes passed in crowded hallways, hidden whispers beneath the covers of her bed before I snuck out the window so her father didn't catch us together. It *was* exciting. There was adoration. We were tender.

And I had thought it was love. For so long, I believed it was love between us. I never considered that it could have been something else.

Not until that moment there in the bar with Sophie almost ten years later.

Sophie said the words I'd never have brought myself to admit before. "The fear from Jaime's death won because it wasn't love, Darren. Not true love, not real love. Not worth fighting for and being brave for and standing up against the world for love."

I stared at Sophie without words as she stared back at me.

"I'm not saying that if it had been love between us we wouldn't have felt fear. Of course we were going to feel fear. But the difference is, and here's the key, true love would have given us courage. And we had no courage, Darren."

Sophie's hand shook a little as she reached over to cup my cheek gently. Her eyes held mine as she whispered, "Not you. Not me. Not us."

I took Sophie's hand by the wrist and pressed my lips to her palm. My eyes closed for just a brief moment. I drank in the memories of us that I held so terribly close that they were almost sacred to me. In that moment, there was a sort of sadness in my heart.

For all these years I had thought that I had let her go there on the front steps of Ma's house the day of Jaime's funeral. But I knew now that I hadn't. I never let her go. I held onto the image of her, the hope of her, the beautiful lie of Sophie: that we were destined to be together, that we were made for one another, that we were in love.

I kissed Sophie's palm once more and then gently rested her hand back on the bar top. I was finally letting go.

With this realisation came a certain sense of freedom. It was as if the anchor that held the ship was cut loose. I was bound now to only the wild, crashing waves.

Where would they take me?

"I think we'll both find it one day," Sophie was saying with a hopeful smile toward me. "Love, I mean. The real thing this time."

I nodded somewhat distractedly. My mind was consumed with the image of a distant shore, and upon that distant shore was a flash of bright red hair twisting in the wind.

"How do you think we'll know?" I asked Sophie with a sudden sense of urgency. I desperately searched those hazel eyes whose warm, comforting flames I prayed would burn for someone else one day. "How do you think we'll know when we've found it? When we've found love? When we've found the one we love?"

Sophie shrugged, finger tracing the lip of her now empty wine glass. "I think we tend to complicate that answer," she said. "But I think it's really quite simple."

I practically leaned in closer to her, heart beating rapidly as I clung to her every word.

"You'll know you've found love because whoever it may be, she'll give you the courage to face that fear you've only ever run from. That's how you'll know."

I sank back into my barstool and stared at the reflection of myself in the long mirror behind the rows of liquor bottles against the back of the bar. I sipped my whiskey as my wind whirled, a chaotic mess. Amongst the churning seas and crashing waves, one question was clear as the glare of a lighthouse through the sleet and rain:

Was I ready to stop running from my fears?

48

DARREN

*I*t was almost midnight. The neighbour's dog was barking incessantly, and porch lights were flickering on one by one on either side of Eoin's townhouse. But it would take the whirl of red and blue lights, the whine of a police car and even the cold metal of a pair of cuffs to get me to stop pounding on his front door.

I ignored the bleary eyes peering out at me from cracked blinds across the street and thudded my fist again against the white painted woodgrain. The doorbell resounded inside as I stabbed the button next to the door repeatedly till I feared it might get stuck. Based on my last interaction with Eoin, I was fully prepared to do this all night till he answered the door.

I was wearing several layers beneath my warmest coat, I brought a sandwich from the local deli, and next to me on the porch a thermos of coffee (mixed with whiskey for warmth…and a bit of extra courage, seeing as I needed all I could get).

"Eoin!" I shouted as I continued to pound his door and ring his doorbell. "Eoin, I'm not leaving here till you let me talk to you. So you better open your door or I'll shout it for all your neighbours to hear!"

I imagined Eoin inside cursing under his breath as he folded his pillow angrily over his ears and squeezed his eyes shut. That was fine. I could shout loud enough to get past a few goose feathers.

"Last chance, Eoin!" I shouted again. "Ye better come let me in. I'm not leaving."

A few more dogs down the street joined in, so now there was a chorus of barking in addition to my very annoying drum solo. A twinge of nervousness made my feet shift uncomfortably on Eoin's welcome mat as several more lights switched on in once dark windows.

"Alright then," I bellowed into the night like a crazy drunk on a city corner. "I'm just going to tell you what I need to tell you out here in the cold for everyone else to hear!"

I paused my knocking and eased up on the doorbell for a moment as I pressed my ear to the door and prayed for the sound of a creaking mattress or steps down the hallway, anything to indicate that Eoin had relented and was coming to let me inside so I didn't have to air our dirty laundry in front of the entire neighbourhood. But there was no sound at all inside Eoin's dark townhouse. If Noah hadn't told me that he was home, I would have just assumed I was shouting at no one.

But he was there.

And I had a choice: should I give in to the fear of admitting my deepest, darkest secrets to not just Eoin, but to all of his neighbours as well and hop on my motorcycle and drive home? Or should I stand up? Should I get loud? Should I fight?

I sucked in a deep breath, wishing it didn't shake so terribly, before exhaling. I stared up at the porch light above me.

"Okay," I whispered to myself. "I can do this."

After one last nervous inhale, I stared at the blank door in front of me and raised my voice loud enough that I knew there was no way that Eoin couldn't hear me.

"Eoin, my greatest fear in the world is losing my family," I shouted. "I am terrified of not having you and Noah and Michael and Ma. It keeps me up at night. It makes me toss and turn. And when I do manage to fall asleep it makes me bolt upright, covered in sweat, and panting from a nightmare where you all are gone."

My heart pounded as the dogs barked and neighbours stuck their heads out of cracked doors, curious as to what in the hell this stranger was shouting into the once calm night. These were secrets that I wouldn't even admit to myself; they were secrets hidden in the deepest, darkest, most remote corners of my soul. I didn't let anyone see them.

Now I was laying them bare for all to hear.

My palms were sweaty, my cheeks red, and my heart seemed to thunder a dangerously inconsistent beat. This was fear and I was facing it.

"Eoin, when Jaime died I missed saying goodbye to him like the rest of you because I was with Sophie," I shouted, even going to the extra measure of cupping my hands over my mouth. I could see my breath as I shouted in the cold, as if my ghosts were escaping the prison I created for them in my heart. Each one leaving was agony. I resisted the urge to cling to them, to shove them back inside, to lock the doors once more. Forever.

"I was running away with her," I shouted despite my shortness of breath. "The only reason I knew about Jaime was because I called home from a pay phone to tell Ma I was leaving, that I was safe. I tried to rush back when she told me what happened, but that old piece of shite car of mine broke down. I tried to...I tried."

I squeezed my eyes shut to try and block off the waves of emotions that swept over me. I had to keep going.

"After Jaime's death I made a vow that I would always put my family first, that I would never let anything get between you and me ever again," I shouted over the barking dogs down the street. "Because there is nothing I fear more than losing another one of you like I lost Jaime. It is the single thing I fear in this world."

I sucked in a deep breath, my harsh panting loud in my ears.

"I've been running from my fear for so long," I continued. "I've been using it as an excuse to hold onto my guilt, to make myself miserable, to push away happiness and joy and love."

On Eoin's porch I leaned back and craned my neck to spy down the street for any sign of red and blue flashing lights. Surely by now one of the neighbours had grumbled "This is enough" and reached for the telephone to report the madman bellowing into the night, causing quite a scene, and generally disturbing the peace. I certainly felt mad.

My eyes were wide, my heart rate pounding, my palms sweaty as I cupped my hands again over my mouth and shouted, "But I've finally found a love that I don't want to run away from. I've finally found a love that makes me want to stand up to my greatest fears instead of cowering in the dark. I've finally found a—oh."

I stepped back in surprise when the front door opened. Eoin blinked at me with bleary eyes in the dim light of the hallway. I shook my head in shock that he was there in front of me. Well, and that his fist wasn't launching in the direction of my nose.

"Eoin, I—"

"Jaysus, get the fuck in here, alright?" Eoin interrupted, holding open the door just enough that I could slip past if I turned sideways and sucked in as much as possible.

"Hopefully you weren't sleeping," I said sheepishly as I did just that, avoiding Eoin's eyes narrowed on me.

"The whole bleedin' street was sleeping, Darren."

I paused in the living room and fidgeted with my fingers in front of me, suddenly unsure of what to do next. I hadn't expected to get this far. Jail? Sure. The emergency room? Perhaps. But inside Eoin's townhouse again? No, not really.

"Tea?" Eoin asked, his slippers padding across the kitchen floor.

I turned around to look at him with a raised eyebrow. "Tea?"

Tea was quite the turnaround from the bottles of whiskey and kegs of Irish red ale that littered the place the last time I was here. In fact, now that I realised it, there wasn't a sign of alcohol anywhere. No takeout boxes littering the coffee table. No random bras flung here or there. No evidence at all of a spiralling man.

"Tea?" I repeated, still a little stunned and surprised.

"As in them dried bits of leaves in boiling water," Eoin grumbled as he turned the kettle on.

I scratched at the back of my neck awkwardly. I fumbled over my words like an idiot, not sure what to even say. "No, I know what tea—it's just that, I—"

"I'm not leaving you," Eoin interrupted. His eyes were not on mine as he said this. He was focused on taking two Lyons teabags out of the box at the kitchen counter.

I stared at him for a moment, not even sure that I had heard him correctly. He had said it so nonchalantly, so casually, so matter-of-factly, I almost couldn't believe he'd really said it.

I took a hesitant step toward him, opposite the kitchen counter. "What did you say?"

Eoin sighed as he fidgeted with the little string attached to the teabag. "I'm not leaving ye, Darren," he repeated, his words soft-spoken. "I'm not leaving you, alright?"

Eoin finally looked up at me. It wasn't much, just the tiniest tilt of his chin upward so that he could see me past his long boyish eyelashes.

"Alright?" he pressed, not breaking eye contact.

I was frozen. My mind, my body, my heart: all frozen, paralysed, petrified even.

Eoin then stretched his arm out across the kitchen counter and squeezed my hand. "We're brothers," he said. "I'm not leaving you."

The tea kettle began its dull boiling roar before it turned itself off automatically. Eoin didn't let go of my hand and his intense gaze didn't let go of my eyes. "Alright?"

I tried to fight back the mist that threatened to turn into tears as I managed a quick nod.

Eoin shook his head. "No," his voice firm. "I need to hear you. Jaime never left me. He never left you. We never left him. And *I'll* never leave *you*, Darren."

Eoin's fingers gripped my hand more tightly, as if to punctuate each and every word he spoke, as if to tattoo them onto the inner side of my wrist, as if only a brother's touch could speak to a soul.

"I need to hear you." I heard the slight quiver in Eoin's voice.

With my eyes still locked on his, I whispered, "You'll never leave me, Eoin."

Eoin nodded. "And you'll never leave me," he said, gaze fierce before adding, "because we're brothers."

It was my turn to nod, though I only nodded just slightly for fear that I would jar a tear loose. "Because we're brothers," I repeated.

Eoin nodded once more, cleared his throat, and turned his attention back to the tea.

"Grand," he said, voice deep and low despite the fact that I saw him swipe the back of his bear paw-like hand across his face when he thought I couldn't see. "Grand like."

I at least had the advantage of wiping my tears away without him noticing. Though perhaps that was why he turned away in the first place: to give me that opportunity.

Eoin sorted each of us a cup of tea with milk and we sat next to each other on the couch.

"I'm still pissed at you," Eoin said first, glancing over at me with a fixed eyebrow. "And I reserve that right for as long as I deem appropriate."

I raised my hands. "Fair enough."

"I might still slug you."

I raised my own eyebrows at him over the lip of my teacup.

"Fine," Eoin grumbled, crossing his muscular arms over his chest. "Maybe no more slugging you."

I chuckled softly and sipped my tea. We sat in silence for a long while.

"I didn't understand what Kayleigh was saying when she told me about you and her," Eoin finally said. "I didn't understand the kind of love she was talking about. Love that changes you and makes you fearless. Love that's worth fighting over, fighting for." Eoin leaned forward to set his empty mug on the table. "And I definitely wouldn't have understood what in the hell you were hollering out there tonight..."

"But...?" I prompted when Eoin was silent.

Eoin bit his lower lip and tapped his finger nervously against the side of his cup. I watched him curiously, studying his obvious discomfort. "But I might have met someone..." Eoin said slowly, glancing over at me out of the corner of his eyes.

I nodded, trying to be patient. "And...?"

Eoin sighed. "I think maybe I wanted to be in love so terribly that I just convinced myself it was love with Kayleigh." Eoin paused for a moment, contemplative for perhaps the first time I'd ever seen in my life. "And I want someone to feel toward me the way Kayleigh obviously feels toward you," he finally said.

His words made my heart rate quicken. I tried my best to keep my breath steady as I exhaled.

"I'm sorry all of this happened the way it did," I said. "It's certainly not how I would have planned it."

Eoin laughed and shook his head. "It happened just the way it was supposed to happen, Daz."

Eoin using my childhood nickname was the greatest relief I'd felt in years. It was what finally gave me peace that everything was going to be alright, *we* were going to be alright. I sagged into the cushions of his couch and briefly closed my eyes.

When I opened them I dared to reach over and squeeze my brother's shoulder. "So tell me about this 'someone'," I said. "Bra size, favourite position, any interesting tattoos. You know, the usual."

To my surprise (and perhaps Eoin's himself), he didn't hit me. Instead he just smiled. "That's a story for another time," he said with a wry wink. "You've got somewhere to be."

I raised a curious eyebrow. "I do?"

Eoin reached over and took my cup of tea from me despite the fact that there was still some left. "You do," he said, placing it on the coffee table and nodding toward his front door down the hall.

"Um, where?" I asked, glancing between him and the door I was suddenly getting kicked out of.

Eoin grinned. "You've got to go get your girl."

49

KAYLEIGH

I sat in my car for almost twenty minutes before finally working up the nerve to open the door. It was the first day of my apprenticeship, and to say that I was apprehensive would be an understatement. As I walked along the sidewalk toward the mechanic's shop already bustling with activity, my palms were coated in sweat despite the morning chill.

From just down the road I could see men in blue coveralls working quickly and confidently on engines, changing out tyres skilfully, and using pieces of equipment I'd never even seen before, let alone knew how to use myself. I was throwing myself into waters well past my depth and my heart was racing.

I was so nervous that I was almost at the garage doors before realising that I'd forgotten my tool belt along with all my tools, naturally, on the passenger side seat. Cursing my scattered brain, I hurried back to my car and leaned inside to grab the tool belt Darren got me for Christmas. As I tightened it around my hips, my fingers grazed the inscription: *Kayleigh Scott: Mechanic.*

I didn't have a degree in car engineering. I didn't have formal training of any kind whatsoever. I couldn't even properly name every component hidden in grease and oil beneath the hood of a car.

But Darren believed in me.

And that was enough.

With a renewed sense of determination despite the considerable amount of palm sweat, I strode down the sidewalk toward the mechanic's shop. I kept my chin high, because Darren gave me this tool belt. I kept my back straight, because Darren saw my potential. And I kept my chest forward, because it was my feckin' name on that belt. *Mine.*

Loud music played over a stained and dusty boombox player much like the one in Darren's shop as I stepped inside the garage doors. A big man with a backwards baseball cap emerged from under the hood of a brand-new car. He nodded toward me in acknowledgement.

"Dropping off a car, little lady?"

I shook my head as I tapped my hips and the tool belt draped over them. "I'm the new apprentice," I said over the blaring music. "I'm looking for Eddie."

The big man stood to his full height and twisted around his baseball cap as he assessed me from head to toe. He switched the toothpick between his lips from the left side to the right side as I tried my best not to squirm beneath the pressure of his doubtful gaze. I kept my mouth in a stern line, my eyes drilled on him.

Finally the big man thumbed over his shoulder and said, "Eddie's out in the alleyway having his morning smoke. Might want to wait till he's done to talk to him though."

"I'll take my chances, thanks," I said before striding as confidently as I could past the big man and the new shiny black car and the array of tools I didn't know from one another.

As I walked along the line of cars in for repair, drawing the curious eyes of each mechanic I passed, I again ran my finger along my name etched into the smooth, warm leather of my tool belt.

Kayleigh Scott: Mechanic. Kayleigh Scott: Mechanic. Kayleigh Scott: Mechanic.

Maybe if my fingers remembered the words, my heart would too.

My hand hesitated just for a moment at the door to the back alleyway. Just a moment.

I stepped out into the alleyway and into a cloud of cigarette smoke I tried not to choke on.

"Someone can help you with your car up front, missy. I'm on break," an old man in grease-covered coveralls two sizes too big for him barked irritably between long drags of a cigarette. He then mumbled to himself as if the curtain of smoke somehow blocked the noise as well. "Can't have five feckin' minutes to myself in this bleedin' dump."

With one last push of confidence, I extended my hand into what felt like the gnashing teeth of a junkyard dog on a too-long chain. "Eddie, hi, I'm Kayleigh Scott," I said, trying to win over the cranky old man with a charming smile. "I'm your new apprentice mechanic."

Eddie's eyes darted over to me, giving me a once-over. He shook his head as he reached into his breast pocket for his pack of cigarettes. "No you ain't."

I wasn't expecting balloons and a cake on my first day of work...but I also wasn't expecting this kind of response either.

"I'm sorry?" I asked, fingers instinctively falling to my tool belt.

Stay strong, I heard Darren's voice in my head. *Fight for what you want.*

"You're not supposed to be here, girlie," Eddie grumbled.

A flash of heat swept over my cheeks as Eddie lit up another cigarette as if nothing at all had happened. The old Kayleigh would have slinked away, embarrassed and blushing. The old Kayleigh would have mumbled a timid apology for wasting the man's valuable time. The old Kayleigh would have left without a word.

But I was not the old Kayleigh.

"Excuse me, but I should absolutely be here," I said. "I'm smart and hardworking and I learn fast. I'd dedicated to the craft and will put everything I have into this apprenticeship."

The only movement from Eddie was a lifting eyebrow as I continued passionately.

"I want this to be my career, my future, and I won't let anyone, especially an old misogynist stand in my way."

Eddie snorted at this and leaned his head against the brick wall to stare up at the roof line above him.

"You're really missing out on a great mechanic by letting your prejudices get in the way, and I hope you remember that, sir." Chest huffing and puffing indignantly, I reached for the door handle to go back inside.

"Are you done?" Eddie's voice made me pause.

I turned back. "What?"

"Are you done," Eddie waved his cigarette about, "with your little speech?"

I hesitated. "Um, yeah," I said slowly. "I guess I am."

Eddie nodded. "Good," he grumbled, clearly more bored than anything. "'Cause what I meant is that another shop owner called and needed an apprentice. Said he'd pay me to have one of mine. I sent you an email about it this morning. Don't you check your phone?"

I masked the embarrassing fact that in my current financial situation, I couldn't afford a phone plan and cleared my throat and asked somewhat meekly, "Do you have an address then?"

∾

"THIS CAN'T BE RIGHT," I mumbled to myself in my car as I squinted at the messily written directions from Eddie to the new mechanic shop. "No, this can't be right."

I pushed my sunglasses up onto the top of my head and switched off the staticky radio. Normally this was a sure-fire tell that someone was lost. But the trouble was I wasn't lost; I wasn't lost at all. I knew exactly where I was in Dublin.

As I passed street after street that became more and more recognisable, I glanced again at the directions.

"This...this can't..."

Maybe Eddie was simply sending me on a wild goose chase. Maybe he just wanted to get rid of me and figured a little fib for a "little girl" would only be a little bad. Maybe this was just the easiest way to get rid of me and I was on my way to a McDonald's.

Or maybe there was another mechanic shop in the very neighbourhood as Darren's shop, Kelly's Garage. Maybe there was another mechanic shop on the exact same street as Kelly's Garage. Maybe, just maybe there was another mechanic shop that I never noticed directly next door to Kelly's Garage.

But as I stopped my car at the address Eddie gave me, I was, to my surprise, *not* at Kelly's Garage.

My heart started thundering as I stared out my dirty car window at O'Sullivan's Garage.

There, in place of the old sign, was the sign that I ordered for Darren on my very first day on the job. There, proudly displaying Darren's family name, was the sign I watched Darren haul angrily out to the trash in the alleyway behind the shop. There, glistening in the morning sunlight, was a sign—a sign of hope.

50

DARREN

*E*oin, still being quite the hopeless romantic and believer in fairy tale endings, was quite disappointed when I shot down his suggestion that I go catch Kayleigh at the airport like they did in all the romcoms he would never admit to seeing in theatres.

"But Eoin," I said as gently as possible, "Kayleigh would have to be at an airport..."

Eoin considered this minor hiccup for a moment before shrugging. "I could buy her a ticket?"

In the end I kindly refused my little brother's help in winning Kayleigh back. I'd returned to my apartment and called her roommate Candace at The Jar.

"Kayleigh left, *idiota*."

Even a mechanic such as myself could translate that one from Portuguese.

It took opening up my soul to Candace and telling her the whole story of Kayleigh and me, while drunk guys in the background hollered for beers, for Candace to tearfully give me a number for Kayleigh in Cork.

"*Boa sorte, amigo.* Good luck," she said before asking about whether Eoin needed a curvy Brazilian friend to help heal his heart.

It took calling the number Candace gave me till my fingers were numb before someone picked up.

"Yeah, she *was* crashing here on my couch and eating like all of my Ben & Jerry's," Kayleigh's friend said irritably (perhaps because it was 4:36 in the morning). "But she left."

"Left?"

"Something about an apprenticeship in Dublin. Hey, can you tell her she owes me for the ice cr—"

At this point in my search for Kayleigh, I realised just how many mechanic shops there were in Dublin. I didn't care. I kept calling and calling and calling until—

I nearly cried in relief when I finally got the answer to my question "Is Kayleigh Scott apprenticing with you" as a gruff "Yeah, so what of it?".

"I need her."

The owner of the shop, Eddie, was immediately confused. "Need her?"

I cleared my throat. "Um, what I mean is that I'm low on staff here and could really use the extra help. I'll pay you."

The old man grumbled what sounded like, "Yeah, whatever."

All there was to do was wait till Monday morning. On the Sunday before, Michael, Noah, and Eoin all came to help me dig out from the office the O'Sullivan sign Kayleigh ordered on her first day and replace the old faded sign with it. We shared a round of beers for the first time together as brothers since my fight with Eoin.

Eoin even wished me good luck on his way out.

I tried to keep busy that Monday morning, but I couldn't stop myself from looking up from beneath the hood at the sound of every passing car. I imagined Kayleigh driving up, realising where she was going, and continuing straight past all the way back to Cork. So with each rumbling engine, I leapt up to check, terrified that it was her not stopping.

When I heard brakes for the first time outside my garage, my heart seized.

My wrench clanged to the concrete floor as I stood and wiped the grease from my fingers. I hurried past the line of cars needing repairs and blinked in the morning sunlight just as Kayleigh stepped out of her car.

Her eyes found mine as I stopped just at the garage door. I'd dreamed of her eyes every day for the last few weeks, and every night they grew more and more vivid green. Every morning I woke up and shook my head: no, surely they weren't that *green*.

But the green of my dreams was nothing compared to the way her emerald eyes sparkled.

I swallowed heavily, suddenly nervous and conscientious, as Kayleigh closed her car door, leaned against it, and crossed her arms over her chest as she stared at me from across the driveway. All the city noises seemed to disappear. Or maybe I simply couldn't hear them over the pounding of my heart.

After a moment of tense silence, Kayleigh finally nodded up at the new sign. "Did you order a new one?"

I shook my head.

Kayleigh frowned. "Go dumpster diving then?"

Again I shook my head.

The silence hung heavy between us. It was the silence of the first time we laid eyes on one another: her in her bath towel, me with my hand on the door, neither moving, neither saying a word. It was the silence of the dark road the first time I took her on my motorcycle: her hands around my waist, her cheek against my back, my headlight the only source of light, save for the stars above and the city below. It was the silence beneath the hood during all those times we worked alone in my shop: our breaths humid in the cold air, our fingers grazing one another's, our hearts beating in time. It was the silence of Ma's foyer: stuffed in close to one another as we took off our shoes in the dark, completely unaware of what was to come.

And it was the silence of our separation from one another: aching and painful and unbearable.

Kayleigh's voice was like the splintering of thin ice on a mountain lake. We both knew we were going to fall; we both wanted to be dragged under. It was only a matter of when.

"How then?" she asked, her voice breaking.

I swallowed, hoping that I could push back down the wells of emotion that made my throat tight. "I never got rid of it."

We were far apart, but my softly spoken words carried as if my heart had a direct line to hers.

Kayleigh glanced at the sign. Then back at me. "You never got rid of it?"

"I couldn't," I said simply. "It's been here this whole time."

Both she and I knew we weren't talking about that stupid sign. Silence descended back over us. It was soon clear that I had to be the one to break it. Kayleigh started the crack in the ice, but I had to be the one to shatter it if we were to fall together.

I cleared my throat nervously and said, "Sounds like your brakes could use some work."

Waiting for Kayleigh's response was agony. Finally she nodded, kicking at her front tyre with the heel of her boot.

"Yeah," she said, pausing for a terrifying moment. "Um, maybe we could take a look at it together? I heard you're looking for an apprentice."

I tried not to let the spring of joy just explode inside my chest. It took every ounce of restraint to give only a small nod. "Why don't you pull it on in then?"

I stuffed my hands into my pockets so that she wouldn't see

how terribly they shook as I made room inside the garage for Kayleigh's car. She drove up the drive, pulled in, and I lowered the door behind her. The garage was plummeted into a hazy orange glow from the early morning light. I exhaled shakily as I stepped toward her driver's side door.

It opened as I reached for the handle.

I expected Kayleigh to step out so that we could put the car up on the winch to take a look at the brakes. I even held out my hand for her to help her out. But she didn't move.

A fire burned in her eyes as she stared up at me. Her chest rose and fell quickly and she swallowed heavily. She bit at her lower lip before glancing at my offered hand. I couldn't breathe as she slowly reached out to me.

But Kayleigh did not slip her hand into mine.

With her eyes searching my face, she gently traced her fingers along mine, ran them along my palm, and pressed them against the racing pulse of my inner wrist. Her quiet exhale came out shakily as she licked her lips and slowly wrapped her fingers around my wrist, her thumb smearing the smudge of grease over my wrist bone.

I could hardly breathe as I stood there next to her car with her eyes on mine. Kayleigh held me in the dim light and heavy silence as she stared up at me.

And then she tugged me gently toward her.

51

KAYLEIGH

I wondered if he would let me.

After all this time, I wondered if Darren would finally let me pull him in tight, hold him close, *love* him. There in the driver's seat of my car parked in his garage, I wondered if he was finally ready to leave the past behind him. I wondered if he had finally forgiven himself and decided he deserved happiness and peace just like all of us. Was he finally done running from his fear? Finally willing to give himself to me?

I'd never been more terrified in my life than I was in those tense, silent moments as my hand reached for his, as I slipped my fingers past his, as I circled his wrist in my grip and waited. I wasn't sure I could handle him pulling back from me again, retreating, *running*; I wasn't sure my heart could bear it.

So tugging at Darren's wrist felt like the single greatest risk I'd ever taken. Greater than standing up to Andy in front of that bar. Greater than quitting with no other job prospects and no savings. Greater than signing up for an apprenticeship in a mechanic's shop. Pulling Darren into the car, silently asking him to fall for me, fall *with* me felt like diving off a cliff and not knowing whether it was cool waters or deadly rocks down below.

I thought my heart would leap out of my chest as I gave his wrist just the slightest tug.

And he followed.

Despite the shadow of the garage, I could see the trust in Darren's eyes. There was still fear, too. But he followed.

He fell.

It was clumsy and awkward and difficult, but so was love. With my heart pounding and my eyes never leaving Darren's, I manoeuvred myself into the backseat of my car. My head bumped against the ceiling more than once and my shoulders nearly got wedged between the two front seats. It wasn't graceful how I collapsed in the back. But when I tugged Darren after me, he came.

That alone sent shivers down my spine.

Darren paused only once on his way to me in the backseat of my car, and that was only to reach back and close the driver's door. The sound of it closing made me lose my breath: this was happening, this was finally happening.

I kept my fingers wrapped around Darren's wrist as he ducked down to crawl into the back, not because I didn't trust him to follow, but because the touch of his skin was the only thing keeping my heart from exploding. I was trying to stop myself from gasping as he sat next to me, our knees the only other points of touch in the tight space.

Though not for long.

The air in the car was like the air beneath the hood or beneath the undercarriage: hot and dense and humid. I was struggling to breathe, but I didn't think this was the cause. Not when Darren's eyes, pupils blown widen open, were fixed on me like they were.

"Darren," I whispered, my voice shaking around his name.

Darren's free hand moved to cup my cheek as we gazed into each other's eyes. His other was still held in my desperate grip.

When he whispered back "Kayleigh", I couldn't help but sob. I didn't want anyone else in the world to ever say my name again. No one but him. Because no one but him made my name sound like a prayer, a desperate plea, a last gasp. No one else made it sound like the name of a terrible storm, wild and strong and all-consuming. And no one else said my name like it wasn't just stamped in leather on a tool belt, but seared across his own beating heart.

"Kayleigh," Darren whispered again in the hot, dense air of the backseat before leaning his head forward and pressing his lips to mine. "Kayleigh... Kayleigh... Kayleigh..."

He sighed my name against my lips as his hand moved from my cheek to hold the back of my neck. I moaned when his fingers slipped into my hair at the nape of my neck. He twisted his grip and tugged my head back just slightly so that he could suck at the sensitive spot of skin just below the ear. Goose bumps erupted up and down my arms.

My breathing grew shallow as Darren's searing kisses burned a trail down my neck. He nipped at my collarbone and then his fingers gripped the neckline of my shirt. He pulled back just enough that I could see his dark eyes in the dim light. He spoke without a single word, but the only thing more obvious than his question was my answer.

"Yes," I gasped.

Buttons scattered across the backseat of my car as Darren ripped apart my work shirt. I hit my arm on the headrest of the front seat and he banged his head against the ceiling as we rushed to get our clothes off. I wanted his hot skin against me. *Now.*

When I was down to just my bra and underwear, Darren gripped both sides of my face as my fingers fumbled blindly with the button of his jeans. I could feel his throbbing need beneath my palms and it turned me on so much that I sank my teeth into his bottom lip.

Our harsh pants were only interrupted by our curses as we banged our heads against each other and the car. Clothes were ripped at, shoes slung hastily aside, and underwear not even fully off as I straddled Darren's hips, both of us finally naked.

We didn't stop to admire each other's exposed bodies or press palms to every delicate square inch of skin. We were driven solely by our pounding, pulsing need for one another: like magnets held apart for far too long, striving and yearning and demanding nothing but to collide against the other.

Darren's fingers dug into my hips as he pulled me down on top of him. My fingernails clawed into his shoulders as I took his long cock fully inside of me. Before either of us could catch our breath, I started to ride him hard and fast and desperate. It was obvious that neither of us was going to last for long.

Darren's hands moved frantically up and down my back like he was falling and trying to catch himself. My head banged up against the ceiling of the car, but I kept going faster and faster, my tits glistening with sweat and bouncing. My thighs clenched together and I felt myself getting close as my shaky gasps grew more and more erratic.

"You love me," I breathed against Darren's lips, emotion flooding over me.

Darren's hands slid down my slick sides and gripped my waist. His eyes were locked on mine, pupils hazy with lust and desire. "And you love me."

I held his face in my hands and pressed a shaking kiss to his lips as he lifted my hips and drove me back down onto him. It only took a minute more before I came, screaming his name against his mouth as my body shook. As I buried my face in the crook of his neck, Darren lifted me and thrusted into me till he came as well.

I collapsed against his sweat-slick chest and breathed in deep the musk of his cologne against his neck. I knew, in the backseat of that car, that I'd found home. His arms caressed my back as I stilled.

I chuckled, interrupting the humid silence. Darren stirred under my cheek and craned his neck so he could see me against his chest.

"What is it?" he asked, gently brushing a strand of red hair behind my ear.

"Oh, it's nothing," I said, grinning at him. "It's just a little funny how out of order we've done everything."

I noticed Darren's quirked eyebrow and shifted so I was sitting up. I picked up Darren's hand and pressed my lips to the back of it.

"Well, normally you meet the family once it's serious," I explained. "But I met your family before I even met you."

Darren grinned. "And I fell in love before we'd even ever kissed."

It was my turn to lift an eyebrow in surprise. "Really?"

Darren nodded. "As silly as it sounds, I think I fell in love with you in Ma's bathroom that morning," he said. "When was it for you?"

I opened my mouth immediately, because I assumed it was an easy answer. But I could only stare at Darren in confused silence for a moment before saying, "I can't think of a time when I didn't love you."

Darren again kissed me sweetly, softly, warmly.

"And!" I said, pulling away from his kiss and making Darren laugh. "And we just made love and haven't even been on a date."

Darren held my chin between his thumb and forefinger. "I can fix that."

"Oh?"

He nodded. "Go on a date with me?"

I smiled. "Yeah."

But it didn't matter where we started: the beginning, the middle, or the end. Because my forever was with him.

EPILOGUE

KAYLEIGH

ne year later...

IT WAS two days before Christmas. O'Sullivan's Garage was filled with twinkling Christmas lights, the sound of merry carols on the radio, and mistletoe I actually wanted to be caught beneath. Tiny hints of snow fluttered outside as Darren and I finished up our last work orders before the holidays.

I wasn't nervous about the Christmas rush. I'd done all my shopping, wrapped all my presents, bought all the groceries I needed to bring to Ma's place. Finances at the shop were doing fine, great, even. I had a secure job as a mechanic at the shop, wonderful friends, and a warm bed to lay my head every night.

And yet, I could not have been more nervous as I was then.

I was pretending to work on the front wheel of a motorcycle, but really spending all my time peeking across the shop at Darren. I could just see the white poof of his red Santa hat from atop the open hood of the car he was working on. Every time I saw it, it made me smile, because it showed me just how far Darren had come in the last year.

He would have burned a Santa hat at just the very sight of it twelve months earlier.

As I kept craning my neck to spy on Darren, I tried my best to keep my toe from tapping, my palms from sweating, and my heart from racing faster and faster. But it was no use.

Our lives were about to change.

"Hey, babe," Darren called out across the garage, "I can't seem to figure out what's wrong with this radiator over here."

My chest seized as I froze on my work stool. "No?" I called out tentatively, eyes fixed on that white poof just visible above the hood.

"No," Darren grumbled as he struggled with something. "It seems like something is wedged in—what the…"

Darren's words trailed off and my heart beat so terribly that I thought it was going to beat straight out of my chest as the silence in the shop stretched on and on. Darren's Santa hat remained still as I watched…and waited.

When Darren finally came from around the car and looked over at me, tears were already in his eyes. In his trembling fingers he held the sonogram I brought from the doctor and hid for him to find in the radiator.

He couldn't find words for a moment as I started to tear up myself.

"Are you…I mean…are we…are we?"

I managed a teary, messy, elated nod and Darren rushed across the shop to sweep me up into his arms. He hugged me and kissed my wet cheeks and spun me round and round as he laughed with pure joy.

"I can't believe it," he kept saying. "I can't believe it. I can't believe it."

He set me down and kissed me long and hard and so

passionately I got butterflies just like the first time. I laid my hand against his chest and felt his heart racing just like mine. We were both shaky and giggly and teary-eyed and it was perfect.

A few minutes later I couldn't help myself from laughing just a little bit as Darren stared down at the sonogram with such awe, the touch of his thumb already gentle and tender despite the obvious fact that he was only holding a picture. He looked up at me in slight surprise, tears still clinging to his long dark eyelashes.

"What?" he asked, his voice still thick with emotion.

I reached up and brushed a tear from his cheek, smiling as I shook my head. "It's nothing," I said. "It's just that we're doing it again."

Darren raised an eyebrow at me after glancing down again at the sonogram, as if he couldn't resist looking away for longer than a moment or two. "Doing what again?"

I grinned and moved beside him so that I could rest my face against his shoulder and look down at the first picture of our daughter with him.

"You know," I said. "Doing everything out of order."

To explain even further I wiggled my bare left hand over the sonogram. I was surprised when Darren stepped away from me with wide eyes.

"Oh shit, I forgot."

I frowned in confusion. "Forgot what?"

I would have expected Darren to say many things in that moment, but never, "You know the exhaust on that Honda has to be fixed tonight."

I glanced over my shoulder in confusion at the blue Honda in the corner. It was next on my list of work orders, but was this really the time to be bringing this up? My face was not happy when I looked back at Darren and crossed my arms over my chest. "Excuse me?"

My ire did not seem to be affecting him, because his eyes were alight even as he tried not to smile.

"Kayleigh," he said slowly, "the *exhaust* on that Honda *really* has to be fixed tonight."

If he thought he was making the situation better, he was wrong. Dead wrong.

"Pregnancy doesn't affect my hearing, Darren."

Nor the strength of my fist.

Darren sighed and then came over to twist me around with a smile playing at his lips and guide me toward the Honda at the back of the shop.

"Kayleigh," he said patiently, as he helped me to my knees behind the back of the car. "I think there's *something* blocking the *exhaust*."

"Well, you fix it," I grumbled, trying and failing to stand up as Darren held me tight.

"You little spitfire," Darren laughed. "Why in the world did I decide to marry someone so stubborn?"

"Probably because you li— Wait." I stopped and glanced at Darren. Darren, who was on one knee next to me. "Did you say marry?"

Darren, with the sonogram still held tightly in his grease-stained, scar-covered hand, nodded toward the exhaust with a smile. I held his forearm him to keep myself steady as I leaned down farther to look into the grey pipe.

And there I saw it: the glint of a diamond in the darkness.

Just like my one true love.

BOOKS BY SIENNA BLAKE

Irish Kiss

Irish Kiss

Professor's Kiss

Fighter's Kiss

The Irish Lottery

My Brother's Girl

Player's Kiss

My Secret Irish Baby

Irish Billionaires

The Bet

The Fiancé

The Promise ~ *coming Dec 2021*

Billionaires Down Under

(with Sarah Willows)

To Have & To Hoax

The Paw-fect Mix-up

Riding His Longboard

Maid For You

I Do (Hate You)

Man Toy (Newsletter Exclusive)

All Her Men

Three Irish Brothers

My Irish Kings

Royally Screwed

Cassidy Brothers

Dark Romeo Trilogy

Love Sprung From Hate (#1)

The Scent of Roses (#2)

Hanging in the Stars (#3)

Bound Duet

Bound by Lies (#1)

Bound Forever (#2)

A Good Wife

Beautiful Revenge

Mr. Blackwell's Bride

Paper Dolls

ABOUT SIENNA

Sienna Blake is a dirty girl, a wordspinner of smexy love stories and an Amazon Top 20 & USA Today Bestselling Author.

She's an Australian living in Dublin, Ireland, where she enjoys reading, exploring this gorgeous country and adding to her personal harem of Irish hotties ;)

Printed in Great Britain
by Amazon